THE MOUSE GOD

Susan Curran was born in Aylesbury and read English at the University of Sussex. She worked in insurance and computing before beginning her writing career in 1979. She is the author/co-author of sixteen books on computers and new technology, including *The Penguin Computing Book*. *The Mouse God* is her first novel. She now lives in Norfolk, and has two sons.

THE MOUSE GOD

Susan Curran

■

FONTANA/Collins

First published in Great Britain by
William Collins Sons & Co. Ltd, 1987

First published by Fontana Paperbacks 1988
Copyright © Susan Curran 1987

Made and printed in Great Britain by
William Collins Sons & Co. Ltd, Glasgow

For Ray

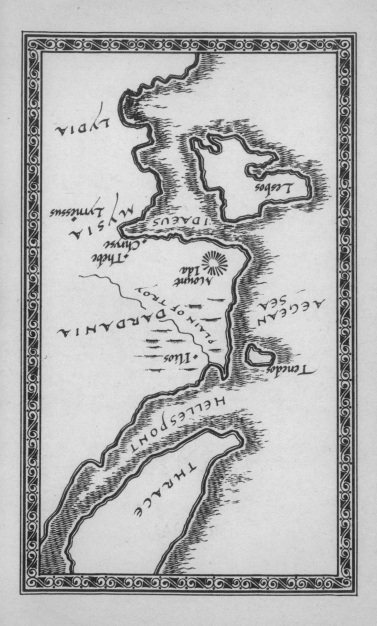

Prelude

CHRYSE

■

CHRYSEIS FIRST LET OUT the sacred mice in her third summer. She would have done it sooner, but until then she could not work out how to untie the fastenings of the cages.

She did not want to set the mice free; just to play with them. When the front of the first cage was open she reached in and picked up one of the mice. It was white, with pink eyes that reflected the sunlight. It looked up at her for a moment, then with a wriggle it was out of her palm and gone, across the courtyard, up the low stone wall and lost in the brush that wove along the top. The other mice crouched in the cage, watching. As she turned towards them, they too were out and away.

She had not expected them to move so fast. She was surprised, and impressed. She moved to retrieve one mouse which was still in the centre of the courtyard, sniffing at the ground, but it ran faster than she did, and was through the gate and into the field beyond before she was halfway towards it.

Barely a moment had passed, and not a mouse was to be seen. Chryseis felt a twinge of annoyance. She was not frightened. Nobody had ever told her not to open the cages; they had all assumed that she would not be able to. She opened the second cage, telling herself that she would be quicker this time, and hold the mice tighter. She picked up two, one in each hand, and squeezed them as hard as she dared. She did not want to hurt the mice. That left her without a hand free to fasten the cage again, and as she turned away the other mice slipped out. What now? It would be difficult to play with the two mice out in the courtyard without letting them escape from her. Chryseis decided to take them indoors, to the big room where Rhene was preparing the supper.

Rhene looked up, and let it out a shriek as she saw the girl with a mouse in each hand. That surprised Chryseis too. Rhene was not afraid of mice, nobody in the sanctuary was. Chryseis started, but she did not let go. 'Can I play with them in here? Over in the corner?'

'Apollo! What has the girl done? Oh, the cages!' Rhene pushed past her towards the door, rubbing her hands on her apron as she went. Chryseis followed her outside. She stopped in the middle of the courtyard, looking across at the cages: two open and empty, and only the third the full of mice, squeaking with excitement.

Chryseis realized then that she must have done something very naughty. Rhene did not even turn to her. 'I'll go and fetch the master. Stay here.'

It had to be bad. Father did his work, his writing and his calculations, in the afternoons, and nobody ever disturbed him then. Chryseis stood waiting as she had been told to. She wondered what she should do with the mice. They were still in her hands and she was afraid she might lose one if she tried to put them back. She looked down and whispered to them, telling them that it would be all right. Father never punished her, though Rhene sometimes did when Father was not around. The mice looked back, their whiskers twitching. She would have liked to stroke the whiskers, see what they felt like, but she dared not move her grip.

Her father arrived at a run, with Rhene panting behind him. Chryseis looked up at him bravely. She did not want to let him see that she was frightened. 'I only wanted to play. The other mice all ran away. Shall we go and look for them?'

Chryseis shook his head and crossed over to her. 'Here. Give me those two. Rhene, will you hold the cage door up a little while I put them back?' He concentrated on the two mice for a moment, and then turned back to Chryseis, as if he had just remembered her question. 'The mice are gone now, Chryseis. I doubt if we shall find any of them today. Perhaps one or two will come back tomorrow, if they are hungry.'

'Are you very angry, Father?'

The priest shook his head. 'It is not my anger you should worry about, my dear. It is Apollo's anger. You know the mice belong to Apollo, don't you?'

She nodded. Apollo was very important, so important that they never saw the real god, only his statue, though he was always in the sanctuary, Father said. 'Shall I go and say sorry to Apollo?'

Chryses looked at her. She was frowning a little and wringing the edge of her skirt.

'I think you should. Let's go and do it now.' He took her hand and they walked together through the olive grove, and up the low hill to the clearing. This was something special and new. Of course Chryseis had been to the shrine before, but only when there were rites, when the serving boys were there, and people from the village. Today the two of them were alone, and the smell of incense was missing.

Chryses drew her across the main clearing and through the screen of bushes past which only the priests and suppliants were permitted to go. He went to the priest's hut and emerged carrying his golden staff, with the white ribbons fluttering from the top. He told her where to stand and crossed to the altar.

He bowed low before the big statue of Apollo – sitting with a mouse trapped under one foot – then lifted up his hands and head and began to speak. At first the words were simple, and Chryseis listened to them, but after a while they grew more complicated, and she did not try to listen any more. It seemed to her that her father had forgotten she was there. She stood still, watching him at the altar and wondering where the real Apollo was hiding. Perhaps the mice had gone to find him? She would have to ask Father when he had finished.

She did ask, but her father just looked stern and told her that she was too little to understand these things and she should go off and play. And never, ever do it again.

There were not many things Chryseis was forbidden to do. There was nobody to forbid her most of the time. Chryses was in his hut working, or at the shrine with the God, and Rhene was always busy in the house or the home fields. They did not like her to go as far as the harbour on her own, but she could do even that if one of the servants from the shrine, or one of the village boys, was with her. She was not allowed to go to the shrine alone, but she never wanted to do that. It was a frightening place, and the boys told her horrible tales of the animals that were killed there.

The mice were not frightening, even though they belonged to Apollo. Because they belonged to the God, they were special. As Chryseis grew older she became more conscious of their specialness, of the aura of mystery that hung around them. They were never killed at the shrine. Their part in its life was secret and inexplicable. She liked to think that Apollo took them out to play with, when nobody was around to see him. She wished she could be like the God, and play with them herself. Increasingly too she felt sorry for them, being shut up in the heavy wooden cages. They would gnaw, gnaw at the sides, as if they longed to be free, but when the wood got thin and they must have been hopeful, they would be taken out and put into new cages with thick sides.

She often thought about letting them out again. Being forbidden to do it gnawed at her mind, as the mice gnawed at the cages. She would have played with them for a little while, she thought, and then let them go free if they wanted. But she did not want to make Father or Apollo angry, so she did not do it. Until her seventh summer, when Phegeus, one of the village boys, dared her to.

He promised to give her the doll he had been whittling, if she did it. She wanted the doll, and she wanted to do it. The combination was irresistible and one afternoon, when Rhene was away at the lower field, she went over to the cages. Phegeus and three other lads from the village were watching her and she turned to look at them, not at the mice, as she unfastened the twine. There was something delicious about their complicity.

She picked up just one mouse as the rest scrambled out. One or two went straight for the wall and the outhouses, away from the boys, moving just as fast as she remembered. The others, bolder, stopped to sniff around. Before the last mouse had left the courtyard a shadow crossed the sky. Hurry, she felt her mind telling the mice. They seemed to have frozen in their tracks, all their energy taken away by the hawk that swooped down. It caught a mouse in its claws – not a baby, a big, fat one – and was away in a flash.

Chryseis was shaking, the tears running down her cheeks. Why had the mice not run? Why had they not fought back, ganged up on the big bird and sent it packing? Why had they given in so easily? She had thought them fast and fearless, but now they seemed lily-livered little creatures, not fit to belong to the God of the Rising Sun at all.

The boys were gone almost as fast. She was not sure if it was the bird or her tears that had scared them away. Cowards. Chryseis despised them at that moment almost as much as she despised the mouse that had let itself be caught. She turned to the mouse in her hand. It lay limp and lifeless as she uncurled her palm, its whiskers trailing helplessly. In a single swift, angry movement she hurled it high in the air, over the wall and far beyond.

The wooden doll lay abandoned by the wall of the house. She crossed over to pick it up. It did not seem so pretty now, and there was something smug about its blank face.

Rhene did not notice the empty cage on her return, so Chryseis told Father when he came back for supper. She did not mention the boys who had been watching. Chryses listened in silence and then looked at her for a long moment, so that she could read his face. There was no anger in it, but there was disappointment.

'Are you going to punish me?'

'I do not think that would do any good, do you?'

'It won't bring the mice back.'

He was silent for a moment, as if he wanted her to feel that he disapproved of her taking it all too lightly.

'What do you think you should do, Chryseis?'

She thought. 'I think I should do something to tell Apollo I'm sorry. Something that hurts.'

Chryses looked down at the floor. The wooden doll lay there and he bent and picked it up.

'Is this yours?' He was always vague about her things and would not notice that it was new, any more than he would notice a new ribbon in her hair, or different spices in the dinner.

'Yes.'

'Perhaps you should give this to Apollo. As an offering.'

Chryseis hesitated. She had been tempted earlier to throw the doll away, into the bushes after the mice. 'That would not hurt enough. I'll give Apollo my other doll. I like that one better.'

'Good girl.' He waited while she fetched the doll, and they walked together up to the shrine. It was growing dark when she placed the doll on the altar. There were always offerings there: fruit, woven wreaths of corn, little terracotta statues, but the doll looked to Chryseis to be better than the rest. Apollo ought to forgive her, she thought, if he was a fair god.

Chryseis did not turn back to look at the altar as they left it to return to the house. In the morning she came, however, when nobody was around. Not to take the doll back – she knew it belonged to Apollo now – but just to make sure that it was still there.

The altar looked somehow smaller in the daylight. The offerings had a depressing ordinariness about them, as if they were no different from the clutter in the house. There was no sign of the doll.

A wave of panic washed over her. Had someone taken it? Had a big bird carried it away? She dared not rummage among the offerings, but she crept from side to side of the altar, trying to see if the doll had slipped under some other gift. There was no trace of it at all.

In an agony of fear she slipped to the grass, twisting onto her belly and beating the ground with her fists. The world was hazy to her, as if she had been looking too long into the sun. What did it mean? Had Apollo rejected her offering? The thought brought a cold, hollow feeling to her insides.

Then her sight cleared suddenly and focussed on an expanse of rough grass. In the centre of it, almost within her grasp, was a white mouse.

The mouse and the girl regarded each other in silence. The tiny pink eyes had a jewel-like clarity. The mouse's nose shone damply, its whiskers agitated the sunlight. Slowly it turned and began to creep away. Even more slowly, Chryseis pushed herself to her knees. She squatted there alone for a long time. Then she roused herself and set off down to the house.

In the middle of the night she awoke and thought, quite suddenly, that her father must have taken the doll, to make sure that she would not come to retrieve it. It made a cruel kind of sense. Yet, at the same time, it was not the sort of thing her father did. Rhene, yes: but her father had never cheated her, and it seemed to her that that would have been cheating. She did not want to think that it might be true. She let the image of the mouse come back into her mind, its eyes fixed unblinking on hers, its whiskers aquiver. It was surely a messenger from the God. It had brought her a feeling too rare and precious ever to be shared.

She never asked her father about the doll, and she never saw it again.

She did ask Chryses about the mice. It still bothered her, the thought that the mice were not worthy of Apollo. Why were the mice sacred and not the big bird? Chryseis was not sure that Rhene would know the answer, but she felt that Father should, and she asked him one evening after supper.

He looked at her thoughtfully. 'That is a good question. Why do you ask it?'

She told him the story, just as it had happened in the court-yard.

'But that is the nature of mice, to be caught by hawks and eagles, and owls, and bigger animals. They know it is. They know there is no good in escaping their destiny when it comes, and they wait patiently for things to happen as they must. Do you think it is unworthy of Apollo to behave like that?'

'I think it would be better to fight back.'

He laughed. 'There are times when you must fight back. With Apollo's help, you will know them when they come. You fight then to fulfil your destiny, and to do the will of the gods. But there is no honour in fighting against your destiny. When you know that the gods want something that comes hard to you, the honourable thing to do is to accept it gracefully and willingly. That is what we always hope the animals will do when we sacrifice them, and that is what we must do too.'

'But what happens if the gods do not tell you anything? If it is all left up to you?'

'They will tell you, if you listen to them. And you must listen to the priests too. It is our task to ensure that people know what is required of them.'

'Does Apollo really talk to you, Father?'

'Sometimes, yes. I think so.'

'Would he do things for you in return, if you asked him?'

Chryses looked narrowly at her. 'You must not go expecting Apollo, or any of the gods, to help you, my dear. They do not work like that. We do not worship them so we can ask favours of them. We worship them to please them, to do them honour and to avoid their rage. Sometimes we ask things of them, but it is not good to ask too much of the gods. And when they do answer our prayers, it is not always in the way that we expect.'

'It sounds very difficult to me.'

'You will understand when you are older.'

'Will I be a priest then, like you?'

'Not quite like me. You will be dedicated to Artemis, the Goddess of the New Moon. That is what your mother wanted, and I think it is right for you.'

Chryseis did not answer. She was surprised, and a little disappointed. It would have been all right to serve Apollo. She knew him, and trusted him. But she knew almost nothing about Artemis, and she had a feeling that she would not like serving her. Was that the God talking to her, telling her that her father was wrong? The episode with the doll had made her uneasily conscious of her father's fallibility. At the same time, she thought he would be angry if she suggested that it was.

That summer Chryses took his daughter up to the sanctuary of Artemis, which lay high in the hills above their village of Chryse, even beyond Thebe, the town inland from them. It was the first time she had ever left her home village.

There was a wooden stockade around the sanctuary. Chryses waited with Chryseis at the big gate until a woman came, but he did not come inside with her. Men were not allowed in Artemis' sanctuary, he told Chryseis. He would stay at the gate until the priestess had finished talking to her.

'Must I stay here, Father?' Chryseis did not want to stay. The stockade felt imprisoning to her, even from the outside.

'Not this time, no. I have brought you to see what it is like. You will return two summers from now, in your ninth year, and be dedicated then.'

The priestess came and led her away. It was quiet and still inside the sanctuary. There were no little children, no men there: just women, moving slowly as they did their work. The priestess led her to a hut, neatly made but almost empty inside, and made her sit on a low stool. Then she talked. Artemis was the goddess of mountains, she said, and of hunting. Like the mice, she was swift; unlike them, she was fearless. She was the goddess of childbirth, and of little children. She was a virgin goddess. Her priestesses must never marry, or lie with a man.

'Do you stay here always?'

The priestess smiled. 'Yes, always. It keeps us close to the Goddess.'

The priestess was tall and fair, and a little moon-like herself. There was something clear and cold about her, like a mountain stream. Chryseis had an uneasy feeling that she too would become cold inside if she were to live at the sanctuary. It was a relief to know she was going to go home.

They stayed at Thebe on the way home. Chryses was a distant relative of the King of Thebe, Eetion, and he went to the shrines to make sacrifice and to the palace to talk to the king. Chryseis was sent to play with the palace children. There was a great crowd of princes, seven of them, and just one princess, Andromache, a few years older than Chryseis. Chryseis had little interest in Andromache, a placid easy-going child who sat and chattered with the palace women all day, but the boys were fun and she went wild with them, clambering up and down the steep sides of the dried-up river course and running through the corridors and anterooms of the palace. It would be difficult, she thought, to live in a place without boys, a place where nobody shouted or laughed out loud.

Chryses asked her, when they arrived back home, what she had thought of the trip.

'I liked Thebe. Towns are exciting, aren't they? So many people, and so much going on. I liked Maris and all the other princes.'

He smiled. 'Thebe is a very small town, my dear. Perhaps one day you will see Ilios, the sacred town of Apollo, where there is a great citadel and the streets are paved with stone.' Then he remembered. 'But the sanctuary is more important. I know there was not so much happening there, but you liked the priestess, surely?'

'She was very kind.' Chryseis hesitated. She had a feeling it would be best to say something right away, so that Father could have plenty of time to get used to the idea. 'But I do not think I should go to live there, Father. It would not be right for me.'

Chryses looked at her sternly. 'This is what has been planned for you, my dear. Perhaps it did seem strange after here, because this is what you have always known. But it will be familiar to you when you have been there a while.'

'Thebe did not seem strange, and that was new to me too.'

Her father seemed only half to listen to her. He said thoughtfully, 'Perhaps I should have taken you there in the spring, when they have the festival of the moon maidens. It would not have been so quiet then, with the visitors and the singing and dancing.'

'I'd rather you took me to Ilios.'

He frowned. 'It is a long way, Chryseis.' He was tempted to bargain with her, but that seemed disrespectful to the gods. Still, it would not do to have the girl go to Artemis unwillingly. Such a sacrifice of one's life had to be made wholeheartedly or it was worth nothing.

Chryseis had no such reservations. She said carefully, 'I think perhaps I could accept the sanctuary more easily if I had seen Ilios first.'

Chryses looked at her. There was an eagerness in her face that had not been there when she had come away from the sanctuary. He loved her dearly and did not want to see her made unhappy. 'Then I will take you there, my dear, when I next go. Next summer, perhaps, or the summer after.'

'You promise?'

He smiled. 'Yes, all right. I promise.'

The following spring the war began. A great alliance of Achaeans from the lands to the west came to attack Ilios, the capital of Troy. It was no surprise. There had been a series of petty raids by both sides on the other's lands, growing steadily more serious, until in nominal revenge for an early kidnapping the Trojans had made an attack on the Achaean kingdom of Sparta. The Ilian prince Paris had carried off treasures and the Spartan queen, Helen. Helen's husband Menelaus, his brother Agamemnon, King of Mycenae and High King of Achaea, and a host of others sailed across the Aegean to win her back.

Priam, King of Ilios and High King of Troy, refused to negotiate with them. It was whispered that he believed he could defeat the Achaeans, far away from home and with no allies on the mainland, and become master of the Aegean Sea. A grand ambition: but those who had seen the Achaean landings spoke of hundreds, perhaps even a thousand ships. There were fifty thousand warriors or more. The whole affair was a madness, a disaster. It would be a war great enough to bring down empires, let alone a modest kingdom such as Troy.

The implications of the war occupied Chryses all the time. Ilios had always had the protection of Apollo; yet Apollo was the god of reason, of order, the god who insisted that men and beasts alike keep to their appointed roles, and ask no more for themselves than those roles offered them. Chryses was not sure that Apollo would give his protection to this rash enterprise. He did not want to endorse it himself, though he feared the consequences if he did not.

The sanctuary at Chryse lay in Mysia, to the far south of the Trojan lands. The Mysian kings, reluctantly acknowledging Priam's overlordship, agreed in alliance to offer token help to the High King. It seemed to Chryses a policy that could only lead to disaster. The signs of disaster lay in every sacrifice he dissected, in every portent in the sky. But Eetion of Thebe, Evenus of Lyrnessus and the other more distant Mysian leaders were in no mood to listen to him.

If only he could show them some sign so unmistakable that he could force them to listen, Chryses thought in anguish. He spent days shut away in his hut, working with the precious documents from Egypt and Babylon which told him about the sun. He knew what he wanted. It was at the core of the Mouse God's power, the knowledge that sometimes the weak could defeat the strong, the mouse take a bite from the sun itself. Would it happen soon? Even the Babylonians could not be sure about such things, and his ability to do the calculations was much poorer than that of their great astronomers. He prayed daily to Apollo that it would; and that he would foresee it, so he could be there, in Thebe or Lyrnessus, Evenus' capital, or even in Ilios, and make it seem terrible to a king.

The lads who served at the shrine were biddable, but not clever, and could not help Chryses with this kind of work. Chryseis, he slowly discovered, was different. She learned fast, and she showed a keen interest in the mysteries of astronomy. Her father did not teach her to read the foreign scripts he puzzled over, but he showed her how to do the calculations, and soon she could check the simpler ones for him.

She learned other things too: to speak good Greek, the language of the Aegean, and to sing and dance in the rituals at the shrine. In this way she served Apollo, a god who demanded no initiations like other gods, but who accepted the service of all those who sought the power of knowledge. There was no question of changing the plan to dedicate the girl to Artemis, but it pleased Chryses to see how well she played her part. She had a natural sense of grandeur, of occasion, of style. She had the knack of playing to the human audience, without ever seeming to lose awareness of the presence of the God.

His daughter had her own motives. The war was not real to her. The Achaeans were nowhere near the sanctuary, and less frightening than the boys with whom she played at pirates. The shadow of Artemis had been hanging over her ever since the visit to the inland sanctuary, though, and she was determined to find some way of escaping it. It could only be to her advantage, she thought, to make her father need her to help serve Apollo. It was better still when he travelled to talk with priests and kings, took her with him to Thebe and Lyrnessus.

Chryseis did not run wild with the boys any more. She watched the women. She watched Andromache and her mother Astynome, the Queen of Thebe. She watched the ladies of Lyrnessus who clustered and chattered at Evenus' court. She made friends with Briseis, a merchant's daughter who was Andromache's age. Briseis asked her about the calculations and the letters from Babylon, and the rituals of the shrine. In return she learned from the older girl all the things that town girls learn: the tricks of dressing to please men, of running a house. One day Chryseis was determined to do what Briseis was certain to do: marry a king or a prince. But she would not find him in

Thebe or Lyrnessus. Even the princes there were country boys. She would bide her time, until she got to Ilios.

There was no trip to Ilios the summer after the visit to the sanctuary. Or the next summer, or the summer after. Chryses went once, but he refused to take his daughter with him, saying that it was too dangerous. There would be time enough when the war was over.

But the war did not end. The years followed each other, and Chryseis grew up. Her ninth summer passed without comment, and so did the ones after. Chryses did not seem to notice how fast she was growing, and Rhene, now old and slow, did not trouble to remind him about the sanctuary. Chryseis trusted her father. He would not send her to Artemis till she had seen Ilios. Once she had seen it, she would be a virgin no longer, she hoped, and it would be time to set before him her different plans for herself. She did not think Artemis would mind. The Moon Goddess hardly knew her. And Apollo would be no problem. She talked to him at the shrine, made little sacrifices, to ensure that he would be on her side.

In the late autumn of Chryseis' fifteenth year, everything changed. It was eight years since the visit to Artemis' sanctuary, seven since the war had begun. Prince Maris from Thebe, one of Andromache's many brothers, came to the sanctuary and asked to speak with Chryses. The priest made to take him up to the shrine, where he could make offering, but the lad shook his head. He wanted to talk with Chryses in private, in the house.

The boy asked for permission to marry Chryseis. He had seen nineteen summers, he said, and though he was not Eetion's heir, he reckoned he had a good future ahead of him. He had known her since they were children together. He said he loved her.

Chryses was shaken. He had been wrapped up in his own affairs for years and had scarcely realized that his daughter was growing up. She was too young to marry. Girls in Mysia did not marry until their eighteenth year, their nineteenth or even their twentieth. She was not destined to marry, anyway. He told the boy so, not brutally but bluntly enough, and sent him packing.

'It's all right,' the prince said with a smile. 'I'll be back next year. She will wait for me.'

As soon as the boy had gone, the priest went out to look for his daughter. He found her in the courtyard, sitting in the afternoon sun in front of the cages of mice. The big dog he had bought from a passing trader the year before lay at her side and wagged its tail as he approached. She should have been doing something useful, Chryses thought vaguely to himself. Spinning, or weaving, perhaps. But nobody had ever pressed her to that kind of work, and although she could do it well enough when she tried, she generally managed to avoid it.

She wore girl's clothes: a short tunic of undyed homespun, belted low on her hips, and a pair of rough sandals. The body beneath the tunic was not girlish any more, though. Chryses, who so rarely looked at his daughter, saw her suddenly through Maris' eyes, and realized that she was beautiful. He felt a twinge of anxiety. Then Chryseis looked up as his shadow fell across her feet, and smiled at him – an open, childlike smile. 'What is it, Father? Do you need me to come and help you?'

Chryses told her straightforwardly about the prince, and what he had wanted. Chryseis listened calmly. It seemed the news did not surprise her, or disturb her.

'It's all right, Father,' she said gently. 'I have no wish to marry Maris. He knows it very well.'

'Maybe, but this should never have happened. I should have sent you to the priestess years ago.'

She smiled again. 'But I am useful to you here, Father; and it is a long way to the sanctuary.'

'You should be safer there, my dear. There is always danger here, by the estuary. The Achaeans may not have come here yet, but they have raided Lesbos, and that is close enough. It could be our turn next.'

'I don't want to be safe. I would rather stay with you.'

'That will not do at all. You are a grown woman. You should have been dedicated by now.'

'I still feel it is wrong for me, Father. I would rather marry. Oh, not Maris, he's just a boy, but there will be someone. Let me work it out for myself.'

Chryses sat down heavily on the packed earth. 'Chryseis, you must understand. Of course I do not want you to go to Artemis unwillingly, but I do want you to go. It has been planned for years, you know that. It is a much . . .' – he groped for a suitable word – '. . . finer life than marriage. You will not have to belong to any man, you can be free in the sight of the Goddess. You will not be pulled down by children, and servants, and all that kind of thing. Maybe it seems unappealing now, but you will find a great deal of satisfaction in it, I am sure. I think I should take you up to the sanctuary this summer.'

Chryseis frowned. She was used to getting her own way with her father. This was not the time to make him stubborn.

'I have thought about it a great deal, Father.' She paused, and made her voice lighter and brighter as she went on. 'Remember, you have not taken me to Ilios yet. You promised I should see it before I was shut up in the sanctuary. You know how much I have looked forward to it. I hope you will keep your word.'

Chryses had almost forgotten the promise, but it came back to him now. It was a complication he could have done without. He said slowly, 'There was not a war when I promised, child. Ilios is not what it was. It is under siege and a dangerous place to go to.'

'You have been there, and come back safely.'

Such a stubborn child; she always had been. Perhaps he should have kept her under tighter control, refused her more. It was too late for that now, however. He had always kept his word with her, and he had not the heart to refuse what might be her last request from him. It was time he went again, to talk to King Priam and the priests who served Apollo at Ilios. They could look over his calculations, help him decide if he was right. He did not expect an eclipse to come that year, but he hoped for one in the next. 'Very well. I will take you there in the spring, and to the sanctuary next summer.'

'Thank you, Father.'

Chryses turned to look at her. She sat in just the same position, perfectly at ease. He wondered if he should ask if she was still a virgin. It would be awkward if she was not. Chryseis did not like to be distrusted, though, and they had never discussed that kind of thing. She knows what is expected just as well as I do, he thought to himself. She will not tempt the gods too far. He got to his feet, clumsily. 'I think we should go together and make sacrifice. Will you come with me?'

She smiled brightly at him. 'Of course, Father.' And they set off through the grove together.

Part One

LYRNESSUS

THERE WAS A SUDDEN scuffling noise in the undergrowth. It broke the stillness of the morning. Aeneas stopped in his tracks, his hand reaching for the dagger at his waist. A hare streaked from the edge of the forest, grey-brown against the spring green of the low scrub. He did not turn to watch it. Instead he waited to see what might have frightened it. There were wolves, even a few lions, in the forest; and he was alone, and not well equipped for a fight with an animal as fierce as that. He crouched, waiting to launch a quick attack on whatever emerged. Nothing followed. Some shy animal, then, made cautious by the presence of the man and of his dog, which was already well down the hillside after the hare. Slowly Aeneas' guard fell, and he scrambled downwards to see how the dog was faring.

The dog was a good hunter, and he had been well placed to cut off the hare's escape, but the hare had lured him down the slope and it took some time for Aeneas to reach him. The kill was over by then, and the carcase hung limp in the dog's mouth. The blood was beginning to congeal against the grey fur. With a final emphatic shake, the dog dropped the trophy at his master's feet. He got a rub of thanks as Aeneas bent to pick it up. Not a bad size: it would make a good stew when he brought it back to the palace. He was not making for home yet, however. He wiped the worst of the blood on the long grass, pulled up more handfuls to wrap the remains, and stowed the parcel carefully in the leather pack he carried across his shoulders.

Aeneas was a dark wiry man, a little below middle height. He was dressed for farm work and a stranger might have mistaken him at first glance for a slave. A second glance would have shown that his tunic was recently washed, and well made, with a narrow band of princely purple around the hem; that his leggings were thick, his sandals almost new. No slave carried a bronze dagger as elegantly carved as the one Aeneas now tucked back into his belt; no slave handled himself with such an air of confidence. He had a right to be confident. It was his land, even if the occasional lion disagreed with him.

He was still a young man, with perhaps twenty-nine or thirty summers behind him, but it was easier to see the old man that he would become than the boy he must have been. There was something wary about his face, as if he was used to watching out for danger and rarely let himself relax. He moved quickly, even when there was no evident need for urgency, in a manner that suggested that his mind was never still.

There was nothing unusual about catching a hare, even alone and by chance. But it had distracted him and it was a few moments before he began to piece together, behind the pants of the dog and the rustles of his own activity, the threads of something different and alarming. There was a distant clashing noise, faint and yet too metallic to blend into the background. He could hear the cattle lowing, though they were several fields away. Then came a scream, cut suddenly short – perhaps only by a change of the wind – and leaving a moment of silence. Aeneas' concentration was fully focussed now. The dog, too, tensed and pricked his ears.

Aeneas had been on his way to the far pasture. He spent many of his days doing this, walking across to the outlying reaches of his land, checking that the animals were well tended and the herdsmen alert for danger. Wolves and lions were not the only threat. It was the eighth year of the war with the Achaeans. True, most of the fighting had been around Ilios, and Aeneas and the other kings and princes of Dardania had been able to tell themselves with conviction that King Priam's quarrel had little to do with them. A man does not always choose his war, though, any more than he decides to fight with a lion. The danger comes to him, and he must do something about it if he wishes to survive.

It now seemed quite possible that the Achaeans were coming to Dardania. After eight years in which they had backed up a loose siege of the citadel of Ilios with raids along the coast and among the islands, they were clearly running short of pickings there. Wars had to be financed somehow, so they were moving elsewhere on their forays. It was useless sitting at home and arguing that they would never come inland of Mount Ida, when every traveller between Dardania and the coast whispered that Achilles was already on his way.

Aeneas had believed the tales – almost. It was still early in the year and not yet safe sailing weather. He had doubted if Achilles would really come overland. The ground of central Troy was rough and rocky, and any route to Dardania from the Achaean base on the plain of Ilios would involve crossing mountains with steep slopes and sudden drops that would tax the best-trained troops. Surely, he argued, the Achaeans would have the sense to wait till the gales ended and they could do most of the journey by sea. Even if the tales had turned out to be true, Aeneas had reckoned to get a few days' warning, time to shake up his neighbours and plan a resistance stiff enough to turn the invaders back in a hurry. He had even done a little sounding out. He had not been expecting to run across enemy troops that day. But it came to him now that it was just conceivable for a scouting party moving at speed to have outpaced his informants.

There were three herdsmen with the cattle. He had armed them well: they had daggers, bows and long hunting spears. They were not trained soldiers, though, and it was pointless to expect too much from them. If marauders had come, Aeneas reckoned there would be many more than three. His men might have managed to put up a few moments' resistance while their boy ran back for reinforcements from the palace; but if the attackers had surprised them, coming out of the forest and straight onto the summer pasture, they might not have had time to do even that.

It was suspiciously quiet. Was the fighting over and done already?

Aeneas hesitated. It was still some way to the edge of the pasture, but it would take four times as long to return to the palace. There he could rally at most a dozen men: a couple of guards, household servants, farm hands. The Dardanians were not town folk: King Anchises' palace was barely more than an isolated farmstead, bigger but not different in kind from those his dependents worked. Almost half the men from the region were in Ilios, swelling Priam's forces. Aeneas knew he should have started to plan their defences sooner, and worked harder at it. Too late to think that now. If he worked flat out from that moment onwards, it would take maybe two days to raise a decent fighting force. One to call out his father's men, and one more to obtain support from neighbouring kings.

Two days was a long time. Maybe too long. He had an urge to run straight back and get started; but this was no time to delude himself. If he were to go round the farmers with a tale of a few strange noises in the hills, half of them would laugh in his face. He could not oblige them to join him. His authority as prince did not go that far, and nor did Anchises' as king. Likely as not he would have barely more than his own servants to come and check it out with him. And for all he knew yet, it might be just a couple of rustlers, and the nervousness that the imaginary lion had stirred in him.

It seemed there was no alternative. He would have to go on to the meadow, and discover exactly what was happening.

Calling the dog to his heel, he set off: briskly at first and then more slowly, making his way up the slope where the grass gave way to broken rock and brush which offered more cover. As he came closer to the pasture he moved to the edge of the forest and made his way through the trees. The going was hard. He trod cautiously on the uneven ground and the brambles tore at his legs through the linen leggings. He shivered a little in the dense shade.

He had to cut back to the border of the forest before he could see anything of the meadow. It was almost midday and beyond the trees the late spring sun beat down from a cloudless sky. Two butterflies circled around in a shaft of sunlight that cut into the heart of the shade. Behind their moving image the fields were very still. The herd had been moved to the summer pastures only a few days before and the grass was still green and rich. It was reasonably good farmland and there were more than fifty cattle.

Aeneas was looking for the cattle and he saw them first. A dozen men were herding them together with sticks. His second look showed him that they did it awkwardly, as if they were unused to the work. There was something energetic about them, they had none of the apathy of professional herdsmen. They had long hair, tied with twine at their necks, and wore short black tunics. The lowing of the herd mingled with the shouts of the men. Something was missing. No dogs were barking. Aeneas' eyes moved on, to the black shadow at the far end of the field. Squinting against the bright sunlight, he could make out the bodies of the dogs, piled together with their legs splayed out at unnatural angles. A few feet away were more bodies, those of his three herdsmen. No sign of the boy; maybe he had got away.

Beyond the shadows, a troop of men stood. There were thirty or more, all with long hair and black tunics. And in the fields beyond, going back, back across the slopes of the mountain in the direction of the sea, there were more men, more and more. They swarmed across the land like ants. Apt enough, Aeneas thought grimly to himself. They were the ant troops. Achilles' ants, his Myrmidons. Every single one of them.

Well, here it was, no mistaking it. From the little chase of the morning to the big battle of the afternoon. Excitement pulsed through him. He enjoyed fighting, though it was a bad thing to be taken by surprise. Men are like animals under the skin, he thought. The thrill gets to us, and away we go.

The thought swung his head round naturally to where the dog crouched beside him. He did not mean the look as encouragement, but the dog was waiting for a sign and he launched forward into the meadow with a loud bark. Aeneas cursed. He had meant to stay hidden: there was nothing one man could do against an army. It was too late. The eyes of the soldiers at the edge of the meadow were turning towards where he stood in the shade.

Still, he had a good hundred paces' lead over the men at the near edge of the meadow, and it was his land. He knew every hillock, every ditch, every fence between his hiding place and the palace. There was a fair chance of making it back. He was away at a run and did not turn to see if the troops were following him.

They did follow. Six of the nearest men set off in pursuit, and at first they gained ground fast. Aeneas was a strong runner, but the long scramble to the meadow had tired him, and the leading Achaean, a tall man with red hair, turned out to be a better one. He tore in front of the rest and looked to be within a spearthrow of his quarry. The man still held his long spear and he stopped to take deliberate aim and throw it. It fell just wide. Aeneas had heard the men behind him, but he still swerved in surprise and shock. He kept running, however, and the pursuit slowed abruptly, as if the soldier, losing his gamble with the spear, had decided to let him go. There was no sign of the soldiers by the time Aeneas arrived, panting, at the palace gates.

◼

'Bloody pirates.'

The words were vicious, but there was something subdued about Briseus' voice, as if he had not yet picked up energy after his supper. He slammed down his heavy bronze cup onto the trestle, though, making it clear that his annoyance was real. The cup was barely half-full, but a splash of wine crested its side and a puddle spread across the smooth oak surface. Briseus did not glance at it. He threw himself back in his chair and looked over at his wife and daughter with a challenge written clear in his face.

His wife did not react at all, as if she knew that the challenge was not really intended for her. Briseis did. She looked back with an air of slight surprise. Not at her father's words, which were predictable in the circumstances, but at the suggestion that she should argue with him.

It was nearly a year since Briseis had last been in the house. She had left it then to go to her husband's. Her father had blurred in her memory in the interim, and it was disconcerting to be back in front of him now and be treated just a little differently from how she remembered.

Briseus was a big man. He looked plumper to her, and her mother thinner, as if he was drawing all his wife's substance away, bit by bit. He came across as placid in public, but he enjoyed family arguments, where he could insist on the victory that he felt to be his due. In that Briseis – who was as slim and neat as her mother – took after him more closely than she realized. It was not normally she who was given the role of polite dissenter, but her three brothers were not there, and they had no other visitors.

They were all on edge that evening and it seemed to the girl that there was something to be said for a good squabble to clear the atmosphere, even if she was bound to lose. Her father had brought her up to speak her tongue. Annoyance at the silence was beginning to gather on his face, so she launched into the argument without stopping to think too much about her words. 'I hardly think of the Achaeans as pirates. We are too far inland for pirates, surely.' Lyrnessus was a good day's journey by foot from the open sea, though the River Idaeus widened into a salt estuary only a third of the distance away.

'It's what they do that makes them pirates, not where they go. They are out looking for plunder. They've stripped the coast bare, so they have to look inland now.'

'Surely there's more to it than plundering. If that was all they wanted, would they not rustle our herds and then be off without challenging the army?'

A grunt. 'Has your husband taught you no better than that? No army is going to forage three days' march from its base for the sake of a few cows. What they want is the gold and bronze of the town – and its women too.'

Briseus' answer exasperated his daughter. It always had, this side of her father's character, and right on cue she felt a flush of anger. A conservative merchant at heart, Briseus tended to think always in terms of goods taken and lost. Politics interested him only when they threatened to cause interference with trade. He had no time for the supposed causes of the war. In his eyes they were nothing: just a polite excuse to cover up the blatancy of the plundering. So to him there was only the scale of the pickings to differentiate an eight years' campaign from a hit-and-run pirate raid.

Briseis might have tended to agree a year before, but her husband Mynes had quite different views on the war. He had done his best to instil them in his wife, and she was persuaded that she agreed with him totally.

But it was not so easy now, with Mynes away and her father

eyeing her from across the trestle, to recall just what Mynes' position was. Of course he took the politics seriously – she assumed that princes always did – and she had picked up the broad outlines of it all. It did seem immensely complicated, though, all the jockeying for position and meddling with alliances that had induced the Achaeans to attack when they did, not to mention the miscellaneous attitudes people took to the business of Paris and Helen. As Mynes had explained it, it was as naive to think that the war was about one Spartan queen as it was to think it was about plundering. They both came into it, certainly, but they were no more than strands in a complex tapestry.

Briseus listened to his daughter as she worked out her argument, but he kept his expression of faint impatience and broke in before she lost herself totally in the mass of contradictions. 'Oh, that business about Priam and Agamemnon is all very well. Diplomacy and war, I know. Maybe they thought up all sorts of reasons to justify fighting at Ilios; but that has nothing to do with us. Lyrnessus is not Ilios. We are a bloody long way from Ilios, and there is no grand passion to justify this little raid.'

She flinched. All this bad language was not normal. It must be the nervousness getting to him. 'That's not true, Father. We are in Priam's territory, even if we are right on the edge of it, and the Mysians have been giving support to the Ilians. Maybe not as much as the Phrygians do, but enough to make us legitimate targets.'

'Huh. Like Lesbos, I suppose.'

That was true, she had to admit. Lesbos had never been so much as an ally to Priam, let alone part of his territory. It was difficult to think of a reason other than plunder for the devastation of that island, and the others like it.

'All right, that was piracy. But there are plenty of good strategic reasons for the Achaeans to attack Lyrnessus.'

'There are plenty of good strategic reasons for piracy, my dear. It fills men's bellies and puts clothes on their backs. But that makes it no better for the victims.'

'No. Of course it is dreadful. All the same, I think it helps a little to see why the Achaeans are doing it.'

At least, it had helped her. There was an abstract kind of

comfort in knowledge, even if the facts themselves were cheer-less. So it seemed to Briseis. Mynes, a thinker and talker himself, had taken it for granted that she wanted to know as much as possible. He had always talked to her about the causes of the war and its progress, but it had been largely out of general interest until it had become clear that the Achaeans were head-ing for Lyrnessus in pursuit of Aeneas and his Dardanian army. Now it was horribly, disastrously real to them both.

On each of the last six days, messengers had come to their estate with the latest news. Mynes never kept any of it from her. They had listened together to tales of Aeneas' escape from Achilles on the slopes of Mount Ida. To the account of his mustering an army of Dardanians, while Achilles sat calmly by. That was not a pirate's style, it seemed to Briseis. Pirates would rush in, taking little victories as they came to hand, but it had appeared to be Achilles' deliberate policy to hold off until he could force a major battle. Presumbly he was confident of winning it.

It had seemed unlikely at first that the fighting would involve Mysia, the country to the south of Dardania, at all; but evidently Achilles had liked the idea of taking on the Mysian army at the same time. He had harried Aeneas' men steadily southwards, never giving them time to group properly until they came to Lyrnessus, and then he had settled his mass of troops down in the plain by the river, making it quite obvious that this suited him nicely, thank you, and the battle was going to happen now.

Mynes' estates were to the north of Lyrnessus, almost directly on the route of the advancing armies. It had become clear that his household would have to pack their possessions and take refuge in the town. It would be Mynes' job to lead the Mysians, since King Evenus was too old and sick to fight. He had delivered Briseis at the palace the day before. It was packed to the rooftops with refugees, and though she had worked dutifully there all day, she had escaped in the evening to the quiet of her parents' home just down the hill, and to the attic room where she had slept as a child.

The point about Achilles struck her as a good one and she felt that she had made it quite well. Briseus looked at her for a moment as if it impressed him too, or she did. But he was not prepared to give ground and tried a different tack. 'These are Mynes' arguments. You get them all from him.'

'Of course I do. He understands it all much better than I do.'

'Always did think there was something schoolmasterish about Mynes.'

That stung, particularly since he was right. Mynes was fifteen years older than Briseis, and much more experienced. It was the path their marriage had naturally taken, for him to play the part of the teacher, and it suited his character. Briseis, though she was bright enough, was not confident in her own opinions and had easily absorbed her husband's. It worried her sometimes that he and her father differed so markedly. It had seemed quite reasonable to her before to resolve the differences by switching from belief in one of them to belief in the other. The argument made it a less comfortable choice. She did not wish to appear disloyal to either man.

She said cautiously, 'I think there's a deal of truth in what he says.'

'Maybe.' Briseus felt slightly guilty about the remark. Mynes might be dead, he thought, by that time tomorrow. 'I suppose it suits a general to take the politics of it seriously.'

'I think that is ever so important, more important than anything. To know what you are fighting for, and what the other side is fighting for.'

This was Mynes again. His enthusiasm for the coming battle was based on his deep sense of honour. And honour to him, Briseis knew, was not just one man's business: it was an inextricable part of the whole war. It was important that both sides felt themselves to be in the right, that every soldier launched himself into battle with heart and soul in the service of a noble cause.

Briseis did not expect her father to disagree. He did. 'Damn the other side. It's what we are fighting for that counts.'

'I don't think that's right. It wouldn't be the same if both sides didn't go about it honourably.'

'I dislike that word honour. It messes things. It leads people to think they are fighting for something distant. There is nothing distant about this damn battle. The men are not fighting for Helen and her pansy of a prince. I don't give a fig for Priam and his bloody taxes. We are fighting for our own safety and possessions, against a gang of greedy and bloodthirsty pirates. And don't you ever forget it.'

Briseis looked at him in surprise and alarm. His view was beginning to make sense to her. Not that she agreed with it — she was too committed to Mynes to do that — but she saw now that it had a terrible consistency. She suddenly understood why Briseus had reacted to the threat as he had. He had consistently resisted his sons' pleas to be permitted to travel to Ilios to fight with the main Trojan army: he preferred to pay the heavy taxes levied on those who refused to go. Now, though, he had sent them out onto the plain below Lyrnessus without hesitating at all. He might even have gone himself, had it not been for the lame leg he had earned fifteen years before, when a boar's tusk had caught him above the knee.

A shiver ran through her. She and Mynes had burst into the town the previous day on a wave of enthusiasm. Now it all seemed to have been washed away, and a dim shadow of resentment crept over her in its wake. It seemed that the people of Lyrnessus had nothing to gain, and everything to lose. They were no more than tokens in a war which they had not asked for, and in which they had not wished to take sides. Her husband, her brothers, his brother, were risking their lives not in some glorious endeavour, in which success would win them honour, riches and immortal fame, but in a squalid scrap. They were not heroes, they were barely different from alleycats defending their midden.

It was not the danger that worried her, though she was well aware of it. Mynes had spelled out all that too. If his troops were to lose the battle, Achilles would storm the town — even though it would not be easy to attack. The Achaeans would take it all: the gold, the bronze, and the women, just as Briseus had said.

She turned to look around the room. Briseus had a big house, built in the style that the architects of Ilios had spread across half a continent. The stone and brick were plastered inside, the floor was paved in gypsum. It was solid and elegant. Almost the whole of the ground floor was taken up by the megaron, the pillared great hall in which they sat. There was little sign of hardship, though trade had been hampered by the war. Briseus had always struck hard bargains, and he enjoyed surrounding himself with fine things. He ate from bronze dishes and drank from a cup that would have suited a king. More bronze shone on the trestle, in the light of half a dozen lamps. His tunic and his wife's were of fine, soft wool, the borders worked in several colours. It was a lot to lose.

It did not seem to Briseis that her parents had made any preparations for the attack at all. The rack for hunting spears by the door was empty, but otherwise things looked to be just as they always had been. The forthcoming battle was real enough to them, with their sons camped out with the army on the plain below, but not, as far as she could see, the storming that might follow it. Had Briseus not thought of hiding his valuables? His daughter decided to ask him.

The question clearly came as a surprise. It was as if Briseus' normally robust, even brutal realism refused to go that far. In a way, he mentally switched sides when he thought about the aftermath of the battle. The picture was there, but he saw it from the position of the conquerors surging in, not from that of the dregs of the defenders struggling against them.

'It will never do, to think about losing.' There was despair, but also a hint of decision in his voice.

'We have to. To prepare for it. It will not be the end of everything. People will survive.' Well, some of them, she supposed. 'And recover afterwards.'

Briseus shook his head. 'To me, it seems that there is something dishonourable about that. Something pathetic about the whole business of getting ready for a defeat. I'm not going to bury my valuables in the hope of coming back later to dig them up when the Achaeans have gone. If it comes to that, I'd rather kill myself, if they don't do it for me.' He paused, then added, with a sly note, 'I cannot see Mynes doing it either.'

There he was mistaken. Mynes and Briseis had done just that. Before they left their house they had sent the servants away while they dug a pit in the orchard, and placed in it everything of gold and bronze that they possessed, wrapped in an old coverlet. It had not seemed pathetic to Briseis, perhaps because Mynes did it in so matter-of-fact a way. She had not let herself think about the implications too deeply. There was something desperate about the deed, when you started looking at it that way. It would not do at all to have nightmares about it, imagine herself coming back, alone and in mourning, to dig up the bundle. She simply thought of it as a necessary and very sensible precaution. It was not really tempting fate. Of course they had left the finest dish in the household shrine, an offering to the snake whose presence, half-dangerous, half-protective, governed the future of the household.

She did not tell her father that. Instead she replied quietly, 'I think it would be a comfort to Mother if you did something.'

Her mother refused to return her look. Nevertheless she expected for a moment that the appeal would work, and that Briseus would rise from his chair to make some sort of preparation before it was too late. No. He turned instead to call the maidservant to pour more wine. There was a short silence, broken by the whimper of Briseis' baby as she awoke. Just as well, for there was nothing more that either of them could face saying. The girl hurried to fetch Ianeira from the nursemaid, and feed her before the cries grew louder and upset them all.

When she returned downstairs it was to find all but one of the lights extinguished. Her mother had gone to bed, but her father was standing by the door, his red woollen cloak thrown over his shoulders, as if he were waiting for her. He had been. 'I cannot go to bed yet. I thought I would walk down to the walls. Will you come with me?'

It was not usual for anyone to walk out after dark, but this was not a usual evening. Briseis did not reply, but she went to fetch her own cloak while her father lighted a torch. They made their way in silence through the porch and across the courtyard.

Lyrnessus was a small town and the walls were only a short walk away. It was a dark night and the path was littered with manure. All day flocks of cattle, sheep, geese and goats had been herded into the stronghold until they filled the main square in front of the palace, and the yard and ground floor of every peasant's hut. The town smelled of animal fear. Briseis took her father's hand as he limped down the hill. There was no sign of anyone else until they came to the watchpost at the end of the street. The sentry turned to watch them coming and then, when Briseus had hailed him, moved back to his post.

There was no stone wall around the town, as it was said there was at Ilios; but the site was strong, and there was only one track, up to the gate, shut firm, with a stone guard tower by its side. Round the rest of the town – except where the slope was too sheer to climb – was an earth rampart, with a ditch beyond, and a wooden stockade along the top. Briseus stayed at the foot, but his daughter scrambled up the slope to join the soldier who looked out at the plain below.

She stumbled as she reached the summit, and the guard turned again to take her hand and pull her next to him.

'It felt like stones underfoot.'

'There are. We are to throw them at the invaders, if it comes to that.'

She bent down, curious, and her hands felt round the shape of a pile of smooth river stones. 'They're big. I doubt if I could throw them far.'

'You won't do that, lady. It's for the soldiers who come back up to the town, or maybe the farm girls.'

'I shall do something, though, if they come.'

'They'll not come.' He was a young lad, in perhaps his thirteenth or fourteenth summer, and she could sense his smile in the dark.

Briseis did not answer, but turned to look out over the stockade. It would have been chest-height on a man; she could just see over it.

'You won't see much, miss.'

At first it was true, she could not, but as she continued to look she made out the lights, barely more than pinpricks, that shone across the plain from the near edge to the far distance. 'Those are the watchfires, are they?'

'Really more like campfires, lady. The soldiers sleep round them, to keep away the wolves. The ones nearest to us are our men, and then you see the break, and over there, down by the river, are the enemies'.'

The break was clear, once he had pointed it out. 'I see it now. They all look so tiny, like fireflies in the dark.'

'In daylight they are like ants. Thousands of them.' The boy paused, perhaps thinking it sounded too scary.

'The Myrmidons, yes. The ant troops who come up from the ground.'

'You don't want to believe those old stories, lady. They are only men. I reckon Achilles is no better a fighter than Prince Mynes, for all the tales they tell of him.'

'I am sure he is not.' Her gaze moved away from the horizon down to the fires nearer the town, where Mynes and his brother must be, and all the other men she knew.

'Your sweetheart is out there, is he?'

She smiled. He would have known her in the light, but the dark was deceptive. 'My husband, yes.'

'He'll be back to you by this time tomorrow.'

She was quiet for a moment, looking down at the fires, and then she said slowly, 'I hope so.'

Briseus shouted from the foot of the slope. He was growing impatient, and his torch was burning low. Briseis turned and slid back down to join him, and they made their way back to the house to get what sleep they could.

Lyrnessus stood on the edge of the upland that led to Mount Temnus. From its highest buildings you could look over to the west on a clear day and see, across the low-lying plains, the blue-green waters of the Edaitic Gulf, with the island of Lesbos close at hand and the open Aegean beyond.

In the morning Briseis looked at the familiar sight from her attic window, and then turned to feed Ianeira and to comb and braid her own long brown hair. She came downstairs to find the household seemingly as usual, with the servants sweeping and cleaning and her mother at her loom. 'Briseis, my dear. Could you fetch me another hank of this red-dyed wool from the storeroom at the back?'

'You're not coming to the palace?'

'I'm sure there is no need for that, dear. There are plenty of slaves at the palace.'

'Did the Queen not ask you to come to help?'

Her mother's brows lifted. 'Of course not, Briseis. She did mention something about bandages and I sent the cook's girl across. I told Melite to be ready to go as well, if she asks for more help. I would hardly go myself, would I?' Seeing Briseis' expression, she added after a moment, 'And I do think Mynes would be happier if you stayed here with us.'

'We shall need all the help we can get.'

'My dear. The battle will be over by midday, King Evenus told us. I do hope you are not getting into a state over it.'

Briseis opened her mouth to retort, and then shut it slowly. It would do no good, she admitted reluctantly to herself, to frighten her mother. If she was worried enough to come to the palace, she would doubtless be too over-wrought to prove any help with the work there.

'Mynes is expecting me to go there,' she said quietly.

'But you will come back at midday, dear? To feed the baby.'

'I'll be back at midday.'

As Briseis made her way up the hill to the palace, her annoyance with her mother evaporated. It was exasperating that she did not show more sense at times, but her optimism was not unique to her: it was very much a common attitude in the town. No, it was not optimism: it was more a placid complacency. King Evenus was a shrewd propagandist and had taken care to foster the conviction that the battle was little more than a formality and that Achilles would soon be sent packing. By the standards of the townsfolk, Briseus was a pessimist. So he must have seemed to his wife: and just as Briseis had been torn between her husband's view and her father's, so her mother had been divided between Briseus' and Evenus'. Clearly Evenus, whose opinions were more to her taste, had won hands down.

The town was crowded with women, children and animals, most of them standing about aimlessly. There was nervous anticipation but, as far as Briseis could see, there was no panic. Few people really believed that Achilles would win the battle; even fewer, that he would follow up a victory by attacking the town itself. Even the sacrifices and prayers had been done in a spirit that suggested that though the favour of the gods was essential, their help would hardly be needed.

Perhaps Evenus was right, Briseis tried to tell herself. Not in his beliefs, but in his strategy. For once there seemed to her to be disadvantages in Mynes' policy of facing up to everything. It was as if she were alone in expecting the Trojans to lose, and it felt like a guilty secret. Briseus was right in that respect: there was something dishonourable about dwelling too soon on defeat.

There were two companies of Mysian soldiers, one commanded by Mynes and the other by his brother Epistrophus, and almost as many Dardanians, with Aeneas at their head. It added up to a respectable force and the Achaeans probably did not outnumber then by much. The black Myrmidons were in a different class as fighters, though: Mynes had made that very clear to his wife. They were all seasoned warriors, while most of the Mysians were farmers and tradesfolk who had played no part in the earlier phases of the war and had no experience of fighting on this scale.

Briseis found it a relief to get to the palace, with its air of purposeful activity. The walking wounded were to be sent back there throughout the battle and the last preparations were being made for treating them. The troops' surgeon was holding court in the megaron, shouting out orders to his female helpers. Briseis spent till mid-morning tearing up old tunics for bandages, and then the wounded began to arrive and there was no more time for thought.

She had nursed men before, after hunting accidents or skirmishes with other tribes, and the work was nothing new, nor did the blood worry her. Some of the men talked continuously, some were silent as she went about washing their wounds, staunching the blood with yarrow powder and wrapping around the balm leaves, and bandaging, bandaging. She did not listen to half they said, and the other half did not make much sense at first. Every man had a different opinion of how the battle was going.

At midday she returned to her mother's house to feed the baby. Her mother and the servants seemed much as she had just left them: a shade apprehensive, but not panicky. There was no sign of Briseus. He had gone to the walls to watch the battle, apparently.

Had he given his wife any instructions? Briseis wondered to herself. Had they planned their escape, if it proved necessary? She was conscious of the contrast between her mother's determined blindness and Mynes' methodical pre-planning. Her own instructions had been very precise.

She went over them, upstairs, with the nursemaid. The trumpet calls that would signal the army's retreat to the town; the different sequence of calls that would warn the inhabitants to evacuate it. The locations of the rope ladders over the stockade, at the far side of the town. The clearing in the forest where their household would gather, to wait until it was safe to travel back to the villa. The secret caches of food. It was all as clear and certain as Mynes had been able to make it at short notice.

'Try to make sure my mother and the women come with you,' she added in an urgent undertone. 'But if they hesitate for too long, then you must leave without them. Don't wait for them. I will leave from the palace and meet you and Ianeira in the forest.'

'Yes, ma'am,' the girl muttered. Briseis looked dubiously at her. Maera was a biddable girl, but slow-witted and lacking in spirit. How would she cope, Briseis wondered, when the precision of the plans gave way to the chaos and terror of the moment of action? Briseis had a sudden longing to stay with Ianeira, or even to take both her and Maera to the palace, but she was conscious that such a move might push her mother into panic. The house was a safer place, in any case: if the Achaeans did break into the town they would make straight for the palace.

She settled for repeating Maera's instructions to Melite, her mother's girl, and took a couple of the other maidservants back to the palace with her.

A short while after she resumed her work the soldiers' stories began to change. Most of the wounded said nothing now, but their haunted eyes repeated what the others told her: that the battle was being lost, and fast.

More wounded came, and more, and then they stopped coming. She did not notice straight away, there were so many of them to be seen to and never enough women willing to do the job. The trumpets sounded the evacuation signal, a blare of alternate short and long notes, distant but insistent. But how could she leave the man whose leg she was bandaging? Another soldier had dragged him up the hill; he could not have walked, even with her help, could not have climbed the stockade. She worked doggedly on, willing her hands to keep steady.

Finally the surgeon came over to her. 'That's enough. It's time to get out of the town.'

'But this man: I cannot just leave him. And there are so many others who cannot walk.'

'There is nothing you can do.' The surgeon's voice was firm and Briseis looked up from her work. Her eyes moved from his face to scan the room. It was emptying fast and the line of men who had been waiting for her to see to them had disappeared.

'This man cannot move, though. What are we to do with him?'

'What do you think? Commend him to Zeus.'

The surgeon did not tell her to look away. Instead her eyes went down to his hands, and though he was quick, they followed the knife as it moved to the man's throat, and across it. She turned away, suddenly sick.

'Will you get going now?'

She went without saying another word. There was no sign of her mother's women. The square was full of animals, half of them not even penned, but there was no trace of the children who had been minding the flocks. Down the side alleys she glimpsed a couple of fleeing figures; otherwise, the town seemed deserted. In the open air the noises of fighting were loud: screams, yells, crashes and thuds, mingling in a cacophony of terror.

The baby. Had Maera left, had she followed her instructions? Had she taken Ianeira with her? In a sudden panic, Briseis veered from the main street towards the alley that led to her parents' house. She lifted her skirts as she ran down the hill. Somewhere behind her, a trumpet blared again, an unfamiliar sequence of notes that rose over the din of the battle. She almost fell through the open door into the big stone house.

The thick walls dimmed the noise. The house was very still. The cooking fire was roaring unchecked in the hearth. Briseis did not dare to call into the silence. Instead she ran up the stairs. The crib was there. She bent over it. Ianeira lay dozing, alone. Briseis plucked her swiftly out of the crib, and was at the door of the room, and on the stairs.

She heard the shouts when she was halfway down. They were loud: men in the street, surely, not far from the house itself. There was no rear way from the house: the back door led into an enclosed high-walled courtyard. She ran along the corridor and into the megaron and made straight for the high shelf by the hearth, where the knives were kept. Amazingly, the women had not taken them. She grabbed a short, sharp meat knife with a worn wooden handle. It felt oddly comforting in her spare hand.

As she turned from the hearth, the outer door slammed on its hinges. Dark shadows filled the porch. The soldiers were there.

The first soldier peered into the room. Briseis pressed herself against the wall of the hearth. She believed for a wild moment that he had not seen her; he turned, then shouted to the men behind him, 'We're in luck, boys!' He stepped a pace into the room, and two other soldiers followed him.

Briseis, backed hard against the wall with one arm clutching the baby, held the knife out in front of her. The soldiers circled warily towards her. They wore black tunics. One had a battered breastplate, another carried a shield. They did not meet her eyes; theirs were on the knife, and as she drew her hand back a fraction, the nearest man reached to pull out a knife of his own.

She moved, as swiftly as she could, away from him and towards the central soldier, who had no shield. She feinted a dash past him. His arm came out to stop her and she slashed with the knife, high, as she collided with it. The blade slid across his cheek, scoring deep into the flesh. Then her legs were kicked from under her and she was falling to the floor.

The child was ripped from her arms, and above the shouts she heard a sickening thud as its body was flung across the room and against the wall.

'Bloody bitch! Got me right across the face!'

'You take her first. I'll hold her down.'

Her head and shoulders were pinned down; she could see nothing, but she heard the rip as her dress was torn from neck to hem, and smelled rank sweat from the tunic of the soldier who was half suffocating her. She kicked out, wildly, and heard a string of foreign oaths. A firm hand caught her legs and another hit her, hard, on her bare thigh.

'Hold her feet down for me. She kicks hard, the bitch.'

She kicked again, as hard as she could, and tried to twist her face to bite the soldier who was pinning her down; but her captors were in control now and she could barely move her arms and legs. The pressure on her intensified; then suddenly, it loosened. Briseis kicked out again, connected with nothing, and then a hard foot landed in her ribs. She rolled onto her side, sick and winded.

There were soldiers' voices somewhere in the room, but she did not take in what they were saying, and nobody was touching her. Sobbing for breath, she half-slid, half-crawled across the floor to where the tiny bundle lay against the wall.

There was no blood to be seen, but when she picked it up the baby's head lolled unnaturally, and the open eyes saw nothing. Hers were blinded a moment after by the flood of tears.

The soldiers were forgotten. It was as if she and Ianeira were alone. Then a man's hand touched her shoulder, and a spasm of shock ran through her as she flinched instinctively.

A firm hand tightened on her upper arm, and another reached out for the bundle. 'There is nothing you can do for it now. Give it to me.'

'Not it, her.' She said it automatically, and looked up. Disoriented, she somehow expected the face to be Mynes'; but the eyes that she saw through her tears were not Mynes' brown ones. These were the dark grey of storm clouds, and there was anger, not love, in them.

'Give her to me.' The man had a harsh, commanding voice, but she did not move to obey. He added, more gently, 'I will see that she is put on the pyre.'

And not left for the dogs or the kites. The tears came back in a rush, and she hardly felt the soldier take the tiny body from her, or heard him say as he left, 'Automedon, get her to put on a decent shift and send her to wait with the other captives.'

The other man gave her a moment, then he came across to pull her to her feet. He slapped her hard across the face, to bring her to her senses, and she stood, suddenly still, in front of him.

'Find yourself a dress.' He said it in Greek, the tongue the other soldiers had used, but when she did not respond he repeated it in bad Trojan, and added, 'You cannot stay here, it's dangerous, you've seen that.'

She turned to obey him without saying a word. She went upstairs to the attic. A couple of her mother's maids had been sleeping there before she returned home: their chest was in the corner, and she opened it and withdrew a rough tunic of homespun. She turned from the man as she slipped off the torn dress and put on the tunic. He stood by the door, watching her.

'What is your name?' He said it as she was turned from him, and she did not reply. Again he repeated the question in Trojan. Briseis fastened a tin brooch at the shoulder of the tunic, tied a thin leather belt around it, and turned to him, saying with a dignity that sat strangely with her tearstained face and rough clothes, 'I am Briseis of Lyrnessus, wife to Prince Mynes.'

She said it in Greek almost as good as his, and much better than his Trojan. A smile came across his face. It was a square plain face, with honesty and intelligence written in it, and if she had met him in different circumstances she might have liked him.

'Indeed.' Automedon watched her for a moment, and then said, 'I think I will ask Achilles if I may have you.'

He could hardly have expected gratitude; he certainly did not get it. She walked across the room, pushing past him, and went down the stairs and out of the house for the last time.

Automedon followed her, and when they reached the street he said quietly, 'Mynes is dead, and his brother. Achilles killed them both. There will be nobody to ransom you.'

Briseis did not answer him.

When Briseis looked back on it all, she could see scattered scenes from the rest of that day in her mind as clear and distant as if she had watched them in a play. Nobody had taught her her part, and she seemed to have stumbled over her lines, but the soldiers had the confidence born of a hundred rehearsals and they swept the women along in their wake as they cleared the town.

She saw a group of captives standing at the foot of the hill, watching a band of soldiers manoeuvre a heavy wagon down the slope. It should have been pulled by oxen, but they could not have found any and had yoked a couple of mules to it instead. The cart was piled high with the goods they were taking from the town. The black tunics showed the men to be Myrmidons. She heard their shouts: they seemed boisterous, even merry, in the aftermath of the fighting. Mingled with the noise was the high whinny of the mules as they shied away from the bodies that still sprawled across the path, and unfamiliar hands fought to control them.

Two soldiers stood apart, watching the activity. Both were tall, strongly built, with a natural air of command. The taller man by a finger's breadth turned to say something to the other, clearly his superior. The second man laughed: no whisper of the words came to her, but she heard this sound ring out in the still air. He had taken off his helmet, and a glint of the late afternoon sunlight caught the red-gold of his long hair. His bronze breastplate was emblazoned with golden stars. It was dusty, and there was blood on the sword that hung from his belt.

The next scene came back to her repeatedly. The band of women and children stood huddled together in shared desolation; among them she saw her own face, dirty and streaked with tears. Around them, the black soldiers gathered. The man Automedon walked up to the two tall men; she saw him talk with them, and all three look in her direction. She watched herself look up in a gesture of defiance. She met the eyes of the tallest soldier, a fair-haired, handsome man. They struck her as a surprisingly soft blue: perhaps they had hardened in the heat of the fighting, but there was no aggression left in them. Then her eyes were forced to the second man, the commander, by the strength of his gaze, which struck her as hard as if he too had hit her. Only then did she realize who had saved her from the soldiers. There was no need to watch the rest of the scene. Even without looking at Automedon or hearing their conversation, she knew that she would not go to him. Later, it would seem to Briseis that there had never been a time when she had not known that she would belong to Achilles.

A last image. She saw herself again among the band of captives who had been set to trudge from the town. Alongside them were the wagons and a train of donkeys, mules and cattle, every one laden. Among the goods they carried she could make out the copper cauldron from her father's hearth, the silver trimmings of his harp. The black troops guarded the captives, but there were fewer of them, and Automedon and the two tall men were not to be seen. In the background, the walls of Lyrnessus rose up against the evening sky. A flame appeared from the house by the gate, and died down almost immediately. Then the flame could be seen again, reaching high into the sky, and the buildings burned with a fierce yellow light that shamed the setting sun. The wind had risen, and the charred rushes from the roofs drifted on the breeze and settled over the procession, turning the captives as black as their guards. It would have to do for mourning. There would be no other.

The force that had carried her through the early part of the day had gone by then. She did not care much what would happen to her. Perhaps she had been wrong when she told her father there would be survivors. She did not feel like one of them.

Priam was late coming to the council meeting: a king's privilege, and one that he always took. That day it exasperated Troilus particularly, and he shuffled on the hard stone bench as time passed and the chatter of the princes and generals rose and fell.

It was past midday already and the sun shone strongly though the high windows of the council chamber, catching the golds and silvers, reds and blues of the frescoes: a procession of tributary kings, another of priests and priestesses, and on the wall behind the throne, two great red and gold dragons breathing fire, the symbol of the royal house of Troy. Some of the frescoes were in need of retouching; the paint on the floor was faded and scuffed. Troilus' foot moved to rub dust into the eye of the octopus on the square by which he sat. There was something baleful about it, he did not want it staring up at him.

When he looked up, he discovered that Helenus was standing

expectantly in front of him. Troilus had not noticed him coming, with the crowd in the chamber. It had not been made to hold so many.

Troilus had the impression that Helenus had said something, but his mind had wandered far away, and he had missed his brother's words. Helenus laughed and repeated them. 'It's nothing urgent. I wondered if you were coming drinking this evening. There's a messenger in from Lyrnessus, and Ennomus and I were going to grill him for details of the Achaean attacks. You know they were moving south from Aeneas' territory, in that general direction. We'll start off in one of the taverns, then later we'll maybe take him down to the lower town.'

By that he meant the whorehouse. Troilus hesitated. He planned to expend his energy in a different direction, and he thought it might be easier to cut out of the entire evening rather than skip off halfway through. 'Will the messenger not report all that to the council — if it ever starts?'

Helenus laughed curtly. 'You must be joking. He'll give the council the bare details, and then pass the rest on to the Mysians in the camp. I'd not reckon to get anything out of him myself, had Ennomus not promised to come.'

Ennomus was a Mysian himself, though his lands were well to the east of Lyrnessus. True enough. Troilus knew he ought to show more enthusiasm. Helenus was an indifferent fighter, but he always knew the latest news. It was generous of him to offer to share his sources. 'When are you meeting?'

Before Helenus could reply the heavy doors at the end of the chamber swung open and the herald announced Priam's arrival. Dozens of conversations came to the same abrupt halt, as the assembled counsellors rose to their feet.

A priest came first, white-robed and shaven-headed, bearing the symbol of the King as High Priest and God on Earth, the great golden double axe. Then came the mace bearer, with the jewelled mace set with rubies and emeralds that represented the King's temporal authority. He halted to the left of the throne, leaving the priest to the right of it. A herald brought the speaker's staff, and laid it on a low table immediately before the dais. A long pause: then the bent figure of the High King came into view, swathed in a purple cloak encrusted with silver and gold embroidery. Every man in the chamber watched as he made his painfully slow progress to the dais, supported by a manservant on either side. As he came to the throne he reached out to grip the heads of the pair of carved dragons that formed its arms; then paused, and dragged himself slowly round to face the counsellors.

When he declared war on the Achaeans, the High King had been a vigorous and forceful man, a dominant ruler throughout the federated kingdoms of Troy. Its eight-year progress had seen him descend into old age, his body twisted by currents of pain, anger and determination. It seemed at times that only his iron will held him together, as it held the Trojans and their allies. Gazing now on the kings who paid tribute to him, the soldiers who fought for him, the priests who prayed for him, Priam's ravaged face quivered and stilled – the effort visible in every deep-cut line – into a mask of majesty.

He spoke the words of the invocations to the gods in an old man's voice that carried, nevertheless, to the farthest corners of the long room. He paused again, as if he was enjoying the total silence that he had enforced upon more than a hundred men. Then he sat, slowly and painfully, and received the mace into his hands.

There was a power about it all, the kingship and the familiar routines, in the heart of a citadel that had stood on this spot since time began. Even the bent figure under the heavy cloak could not diminish the effect. When he glared outwards at the council, it seemed as if the High King did not merely depend upon the power: he positively created it, reinforced it and radiated it in every direction.

With a murmur and a shuffle the men of the council sat too, on the stone bench around the perimeter and the serried wooden forms that filled the body of the chamber. Helenus nudged his way onto the bench next to his brother and whispered in his ear, 'Just after supper. I'll catch you in the palace and walk down there with you.'

Troilus was not certain he would be back before suppertime, but this was no time for argument. Both men turned their heads to the throne, and fixed suitably attentive looks on their faces.

At that time the council acted as a military assembly, though priests and old men who could no longer fight came to it as well. Troilus knew it was important, in a way. There was no other opportunity for the commanders to talk openly together, except in the few moments before a battle. Unfortunately it also tended to be boring. The council had no power to make decisions. Its members could only try to influence Priam; and if Priam was ever influenced – which his young son sometimes doubted – it was not here, where the issues were bogged down in a mass of formal procedures and arguments about minutiae.

At times Troilus felt that Priam did not notice anything that went on in the council chamber. Always despotic, the High King had become even more closed within his own thoughts over the past few years. He was old and seemed to doze sometimes in the tall throne. But then he would open his eyes and sweep them round the room, and nobody who caught his gaze would think it unseeing. Advice on policy he might disregard, but Priam did not tolerate disrespect or inattention.

All the same, Troilus let his thoughts drift while he kept his face frozen in the proper expression. The High King's preamble seemed to go on forever and there was little information in it. Priam had his own sources, but the snippets that they brought him were not for public consumption. He saw the council as an opportunity to obtain information, not to offer it.

Troilus' thoughts went straight to Chryseis, like a hawk homing in on its prey. Oh, he had laughed so much that morning over the business with the dog and the loom weights. When he had realized that she had planned it all so she could get her message to him in the confusion, he had laughed even more. Finally Cassandra had told him waspishly that if he must gurgle like a drain, she would fetch her chamber pot and tip it down him.

He did not usually think so much about his girls, most of them were forgotten the moment he had left them. It was surely the frustration. It was, what?, two days since he had been alone with her, and it had been three before that. Much too long. He had not thought of turning to any of his other girls, but he would have made love to her ten times a day, given the chance. And she would have let him. She would have smiled that sneaky smile, and laughed out loud in that funny mixture of shock and triumph each time he came into her.

He was hard at the thought of it, his face dissolving into its slow smile. Helenus turned a fraction and kicked him on the shin. Troilus sat up straight and mentally poured a jar of cold water over his head.

Priam's long speech was drawing to a close. The High King hunched forward in the high-backed throne, his hands with their jewelled rings gripping the carved dragons' faces, his tired eyes peering out at the men in the shadows of the chamber. He spoke rhythmically, almost musically, with more apparent concern for effect than for meaning.

It was the usual sort of stuff. Rations and troop dispositions, enlivened slightly by the prospect of a delegate mission to the Hittite King. It grated on Priam that the Hittites did not give him more support, though he had never done much for them and knew as well as anyone that they had trouble to deal with in the east.

A few moons before, Troilus would have pressed to go on the mission, though it could hardly hope to achieve much. There were few chances to escape from the citadel. Now he was reluctant to cut short his time with Chryseis before she was sent back home at the next full moon. Still, perhaps the delegation would not set out till after then. He considered the effect of volunteering to take part, then decided that it might as likely prejudice Priam against sending him. Best to say nothing.

Troilus would have expected the man from Lyrnessus to be introduced next, but there was no mention of him from the High King and instead the speaker's staff passed to the floor. Strange. Was the news from Mysia and Dardania so insignificant, he wondered, that it rated a lower priority than the arguments about rations for the horses? Or was it so bad that Priam was deliberately trying to dull its edge by postponing it till later in the meeting? Very few details of the latest Achaean raids had reached the citadel and he really had no idea what to expect.

Hector spoke first. A tall, strongly built man, he had established himself as Priam's heir amid competing claims from Paris, Deiphobus and the High King's many other sons, and as supreme commander of the allied troops amid equally strong competition from the more powerful of Priam's tributary kings. He exuded a quiet confidence that suggested he had never doubted the outcome of either struggle; indeed, that he had barely noticed there was any struggle. His features were large and well made, his hooked nose a replica of Priam's own; his voice was deep. He gave a deceptive impression of thinking and moving slowly, which made his sudden turns of speed all the more unnerving.

There was no rapidity about him that day. He made the usual complimentary remarks to his father, and then went on, 'Might I suggest Prince Helenus, sir, as leader of the delegation to the Hittites?'

Troilus' eyes moved to his other brother at his side. Helenus' insouciant expression gave no indication of whether he had expected this. He rose to his feet lazily and moved to the front of the room to take the staff. 'My brother flatters me. However, in the circumstances I feel that one of the southern leaders might be a more appropriate choice. Antiphus, perhaps? Or Aeneas, if he returns soon to Ilios?'

How typical of Helenus, Troilus thought. Letting Hector set up everything for him, then throwing it all away for the sake of a little easy popularity. Antiphus, the dark, heavy-faced commander of the Lydian forces, was sitting with a group of other southern commanders near the front of the chamber. Helenus glanced towards him and held out the staff as if he expected the Lydian to take it from him.

Instead he was rewarded by a nudge from the herald, and by Priam's voice cutting in firmly, 'Prince Paris will lead the mission. I shall select the other delegates later.'

There was a low rumble from the front benches, then the Thracian leader Peirous took the floor. As a northerner, he could and did argue strongly in favour of a southern-oriented delegation. Priam's eyes closed even as he was speaking and the High King's hand made a small, impatient gesture, as if to underline the fact that he was not prepared to be influenced. Sensing, perhaps, rather than seeing the gesture behind him, Peirous let his argument trail to a halt.

There was a short silence as the Thracian resumed his seat, then Antiphus rose to take his place. Taciturn with outsiders, he rarely spoke in council, and Troilus felt a mild curiosity to see how he would put a case that appeared to be doomed before he began.

The Lydian made no mention of the delegation. Instead he embarked on a lengthy discussion of the respective merits of alfalfa, chopped straw and barley mash as horsefeed. Important to the winning of a war, but hardly gripping. The attention that he had won initially was dissipated by the time he drawled in his thick Lydian accent, 'Of course, if the Achaeans establish a base on the Idaeus now that they have defeated the Mysians and sacked Lyrnessus, it will affect our supply route for the barley from Lydia and Caria.'

It was perfectly deliberate, and better done than Troilus would have credited. Antiphus paused for just long enough to under-line the effect, then he went on to enumerate some alternative sources of fodder. He had barely embarked on his next sentence when the chamber erupted with shouting. He ambled over and handed the staff to the herald at Priam's side, then sat down, thick with satisfaction.

Whatever Troilus had expected, it had certainly not been that. He had thought there might be news of losses in Dardania and perhaps a request from the messenger for help for Evenus. He had had no idea that Lyrnessus itself had been attacked, let alone that it had fallen. Had Helenus known? He glanced sideways. Helenus' face was drawn into a frown.

It was no great surprise that the Lydians already knew what most Ilians clearly did not. Antiphus' territory lay south of Mount Tmolus, not far distant from Lyrnessus. Of course his spies would get to him fast with news of anything so vital. The surprise was that he should let his secrets out, show the council how good his intelligence sources were. Troilus, too, frowned. Was it only an attempt to barter himself a place on the delegation – and if so, why had he not done it in private? Or had he some other motive, still to emerge? It seemed there was yet another person playing a murky and dangerous game.

All round Troilus there was excited argument. Evidently he was not the only one intrigued by the politics of it. We are becoming corrupt, he thought to himself. A city burns, hundreds of people die or are enslaved, and instead of being stunned into silence we burst into activity like a flock of vultures, all concerned to win advantage out of it. Whatever Antiphus' motives for talking, he made it clear that he would not really give a bean for Lyrnessus. It was just a staging post on his supply trail. Yet the man must have been there, surely knew people who were trapped in the city when it fell. Troilus himself knew nobody from Lyrnessus. If he could not grieve for the people of that city, though, he could grieve for those of Ilios, reduced by the war to indifference and callousness.

The herald was calling the meeting to order and Priam sat up straight in his chair. On him indifference sat kingly: it was beneath his dignity to express excitement or interest at the news. Behind the impassive mask he must, however, have been calculating hard. Would he call on the messenger now? Troilus' eyes strayed to the inner door of the council chamber, where in the shadows he could make out the shapes of two men. The messenger, and a servant sent to summon him to the meeting? The men stepped a pace into the room: yes, a stranger who was surely the Mysian, and one of Priam's household boys. The herald crossed over to them. He spoke fast, in a low voice. On the face of the stranger, sheer disbelief. The herald gestured to where Antiphus sat, and what the stranger read from the Lydian's fleshy face must have convinced him. He drew back, his hands coming up to his face. No, Troilus decided: he will make a poor show for Priam. The High King will be forced to return the staff to Antiphus.

Silence for a long moment, then Priam evidently concluded that there was no alternative. He gestured to the second herald, who handed Antiphus the staff. The Lydian rose again, this time to a chamber alive with concentrated curiosity.

What he had to say was, nevertheless, brief and disappointing. Aeneas' men, he understood, had been pushed south as far as Lyrnessus, with the Achaean forces in pursuit. The Achaeans had circled around the eastern flank of Mount Ida, rustling cattle and devastating villages and farmsteads in their path. Then Mynes of Lyrnessus and Aeneas had led a Trojan force in a pitched battle against the invaders. Achilles' victory had been decisive and he had followed it up by sacking the town. Presumably his forces were still on the shores of the Idaeus, taking advantage of the chaos following the victory to acquire further plunder before retreating back by sea to their base camp.

It was little more than the council could have deduced from his earlier statement, and the questioning that followed was so fierce that Troilus could not believe the man was keeping back anything else. The Lyrnessian, devastated by the news, was in no state to add more, and the curiosity of Ilios would have to wait until refugees from the battle reached the town. Priam, catching the mood of the assembly, brought it abruptly to a close, and his men spilled out noisily into the afternoon air.

After the press of the council chamber it was a relief to escape to the small, shady courtyard. Troilus paused, drinking in the clear air; then turned abruptly at the touch of a hand on his elbow. It was Helenus, who had followed him outside. 'Not much hope of a cheerful drink with that man tonight.'

'You had no idea?'

'About Lyrnessus? None. Of course the earlier exchanges were all planned, though we hadn't bargained for Priam intervening when he did. Antiphus was supposed to argue in favour of Aeneas, then we reckoned the delegation would go to one or the other of them. He might have told me or Hector something when we were planning it with him.'

'You didn't want Hattusas for yourself?'

'Me go to Hattusas? At midsummer? Zeus, credit me with some sense!'

A slight frown appeared on Troilus' open face. Helenus had a knack of making him feel like an unsophisticated child. He had a mind like a snake: every time Troilus felt close to understanding him, he would somehow slither away.

The two men made a striking pair, in the purple-and-gold-edged tunics that marked out Priam's sons. They were much the same height and had a similar manner, alternating between absent-mindedness and a rather boisterous charm. Troilus tended to copy Helenus' style of dress, which gave an impression of slightly dishevelled elegance. They might have been taken for twins, had Troilus not been as dark as Helenus was fair. Helenus' boyish look was deceptive, though. He was nearly ten years older than his brother, and in a harsher light it would have been easy to see the lines that had worn his face into an expression that some took for good humour, some for cynicism. Only the cruel would yet have seen cynicism in Troilus' face.

'So you'll stay in the palace tonight?' Troilus ventured.

Helenus glanced at him, then looked around at the other men who were beginning to make their way out of the courtyard, through the passage that led to the Palace Square, and down the hill to lower Ilios and the allied camp. 'I cannot see Ennomus, but I guess he'll still be ready to join us. He can tell us what sort of a man Mynes is, before he gets to Ilios. As he must do now, I expect.'

'You haven't met Mynes?'

Helenus shook his head. 'Never, as far as I can recall. Hector knows him well, but then Hector doesn't see the things that Ennomus does.'

Troilus stopped to consider that. It was true. Hector would give a solid, clear description of the man, while Ennomus and Helenus would build up his character out of hints and intuitions. If Hector saw a man as other men saw him, Helenus and Ennomus both seemed to see men as the gods did. It could be an intriguing evening, Troilus thought: watching them strike sparks off each other and generate pictures in the flames. 'I might be rather late for supper.'

Helenus grinned. 'Where are you meeting her?'

'Mind your own business.'

The retort had no visible effect. 'You want to be careful, Troilus. Hector wouldn't take it kindly if he knew, not while she's staying with him and Andromache.'

The frown developed into a scowl. Troilus had had no idea that Helenus had seen quite so much. 'Ah,' he said viciously, 'but Hector doesn't see the things that you and Ennomus do.'

'Other people do, Troilus, and one of them might feel inclined to tell him.'

Troilus made no reply as they clambered down the steep streets of the upper town. After a pause Helenus added, 'There was a pretty blonde I met in Asius' tavern the other evening. I could track her down for you tonight . . .'

'No thanks,' his brother retorted with venom.

'Got it that badly? Well, I'm off to the stables. See you later. Don't do anything that I wouldn't do.'

That left plenty of scope, Troilus thought to himself. Helenus was notorious for his women – not that he would ever consider marrying any of them. But then Troilus had no intention of doing that either.

The meeting had finished earlier than Troilus had expected and he was confident of beating Chryseis to their meeting place. Just as well: there was danger from snakes, scorpions and rats in the abandoned barn. She hated to wait there alone for him, even with her father's big dog to protect her, and had he been as late as he had feared he might well have found her gone.

Through the Dardanian Gate the paved road continued as far as the bottom of the slope, then the flagstones gave way to beaten earth and pebbles. The road remained wide as it curved to the west to follow the valley of the Scamander, but Troilus soon turned off it, taking a sidestreet that led eastwards.

Before the war almost all Ilios had been contained within the walls of the citadel. Ilios was not so much a town as a palace-fortress in the old style, built to house the royal family that ruled over the lands around, their servants, suppliers and dependents, an army of priests and a small garrison of troops. There had been just a few streets of houses, the homes of merchants and rich tradesmen, immediately outside the walls and straggling along the road that led up to the Dardanian Gate.

The population had grown many times over in the years of war. A camp had been established for the masses of allied soldiers, with a strong wooden stockade around it; and a shanty town of camp followers and refugees from territories devastated by the Achaeans had grown up in the shadow of the great stone walls. When the war went badly, and the Achaeans pressed the Trojans hard, it was just about possible to pack every inhabitant into the citadel. Most times, though, the lower town was safe enough.

Inevitably the big houses of lower Ilios had been neglected during the years of siege. Most had suffered damage in the raids and they had been rebuilt haphazardly, with rubble or mudbrick walls where once fine stonework had been used. Few windows faced onto the street. Even with the Achaeans plundering far afield, the street was almost deserted. People worked indoors, or in enclosed courtyards.

Further out from the citadel came the shanties. There were no streets there, just a mass of alleys winding between the shacks. The ground was littered with rubbish. Mangy dogs, and equally neglected children, scuffled aimlessly in the dust. A stench of excrement and decay hung heavy in the still air. No wonder Chryseis refuses to take this path, Troilus thought. His pace quickened, then slowed cautiously as a dog turned to sniff at him.

It was a relief to reach the edge of the pastures. The fields near the town had once been used for wheat and barley, but it was not thought safe to plant crops on this unprotected land any more and instead the plots were given over to rough summer grazing. The land stood high, looking out over the plain, and there would be enough warning of an attack to get the animals to safety. The fields were rutted with old furrows, now grassed over. Troilus skirted them carefully, tracing the narrow footpath that ran between the plots.

The crumbling stone barn, turf-roofed, stood at the far end of the fields, shaded by a large ash tree. No crops were stored here any more: they went straight to the jars in the vast storerooms within the citadel. Troilus and Chryseis had met there half a dozen times and only once had a herdsman given them a second glance. It was private, reasonably safe, and to Troilus that more than outweighed its disadvantages.

She stood against the jamb of the door at the barn end, watching him make his way across the final field. The dog made to trot towards him and he heard her call it back. She hated to be alone, even in the sunlight, and even with the sight of him coming to her.

He caught her about the waist and pulled her into the shadows for a long kiss. When he released her she took a step back, catching his hands in hers and inspecting his face thoughtfully.

She had the look of a play-actress who has rehearsed her lines, but is thrown off balance when her partner messes up her cue. Of course, he was not smiling. His mouth worked rapidly into a grin. 'You should train that dog to disobey you sometimes.

Otherwise people are going to wonder about those little accidents.'

'Oh, but it was so funny, wasn't it? And Helen was so furious. But you haven't heard yet what happened afterwards. You know Helen has a big jar of rose oil in her room, and she dips into it and sprinkles some on her dress whenever she passes by? Well, Cassandra tipped all the oil into a wine jar, and she filled the perfume jar up with runny honey. And then . . .'

The smile had reached his eyes. 'Later. Tell me later.' He was pulling her into the barn as he spoke.

'But Troilus, I must tell you . . .'

His kiss smothered her words and she gasped as he pulled her tightly against him. Her arms drifted about his neck, and her hands traced the path of Cassandra's runny honey, all down his back. She licked his nose with a giggle. 'All right. Later.'

It was much later before they talked again. They lay entwined on the pile of straw in the corner of the barn. Chryseis sighed and moved to lie half-across Troilus. There were faint lines scoring his forehead and she tracked them thoughtfully with a long-tipped finger. 'You were so serious when you came this afternoon. Had you been talking to someone?'

'I was thinking about the council meeting. There was news about the Achaean raids.'

'Oh.' She hesitated. It crossed his mind that she had been expecting his mood to have been caused by some more personal matter. Not another argument about marriage! He carried on, hoping to divert her. 'There was a battle at Lyrnessus – three days ago, I think, or maybe four. Mynes lost, and the Achaeans stormed the town. The news came as a shock. I had heard it was a fair stronghold, and nobody had expected it to fall so suddenly.'

Chryseis sat up, suddenly alert. 'Lyrnessus? The Achaeans are at Lyrnessus?'

Her reaction surprised him. She rarely showed an interest in the progress of the war, and he said without thinking, 'That's what I said. Why, what is it to you?'

As soon as the words were out, he realized. 'Sorry, that was a stupid question. It's not so far from Chryse, is it? Did you have friends there?'

She looked at him blankly for a minute, pulling at the heavy braid that fell over her shoulder. Then her eyes fell and a frown crossed her face. 'They came up the river, then? Past Thebe?'

Troilus was not even sure which side of Lyrnessus Thebe lay. Was it on the south bank of the estuary, or was it further inland? No Trojan ever liked to admit his ignorance, and an easy lie was on his tongue when it struck him that he knew the answer: the Achaeans could not have come that way at all. 'No, they had been raiding in Dardania. There was a strange tale about Achilles throwing a spear at Aeneas in his meadows. Maybe you heard it – it was going around the town a few days ago. There was some sort of a confrontation – I'm not sure what happened, the stories varied – and then the Dardanian forces went south to take refuge in Lyrnessus. A long way to go, but there are no good strongholds in Dardania. Achilles followed them overland. It's only two days since a messenger came from Aeneas, so the Myrmidons can hardly have attacked anywhere else on the way.' He thought a moment more, and added, 'They must plan to get back by sea with the captives, though. Would that put Chryse in danger? Anyway, it's no time for travelling in Mysia, so perhaps your father will stay a while longer in Ilios.'

The thought cheered him. It had not seemed as if there was any prospect of the priest extending his stay after the new moon, but if there was serious fighting around the Idaeus, surely he would not return until it was over.

Chryseis frowned again, as if to contradict him. Then she looked across at Troilus and seeing his grin reached over to hug him. 'Maybe. I have no wish to go home yet. You must know that.'

He laughed, and kissed her again. 'I won't let you go home yet. I won't even let you out of the barn, not till you've finished the story about Cassandra's honey.'

The sun was low in the sky before they slipped out of the barn, and Troilus had to run all the way to get home in time for his meeting with Helenus.

■

Just within the East Gate of Ilios was a quiet quarter which was the haunt of the city's goldsmiths, silversmiths, enamellers, bronze- and iron-workers. It was a maze of small alleyways, lined with smithies and one-man workshops, which intersected at a little paved square. In the centre of the Square of the Smiths was one of the city's two wells. There the smiths' wives and servants would come at sunrise each day to fetch water, and at sunset to chatter amongst themselves.

The square was unusually deserted on the afternoon of the council meeting, and when Andromache lowered herself onto the raised surround of the well there was nobody else in sight. She let out a little sigh, more of fatigue than of low spirits. It was several minutes' walk to the Square of the Smiths from her house on Palace Square and it had been enough to exhaust her, even in the cool of the late afternoon. The shade from the wild pear tree made the stone chilly to sit on; when her breath came back she shifted a little further along to sit in the sunshine.

Andromache was fond of the Square of the Smiths. It was the one place in the citadel that reminded her of Thebe. The square was shady and the buildings that surrounded it were old and unpretentious. They were taller than any buildings in Thebe, but she could forget that if she kept her eyes downwards. Clumps of amaranth stained the shadows at the foot of the walls a brilliant purple. All the other flowers Andromache had seen in Ilios had been painted ones. There was barely a trace of the inexorable wind that washed day and night over the heights of the citadel.

From the alleyways came the usual noises and smells of the smiths' quarter: the low hiss of fire and bellows, the tap-tap of hammers, the unmistakable smell of charcoal and paint mingled. A louder scuffling noise in one of the alleys made Andromache look up sharply. A moment later a small boy emerged, struggling to carry a large trussed lamb. A flicker of annoyance shone in her face. She came to the square to gossip; it was unusual for her to have to wait for a chance to indulge in her favourite pastime.

Andromache was a plain woman, with a snub nose and wispy hair, but she had an easy manner and a ready smile. She wore a dress of fine-quality wool, dyed a rich red, that had no pretensions to fashionableness. Her neck was looped with gold and her fingers were laden with rings. Her feet, hennaed in an intricate pattern of curves and circles, tapped out their mild impatience on the paving stones of the well surround.

Shortly afterwards the swordsmith's wife Eirene emerged from a sidestreet and crossed to the well, with a stirrup jar balanced on her head. She lowered it carefully onto the surround, peered inside as if to satisfy herself that it was clean, and turned to nod at Andromache. 'Good afternoon, my Lady. How's the baby coming along?'

Andromache beamed. The midwife had been with her that morning. She had felt the baby, pronounced when it was due, and sworn that it was a boy because it sat so high up in her belly. The general belief in Thebe had been quite the opposite: that this was a certain indication of a girl. Was she usually right? Andromache had been waiting for someone to ask ever since.

Eirene listened carefully but impatiently, as if she could hardly wait for her turn to speak. 'Oh, she says it will be a boy every time. It's what we all want to hear, isn't it? And she'd never say anything else when the baby's as important as yours, my Lady.'

Andromache smiled. She always enjoyed Eirene's peculiar blend of tact and frankness. 'So you reckon it's a girl?'

'Well,' said Eirene, settling herself comfortably next to Andromache and abandoning her token formality, 'I always thought like you did, dear. I've had four girls, and they always sat high in me like yours, and two boys who lay differently, lower down, like. So I wouldn't like to say as the midwife is right. But then again, she just might be, mightn't she?'

'It's hard to know, if you haven't had one before. If this is high or low, I mean.'

'Stand up a moment.'

Andromache stood, giggling, and after a quick check that nobody was around Eirene reached over to feel round her belly.

'Ooh, it kicked me! Kicks hard enough, so maybe it is a boy.'

Andromache settled down again, reached out a hand and caressed the spot where the baby's foot had kicked. 'I think,' she said cheerily, 'I'll tell myself it's going to be a girl.'

'Would you mind if it were? Would he mind?'

'Prince Hector? Oh, I don't think so, so long as I have a boy afterwards. He'd be a little disappointed, I suppose, after we waited so long for it to be on the way.'

'It wasn't all that long. What was it, a year last midwinter you married him?'

'It seemed a long time.' Andromache sat silent for a moment, as if she was reviewing that long miserable first year in Ilios, and then brightened up, afraid perhaps that she had shown feelings she would have preferred to keep to herself. 'Really,' she went on, 'I'd quite like a girl for myself. They're not so much trouble, are they?'

'Not when they're babies, they're not, but they can be terrors when they're growing up.'

'I don't think I was a terror. It would be fine if I had a daughter just like me. Or one like Hector.' An involuntary image of Hector's sister Polyxena, who was very like him, came into Andromache's mind and gave her a momentary thought that this was not entirely true. 'Or like my mother or father, even.'

'I can't imagine a little girl like King Priam.'

Another giggle erupted from Andromache. 'Oh, she couldn't be. Think of a girl with that kind of nose! Mind you, Hector has it, but women don't get noses quite like that, do they?'

'Hardly ever,' Eirene said convincingly.

'It would be nice if she were pretty. I wouldn't want her to be plain like me.'

'You're very nice-looking,' Eirene retorted quickly. 'But there are some real beauties in the family. Chryseis, for instance — she's related to you, isn't she?'

'Not very closely,' Andromache said doubtfully. 'Anyway, I don't know that I would like a daughter quite like Chryseis.'

'Oh, not quite like. She's a nice girl, of course, but it must be a worry keeping an eye on her.'

That was not entirely what Andromache had meant. Though

she had a vague awareness that she ought to keep an eye on Chryseis, who had no mother after all, she had always found herself extraordinarily reluctant to do so. She could hardly say it was a burden, looking out for a girl who was never in the house. It was more that she did not . . . she just did not get on with the girl. She was still trying to frame a suitable reply that admitted some of this, but not too much, when Eirene said, 'Do you think Prince Troilus will marry her?'

'Troilus?'

'Oh, didn't you know?' Sympathy, mild embarrassment, and pleasure at the prospect of telling a choice piece of news mingled in Eirene's expression. 'Of course,' she added quickly, 'I only found out myself the other day.'

Andromache took in the expression without pleasure. Reluctantly she said, 'Found out what, Eirene?'

Eirene glanced around, as if to ensure that they were still alone. A slave girl was just making her way into the square, but she passed through without coming near the well. As the girl disappeared in the direction of Silversmith's Row Eirene slid a little closer to Andromache, and said in a piercing whisper, 'There's been talk about it in the lower town. Apparently he meets her in a barn out by the east fields. One of the herdsmen saw them together there and it could hardly have been by chance. I wouldn't say anything just for the sake of gossip, but it would be a pity to see her get into trouble. A priest's daughter, and a relative of yours. They say she's clever, but the clever ones are not always the sensible ones, are they? There was a tale, too, that she's been promised to Artemis — or did I hear that wrong? I wondered if people had been making it up to add a bit of spice to the story. She doesn't seem the type for a virgin life, does she?'

Andromache's mouth opened momentarily and her face, normally so placid, seemed to have lost all its shape. The embarrassment won out in Eirene, who turned to the well and busied herself with the rope and leather bucket until she heard Andromache's voice, as steady as ever. 'That last bit is true, at least. Chryseis' father does mean her to go to Artemis. As for the rest, Eirene, I'm surprised to hear you repeating such rubbish. It's just as well I trust what you say about the baby, because you seem to have this story completely round-about. Distrusting the truth, and believing what I never would!'

Even the little laugh that she brought out did not take the sting completely from her words. Eirene's face grew red and her hand shook slightly as she poured the water into her jar. 'I didn't mean to give offence to you, my Lady.'

'You haven't, Eirene. I'm sure you meant well. But I should be offended if I thought you had repeated this to anyone else. It may be meant as a bit of fun, but it could do a great deal of harm to Chryseis if people did believe it.'

'Nobody means that, not at all. We'd just like to see a nice wedding to brighten up the town a bit. And they do make a lovely couple, don't they?'

A lovely couple. It annoyed Andromache, that phrase. It was not just trite, it was positively plebeian: the kind of thing nobody in the palace would ever say. It seemed to summarize, in three innocent words, all the reasons why it was inappropriate for her to be sitting here on the bench round the well chatting to a swordsmith's wife. She had a sudden urge to stand up, make a cutting remark, and sweep off in aristocratic fury and disgust. She fought the urge with difficulty, and said instead, 'It would not do at all, though. I am sure Chryseis knows that very well and it will all turn out to be a mistake.'

'I dare say I was wrong, ma'am,' Eirene said without troubling to disguise her annoyance. She tipped a last bucketful of water into the stirrup jar and made it politely clear that she was ready to make for home as soon as Andromache had left.

Andromache kept a determinedly neutral expression on her face as she made her way slowly back up the hill. You never knew who was watching you in Ilios – as Chryseis, it seemed, would find out soon enough. She could feel the frown aching to emerge beneath it. The news had ruined her afternoon.

Chryseis was not there when she reached the tall house opposite the palace, with its slightly faded white stucco and dark timbers. Andromache's housekeeper was at the door to the courtyard almost before she could get her own hand to it. She frowned at Andromache, as if to express her disapproval of these low-class jaunts without any attendants, and said, with a note of triumph, 'Lady Polyxena has been waiting for you, ma'am. She's been here for a while. I showed her to your room and took the liberty of offering her some wine.'

'I hope you watered it well, Helike.'

'Of course, ma'am,' Helike replied with patent insincerity. She trudged deliberately up the stairs in front of Andromache so that she could announce her properly to the visitor.

Andromache's private room was on the second floor. It was smallish, almost square, high-ceilinged and airy. A long narrow window looked out over the flat rooftops of the citadel to the plain below. On the walls, a fresco of country scenes echoed and romanticized the view outside. Two aggressively fashionable women sat in the painted landscape, sharing a picnic. They wore court dresses, ridiculously inappropriate in the countryside, with long tiered skirts and tight bodices that exposed their breasts. One was in red, the other in a harsh blue.

There was a heavy wooden bed, draped with a brightly coloured Cretan blanket, a small inlaid table awash with perfume bottles, and a carved chair. Polyxena rose gracefully from the chair as Andromache entered. Tall and vivacious, she had the knack of persuading people to think her pretty before they looked again and noticed that her features were disturbingly like Hector's. Her dress was similar to those the women in the fresco were wearing, but heavily trimmed with the red ribbons that were the latest fashion, and there was paint of a matching shade on her cheeks and nipples.

'I'm sorry if you have been kept waiting,' Andromache managed to say with a puff as she subsided onto the bed.

'Do have the chair. You look tired out.'

'No, the bed is comfier. I find the chair too low now. It's just the walk. I'll be fine in a moment.'

Polyxena gave a thin smile. She did not ask where Andromache had been. Her sister-in-law's chats with the tradeswomen were much discussed in the palace. In fact, she thought silently, Andromache could have been taken for a rich merchant's wife herself in that dreadful shapeless gown. But it was no use discussing clothes with Andromache: even a palace reception would not get her into a fashionable dress. 'I came to see what the midwife told you. Helen was asking, and Cassandra. Did she say when the baby is due?'

Andromache's returning smile was more open. Even she could not suspect any bitchiness behind that question. She settled down comfortably as Helike returned with a second cup of wine – heavily watered, this one – and began to relate her news all over again.

Chryseis was forgotten until Polyxena had left, with a promise from Andromache to come to the women's megaron at the palace the following morning. Alone, Andromache sighed. Polyxena on her own had not been too bad. But to face her, and Cassandra, and Helen, all at the same time . . . it made her heart sink to her knees.

Andromache had always liked to chatter, to be one of a group. It was a flock of starlings she wanted, though: she had no skill at being a dragonfly among dragonflies. She hoisted herself back onto the bed and curled up on her side, cuddling the bulge of her belly.

There was something else nasty, at the back of her mind. Oh, Zeus! That wretched girl. The curl of her body tightened and her fists clenched until the fingernails cut into her palms.

It had to be true. Whatever she had said to Eirene, she did not seriously doubt that. She could not remember ever seeing Chryseis and Troilus together, but perhaps that was evidence for, not against, the tale. She could recall, all too clearly now, the flushed excitement on Chryseis' face when she had come back to the house later than she should have, the thinness of her excuses. Talking with Helen till long after dark! Getting lost on the way back from Apollo's sanctuary! She must have been a fool herself to be taken in by them.

It was equally true, however, that Chryseis was intended to be a priestess of Artemis. Spice to the tale! That was an understatement if ever there was one. A priestess would be killed if she was suspected of laying with a man. Not that Chryseis was a priestess yet, but that made only a little difference. People did not question their destinies in Andromache's world, and that was Chryseis'.

Why, why then should she do it? Why should a well-brought-up priest's daughter do something so wicked and dangerous?

Why should a girl who feared the gods as Chryseis seemed to, as every sane person did, do something so totally opposed to the destiny they had set down for her?

Lying there on the high bed, as the sun drew down and the room slowly darkened, Andromache fought to place herself in the other girl's position. To make Chryseis' life real to herself, to gain some kind of understanding of the girl's feelings and motives.

Oh, it was difficult. They had always been so much at cross purposes. The best Andromache could do was to let her mind go blank and invite the images to enter from down the years that she had known Chryseis. The skinny child in Thebe, roaring with laughter as she chased Maris round the corridors of the palace and fell with him, a heap of mingled arms and legs, in the corner by the armoury. The girl at the shrine, unnervingly shot through with the light of the gods, dancing the sacred dance with a dangerous perfection. The young woman who had come to Ilios two moons before, bursting with excitement at the thought of seeing at last the city whose streets were paved with stone. The woman who spent hours fiddling with her clothes and hair, in whose room Andromache always seemed to find her own mirror, who hung on every vapid word Helen had to say about clothes and make-up. The woman who laughed at the soldiers who had lingered about the gate to the tall house ever since she arrived in Ilios, pretending to wish they would go away and yet always managing to find a glance and a word whenever she passed them.

The other images came harder, for they were of scenes which Andromache had not witnessed. A barn in the east fields, long abandoned. She saw Troilus, scowling and then laughing. She saw a pile of straw, and almost unconsciously added to it a few mice, and more than a few spiders. She tried in vain to imagine herself as Chryseis, greeting her lover there in the shadows, and to see the two of them performing an act that she herself knew only from the comfort of the bed on which she lay. There was no ecstasy in her imagination: Andromache knew nothing of ecstasy. She shivered, in fastidious distaste. How could any woman risk so much to do such a thing, in such surroundings? A lovely couple, Eirene had called them.

Nobody had ever called Andromache and Hector a lovely couple. That thought came unbidden and stuck in her mind, like a troublesome tooth she could not help feeling with her tongue. She was – yes, she supposed she was jealous of that. Not that she would ever have wanted to meet a lover in a barn. She had no urgings towards wantonness. She would have appreciated some romance in her own life, though, and Hector had never shown any inclination to provide it.

And Troilus? Asked the day before, Andromache would have admitted to an ambivalence about Troilus. He had a handsome face and a wide smile, and he would extend his charm to her on occasion. But there was something private about him. He had more than a touch of the elegant, impenetrable façade that Helenus showed; that his twin Cassandra showed, and Polyxena, and Helen, and all the Ilios courtiers who made Andromache feel like a stranger up from the country.

Talking to the women from Thebe, Andromache would have called them all hard and cynical. In Ilios, Troilus the lover – another woman's lover – took on suddenly all the desirability of the unattainable. He symbolized for Andromache a whole world to which she had never possessed the password. Now Chryseis, so vain, so entranced by everything about Ilios, by the slick jokes, the phoney glamour of Helen, seemed to have acquired that password. Andromache's distaste for the palace world was not affected, and yet she was conscious that it was not the knowing dislike of one who has tried something and found it wanting: it was the reasoned conviction of one who knows that what she rejects could never have been for her.

Yet it should not be for Chryseis either. Chryseis had a different destiny. Did she not see that?

Love could make men and women do stupid things: do dangerous, wicked things. Andromache knew that, if not at first hand. She thought back to the brightness in Chryseis' eyes. Was the girl in love? Was it no more nor less than that?

If she had seen the pair of them together, or even known the emotion herself, Andromache might have accepted that easily. She had not, though: and even as she thought it there came into view a different picture. Of Maris in Thebe: her favourite brother, aching for Chryseis; and of Chryseis, enjoying his adoration and yet happily immune to it, treating it all as a game.

Maris had not seen Chryseis' fate as immutable. He had hoped to marry her himself, Andromache's mother Astynome had told her. He had wanted it so badly that he had overriden his family's objections and asked for her. Chryseis had surely been told of that, even if her father had refused to consider it. If one man had hoped to marry her, perhaps she expected others to as well? Was that the game she was playing now? Trying to lure Troilus into marriage?

It was not proper for a girl who was intended for Artemis' shrine to make a trip to Ilios. Hector and Andromache had said as much when Chryses had delivered his daughter to them, and the priest had explained it away as a last indulgence before the girl underwent her initiation. Andromache had thought it a dangerous game at best, exploring forbidden territory and yet meaning to turn your back on it afterwards, though she had had no option but to accept the excuse. But perhaps Chryseis had never intended to settle for just a taste of the forbidden? Perhaps she had always intended Ilios to bring her a husband?

That made sense. Andromache could see it, angry though it made her. How could the girl be so arrogant? However Andromache looked at it, it seemed to her hopelessly wrong. Wrong of Chryseis to dupe her father, wrong to risk the wrath of the gods, even wrong, perhaps, to ensnare Troilus.

It was not as if Andromache had found her own fate particularly congenial. It had been the hardest thing she had ever done, to leave her home and the family she loved, and come as the wife of a man she barely knew to this alien city. Every day of her first year she had fought the longing to rush home to Thebe. But it was necessary to fight. Everybody did. And slowly she had begun to find ways of living with her destiny, to discover sources of pleasure that did not conflict with it. She saw the chats with Eirene and her friends as a kind of halfway stage, a prop that she would have to cast aside before she emerged as a fully fledged princess of Ilios. An indulgence, yes, but they were intended to help her come to terms with her fate, not to change it.

The priest Chryses must surely have seen the trip to Ilios in that light: as a palliative for his daughter. It was her wickedness, her madness that had made her see it instead as the mooring from which she would launch herself in a different direction.

It was done now. If the girl had lain with Troilus she had changed her fate irrevocably. Its alternative was not yet shaped, however. It was up to not only Chryseis, but her father, Hector, Andromache herself, Troilus even, to play a part in determining it.

What should Andromache's own part be? She consciously asked herself the question, and found it impossibly difficult to answer it. Should she urge that the girl be punished, be sent to the sanctuary regardless, but in the ignominious role of an uninitiated servant? Should she help the girl towards a marriage with Troilus? Should she urge Hector and Chryses to send her back home? Not – please Artemis, not – to a marriage with Maris. That would be too cruel. Chryseis could not stay in Ilios, though, unless it was to marry Troilus. The only alternative would be for her to become a hetaira, a high-class whore, and that was no fate for a priest's daughter.

Andromache had never consciously failed to do her duty. She wanted to do it now, but she had no wish to do anything that was unpleasant or embarrassing unless it was really necessary. The more she thought about it, the less certain she was what her duty consisted of. She was not even sure what was right for the girl, let alone how to bring the right thing about. Should she tell Hector? She balked at that: he was not a man to sort out this kind of womanish mess, and any attempt to tell him might destroy their carefully built-up accord. Should she talk to Chryseis herself? There was nothing she relished less. Nor was there anything she could imagine saying to Troilus, and she could see that even a tactful word with Chryseis' father would probably have a disastrous effect.

She had just about persuaded herself that the proper course was to watch and wait while doing nothing when a clatter below told her that Chryseis had returned. Guilty at having made such a cowardly decision, she hefted herself off the bed, determined at least to go downstairs and do nothing without any further delay.

It was not Chryseis at all. Hector stood at the foot of the stairs, looming large as a giant in the dim light. There was an air of resolution about him. He was wearing his bronze breastplate. It was dulled by a film of dust, but the entwined dragons still gleamed faintly in the gloom. He had the look of a man who had just been fighting, but it was not clear to Andromache if he had won.

The shock of seeing him so unexpectedly brought to her a surge of fear, as if he had come to fight her. She did not move from the top of the stairs and the colour washed over her face.

Hector seemed momentarily at a loss. Then he gave a rather forced smile and moved up the stairs towards her. 'Helike told me you were resting. I thought for a moment that it was Chryseis rushing to meet me.'

If it was intended as a joke it did not strike Andromache as very funny. All her elaborately rationalized empathy for the girl was washed away by a torrent of sheer hatred. The words came out before she could stop them. 'Apparently it is Troilus she rushes to meet. She's probably with him now. They meet in a barn by the east fields.'

She stopped short, horrified. So was Hector. He gaped in amazement for a moment, then moved forward to hold her as she sagged by the side of the stairs. 'What nonsense have you been listening to now?'

That was unjust: she was not really a gossip, and she took the words more harshly than he had intended them.

'Eirene told me. The swordsmith's wife.' Guilt made her admit this before Hector asked her. 'A herdsman saw them going inside. It's all round the citadel, it seems.' Appalled at the flood of revelations, Andromache was coming close to hysteria.

Hector regarded her with mingled annoyance and concern. 'You are making yourself ill. I'll call Helike. She must help you upstairs and give you a draught of something. Leave all this to me. I'll go and find the girl, and sort it all out.'

Weak from the excitement of the afternoon, Andromache did not try to stop him. She let Hector carry her back to the high bed, and she was asleep from the mixture that Helike forced down her before he returned.

■

Chryseis came back to the citadel across the fields, on the path that led to the Phrygian Gate. It was the quietest path, and the fastest, but she hated the gate itself. There was a long, narrow passage between the walls, overseen by the watch tower, and the gate at the top was normally shut, so that she had to call out to the guards. She had a recurring fear that the guards would ask what she had been doing out in the fields. They had a right to question strangers, but she had never known them ask any Trojan such questions. Still, a stubborn place in her mind refused to prepare an innocuous answer.

She had always enjoyed acting, behaving like someone who was, and yet was not, herself. In Chryse she would flirt with Maris and the other boys, secure throughout in her underlying innocence. Nobody thought of her as a loose girl: she was nice Chryseis, the priest's daughter. Now in Ilios it had all become frighteningly serious. Worse, she was not sure any more which was the game, and which real life; which the feigned Chryseis, and which the genuine. Chryseis the flirt, the girl with the secret lover – surely that was the real Chryseis now? And the role she had to play was Chryseis the virgin, the good girl who kept her eyes down when she met strange men. It was a part for which she seemed to know none of the lines.

'You enjoy all the subterfuge,' Troilus had accused once, with an exasperation that she only half believed. He enjoyed it too, surely, even when he pretended to be annoyed by it? Her indignant denial had been more than an automatic response. It did frighten her. How could anyone enjoy this hammering in their blood, this rush of nervous anticipation?

But it was true: though the anticipation was dreadful, the acting itself was rather fun. Taking a deep breath she forced her feet forward, calling the dog to her heel. At the top of the passage she shouted out. Silence, then footsteps, and a young soldier with a tangled mop of black hair and a sharp, foxlike face drew the wooden gate back, making a gap just wide enough for one person to slip through. He kept his staff across the gap, barring her way. A stricken expression flickered across her face. Laughing, the soldier caught her eye, and there was something not feigned at all in the look that they exchanged.

Chryseis held the soldier's gaze for a moment too long, then looked down with a shy, animal smile. A whistle from behind made her look up quickly: the rest of the guard were standing in the doorway of the tower watching her. She flushed. The soldier drew his staff back but he stayed standing in the gateway, where she would have to rub against him as she slipped through. There was nobody else in the passage. 'Come on, love, I won't bite you.'

'It's not a bite I was expecting.' Chryseis grinned at him and slid between the gates. The soldier caught her arm with his free hand and she stumbled against him in the shadow of the gate where the other soldiers could not see them. He bent to snatch a kiss and pushed her up against the gate, pressing his body hard all down the length of hers. The dog barked, its breath warm against her legs. The soldier loosened his grip as if he feared a bite himself, and Chryseis wriggled away with a look of indignation. How dare he! All the same, there was a new bounce and swing about her walk as she carried on into the town, feeling the soldiers' eyes on her back.

She was conscious, though, that she had mishandled the scene. What would nice Chryseis have done? Screamed? Surely not. The trouble was, the soldier would not have kissed nice Chryseis. She had gone wrong before that. Eyes down, that was it: no looking at men. Her eyes dropped automatically as she thought it, to inspect the cobbles and the gutter.

She did not lift them when she turned the corner into a busier street; and almost ran into Hector. He had been charging down the hill and he pulled himself up sharply, so close in front of Chryseis that she was forced to take a step backwards. She sidestepped neatly out of his path, converting her giggle into a polite murmur of greeting, and was surprised to find him turn to walk with her back up the hill. The servant who had been scrambling after him turned too, and followed a few paces behind them.

'Am I late for supper?' Chryseis knew she was, but she also knew that it was not Hector's style to come scouring the town for absent guests when his own supper awaited him.

Hector let out a deep grunt and Chryseis took a look at him, curious. What was the man about? He had obviously not washed or changed since he had been fighting that afternoon. His face was rather red and there was a contained anger about it. She had rarely seen him so flustered. What could be so urgent, she wondered, that he should rush through the city, and then suddenly so unimportant that he could forget it and walk back home with her?

Aware of her look, Hector turned to her. He saw his agitation reflected in her face and made a conscious effort to cool down.

'Andromache is not well,' he said. 'Helike is helping her to bed.' Chryseis made no response, and he added with a touch of annoyance, 'I expect the supper can wait till we get back.'

Chryseis politely expressed concern, and Hector frowned. He had said the wrong thing and he was not sure now how to continue with the confrontation.

Bloody women. He had done his best to work off the black mood into which the council meeting had thrown him by a good hard ride into the far fields. Fighting – yes, he had been fighting, but his enemies had been private demons, not Achaeans. Then he had come back to a hysterical wife, and now this jaunty trollop. Her hair was escaping from the neat plait she normally wore across her shoulder, her dress was crumpled at the back. She looked exactly as if Troilus had just tumbled her in a haystack. Hector had never paid much attention to the nudges, winks and comments about Chryseis, but now he saw them in a new light. She's a common little tart, he thought viciously.

And unfairly, he knew, because without Andromache's revelations to guide him he would not even have noticed her disorder. Hector was in no mood to be fair, though. He had rushed out of the house, not in any urge to confront the girl immediately, but rather to get away from the heady atmosphere of hysteria and the sight of Andromache's tears. Now he would have to do something. But what? He could hardly accuse her outright of carrying on with his brother, and what was it to him if she did? Troilus would give him no thanks for interfering, he could be quite sure.

Chryseis was his guest, however, and a distant relative of Andromache's. Troilus might have half a dozen bastards in the town, for all Hector knew, but it would not do for him to get another one on this girl while she stayed in Hector's house. Hector had had no time to consider the implications, but it seemed clear to him then that he would have to get her out of Ilios. He said in a curt voice, 'When is it you go back home? At the next full moon?'

Chryseis gaped at him. Hector gazed steadfastly ahead. He realized belatedly that he had been more rude than he had intended.

'That's what Father had planned, but with . . .' Chryseis pulled herself up sharply, and continued as smoothly as she could, '. . . with all this trouble in Dardania, I doubt if it will be safe to travel to Chryse.'

Hector appeared to consider this new dimension of the problem. Finally he said, 'It should be safe enough. Dardania is a long way away, on the other side of the estuary, and there is no reason for the Achaeans to go anywhere near Chryse. Even if they go south, they will take to their ships from the north bank of the Idaeus. If you travel overland and skirt round the west of Mount Ida, you'll not cross their path. It might be best if you leave a few days sooner than you had planned. I shall arrange an escort for you and Chryses, of course.'

You sneak, Chryseis thought with a mixture of annoyance and admiration. It had become embarrassingly clear to her what the conversation was about. And this was how Hector planned to play it: no outright lies, but plenty of omissions. She had had few dealings with Hector and had been inclined to dismiss him as a slow-moving and slow-thinking giant, but it came to her suddenly that he might prove more than a match for her in a duel of wits.

Hector seemed to think the conversation was over. Chryseis examined his set profile, and said slowly, 'There was no news today, sir?'

'News?' he enquired with no apparent concern.

'Of the Achaeans? I heard a rumour that a messenger was to report to the council meeting.'

'There was a messenger from Lyrnessus, yes, but he did not speak.' That was true enough. 'The news we have is very confused at the moment.' A pause, and he added, 'I think perhaps I should have a word with your father. He can decide what it is best to do. I am sure he will be anxious to get back home.'

That was alarming. It was the last thing Chryseis wanted: to drive Hector to talk to her father. She wished she had a way of finding out how much he knew, but she doubted now if she would discover any more than he intended.

'I shall talk to him myself tomorrow. He may not quite have finished his work in Ilios, but he should be able to estimate how much time he needs.'

Hector met her look head-on, and Chryseis found her eyes moving downwards. 'Leave it till the afternoon,' he said. 'Then I shall have a chance to discuss it with him first.'

Danger was not like play-acting: the reality was worse, not easier, than the anticipation. Chryseis found her heart hammering harder. She had imagined scenes in which Andromache or Helen revealed their discovery to her and she blushed prettily before admitting her passion for Troilus and enlisting their help in persuading him to marry her. But Hector! Hector unnerved her. Troilus' powerful brother seemed immune to her charms, and she had no idea how to try to enlist his support, especially when he had virtually declared his opposition.

She could see no way to counter his final move and was still silently mulling over the disaster as they came into Palace Square. Did Andromache know too? Had she told Hector, or had he learned from someone else? At least, Chryseis thought, she should be safe from confronting Andromache until the morning. That would perhaps give her time to get a message to Troilus.

Hector felt his small victory, and over supper he said no more. For him the affair was almost forgotten: the demons were settling back around him. Disaster at Lyrnessus, no news of Mynes, his close friend, or of Aeneas. No friend, Aeneas: Hector had always thought him wily and cunning, but the Trojans could ill afford to lose him. It must have been divine inspiration that had given him the idea of sacrificing to Apollo the next morning, he decided. It would help to ease his worries over the Achaean raids, and he could speak to Chryseis' father afterwards.

Chryseis rose early in the morning. She looked out Andromache's maidservant and offered to give her a blue glass brooch, a present from Helen, if she would go to the palace with a message for Troilus. Then she set to work on her dress. It took her an age to pick out the sharp twists of straw, and even then there was a dark stain at the back. She knew Andromache would not welcome her asking to have it washed, so she shook the dress out as best she could and belted it loose and low. It was how the girls dressed in Chryse; she had moved her belt upwards when she saw how Helen arranged her dresses.

When she heard Andromache make her way downstairs she slipped into her room to borrow the silver mirror and with it propped up by the window she set about her hair. She had worked out a new style for that in Ilios, too, with a mass of tiny plaits around her head to complement the heavy braid that fell across her shoulder. Now she untwisted them all, then combed her hair through before pulling it back into a simple braid and tying a white ribbon about the end.

From the depths of the mirror, a wan-faced maiden looked out at her. She frowned. Her face looked round and plain. Patiently she teased out some loose strands and twisted them round her fingers. That was better. Was the change of image too blatant? If Andromache noticed, Chryseis decided, she would take it for contrition.

The servant came back. Prince Troilus had left with his brother Helenus after supper the previous night, and had not yet returned. The message would have to wait. The girl sounded genuine, so Chryseis dismissed her – clutching the brooch – and sank back onto the bed. There was nothing to do but cry. She indulged in a good sob before splashing her face in cold water from the basin. There were dark shadows under her eyes now, but that was no bad thing. Along the corridor to return the mirror, and then she made her way down the narrow staircase.

The megaron of Hector's house was a vast echoing room, with a deep porch that made it dark even in broad daylight. The ceiling was intricately carved and gilded; the pillars were painted a dark red, and the frescoes were old and sombre: scenes of battles and feasts, with borders of stylized palms. Around the hearth servants were busy grinding corn, baking bread and spinning; in a corner near the porch, Andromache sat at her great loom.

It was not early any more. Andromache's hands were not working, though, and her head was bowed down. As Chryseis approached she looked up to reveal a face as pale as Chryseis' own and streaked with tears.

It was apparent from her expression that the tears were not for Chryseis, so the girl moved swiftly to comfort her cousin. Andromache clung to her and sobbed with renewed fervour for a few moments before the gasps subsided and her body slumped.

She pushed Chryseis away gently, sat down in one of the high-backed chairs that lined the room, and managed an unsteady laugh. 'I get so weepy at the moment. Everyone tells me it's the baby. I do hope so, then I can cheer up by midsummer.'

'I'm sure it is,' said Chryseis, slipping dutifully down to sit at Andromache's feet. 'I've heard it affects lots of women that way.'

'Hector told me the news. So dreadful.'

Chryseis tensed, then relaxed. Hector must have told her about the fall of Lyrnessus.

'Yes, terrible. I never expected the raids to come so close to home. It makes you wonder if Thebe will be next, or Chryse.'

'Surely not; but those poor women and children in Lyrnessus. You knew Briseis? And the Queen?'

'Briseis? Why, have you heard anything? Is she dead?'

Andromache glanced deliberately up to the carved wooden figure of Athena on the wall by the hearth. 'I suppose we must hope so. The alternative is too awful to think about.'

She meant being taken captive, presumably, and being raped by the soldiers. Chryseis' private opinion was that to be an Achaean slave would be infinitely preferable to death, but it seemed inappropriate to express it just then. Anyway, she thought to herself, Andromache was being unnecessarily morbid. Cheerful, tidy-minded Briseis had never seemed to carry the shadow of doom with her. 'Perhaps Briseis was not in Lyrnessus when the Achaeans came. Mynes' house is quite a way from the town, surely? Did you not go there for their wedding? If she stayed at home, she could be perfectly all right. Achilles might be godlike, but he doesn't get his hands on every woman in Troy.'

'It's up in the hills towards Scepsis. Maybe you're right. But if the Achaeans came down from Dardania they must have passed close, and I cannot imagine Mynes leaving her there alone. Still, it's wrong to imagine the worst before it happens.' Andromache smiled wanly. 'Thank you for cheering me up.'

Chryseis smiled back. She was fond of Briseis. In fact she probably knew her better than Andromache did. It embarrassed her a little to see Andromache cry so readily for the girl while she did not. There had been a rumour, she recalled, that Mynes had refused a match with Andromache because he wanted a prettier wife. Chryseis had half expected Andromache to resent Briseis because of that; but Andromache had married first, and Hector, though stolid, was a better catch and seemed to suit her well. Perhaps Andromache and Briseis got on better than she had anticipated. She was conscious that she was still outside the charmed circle of married women, with their chatter about their husbands and worries about the servants, and that it was not easy for her to judge the currents of affection and disaffection that prevailed within it.

The encounter had not begun at all as she had expected, but it was not going badly from her point of view. After hugging her, Andromache would find it difficult to do an about-face and start to upbraid her about the meetings with Troilus. And she could see a way of turning the conversation to her advantage.

Now she thought about it, the possibility of being taken captive did seem quite bad enough for tears. She felt a renewed pang of sympathy for Briseis. 'Andromache, what happens to captives?'

'They become slaves, of course. I have no idea exactly what happens. I suppose the traders take them off to Hellas or the islands, and sell them.'

'They are not kept by the soldiers?'

Andromache frowned. She wanted to be cheered up now, not to dwell on unpleasant possiblities. Anyway, it was not suitable to be too explicit with a young girl. Looking at Chryseis this morning it was difficult to believe that she was not innocent. She seemed barely more than a child, solemn and pale. 'Maybe some of them are sent back to the leaders' estates. They can hardly be kept in the camp, it would not do at all. I am sure most of them are sold. Most of our household servants were captured in raids.'

Chryseis' lips thinned. Becoming a slave was beginning to sound a dull business, rather than a terrifying one. She wanted lurid tales of ill-treatment. There were few dramatic possibilities in a potential future full of floor-sweeping and bath-cleaning. 'It must be a dreadful life.' That sounded weak. 'To be torn from your family. And not all masters would be as considerate as Hector, would they?'

'I am sure it is dreadful. We must take whatever the gods send us, but it would be very hard to be a slave. There is no honour in it.'

That would have to do. Chryseis pressed on. 'It worries me so much now, to think of going back to Chryse. The Achaeans are so close to home. I feel safe in Ilios, there is no way they could get to us here, but Chryse is terribly exposed. If they could take Lyrnessus, with crags all round it, I suppose they could burn Chryse to the ground in an afternoon.'

Andromache hesitated. She had an uneasy feeling that Chryseis was trying to manipulate her. Was she about to be trapped into promising to keep the girl in Ilios? No, she decided, she would not be caught out so easily. It was in Hector's hands now, and she had no intention of saying anything that might set her against her husband. 'I am sure your father will not let you return unless it is safe enough. Hector plans to talk to him this morning.' She added quietly, 'It is your duty, Chryseis, to do what your father orders. I am sure you realize that.'

Chryseis was silent. She mentally rehearsed a sudden confession to Andromache. Though nothing had been said, she had no doubt now that Andromache knew about Troilus. But she longed for a sympathetic response and she knew that she would not get one. Andromache would never condone an illicit affair.

She would only go on about honour and duty. There was nothing more Chryseis could do just then. She rose awkwardly from the floor. 'It is in Apollo's hands. I shall go myself to the shrine in a little while, to talk to Father. Shall I ask one of the ladies to come to sit with you? I could call on Cassandra? Or Polyxena, perhaps? Or would you prefer to be alone?'

Andromache wanted very much to be alone and lose her thoughts in the rhythm of the weaving. It crossed her mind that a spell of work might do Chryseis good too. But she would not insist, and she let the girl go.

Chryseis thought of going first in search of Troilus; then she remembered Hector's set face the night before and decided it would be as well to talk to her father as soon after Hector as she decently could. Rearranging her dress so that it looked a little more fashionable, she set off to the Scaean Gate.

There was a shrine to all the gods of Ilios in the tower alongside the Dardanian Gate, the main entrance to the citadel, but Chryseis knew that her father would be not there, but in the big grove dedicated to Apollo which lay outside the city to the north. She stopped at the gate to take one of the little staffs, white-ribboned like the priests' staffs, which would mark her as under Apollo's protection. Achaeans too went to the shrine, she knew. The priests had insisted from the start of the war that it should be treated as neutral territory, and Trojans as well as Achaeans occasionally found it convenient to use the shrine as a private meeting place.

It was laid out like the shrine at home. There was a low hill with the priests' houses at the foot, and a thick belt of bushes and small trees surrounding the clearing at the summit. A processional way led up the hill to the dancing floor for the sacred dances, the small altars where offerings could be laid, and the great altar with its massive stones and its brooding statue of the God. All this was familiar to Chryseis. She could find nothing familiar, though, in the bitter herbs that grew around the clearing, or in the massive snakes that lived under the great altar. They frightened her, hinted of dark deeds. The Apollo Ilios knew was not the Apollo of the bright mornings when the sun had risen, but the Apollo of the darkness, before the sun came out. He was the Snake God, not the Mouse God.

To Chryseis this Apollo was a different God entirely from the one she had known at Chryse. He was a dangerous God, a God whose knowledge she had not yet received; nor was it knowledge, she felt, that anyone would look to receive. But to some it came regardless. Perhaps it came through danger, through attack, capture, slavery; perhaps it had come in that way to Briseis. Chryses had endured none of those things, as far as his daughter knew: but she was conscious that, nevertheless, this dark knowledge had come to him. Perhaps in time it would also come to her.

The priest on duty greeted her warmly at the entrance to the shrine. More warmly than she deserved, she realized, as she remembered belatedly that she had brought no offering. Really there was nothing she could have brought, except the blue glass brooch, and she had already disposed of that. The priest's manner cooled, however, when she asked to see her father. He was busy, the priest said curtly. Tomorrow, perhaps?

Hector's orders, perhaps? Chryseis echoed under her breath. Outmanoeuvred again. Accepting defeat with the grace her father had taught her to muster, she made her way slowly up the paved way that led to the altar.

The snakes were nowhere in sight, and she did not look for them. Instead she sent up a quick private prayer to this God she knew and yet did not know, and then turned to make her way back to Ilios.

Aeneas halted his men as soon as they reached the top of the slope and had their first view of Ilios.

They were on one of the northern foothills of Mount Ida. The land between the mountain and Ilios was bleak and deserted, so the citadel stood out all the more aggressively from its surroundings. The high stone wall, steeply cambered, the shape of a squashed plum, with its seven gates: some large and imposing, some little posterns barely wide enough for a war chariot to pass through. The towers with their battlements. The houses, their chequered beams pitch black in sharp contrast to the brick and stucco. And at the very summit of the hill, the palace, its gilded pillars gleaming in the sunshine, its red and white paint as pristine from the distance as a child's new toy.

Spreading out from the high walls, in the direction of the hills, were the irregular shapes of the lower town and the camp. The lower town was as formless and loose-edged as a blob of dye dropped onto raw linen. The camp, in contrast, was tightly confined by its wooden stockade. Within the stockade it was still possible to make out the grid pattern of the huts, though over the years as contingents had expanded and shrunk, amalgamated, disappeared and reappeared, the original design had been steadily altered and adapted. Aeneas could see the empty space of the parade ground, and cupping his hands round his eyes to shut out the glare of the sun, he tried to make out the standards that flew at the entrance to the camp. But they were still too far away, and he could not even be sure how many flags there were, let alone decipher their devices.

His eyes moved on. The sea stretched from his left in a wide arc around Ilios, and far beyond the citadel he could make out the faint shape of the hills of Thrace. The island of Tenedos, with Imbros and Samothrace dim shadows beyond. And by the narrow neck of the Hellespont, the forbidding dark mass of the Achaean camp.

He turned to look at his men. There were less than fifty with him, the bare minimum with which he had been prepared to risk the three-day march. He had mustered the remains of the Dardanian and Mysian army half a day's march from Lyrnessus, but most of the men he had dispersed again en route, sending them to patch up the fired buildings and retrieve the scattered inhabitants of the villages before returning to their homesteads. The men had almost all fled from Lyrnessus empty-handed. Aeneas had brought his little troop through Dardania along a track the Achaeans had not used, and they had requisitioned meat and bread and wine on the way, but sparingly, so they would not be weighed down.

All of them were grey-faced with exhaustion, many of them bandaged and limping. Aeneas had marched them as fast as he dared, and he did not expect any more stragglers to catch them before they reached the citadel.

'We should find a campsite,' his lieutenant, Gyrtius, said. He was a dour, grizzled man who had fought for five summers at Ilios.

Aeneas shook his head. 'We can make it to Ilios before dark.'

'Barely,' Gyrtius grumbled.

'But we must. There is no time to lose.' He had driven the men onwards, knowing how urgent his mission was. Reinforcements must be sent south, and soon: even a day might make a vital difference.

They had barely reached the plain when they saw the chariots riding out towards them. Aeneas formed his men into a tight mass for protection, and they stood with spears at the ready until they made out the devices. They lowered the spears, then: Mysians had come to greet them, and not Achaeans.

It was Ennomus, the slight, fair-haired Mysian commander, with three of his men. Ennomus vaulted down from his chariot and ran across to take Aeneas' hand before his driver had even drawn up his horses. 'Praise Apollo, Aeneas. We feared you were dead.'

'Mynes is,' Aeneas answered shortly. 'And Epistrophus, and most of their men and mine. We have little to give thanks for.'

'You come with news?'

'We are hardly come to fight,' Aeneas retorted, glancing back at his exhausted men for the Mysian's benefit. 'I must beg men from Priam, and swiftly. It is too late to save Lyrnessus, but the Achaeans are moving towards Thebe, and Eetion must have reinforcements.'

Ennomus started to reply, then broke off his words and said instead, 'You are too tired to argue now. Ride with me. Mydon can march with your men, and we will bring the worst wounded in the other chariot.'

Aeneas stopped only to give Gyrtius his orders. Ennomus took the reins from his charioteer and drove them swiftly across the plain. He skirted the stone wall and made straight for the camp. Aeneas looked up as they passed through the stockade. From the beam above the gate, the standards flew: the sunflower of the Thracians, the Mysian poppies, the crossed swords of the Lycians, a dozen or more others.

'You should go first to Acamas and Archelochus,' Ennomus said. They were the commanders of the Dardanians already in the camp: Aeneas knew they would find quarters for his men.

'Can you do that for me?' he asked. 'I should make for the palace, to speak with Priam.'

Ennomus gently shook his head. 'You could speak to his criers tonight; but the High King will not see you before the morning.'

'He must. There is no time to waste.'

'True, Aeneas, but he will not. It is so long since you were in Ilios. You forget how things are done here. The High King does not like to be pressed, and if you do press him you will lose any hope of getting the men you need. Wait till the morning. Tell men in the camp tonight and let the tales spread before you face Priam.'

Aeneas slipped down from the chariot and rested his head for a moment against the polished wood of the side rail. He looked ruefully up at Ennomus. 'I sometimes think to myself,' he said, 'how good it would be to be Achilles. To sweep in like a shooting star for a glowing triumph, and sweep out again leaving somebody else to clear up the mess. Defence is such a messy business, such a joyless business.'

'In Ilios,' Ennomus said, 'everything is messy and joyless. Come to my hut and eat, and I will send one of my men to Acamas, to tell him you have arrived.'

The herald led Aeneas through a winding passage, across a small flagged courtyard, through a series of cluttered rooms, and into another inner court. With a sign for him to wait, he disappeared between the guards and into the depths of the palace.

The courtyard was enclosed by high walls, with a deep colonnade on each side and a little statue on a plinth in the centre. Ignoring the guards as they seemed to ignore him, Aeneas crossed over to inspect it: Zeus, finely done. An offering of crocuses and wild hyacinths lay at the base of the pedestal. The centre of the court seemed to escape the worst of the chill wind that blew in from a narrow passage in the corner and swirled around the edges. It was early morning and the sun was not yet up.

Ennomus had loaned him a thin ceremonial tunic of a fine unbleached linen which emphasized the purple bands round the hem. There was a heavy bandage, roughly fastened, round his thigh. His chin was still reddened from a fierce shave that morning and his expression was bleak. He had left his dagger at the camp. He shivered a little and began to pace up and down.

Ilios might be in desperate straits, he thought to himself, but Priam would hold to his kingly manner till the last. The High King played shamelessly on the citadel's long history, teased out every nuance from its atmosphere of deep-seated power. In reality the High Kings of Troy ruled over a small region compared to the great kings of Mycenae, Hattusas and Egyptian Thebes, but no ambassador to Priam would catch a hint of that. No wonder that it was Priam who, by pushing his powerful neighbours too hard, threatened to bring ruin on the house of his ancestors.

The herald slid silently out of the shadows and Aeneas turned to find the man almost upon him. An attempt to unsettle him? Determined not to show how nearly the man had succeeded, he composed his face into a haughty mask and waved the herald to show him in.

They stopped in the antechamber, where a priestess in white robes stood before the shrine. The herald marshalled Aeneas towards her. She had his offering ready, and for a moment he thought it would be an empty ritual, placing it on the table and bowing low with a few words. But she motioned him to be silent and moved forward with a different expression. Aeneas looked again, and saw the snakes that curled around the statue of Apollo. As the priestess approached, one of them uncoiled its body and flicked its tongue towards her. This time, Aeneas' shiver started at the core of him and radiated outwards. He thought for a moment that they could not be mere household familiars. Surely they were the famous sacred snakes, the snakes which saw everything, and – it was said – had passed on the God's gift to Priam's children Cassandra and Helenus. They were at the heart of Ilios, its power, its knowledge, and its mystery.

He stood motionless, watching the snake wave and hiss, and

then pulled himself together. The sacred snakes never normally left the grove of Apollo, and these were surely much smaller. It was just show, another attempt to bring him off balance.

The offering had been provided for him and at first he assumed that a honey cake was hidden under the cloth in the little dish. Not for the snakes. The smooth scaly head pushed the cloth aside and Aeneas made out the limp shape of two small mice. Dead already, thank goodness. The first disappeared, and already the second snake was pushing forward for its portion. The priestess held the dish still as the great reptiles flicked and hissed around her; and kept holding it, arms outstretched, as she began to speak. The invocation was to the God of Knowledge. Appropriate? For a moment, it seemed not to Aeneas.

'All honour to the God of the Rising Sun,' he said as she came to the close, in a reverent but assertive voice. It was acceptable as part of the ritual; but the priestess turned and gave him an angry look. The herald nudged him to move forward into the throne room and he went quickly.

Though he had been many times to Ilios, and spoken in council, Aeneas had never before had cause to visit Priam's private quarters. His eyes adjusted slowly to the gloom of the chamber after the clear light of the courtyard. There was no fire in the hearth, but smoky incense fumes hung about the room. The ceiling was frescoed in a complex intertwining pattern, picked out in deep reds and gold. On the walls were woollen hangings. They must have been generations old: the colours had faded to a uniform dull brownish hue, and in the shadowy light he could not make out the details of the scenes woven into them.

He took his time looking round before turning to the far end of the room where Priam sat on his high throne. He was not alone and it came as an unpleasant shock. Aeneas had left his own followers back at the camp, understanding that this would be a private audience with the High King; but at Priam's left hand sat Hector, and on his right, Deiphobus.

There was no sign of Paris, whom Aeneas would have pre-ferred to see. Aeneas respected Hector, but regarded him warily. Deiphobus, a younger son, was of a more unknown quantity. It was surprising to find him present, but Aeneas knew that

Priam played off his sons against each other constantly, favouring first one and then another, and preventing any – save Hector – from gaining too thorough a grasp of affairs of state. Perhaps this was some elaborate way of slighting Paris.

'Prince Aeneas, my lords.' The herald had to speak loudly to make his voice carry across the room, for its resonance was muted by the heavy folds of the hangings. When Priam spoke, his seemed to carry effortlessly. 'Zeus and Hera.'

Aeneas started again. 'Pardon, sir?'

'The hangings, boy, the hangings. Don't stand there in the shadows where I have to shout at you.'

The Dardanian stilled the muscles of his face and walked slowly across the room. None of the three men motioned him to sit, and he could see no free chair. Priam's hand lifted a finger's breadth from the arm of his throne, and flapped down. Was it an indication that he was expected to prostrate himself? He was damned if he would to a relative. After a pause he gave a perfunctory bow, and Priam settled back, apparently satisfied. 'About time you came back to Ilios. We need your men here.'

'I have come to requisition men, sir, not to provide them. Achilles is still close to Lyrnessus. We need reinforcements if we are to drive him back without the loss of more strongholds.'

Priam frowned. He glanced across to Hector who looked back, expressionless, and then turned once more to Aeneas. 'Hector will explain my strategy to you this afternoon.'

'It is not a question of strategy, sir. There is a clear need for reinforcements if we are to avoid disastrous losses in Mysia.'

'You are talking rubbish, boy. There is no question of fighting a major campaign in Mysia.'

Try telling Achilles that, Aeneas retorted under his breath. He fixed his gaze on the High King. At close quarters, Aeneas could see the drawn lines of his face. Presumably the incense was intended to mask the smell of sickness. The word was that an ague was eating the King from inside, and looking at him now, Aeneas did not doubt it. Priam had the iron-willed face of a man who expects to be devoured by agonizing pain if he loses his self-control even for a moment. Perhaps it was not surprising that there was no sympathy to spare for the plight of the Mysians.

The High King spoke curtly. 'Only a small detachment of the Achaeans are in your territory. Most of them are still here. You can see for yourself from the battlements: the camp on the harbourside is as crowded as ever. There are as many more troops on Tenedos. We cannot possibly release any men. They are all needed to defend the citadel.'

Aeneas turned to stare at Hector, who returned his gaze unblinking, and then at Deiphobus, who met it briefly and turned to his brother. He looked back at Hector and replied in a measured tone. 'With respect, sir, I think you are mistaken. Even if the garrison were smaller, there is little risk of the Achaeans attempting to storm the citadel. The walls are too strong. Their losses would be suicidal. It is obvious that their policy now is to harry your allies and plunder the countryside, then they will starve you out within a year or two at most. It is essential that you move quickly and decisively to quash these raids.'

For a moment he expected Hector to respond, but Priam reached to place a warning hand on his son's arm. 'The raids are minor. They are of no consequence. What is required is an all-out attack on the Achaean base here. With a full contingent of Mysian and Dardanian troops, and the reinforcements I intend to obtain from Thrace, we shall be in a position to make one before midsummer.'

'You already have a large company of Mysians here under Chromis and Ennomus. The country is scarcely defended at all. Every spare man in south-west Mysia went to fight at Lyrnessus. Did you not hear the news? More than half of Evenus' men were killed or injured. Mynes and Epistrophus are dead. Lyrnessus was sacked. Achilles is still at large in Mysia, and I have word that he is moving north-west towards Thebe. King Eetion is preparing for a major battle there within the next ten days. If he does not get reinforcements, then the Mysian fighting force outside Ilios will be wiped out. Completely wiped out.'

There was a grim satisfaction in his precision, and in his measured rudeness. He stared Hector full in the face, daring the man to disagree. There was no sign of dissent on the Ilian's strong face. He wants to go and fight, thought Aeneas with a sudden surge of lightness. Hector finds this crowded citadel as claustrophobic as I do, with its maze of anterooms, its hedge of protocol and its smell of the sickroom. He too is a man of open fields, where he can wield his sword freely and avenge his country cleanly. With Hector at my side, and a good strong force of Ilians behind us, we could drive Achilles back into the sea, or better still kill him and leave all the Achaeans stunned and hopeless.

But Hector did not speak, and from his father's other side Deiphobus' soft voice took over the argument. 'I think you exaggerate, Aeneas. The loss of Lyrnessus was a dreadful blow, but there is no real reason to think that Achilles will attack Thebe. We cannot possibly divert half the Trojan army down there, just in case Achilles is planning something. It would expose not just Ilios, but all the northern coast. There are more Achaeans raiding to the north, under Ajax. They pose just as big a threat.'

There was something catlike about the tall young man. He preened and stretched in the heavy wooden chair like a prize Egyptian pet. Aeneas looked at him with distaste. This one would keep its claws sheathed, he reckoned, until its own home and family were attacked. But he saw Hector too turn to Deiphobus, with a warmer expression on his face. Hardly relief, for Aeneas was sure that he had been right in catching Hector's mood – but a brotherly solidarity that made Aeneas suddenly feel out in the cold.

Who was not out in the cold in Troy, except for Priam's sons? With fifty of them, including his bastards, the High King had no use for outside counsellors, not even those from other branches of his own family. Even his daughters' husbands had no real status: it was hardly surprising that many of them had not married. The allied commanders were all but ignored, the council was a farce. When the decisions came it was Priam, Hector, Deiphobus, Paris, Helenus, every time. However good Aeneas' advice, it would not be taken. And none of Priam's sons would break ranks in front of an outsider, not even Hector.

Hector hesitated before adding his own reply. 'I am sorry, Aeneas. We do not mean to underestimate the scale of the disaster, but I am afraid there is no question of sending reinforcements southwards.'

Behind the unblinking eyes, Aeneas' body was tensed with anger. The Ilians always seemed to catch him on the wrong foot; he hated each visit to the citadel. The whole place had the air of disaster about it, and its dissolute atmosphere made even the strongest man feel smaller and act more pettily. Already it was plain that there was no hope of winning Priam over at this meeting. He would have to work on Hector, he decided, when he got the man alone.

'Do you still plan to take your own men back to Mysia?' Deiphobus purred into the charged air.

Aeneas turned to look at him again, avoiding the challenge of Priam's gaze. 'I think not, in the circumstances. Without supplies and support from Ilios, there is little we could do.'

'You may give your men three days' rest, before you join the army here.' The High King spoke sharply.

Aeneas' lips curled. 'And they will be re-equipped and maintained from today at your expense?'

Priam appeared to consider. 'In the circumstances, I think that will be possible.' He pressed his hands down hard on the arms of the throne and, rising with difficulty, made his way from the room on the arms of his servants without another word.

The message Troilus received from Chryseis – via Andromache's maidservant – told him that they must meet urgently, and in a new place. It exasperated him. She was growing too assertive, too eager to control things, he thought: she should have waited until he had suggested meeting her. He could not see, either, why she objected to the barn. He could hardly argue with the maidservant, though, and he sent a message back that she should come to a storeroom behind Priam's palace that afternoon. It was the best he could contrive at short notice. The storeroom was close at hand, and there was little chance of a servant coming to fetch wine in the afternoon.

The storeroom was dark. It was barely more than a passage, and as well as the big pithos jars that had always stood in an ordered row along the side, there were makeshift shelves and a confusion of odd containers on the floor. Troilus had forgotten to bring a lamp. He did his best to find the situation funny as he groped around in the gloom, trying to clear a space large enough for the two of them. He hoped Chryseis would catch his mood when she came and not complain about the discomfort.

As his eyes grew accustomed to the light he made out a fat spider busy spinning its web between a couple of stirrup jars on the shelf by his head. She would not like that. He had just trapped it between his hands, ready to let loose in a darker corner, when she came through the door.

'Darling!' Troilus moved forward with a flick of his wrist that was intended to dismiss the spider. It was sticky from the web and did not budge. He could hardly reach out for her with a spider stuck to his palm. Feeling foolish, he had to turn and dispose of it behind a pithos.

'What on earth are you doing, Troilus?' Chryseis' voice was sharp and loud in the narrow room. It brought him a moment of apprehension. He had not stopped to consider, before then, just why she might require this urgent meeting.

'Oh, a spot of housekeeping. Don't you think I've made it cosy? Well, my dear, you should have seen it when I arrived.' He laughed, and pulled her to him for a kiss.

When he let her go she grinned up at him. His unease vanished.

'What a ridiculous place to choose.' She was teasing, not critical. 'It stinks of wine and figs.'

'There's a note of goat cheese, if you concentrate. And I can smell you too, my love.' He kissed her again. 'Anyway, it's all your fault. I was quite happy with the barn.'

'We were seen at the barn.' The sharpness had returned. Chryseis freed herself and made her way past him, deeper into the room.

There was a small high window which sent a shaft of sunlight cutting through the dust Troilus had disturbed. It lit up her face as she turned to look back at him.

There was something different about her, he could see it now.

She looked young, surprisingly vulnerable. She was pale. Her hair hung straight and plain across her tunic. The bright arrogance that he enjoyed in her was gone. He took her in coolly, almost disinterestedly; and then saw the fear in her eyes. A warm rush of love and sympathy brought him blundering forward, jarring his foot on the base of a pithos and reaching out to hug her. She clung to him and he gripped her in return as the words sunk in.

He must have said something, told her it would be all right, not to worry, that kind of thing. Maybe she said something back. She could not have been so desperate to tell him more, though, because her touch changed as his did, as if she was suddenly conscious of the feel of his arms firm around her, of his body pressed hard against hers. The wine around them seemed to have gone to their heads. They were drowning, both of them, in a tide of sensual delight. Her words, the spider and his aching foot were alike forgotten, as Troilus pulled Chryseis down onto the dusty floor.

He made love to her with a vigorous, straightforward abandon that set the winejars rocking and the mice scurrying back to their crevices. She gazed up at him afterwards, her eyes liquid, as if what she saw was very perfection to her. He bent to kiss her again, slowly, and run a possessive hand along her body. She quivered with delight. 'No other man will ever make me feel like this. I love you so much. I couldn't bear to lose you.'

There was nothing rehearsed about the words, nothing manipulative. He believed her. Perhaps that was why he was suddenly conscious of how cold and hard the floor was, how uncomfortably they were squashed between the great jars. He stood up, trying not to be too abrupt, and brushed himself down.

'We have to talk,' Chryseis said, in a voice from which, he could tell, she was trying to keep out a pleading note.

'All right. Tell me what happened.' Troilus sat down, his back to a pithos, and looked at her with a hint of challenge. She moved over to lean against him, her face turned downwards, and began to talk.

She said a lot. It was as if she wanted him to know that any calculation, any reserve between them would not come from her. As far as he could tell, she held nothing back. She told him about the conversation with Hector, on the way back from the Phrygian Gate. About an even more awkward conversation with her father, to whom Hector had told everything and given orders to take her back to Chryse within the next four days. She told him about the coldness of the Moon Goddess – to whom her father had obliged her to make sacrifice – and the warmth of the Sun God, to whom she had asked to make sacrifice. Her father had bartered her a kid for Apollo. She tried to make it real to him: her life and her choices.

Chryseis had already made her choices. There were none left for her now. Troilus and her father would decide what was to happen to her.

Of course she hoped to marry Troilus: he had known that all along. She had more pride than to play on her desperation at the alternatives that faced her if he refused. He would have appreciated that, had he thought about it then. Anyway, he did not know precisely what the alternatives were. Chryseis had told herself it would have been petty to tell him about Maris, or about the other boys, the ones her father did not know about. She had never loved them as she loved Troilus.

She did not mention the dangers of the journey back to Chryse. For that he was grateful. He knew she must realize that it would be dangerous.

When she finished Troilus was silent. Chryseis had not been looking at him as she spoke, but she made herself turn to him now. He looked back at her with an arrogant innocence, with the sort of face little boys assume when they are caught pulling wings off flies and hope that their mothers think them too young to know it is wrong. Chryseis was evidently not fooled. 'You don't love me.'

'Of course I love you.' He said it automatically, but he meant it. 'But you make it all sound so desperate. I just cannot see it like that. I don't want us to be apart any more than you do, but it won't be forever. There is no need for you to marry yet. You aren't carrying a child, are you?' He knew very well that it was too soon for her to tell if she was.

'I don't think so. My father insists that I marry, though. It would be shameful if I did not. Everyone will know soon that I am no longer destined to be a priestess of Artemis. If you do not agree to marry me Father will oblige me to marry someone else.'

'Tell him you are too young to marry, that you want to wait a while.'

She was struggling to keep her face steady, to keep the tears back. He watched her face, and something unfamiliar stirred deep inside him. He had been less cruel to her than he had been to any of the half-dozen girls he had seduced and abandoned before her, and yet his cruelty suddenly seemed unbearable to him. Chryseis looked up at him and said in an unsteady voice, 'If I wait now, will you promise to marry me later?'

Troilus looked thoughtfully back at her. Her eyes transfixed him, and behind the thoughtful look his mind did not seem to be working as he intended. It was an important question, and his answer would be important too. He should have played for time, while he weighed the advantages and disadvantages properly. Instead, he found himself replying almost automatically. 'Yes, if you like. If it means so much to you.'

'It does.' She sounded disappointed. He supposed he had committed himself in a notably half-hearted way. But a commitment it was; and she went on in a brighter tone, as if any commitment would have done just then. 'I suppose we are both young to marry. I think Father would accept that, if I told him you had promised. So long as I am not carrying. If I am, then you'll marry me right away?'

Troilus was taken aback. He seemed to have lost all control of the conversation. He had given her a promise, and it was genuine enough: he would not have thought of retracting it; but it did not yet seem real to him. And here was Chryseis, taking it all pragmatically, playing for more before he had even had time to turn round and remind himself that the gate he had just passed through was now locked against him.

'Troilus?' Chryseis had that worried look that melted his insides. He had to do it. The future was a long time off, after all, and very uncertain.

'If the High King agrees.' It was a fudge, Troilus knew, but so what?

'And otherwise? How long must I wait?'

Troilus shifted edgily. 'Perhaps you could come back with

your father to Ilios next summer. Or I could come to Chryse, I suppose.'

'Will you tell Priam now?' She was pressing too hard, and she knew it. But it alarmed her, measuring the limits of his love.

'No. He will dislike it. I have already told you that. I will tell your father, though, if you want me to.'

'And Hector?'

He sighed. 'Yes, I will tell Hector too.' Then he got to his feet. The storeroom felt claustrophobic. Too many fumes from the wine, he thought. He was trapped. He had stared his future in the face, and dared it to come true. That was a dangerous thing to do. He knew he ought to go to the shrine, appease Apollo, but he felt more like a long hard run.

Chryseis rose slowly after him. She longed to seal the bargain with a kiss, but she was reluctant to ask for one. He might refuse, and that she could not have borne. They left the room hand in hand, but silent, and as awkward as conspirators.

The Dardanian contingent had quarters in the centre of the Trojan camp, overlooking the parade ground. Aeneas had claimed the position years earlier and he was relieved to find that Acamas and Archelochus had succeeded in retaining it in his absence.

He settled easily back into the low hut, wood-framed and turf-roofed, that acted as the officers' quarters. In winter it was warm, keeping out all but a hint of the Ilian wind. In summer it was hot and airless, and they used it only for sleeping.

His first days in Ilios Aeneas spent recovering and briefing the allied commanders. The Dardanians, the Mysians, the Lydians and Lycians all shared his opinion of Priam's tactics; but like him, they felt powerless to change them. Aeneas spoke to Helenus, who also agreed with him, but professed himself even more powerless than the allies. He spoke to Hector. Hector took Priam's line even in private, though with more resignation than conviction, it seemed to Aeneas. He appeared to be anxious to conciliate Aeneas, however. The two men had never been friends before but at this time they met almost daily, to drink, to talk of fighting, and to whore. Hector kept a Nubian girl down in the lower town: one night he took Aeneas to her hut, with Helenus and Antiphus and a couple of others.

Three days after Aeneas reached Ilios his charioteer arrived. He had rested the horses once they were safely away from Lyrnessus and had driven them slowly around the eastern flank of Mount Ida. Aeneas found them clean stalls in the camp stables. He was proud of his team: the best pair of bays in Troy, he reckoned. He gave the horses a day to settle, the charioteer a day to clean off the dust and polish the brass on his chariot. After that he began to fight.

In spite of Priam's warnings, there was little activity on the plain. Most days the Achaeans remained safely behind their own stockade. They were still depleted, with many of their men away raiding, and there was no question of their fighting a pitched battle. Sometimes a few of their charioteers would emerge and engage in skirmishes. These were as ritualized, almost, as funeral games. They were fought as duels: it was considered bad form for fighters to gang up on an opponent. The warriors rarely dismounted. They threw their javelins from the cars, then the team wheeled round and drew back to safety. Finally, the charioteers would jockey for position while their warriors attempted to retrieve the precious weapons. There were rarely any casualties. It was very different, Aeneas could not help thinking, from the battle that would take place at Thebe.

The news came from Thebe ten days later. Achilles had stormed along the shores of the Idaeus, with his troops looting villages and taking captives as they went. His intelligence must have been good, for he had allowed himself a day's rest before attacking the town. Eetion's forces had not been nearly strong enough to force the issue, and their commander had evidently hoped till the last for the reinforcements that never came. He was killed, with his sons and most of his men. The Achaeans sacked the town.

Eetion sent a messenger to Ilios in the last stages of the battle.

The man made his way to the Mysians in the camp, and it was Ennomus who brought Aeneas the news. Aeneas listened in silence as he recited the names of dead comrades. 'Have the Ilians been told?'

'Not by Eetion's man, no. He came straight to me and Chromis. Maybe Priam has his own spies out. I shall send our man up to the palace later, when he has recovered. I thought I would just tell Helenus for now.'

'In that case, do you mind if I tell Hector?'

'You'll not find him in Palace Square. I saw him setting off for the lower town around midday.'

'That's all right. I know where to find him there.'

'Suit yourself.' Ennomus shrugged, and rose to leave. He would go and get drunk with Helenus.

Aeneas went down alone to the tangled alleys of the lower town where the Nubian girl lived. He derived an odd comfort from the dirt and decay, the tumbledown shacks and the shabby, listless people he passed. It was not enough, though. Ilios was still standing, and in Mysia and Dardania there was devastation.

The way was harder to find than he had expected and to his annoyance it began to rain, lightly, but with the promise of getting heavier. At last he turned a corner and recognized the path. The girl's house was built of mudbrick, small and cramped, with a narrow doorway into the single room.

He knocked briefly and entered without waiting for a reply. It was a rough area and he did not want to linger there.

The room was shadowy, barely lit by a slit of a window. Hector's great bulk rose up from the pallet on the floor. He almost touched the roof. He looked incongruous in the mean setting, Aeneas thought: he was made for palaces.

Behind him, Aeneas caught the frightened eyes of the girl. She had pulled a thin blanket around herself as he entered. Hector turned and spoke to her in a low voice. She flitted past Aeneas and out of the door.

If Hector was surprised to see Aeneas there he hid it well. 'Bad news?' he asked calmly.

Aeneas nodded and looked around. There was a three-legged wooden stool by the hearth. He sat down and began to talk as Hector started to dress.

Hector pulled on his tunic and fastened the belt. He bent to tie his sandals and then looked up at Aeneas as the other man finished his account. 'Eetion is alive?'

'Almost certainly not. The fighting had not finished when the messenger left. His sons were dead already and he would hardly run and leave them unavenged – even if there were anywhere to run to. There must be five thousand Achaeans around the Idaeus by now, so I doubt if there will be more than a handful of survivors. You know Achilles' methods: always thorough. He will have stationed troops to cut off the escape routes and make sure nobody is left to harry his captives while they wait for the ships.'

'Did you know him?'

'Eetion? A little. Of course, you must have known him well.'

Hector nodded briefly. 'A damn good man. He was growing too old for fighting, but he was always the sort of commander who kept heart in his men. Very like Andromache, really: plain but reliable.' He must have feared that sounded disparaging to his wife and he added quietly, 'I loved them both.'

Aeneas did not doubt it. Hector might be undemonstrative to his wife, but he certainly cared for her. The Nubian girl had been kept well out of her way.

'You'll want to break it gently to Andromache before the news gets around the town. That's why I came. It's no easy thing for a woman to take, especially in her condition.'

Hector picked up his dagger, which he had placed on the floor by the hearth, and tucked it into his belt. 'Let's go.'

'The girl?'

Hector looked surprised. 'She knows me. There's no need to say anything.'

The rain was coming down steadily by then. The two men bowed their heads and walked in silence until they were nearly at the gate. Then there was a break in the cloud. Hector looked up and shook his head slowly. 'It's a bad business, this. First Mynes, then Eetion. I thought I was used to war and all the losses, but those two hit hard.'

Aeneas could not work up much sympathy. 'You have it too damn easy in Ilios. Oh, I know the rations are tight, but so few men from the town have been killed. People would see it all differently if you died, say, or Helenus. They would see it a damn sight differently if they were Dardanians.'

To his surprise, Hector agreed. 'You are right, you know. But there is no alternative.'

Aeneas turned angrily on him. 'No alternative? When you couldn't make yourself tell Priam to get a couple of companies down to Thebe before it was too late? I reckon that was a bloody good alternative compared to what we have now.'

Hector shook his head. He seemed too drained by the news either to keep to his previous line, or to work up the disagreement into a fight. 'If Priam thought like that, there would be no war at all. It's in his nature to keep the citadel until the end. He will not risk it or his own men until all else is lost.'

'And you think it will come to that? Is it real to you? Or do you imagine Ilios will live on, in the middle of a sea of blood?'

'Right now, I expect us all to die. This year, or next.' The big man was quiet and serious. 'I doubt if there ever has been any way out. But I shall die with all the honour I can muster.'

'So honour to you means this? Messing with a whore in Ilios while Eetion and his sons are cut to ribbons?'

'Honour means obeying Priam. I try to advise him, but I am not the High King. I will not fight battles with my father that I too am certain to lose. There is no honour in contradicting him in front of his allies, or stirring up dissent within the citadel. Could you really expect me to do anything else?'

Aeneas drew breath to retort, and then cut himself short. Hector's heart was not in the argument; and perhaps in the end he was right. It was difficult to doubt a man's sincerity when he chose the course that came hardest to him.

He hesitated at the door to Hector's house, but Hector motioned him to come inside. Aeneas waited in the megaron, ill at ease among the fluster of the servants, while Hector went up to Andromache. He half expected to hear screams, but there were none. She had apparently taken it well. A long pause, then Hector came down alone. 'She's very quiet. I doubt if it has sunk in yet. There will be tears later. Let me send a servant for Cassandra to sit with her, then we'll go off to drink. I cannot sit here and do nothing.'

The two men left, both relieved to escape. Ah well, thought

Aeneas, disaster brings us the strangest bedfellows. And makes us care for them at that. He had never expected to feel close to the big man, but it seemed to him no bad thing that he should.

Andromache sat on the edge of the high bed, her feet dangling just short of the floor. It was a childlike pose. Just then she felt very young, and very small in the face of the big world.

She reached to hug the underside of her belly and feel the weight of the child against her hands. The baby was very still. Stupid of her to expect it to share her mood; but then, she was not moving herself.

She had wept so much lately and now, when duty called her to weep, the tears seemed to have gone. Her father dead. Her brothers too. Doubtless her mother as well. Everything she loved best taken away from her in a single blow. All through the long seasons in Ilios, Thebe, with its low houses and its rustling trees, had meant home to her. Now there was nothing. Nothing there at all.

Her mind seemed blasted as empty as the town itself. She could not think, she could not feel. She stared blankly at the wall in front of her.

She had barely noticed Hector leave, and she made no sign of recognition at all as Cassandra came through the door.

Cassandra hesitated. She had been embarrassed when the servant came to call her to Andromache. They were not at all close, and she had never thought herself any good at offering sympathy. She knew she came across as abrasive; she was not the type for hugs and kisses. How typical of Hector to land someone so unsuitable with the task, she had thought. It would have been rude and heartless to refuse, though. As she had hurried across Palace Square she had tried to recall who Andromache's friends were, so that the servant could go to fetch somebody the girl would be genuinely glad to see, but no names at all had come to mind.

She crossed to the figure on the bed and perched awkwardly next to her. 'Andromache? How dreadful for you. Are you all right?' It sounded all wrong to her, but Andromache was in no state to notice. She looked blankly up at Cassandra. Cassandra was not at all sure if she recognized her.

'Hector asked me to come and sit with you. He thought you would rather not be alone, but I could send the girl for somebody else, if there's someone you would prefer to have with you. Hecuba maybe? Or Helen?' No, hardly. 'Or Polyxena, perhaps?' It was a pity, she thought, that Chryseis was not there – she surely knew Andromache better.

Andromache was silent for a moment, then she seemed to pull herself together. 'I'm sorry. I'm being very rude. Thank you for coming.' She made to pull herself up and off the edge of the bed, and Cassandra reached out instinctively to stop her. She looked far too pale and ill to move.

She flinched away from Cassandra's hand. 'I'm all right, really. I think perhaps I shall go downstairs and sit by the fire. I feel a little cold.'

'I don't think you should move, Andromache. Why don't you get into bed? You could have a fire up here, if you need one.' Cassandra looked around. Yes, of course there was a fire-place.

Andromache did not answer. She rose, then hesitated. She felt queasy and uncomfortable. Her stomach was tight. She reached out to cling to the high side of the bed. Perhaps the pain would subside in a moment. She hardly noticed Cassandra start forward with an exclamation. Then as the spasm died down she followed the other woman's eyes and saw the blood, hot and crimson against the yellows and blues of the Cretan blanket.

Troilus had been on guard duty in the far meadows. He returned to the citadel at dusk to find an aura of expectation hanging over it. It was unlike Troilus to notice the atmosphere but this was so palpable, so obvious that nobody could miss it.

He asked his servant if there was any news, while the boy was unfastening his breastplate and greaves. The servant knew nothing but casual palace gossip, tales of Paris and Helen, Laodice and Polyxena. He related some of these as he was bathing Troilus. Troilus asked him where Helenus was to be found. Helenus was not in the palace, as far as the boy knew.

Helenus did not appear for supper, and nobody else had any real news. Troilus' exasperation grew. He had had the feeling, since Chryseis had left, that he was always the last to hear what went on. He took a torch and set out for the camp to look for Ennomus, in a foul mood. Surely Ennomus would be able to tell him something, he thought, whether Helenus was with him or not.

Ennomus was not in his quarters. The Mysian's herald directed Troilus to the tavern in the Street of the Basketmakers. As Troilus turned to go Chromis' voice behind him pulled him up sharply, and the other Mysian commander fell in at his side. 'I'll come with you, if you've no objection. They'll not miss me here. I've posted half a dozen guards, but I cannot see the Achaeans trying anything tonight.'

'You've heard something?'

Chromis nodded. He was a plump man, with a naturally cheerful expression and a raucous laugh. But that day he was subdued and there was a bitter set to his mouth.

He outlined the events of the battle at Thebe. It came as a shock to Troilus. He had not realized quite how behind he was in his information. Had Hector and Helenus not thought to tell him anything at all? he wondered. He could not recall any news from Mysia since the last details of the sack of Lyrnessus.

He managed a curt 'Thanks for telling me' to Chromis. It did not occur to him to say anything more. Disasters were coming to seem commonplace. The two men walked on in settled misery until they turned into the Street of the Basketmakers, in an old part of the lower town.

There had always been a tavern in the Street of the Basketmakers, but it had expanded steadily during the years of war as the basketmakers' trade had waned. A narrow alley led between two tall houses into a small unpaved courtyard with a well in the centre. At the far side of the yard was the storeroom with its sunken pithoi holding Carian wine and ale brewed in the Hittite style, their rims just above the level of the clay floor. The little booths where the basketmakers had worked had all become drinking alcoves, and there were rooms beyond the yard where men smoked poppy in a fume-ridden haze and where women and young boys plied their trade.

It was a soldiers' tavern, favoured by the southerners for its strong wine. The place was unfamiliar to Troilus and he had the impression that few officers ever came there. He recognized Antiphus, though, and the Lycian leader Glaucus leaning against the well surround, and there were a few other familiar faces in the courtyard. Obviously Helenus and Ennomus were not the only ones who drank their wine unwatered just then.

Chromis took his ration stick and disappeared in search of a serving girl. Troilus began to work his way around the booths, looking for Ennomus or Helenus. He saw neither of them; but as he was approaching the far corner he realized suddenly that the man sitting facing him in the end booth was Hector.

Instinctively Troilus drew into the shadows, reluctant to let his brother see him. He was being ridiculous, he decided a moment later. If Hector came there, obviously he was misjudging the place. It was reckoned respectable, he supposed, in spite of the filth.

Chromis had disappeared into the storeroom, so Troilus made his way alone to Hector's booth. Only as he came level with it did he notice that his brother's drinking partner was Aeneas.

That too was unexpected. Hector and Aeneas had never been close, to his knowledge. Had they recently become friends, Troilus wondered, or was it a special meeting to share private news?

It was too late to ask himself if he was bursting in on something; Aeneas had seen him and was rising to his feet. He drew Troilus into the booth, calling out past him to a serving girl, and Troilus squatted on the rough ground opposite Hector. 'You've heard about Thebe?' he asked.

Aeneas nodded. 'Did Chromis tell you, or Ennomus? Mind, the messenger has probably gone up the palace by now. It'll be all round the citadel by morning.'

Troilus hesitated. He was reluctant to make a political remark, for fear it would betray how out of touch he was. 'You'll have known a lot of men in the Mysian army?'

'Quite a few, yes. It has hit Hector harder, with Andromache's family being killed.'

Troilus had clean forgotten that Thebe was Andromache's town. He turned guiltily to his brother. Hector was staring moodily down at his clay goblet, twisting the stem between his fingers.

'Chromis didn't tell me. Are they all dead?'

'Probably,' Hector said. 'The princes for certain, if the news is right. Eetion was still fighting when the messenger left, but I doubt if he has survived. I told Andromache he was dead. It's best for her to get all the shock over at once. Don't let her think otherwise, unless more news comes in the morning.'

'No, of course not.' Troilus thought, with a touch of annoyance, that he was hardly likely to see Andromache anyway. 'More wine?' A girl was passing with a full jug. 'May I set mine to your rations? Chromis has my stick.'

Hector downed the rest of his cup and handed it over with his ration stick. He had been drinking fast and was beginning to feel the effects. There was a whisper somewhere in his mind that he had reason to treat Troilus warily, but he could not pin it down, or make himself care much.

Troilus took a deep draught and almost choked on it. The wine was even stronger than he had expected. He glanced at Aeneas, who stared back impassively. Hector might be out to drown his sorrows, Troilus thought to himself, but there was no sign of unsteadiness in the Dardanian's gaze. It would be just like Aeneas to sip on a single cup all evening while the brothers drank themselves stupid. Well, Aeneas could think what he damn well liked. Troilus drank the rest of the wine down in long gulps and called for a refill.

In fact Aeneas had been drinking steadily for some time, but he had a good head for wine and his mind was still unnervingly clear. He had not dropped his guard completely since he had reached Ilios, and he was beginning to feel that it would be harder to deaden his feelings than he had anticipated. He might as well get to work on Troilus, he decided. Who knew but that Priam might not pick the boy as advisor on his next round of troop dispositions? He leaned forward, his cup forgotten in his hand, and began to outline to Troilus the pattern of the war in Mysia. He would be careful to keep it accurate, but he could phrase his account so as to make clear his conviction that Priam ought to be taking a harder line.

Troilus listened, but he drank at the same time. He was flattered to be taken seriously by the older man, but he could not pretend that his political awareness stretched to a particular interest in Mysia. Getting good and angry about a hefty defeat was one thing; concentrating on the intrigues between minor Trojan allies was another. Aeneas was beginning to bore him, and it was hard to catch all that he said over the shouts of the men in the courtyard. He made an attempt to wrap up the conversation. 'The campaign must be more or less over now, though. Surely the Achaeans will not hang around any longer to tempt us out after them? They must have taken a fortune in loot: they'll escape back to base with it while they are still safe.'

Aeneas caught the curtness in Troilus' tone. 'You're right. Really, it is Priam's approach to the next campaign that matters now. It's too late to set things right in Mysia. In fact, I had word from Antiphus that the Achaeans already have ships in the Idaeus estuary, so they will doubtless be getting back to Tenedos or to the base here as soon as they have stripped Thebe.'

Troilus frowned slightly.

'Thebe is on the Idaeus? I hadn't realized. I thought it was a little to the south.' Surely Chryseis had mentioned it to him?

'It's on the plain around the head of the estuary. It must be half a day's march from the waterside; the plain is wide there. There's a little fishing port actually on the shore, and I gather the Achaeans have set up a temporary base there. At Chryse. Maybe you know of it; there's a shrine to Sminthian Apollo.'

'Chryse? The Achaeans are based at Chryse?' Troilus was suddenly tense. Half rising, he shouted the words at Aeneas. Hector looked up at the pair, frowning. Aeneas, alarmed, was trying to add some kind of explanation, but Troilus blindly ignored him, turning on his brother. 'You knew this. You knew it all along, didn't you? You cunning bastard, you sent her straight to them. You've killed her!'

The words echoed around the little stone booth and reverberated in the courtyard. Suddenly there was silence. Hector was lumbering to his feet. Before he could frame a reply Troilus was at him, his fists striking out wildly. There was a crash as Hector's cup dropped from his grasp and shattered against the rough wall.

Fights were nothing new in the tavern, but a fight between officers and princes was something out of the ordinary. Even as Aeneas leaped up to try to part the brothers, a group of soldiers reached them. Troilus found himself pulled roughly backwards, his hands pinned behind him. He had barely had a chance to land one good hard punch.

'Get him out of here. Gently. He's been drinking too much, but he'll do no real harm.' Aeneas was perfectly in command.

The soldiers did as he ordered, quickly and efficiently. Troilus was frogmarched down the alleyway and shoved into the gutter in the street outside, still panting from the fight. He lifted himself up unsteadily onto hands and knees. A hefty soldier barred the entrance to the alley and looked down at him contemptuously. If he recognized Troilus he chose not to show it.

'Are you hurt? Come on, let's get out of here.' It was Chromis. The look Troilus shot him was not as grateful as it might have been, but he did not argue as the Mysian took his arm and led him away.

The next morning Troilus awoke late, with a thick head and a foul taste in his throat. He stood up unsteadily. His knee ached: he must have twisted it as he fell. Memories of the night before came back patchily. Chromis had taken him to another tavern in the lower town, smaller and even dirtier, and the pair had got extremely drunk together. He remembered ranting about revenge, but Chromis, always even-tempered, had turned his mood, and they had ended up in a haze of sentimental cheer, singing old war songs and reminiscing about girls.

It was generous of the Mysian. He was no particular friend to Troilus, and Troilus could hardly have complained if he had been left in the gutter. He was uneasily conscious that he had acted extremely badly. I owe him a favour, he thought to himself as he dressed. But first, there was work to be done.

His muzzy head needed clearing, so he took the time to get a quick breakfast. The rations were tight, with new shortages every few days, and a rough porridge was all that the palace offered. Pity we are not low on wine as well, Troilus thought wearily to himself. How long before we drink the storerooms dry at this rate? Then he made his way to Hector's house.

The housekeeper opened the courtyard door warily and eyed Troilus through the crack. Troilus mentally cursed. He had expected his brother to be conciliatory by the morning: Hector was not a man to bear a grudge.

He asked for Hector, expecting to be invited in, at least to the yard. The woman kept the door almost shut. 'Is he not here?' Troilus asked, his temper beginning to rise. 'Do you know where else I might find him?'

The housekeeper hesitated, then she opened the door a little further. She was shaking her head to herself. 'Did you not see the signs, sir? We can let nobody in but the priests, not until the house has been purified.'

Troilus had not looked. Hastily he cast his eyes sideways and saw the branches of yew above the door and windows. 'Who is dead? One of the servants?'

'No, sir. It's the baby. The shock of the news yesterday brought it on. Princess Andromache has been very bad. The midwife thinks she will pull round, but there was no hope for the baby. It should not have come for another three moons.'

'Oh. I'm sorry.'

'The priest will be coming this morning to do the rites. You could come back this afternoon, but I think perhaps Prince Hector will go to the palace then.'

Troilus shrugged. Hector was hardly likely to be sympathetic to his schemes in the circumstances. He muttered his condolences and turned away, at a loss. As far as he was aware nobody else knew about his understanding with Chryseis and he did not want to broadcast it around the town, but he needed to talk to someone. Helenus, he suspected, would not show enough concern. Reluctantly, he decided it would have to be Aeneas.

He found the Dardanian commander at the camp stables. Aeneas was pernickety about his horses: he loudly criticized the Ilian grooms, did not even trust his own charioteer completely, and frequently saw to them himself.

He greeted Troilus briefly, then turned back to his grooming. He was in no mood to be hurried, and Troilus kicked his heels while Aeneas rubbed down the horses with warm and cold water, oiled their coats and scraped off the excess with a squared flint, even replaited the tail of one horse.

At last he dismissed the groom who had been helping him, patted the bays on their flanks and went to the trough to wash the last of the oil off his hands.

The Dardanian was brusque, but not unfriendly, as they began to walk to the centre of the camp. 'I obviously said the wrong thing last night. I still have no idea what it was about. Hector refused to say anything, but it seems he didn't blame you for hitting out.'

Troilus explained as best he could. He felt that he made rather a hash of it. Aeneas looked at him narrowly. 'So you and Hector both arranged for the girl to go back to Chryse?'

'Oh no. It was Hector's idea. It's just that I could see no alternative.'

'Except to marry her.'

'No. Yes. I mean, I do want to marry her, but not yet.'

'So there was no point in keeping her in Ilios.' Aeneas spoke with a smoothness that fired Troilus' impatience. He had expected sympathy to come more readily and he had to work at keeping his own voice calm. 'It was not as if I wanted her gone, not at all. And certainly not into that sort of danger.'

Aeneas thought, then said, 'Maybe Hector didn't realize the Achaeans were close to Chryse.'

'Oh, come on, Aeneas. He hears all the news from Priam's spies.'

'But you had not heard it yourself.'

'I have been a bit out of touch recently. I had other things to think about.'

'The girl.'

'Yes, of course the girl. She has a name, Aeneas.'

'You hadn't spoken to Ennomus or Chromis? Or to Antiphus, or any of the other southerners?'

'Why should I? Hector would have heard any news that they had.'

Aeneas gave Troilus a look reminiscent of Helenus at his most exasperating. All right, Troilus added to himself, perhaps he would not.

There was a long pause, as if Aeneas was waiting for Troilus to say something more. Troilus had nothing more to say, though, and at length Aeneas remarked, 'Well, it's unfortunate, but I don't see that you have anything to blame Hector for.'

'Unfortunate! It's a damn sight more than unfortunate.'

'You'll get over it.'

Troilus' temper broke its bounds at that point. 'I haven't any bloody intention of getting over it. I'm going to do something about it.'

Aeneas eyed him with a mixture of curiosity and faint alarm. Troilus seemed so very young. 'There is absolutely nothing you can do. You don't even know for certain if Chryseis and her father did run into the Achaeans. They might have taken refuge somewhere inland when the escort heard that there was fighting around the estuary. She might be dead. And if she is a prisoner there is nothing to be done about it.'

Troilus' voice rose still higher. 'I reckon there is plenty I can do. I can get down there and find out what is going on. I can bring her back, if she is safe. I can make my father ransom her if she is a prisoner.'

'Ransom her? You just told me you didn't even trust his approval enough to tell him about the marriage. As for going to Mysia, that would be suicidal. The place is crawling with soldiers, it's a positive anthill. If you got anywhere near the captives they would cut you to pieces. It would make more sense to wait till she is brought to the camp down on the plain here and walk over to the stockade in broad daylight.'

The boy was not prepared to admit defeat yet. 'I thought perhaps you would come with me.' He watched Aeneas carefully. 'You know the territory much better than I do. And you said you wanted to strike back at the Achaeans.'

Aeneas shook his head. 'Troilus, you are being stupid. If you set about some harebrained scheme like that you are going to end up dying a very inglorious death in some Mysian ditch.'

'That would be better than letting her go and doing nothing.'

Aeneas appeared to consider this. He showed no sign of approval or disapproval. Finally he said, in a careful voice, 'There is something you can do. If the girl is so important to you it would be honourable to avenge her properly. Wait until we find out what really happened. The news will come through once the Achaeans are out of Mysia. If an Achaean has killed her or taken her prisoner, then you may be able to discover which one, and kill him in open battle. There will be plenty of chances when the fighting moves back to Ilios. As it must do, if Priam has his way.'

Troilus was silent and Aeneas examined his expression with sharp eyes. The sulk did not sit naturally on his handsome face. It seemed to Aeneas that the boy might see sense. He would have to be watched, and kept busy. And Hector would need to be told before his brother got himself into any more trouble. Aeneas added briskly, 'You haven't seen to your own horses yet, have you? I'll come over to the palace stables and tend them with you. Then we can go back to the camp and see if the Mysians have any fresh news.'

He turned towards the Phrygian Gate, and though he did not look back he sensed that the boy began to follow him. A deceptively impetuous lad, but bright enough. Indeed he had heard that Troilus was inclined to use his head rather than his heart when he did not rush into things. Aeneas' curiosity was raised about the girl, though She had surely left Ilios only days after he had arrived; it was a pity he had not seen her. Was she really so pretty? He decided he would have to ask Paris.

Part Two

A SUMMER OF WAR

THE CAPTIVES FROM LYRNESSUS waited on the shores of the Idaeus estuary for a night and a day. The soldiers halted them in an olive grove, where the trees grew almost as far as the water. The water was shallow, but a stone jetty had been built out to make a simple harbour. The nearby village was deserted, and the troops burned the fishing boats in case anyone was tempted to escape that way. They built their campfires round the edge of the makeshift camp and slaughtered a couple of the sheep they had taken, feasting noisily on them. The captives were handed a couple of sacks of meal and told to fend for themselves.

On the second day a Phoenician trader came and the soldiers bartered the male captives, the children, some of the women, and most of the goods they had taken, in exchange for ingots of copper and bronze, and jars of oil and wine. Briseis watched the ship leave dry-eyed. It was strange to see how much a woman fetched. The ship's captain had valued each one individually, pinching the flesh on their haunches as impersonally as if they were cattle and barking out questions about their skills in a thick foreign accent. The women who answered back too readily had been downgraded a little, she reckoned; he had rated the meek ones highest. She herself might have been judged worth five oxen, maybe, if she had behaved herself properly.

The youngest and prettiest were left behind. It was not difficult to tell why. She knew some of them: wives of acquaintances, serving girls from the palace or her father's house. There was one servant of her own. The girl crossed over to sit with her on the hard ground beneath the trees.

Althea was her name: a boisterous, highly coloured girl who had worked as a cook. She had seen perhaps sixteen summers. Always submissive to Briseis before, she greeted her now with a mixture of sympathy and boldness. She had taken the capture lightly and chattered on cheerfully about the prospects in the camp. 'The soldiers say you are to go to Achilles. You're lucky. Did you see him when they looked us over? He's ever so handsome, and it's always good to get the leader, isn't it?' Briseis looked at her blankly. 'Not that he's as important as King Agamemnon, of course,' Althea added, mistaking Briseis' expression.

Briseis fought the urge to tell the girl to leave her alone. There was comfort in knowledge. She had said that to herself before. She drove the tips of her fingers into the dry, crumbly earth and set out to discover what else Althea had learned.

There was a lot to discover, for though Althea had cared nothing about the war before the Achaeans came to Lyrnessus, she had worked hard since. Briseis herself could hardly have given the names of half a dozen Achaean leaders. Althea knew at least twice as many and had picked up a fair impression of their characters from the guards. It was her great chance to exchange a dull life for a more interesting one. She was hoping to be allotted to Diomedes, or perhaps Ajax. They sounded like lively men who would enjoy her cooking and share a laugh with her now and then.

'I'm sorry, I've never heard of them.' Briseis was not used to feeling ignorant in front of servants. 'Is Ajax the man who was with Achilles outside the town?'

'Oh no, ma'am.' Althea giggled. 'They say Ajax is even taller than that, and better built with it. That was Patroclus, Achilles' lieutenant. The soldiers seem to like him, but he's not as rich as the leaders.'

Briseis eyed the girl thoughtfully. 'I don't think you should raise your hopes too high, Althea. We are only slaves, you know. I expect they need their dinners cooked in the camp, and we might both end up grilling fish and grinding corn.'

Althea smiled. 'Not fish. The Achaeans won't eat fish. Still, that's life, isn't it? But it's a change. It's exciting. I like to look on the bright side. Maybe it will be a change for the worse, but maybe it won't. The gods might smile on us this time around. There's no point crying until disaster really does come, is there?'

But for Briseis the disaster had come already and the girl remembered it too late. 'I'm sorry, ma'am, I'm being stupid. It must be dreadful for you, losing the master, and your baby too. But you'll get over it, honestly you will. There'll be happy times ahead, I'm sure of it.'

Briseis could not make herself answer. Althea sat awkwardly by her side for a short while longer, then she got quietly to her feet and went to rejoin the other servants.

The Achaean ships came the next day. There were three of them, too many to tie up at once in the deep water at the far end of the jetty. They came in one by one, leaving two to sit like crows on the water. Sleek and black with high curving prows, they looked hard and purposeful after the plump lines of the Phoenician vessel.

The women were all put in the last ship after the goods had been stowed away. In single file the soldiers herded them along the jetty, hoisted them aboard and bundled them into the hold. It was dark, with a musty smell of figs and rotted wheat, and a suspicion of dampness underfoot.

Briseis had not been at sea since she was a child and she found the journey rough, especially after they turned out of the gulf and into the open sea. It took all day to reach the Achaean base camp and she was weak from sickness long before they got there. She did not trouble to stir herself when the ship beached. Soldiers came to fetch the captives, and unfamiliar hands lifted her up to the deck, washed by the redness of the evening sky, and then down to a stretch of shingle that seemed to tilt just as much as the sea had done. She dropped to her knees, her stomach heaving.

'Had it badly, that one.' The voice was male and sounded quite indifferent.

'They're all inland women. From Lyrnessus and round about. Not used to the sea, but they'll get over it. This is the one Achilles wanted. Diomede had better come to fetch her.'

Diomede sounded like the name of the general Althea had coveted, but it turned out to be a woman, quiet and fair, of about Briseis' age. She seemed perfectly at ease among the soldiers. 'Can you stand up? Or shall I get one of the soldiers to carry you?'

'Is it far?'

The girl shrugged. 'Quite a long walk: it's a big camp. These are Cretan ships. The Thessalians are down the side of the bay, over there. Can you see the black standards?'

Briseis could not make them out. She had never seen so many ships before. There must have been hundreds pulled up in rows on the strand. Most had their masts upright and they seemed to crowd around her like an army of giants. She felt dizzy. Perhaps it had been a mistake to stand up. She swayed, and the stones came up to meet her.

She came to in a tent. It was a makeshift arrangement of hide and branches, like the shelters the wandering peasants built on the plain. There was just room for a person to stand where the roof was highest. She was lying on a straw pallet at the side, and two figures stood close together, towering above her: the girl Diomede, and another girl, a little taller, dark-eyed and black-haired. They were talking in low voices. Then Diomede turned and saw her open eyes. 'Oh, she's coming round.' She turned to a low table, picking up a cup from it, and crossed to the pallet. 'Here. Iphis has made you a draught. There's honey in it, and camomile. Drink it down, then you can sleep.'

'I don't think I can drink anything.'

'You must.' The other girl's voice was hard and there was no sympathy in it. Briseis dropped her eyes and moved to sit up and do as she was told.

'You're making it up, Doris. You must be.'

'No, I'm not. Honestly. I got it from Phoenix, and Phoenix would never make up a story like that, would he?'

Doris giggled as she spoke. The women were sitting in the biggest of their tents. A thin canvas roof radiated out from the roof tree to a framework of branches lashed together, giving room enough for three or four of them to stand at once, and for more than a dozen to sit. All the Thessalian girls were there. They called themselves that, Briseis had learned, since they all belonged to Achilles and the other officers from Thessaly. There had been eighteen of them before she arrived; now there were nineteen.

Doris was a bouncy girl, shortish and slim, with a mobile, heavy-featured face that was striking but not beautiful. She settled herself on the pallet where she sat cross-legged, and leaned forward as she went on with the rest of the story. 'They dressed him up as a girl to hide him, you see: from the recruiting officers. Ulysses and his men had come to bring him to Troy, from Lycomedes' palace where his parents had him fostered, and so Lycomedes' wife dressed him up as one of the girls. Ulysses didn't recognize him, and even Phoenix didn't, but then Ulysses made out that the palace was being attacked and Achilles couldn't resist grabbing a spear and joining in the fight. So he was found out, and Ulysses brought him here to fight.'

'But Achilles wouldn't pass as a girl. Even in a dim light he wouldn't, whatever he was wearing.'

Doris giggled again. 'As we all know. Except for you, Briseis, and you'll find out soon enough.' The others laughed too at that. Briseis did not. Doris ignored her set face and went on, 'But it must be true, if Phoenix told it. You've heard the story too, haven't you, Iphis? Being from Scyros?'

Iphis nodded. It was hot in the tent, but even squatting on the ground she managed to look cool and elegant. 'Yes, they used to tell it in the palace. And it is true that Achilles stayed there before he came to Troy.'

'But not the rest of it?'

Doris shrugged. 'Well, I wouldn't fancy asking Achilles to his face. Would you, Diomede?'

Diomede shook her head and Doris said, 'All the same, I think it's true, if Phoenix tells it. Achilles would have looked different when he was a boy. He would have been shorter, and not as stern, I suppose.'

'Eight years ago, maybe nine. He would have been in – what, his sixteenth summer? His seventeenth?'

'He was younger than that, surely. I doubt if he has seen more than twenty-three summers now.'

'But Patroclus has seen thirty summers. Achilles must be older than him.'

'I always thought he was much older than that.'

None of them, it seemed, had much idea how old Achilles was. It was, Briseis assumed, another of the questions they would not dare to ask him.

She wondered if she might fairly set it down as a criticism of him. She was hoarding their criticisms as a miser hoards silver, and so far there were distressingly few of them. He did shout at them sometimes, one of the girls had let slip one day. Apart from that, it had been ten days during which she seemed to have heard nothing but unremitting praise of Achilles.

She allowed herself a sigh as she and Iphis were settling down to bed. She slept in the tent in which she had first woken, an inner tent that gave off the main tent, with Iphis and Diomede. They would have had a little more space than the other girls before she came; now they were decidedly cramped. Diomede was not yet in the tent, or Briseis would have tried harder to hold the sigh back. She might have liked Diomede, she thought, if the other girl had showed any sign of liking her; but it was very clear that she did not. Diomede had no sympathy with sighs. While Doris and most of the others seemed to believe in cauterizing Briseis' grief by boisterous joking about what lay in store for her, Diomede handled it by behaving with icy coldness whenever any inkling of it came to the surface. She greeted sighs with a wave of hatred. As for tears, all the girls had made it clear that they had to be reserved strictly for the dark.

Iphis, who was not prone to laughter, heard her and turned in the gloom. 'Problems?'

Problems? With Mynes hacked to pieces on the field below Lyrnessus, and Ianeira's tiny body tossed by Achaean soldiers onto the pyre? She felt she would never come to terms with the agony of it, the nightmarish unreality of this new life in which everybody pretended it had all never happened.

But even Iphis would not have tolerated her saying anything like that. Briseis said carefully, 'Nothing new. I find it difficult just sitting there, doing nothing. If only we could go outside the tents more often, or we had spindles or looms. Or if you would all talk about something other than Achilles.'

'I'll talk about Patroclus instead, if you like.'

Iphis was Patroclus' girl: Achilles had given her to his lieutenant several years before. If Briseis had been hoarding criticisms of Patroclus her store would have been even scantier.

'That isn't quite what I meant. Do you never want to talk about yourself? Or could you not be more critical of the men?'

Iphis finished combing her hair and tied it with a few concise, expert movements into a tidy knot at the nape of her long neck. She settled down on her back on the thin pallet and appeared to consider this. 'We tried telling each other about our captures and our families and all that when we first came, and it only depressed us. It's better to turn your back on it all and start again, really it is. We are much more interested in Achilles.' She paused, and added, 'And Patroclus.'

'So I hear.' Briseis was silent for a long time. Had Iphis lost a husband too? she wondered to herself. The other girl gave no impression of harbouring unresolved agonies, though Briseis had as yet made no real attempt to penetrate her elegant façade. On the surface, Iphis showed precisely what the others showed: no serious feelings or opinions at all, just a hetaira's fascination for clothes and jewels, and this uncritical admiration for her master. How could any woman lose her family and feel like that about their murderers?

Briseis glanced over to see if Iphis was asleep and found the dark eyes fixed with bland openness upon her. She said more quietly, 'I thought you would hate them.'

'I suppose I did, at first. Now I love them.'

'Both of them?'

Iphis smiled at that. 'Yes, both of them. I think we all do. I love Patroclus more, of course. Maybe most of the girls do, he is easier to love than Achilles. Not that I would dare to say that in front of any of Achilles' girls.'

Briseis smiled too, but her smile was thin and cold. 'You're right there. I'm not Achilles' girl. And I have no intention of loving him.'

'Not yet, perhaps. Maybe you will see it differently when he's here.'

'Maybe you will talk less about him when he's here.'

'There's not that much else to do even then. On the whole,' Iphis said, 'I think we shall talk about him even more.'

Briseis supposed she must count herself lucky that Achilles

was not yet back at the camp. His troops were still campaigning around the Ideaus, and more Achaeans had set out for Mysia over the previous few days. She reckoned she might have till the next full moon, or even a little beyond, to come to terms with what had happened; to get to know the women with whom she would have to spend the rest of her life, and to listen to their tales of Achilles before she had to face the man himself.

The spring series of campaigns was drawing to a close, and with Priam's forces being swelled daily by distant Trojan allies, the whole might of the Achaean army was needed on the plain before Ilios. The soldiers who had been fighting to the north came back in triumph first, with booty from the shores of Phrygia and Thrace. The camp was alive with excitement. The Thessalian girls went down to the harbour with the rest to watch the landings.

It was the first time that Briseis had been beyond their tents since she arrived at the camp. Its size astonished her. The Achaean territory spread right around the great shallow bay, where the rivers Scamander and Simois fed into the sea, that had been Ilios' sheltered harbour at the mouth of the Hellespont. It was tightly packed with a miscellany of campaign tents, makeshift shelters like her own, and wooden huts. She could barely see beyond them to the great wooden stockade, twice as high as a man, that formed the last line of defence against the Trojans.

Thirty thousand fighting men were said to be in the camp, and Briseis did not doubt it was true. The paths were thick with them surging down towards the harbour and almost as many seemed to mill around the huts. Archers, the mark of their quiver belts slashed pale across their bronzed chests; charioteers, light-footed and distant-eyed; spearmen, tall and arrogant. It surprised Briseis more to see how many of the camp's inhabitants were not fighters. There were cripples, men who had somehow survived broken limbs and crude amputations, who dreaded to return home and had chosen instead to work in the camp as cooks and quartermasters. There were priests, formally robed in spite of the heat. There were groups of women much like Briseis' own, and gaggles of small children, born since the war began, playing in the dust.

At first, her impression was of chaos. There seemed to be no pattern in the collection of shelters, or in the pathways that threaded between them. She had to be mistaken, though: that was clear from Diomede's words, as she provided a steady running commentary for the other girls. Diomede knew how to read order into the scene, and watching and listening, Briseis began to trace the signs that she followed. Paths wider and better trodden than the rest, marking the division between one contingent's tents and the next. Consistent differences in the style of huts, from the peasant brushwood of the Ithacans and the northerners to the elegant canvas of the Mycenaeans. Open spaces where each contingent gathered, marked by the profusion of cauldrons, tripods and cooking fires, and littered with debris from years of suppers eaten out in the open. It was not difficult to detect the personalities of the contingents, the well-run sections and the scruffy ones. The Thessalian section was tightly run in comparison to most, she had no doubt about that.

Diomede kept their group close together as they made their way beyond the huts to the open ground near the water's edge. From the shore she led them to a spur of higher ground where the bay curved round. There they could look down on the harbour without being jostled too roughly. They could see further inland too: over the barricade to the plain of Ilios, with the rivers threading across it, and the citadel itself, distant but dominating from its hilltop.

On the shingle around the harbour, the black ships were pulled up in neat lines. The inner rows had their sails furled; on some, the masts had been lowered. These ships were used as stores for the more precious booty, and as living quarters for the helmsman. Closer to the water all the masts were standing, and some of the sails flapped limply in the light breeze. In the bay itself a dozen ships with the standard of Salamis, Ajax's own fleet, mingled with the fifty Athenian ships that had accompanied him to Thrace. The men clustered thickly round each one as it landed, like ants devouring a carcase.

Diomede kept up her commentary, but now she began to differentiate between the troops and their commanders: the small, neat men from Boeotia and Salamis, with Ajax, as massive as Althea had said, towering over them; the Phocians, clean-shaven and close-faced, with the other, little Ajax at their head; the Spartans, cold-eyed men who moved abruptly, headed by the red-haired Menelaus.

'Which is Agamemnon?' Briseis asked quietly.

'The High King?' Diomede flung her a quick glance, then turned to scan the mass of soldiers. She shook her head. 'I can't see him. It would be easy to tell if he were here. He's not a big man, but he always has attendants, and he dresses like a king. He makes you notice him. He probably hasn't bothered to come down to the ships. He will be there when they make sacrifices in the square, and I imagine he will choose a girl. Agamemnon always eyes the new ones. He soon tires of them once he's got them back to his quarters.'

'Not as soon as they tire of him,' said Doris. The others laughed with her. It seemed to be the thing among them, to criticize Agamemnon. Everyone knew, it appeared, that Achilles and Agamemnon were at loggerheads. And Agamemnon's girls evidently had plenty to complain about, for the High King was said to have a sadistic streak and to maltreat his women.

The girls seemed as friendly then as Briseis had known them. The bustle and activity made them less backbiting than they were in the tents, and she herself was not the centre of their taunts for once. It was as if it did them all good to get out of the stale air and catch the salt breeze that blew across the harbour. But the next morning the atmosphere changed. Achilles was expected back and they were tense with anticipation.

'Do you think the Myrmidons will come in today?' Briseis asked Iphis; Diomede was snappy and seemed best avoided.

The dark girl thought before replying. 'I doubt it. There will be ceremonies all morning, in thanksgiving for Ajax's return. He was back too late yesterday, so they put them off until today. If Achilles brought the ships in now he would lose half the impact; nor would it be fair, to steal Ajax's thunder. I imagine he will wait offshore until tomorrow morning.'

'Is that safe?' Briseis was thinking about seasickness and pirates: it seemed to her unthinkable that anyone would choose to stay at sea overnight if they could avoid it. Iphis took her question differently. 'The High King will not like it, that goes without saying, but I doubt if he will say anything. Possibly he will keep away when they land. Still, he was not at the harbour for Ajax, so it will count for little if he stays away for Achilles.'

Briseis was surprised. She had taken the women's chatter lightly and had not realized that the enmity between the two commanders went so deep, or that the High King was so much to be feared by the other leaders. It was nothing to her, though; and it gave her a day's more respite.

Iphis was right. No news came from the harbour that day, then early the following morning there was word from the sentries that Achilles' ships were to be spied offshore. Diomede came to Briseis to tell her to dress for the trip to the harbour.

They had worn their usual clothes, long homespun tunics, to watch Ajax come in, but evidently Achilles rated different treatment from his women. The girl from Lesbos was wearing a dress that Briseis had not seen before, in the court style. It was bright red with thick bands of embroidery in blue, yellow and gold around the edge of the bodice and of each tier of her skirt. There was a glint of gold at her neck and wrists. Her eyes were rimmed with kohl, her lips and nipples were reddened, and her fair hair was darkened and braided in a complicated style, with a mass of ribbons. Briseis had never looked remotely as sophisticated, and she flushed as she replied. 'Must I come? I would prefer to wait here.'

Diomede was curt and impatient. 'Of course you must. You should have been ready by now. Why did you not come to join us, so Doris could fix your hair?'

Briseis had deliberately stayed in the inner tent and ignored the bustle of the others. 'I will go like this, then.'

Diomede looked her over. 'No. Anybody can see you have made no effort. Come now: if we work at it we can soon have you looking reasonable. The ships'll not be in yet.'

Briseis followed her, wretched, and submitted in silence while the girls painted her face and fussed around her. They found her a dress like Diomede's, blue with red trimmings, and pulled and stitched it till it clung to her body. The blue matched her eyes, Doris said cheerfully; she did not answer. When they had finished she peeped into the mirror Doris held before her. She looked barely distinguishable from the others. The doll's face, bright with red and black, and the body that the dress flaunted so blatantly did not seem to belong to her at all. She felt stiff and awkward as they set off, as if she was walking a puppet across the camp.

Iphis drew her a few steps apart from the others as they made their way down to the harbour. 'Try to be nicer to Diomede. This is hard enough for her as it is. You must not make an enemy of her.'

Her remarks meant nothing to Briseis, and she did not trouble to think about them before replying. 'I cannot see why I should look my best for Achilles. I'd rather look as plain as I can manage.'

Iphis, normally so cool, had to work hard to keep her temper. 'Have some sense, Briseis. You cannot bring back your husband by rejecting Achilles. You really are very lucky to go to him. It would be far worse to be Agamemnon's girl, or Meriones'.'

'Nothing could be worse than to be Achilles' girl. He is the one who killed Mynes.' It gave her a grim pleasure to have an excuse to speak her husband's name.

Iphis frowned. Briseis was making this very difficult. 'I am sorry. Really I am. I know how hard it must be.' Her face clouded, as if she were recalling her own pain from a great distance; and then slowly cleared, as newer memories overlaid it. Briseis was not looking at her. Her face was hard-set, and Iphis said more gently, 'Of course you don't want to dishonour your husband's memory; but you have to go on living. Can you not see it as honourable to make the best of things?' She was warming to her theme. The important thing, she reckoned, was to make sure that the first night went well. Then surely Briseis would fall in love with Achilles. It was difficult to hate a man who gave you pleasure in bed. 'If you have to go to him – and you do – then you need not let him know how much you dislike it. That would be another way for him to win out, surely. It would be better to go to him proudly, as if it was what you wanted most of all.'

Briseis did not reply. They walked on for some distance, and Iphis exclaimed with more than a touch of annoyance, 'Say something. Or did you not hear a word I said?'

As Briseis turned to her she thought she saw a softening in

the other girl's expression. Then Briseis managed a rather forced smile. 'I'll think about it.' Iphis relaxed. 'I'm sorry. I know you're trying to help.' Really, Briseis was more grateful for Iphis' gesture of friendship than for the advice she had been offered. 'Come on, let's go and get it over with.'

She quickened her pace and Iphis hurried to catch up with her. She was anxious to bring Briseis back over to Diomede and the others before Diomede grew even more upset.

As they joined up with the main group the dark girl added, 'The men will say nothing to us at the harbour. They never do. Probably they won't even notice us. We dress up to please ourselves really, not for them.'

Briseis gave her a friendly glance and then turned it into a more open smile. She felt almost happy, for the first time since the soldiers had come. It would be a good thing, she felt, if she could make friends with the women. With them to care about, perhaps she could learn to endure life with the men.

Iphis had told the truth too. The soldiers, like the women, were showing off for each other's benefit, and though there were admiring glances from other men, Achilles and Patroclus did not even glance their way. Briseis allowed herself only a brief look at Achilles. He wore the armour she knew from Lyrnessus: a breastplate emblazoned with stars, and a helmet with a tall, nodding yellow plume. Then her eyes moved in a different direction. New groups of women captives had been brought back on the ships and among them were familiar faces. It came as a shock to see women she knew from Thebe, standing where she herself had knelt less than a moon before.

Her companions noticed the pallor under her rouge.

'What's wrong, Briseis? Somebody walk on your shadow?' It was the first time Diomede had spoken to her since they left the tents.

Briseis pulled herself together. 'No, it's the captives. Of course they must have taken many more prisoners since I came to he camp.'

'You know them?'

'A few of them, yes. They are from the country round Thebe, just along the estuary from my home town. That's the Queen of Thebe, the older woman who is being led off.' (A couple of soldiers, Myrmidons by the look of them, had come to escort the Queen away from the group on the shingle. She appeared to be fainting.) 'And there is one I know well: the slim girl over to the left, with the dark braided hair. Her name is Chryseis.'

It was disconcerting to see Chryseis in this alien setting. Briseis had not seen the girl for a year or more, and even from a distance she could make out changes in her: a new softness in her figure, a womanly air about her where there had been nothing but girlishness before. But it was the same Chryseis who looked about her with pert confidence, apparently not at all subdued by her captivity. She carried with her an aura that set her apart from the other captives, who looked as wretched as Briseis had felt herself.

'Agamemnon will pick her.' Diomede spoke crisply.

'Why do you say that?'

Diomede gave a cold laugh. 'He likes them young, and he goes for the big-breasted ones. She looks to be pretty, too.'

Briseis' anger came back in a rush. Diomede seemed hard, even a little vicious, as if the paint on her face had affected her character. There was a hard note in her own voice as she answered, 'Yes, she is very pretty.'

'You Mysians run to type, don't you? If Achilles had not grabbed you first, you would have gone to Agamemnon yourself.'

Briseis' temper rose still higher at that. She had never thought herself anything like Chryseis. She was older, and paler, and not nearly as buxom. Well, perhaps she looked it then, but that was the milk which the baby should have had, making her breasts hard and round. She turned on Diomede and was snapping a reply when Iphis broke in hurriedly, 'We can wait and see what happens to your friend, Briseis. When you know who she belongs to, you can ask to talk to her. Not today, but soon. I'm sure Achilles will arrange it, if you ask him.'

Briseis frowned. She framed a retort that she would never, never ask Achilles for anything; then she caught Iphis' worried look and kept silent.

The ships had been beached and emptied, and the Myrmidons had disappeared. The girls followed the rest of the soldiers up the wide track from the harbour to a big square at the heart of the camp. It was large enough to hold all the soldiers, and there was an empty space in front of them, before the rambling sprawl of Agamemnon's quarters.

It was easy to tell which was Agamemnon now. The High King stood in his appointed place before his men, resplendent in long purple robes, with a great diadem on his head and a sceptre in his hand. Fawning priests and servants surrounded him. In a loud, straight-edged voice he harangued the troops for what seemed like an eternity. Then his High Priest Calchas made sacrifices to Zeus, Athena and Poseidon, and the leaders of the returning troops, now wearing the oiled tunics of the supplicant, came to be blessed and purified. They took the champion's portions as the sacrificial animals were cut up for the feast. There was no meat for the women; but then they had not expected any.

The troops shuffled back into their fixed ranks when the feast was over, to watch the division of the spoils. Diomede nudged Briseis. 'You have to go and join the captives now.'

Was she being deliberately nasty? Briseis saw no sign of it in Diomede's face and when she looked back at the square she could see other women moving towards the huddle of goods and captives just in front of the altars.

She went to stand close to Chryseis. She doubted if her friend would recognize her in the fancy Cretan costume. Nobody wore clothes like those in Mysia. She hesitated, then decided not to say anything. Chryseis seemed to be coping well with the ordeal, but Briseis feared it might upset her to learn that someone she knew was watching her.

The girls had described the division of the spoils to her as a lottery, but Briseis already knew that the outcome was fixed. Looking across at where the commanders stood, she could make out Achilles' tall figure. Even in the plain undyed tunic that he had worn for the purification, he had the arrogance and power of a master of men. There was no expression to be read in the strong, straight lines of his face. He was now standing next to Agamemnon, who was much closer to her than when she had seen him before. She could make out his features clearly now. His mouth was wide and tight-lipped; his eyes were deep-set, and a livid pale brown. As she caught their gaze a slight shiver went through her. There was something terrifying about him. Perhaps she was lucky, after all. The two men both looked her way and then turned to talk to each other. Briseis remembered Diomede's taunt and stood still, cold in the afternoon sun. Then Achilles crossed over to her and held out his hand. She took it without hesitating and followed him back to his men. He did not smile, or speak to her at all.

Chryseis went to Agamemnon, as Diomede had prophesied. She was by far the most beautiful of the women captives and there was a murmur as he led her out from among the rest. Briseis looked out for the girl Althea, but her friends did not recognize the man who took her. Not Ajax or Diomedes, she thought sadly. It would have been nice to see one woman happy at the outcome. Not that Chryseis seemed sad; her confidence fed on the admiration of the troops, and (thought Briseis) she flirted openly with their leaders.

When the distribution was finished Achilles turned and told her to return to the other women. He would go with Agamemnon, he said, to give the commander-in-chief details of the campaign. She slipped thankfully away to where the girls were waiting to make their way back to the Thessalian tents.

It was a long walk, for Achilles' men had their section at the far end of the camp and the women's tents were towards the centre of the section. The whole camp was thronged with troops and the women walked back slowly, cheerful and laughing after the wine of the feast. Nobody mentioned the men.

Back in their tents the girls hurried to remove their finery. The gold necklets and bracelets went into a small bronze casket, the fancy dresses were folded into a wooden chest. Doris produced a pot of cream, greasy and sweet-smelling, and they used this to wipe the kohl and rouge from their faces.

Briseis began to untie her own belt, but Iphis reached out to stop her. 'Do not change yet. Wait till the others have finished, then they will get you ready.'

They had all been chattering about the feast on the way back and Briseis had momentarily forgotten about the night ahead. She flushed. 'Do I not stay like this?' It would be good, she thought, to change into a more modest dress. It was one thing to strut through the camp with half a dozen others, but it would be another to stand alone in such a get-up and wait for Achilles to tear it off her. She rather liked the thought of keeping the heavy make-up, though. It made her feel unreal. It would armour her, in a way, against what was to come.

'No.' Iphis gave a slow smile. 'Achilles doesn't like his girls looking like that. I told you, we did it for show, not for him. You need something softer and more subtle.'

'I'll put on my usual dress, then. I don't need any help to do that.'

The dark girl shook her head. 'Briseis, you have to do it properly. Leave it to Doris. She's the expert.'

Doris caught the mention of her name and turned. Half the kohl was gone from her face and she looked strangely piebald. 'Won't be a moment. I've just the thing in the chest. You want to look wonderful for your wedding night, don't you?'

Briseis was trembling. But Doris was skilled, and it was a relief to leave herself in the other girl's hands. She took over the tent, sending the other women to fetch water and heat it, wash Briseis – the first good wash she had had since she arrived in the camp – and then keep out of the way while she was being dressed. The dress turned out to be a soft creamy wool one. It was not a straight tunic of the kind everyone wore in Mysia: it had been cut and shaped to fit. Doris arranged the girdle carefully so that the skirt hung in loose, even folds.

'Did the kohl come off?'

'Yes, most of it. He'll not see it in the dark. But I'll put back a little, if it makes you feel better.' She worked it around Briseis' eyes as she spoke, with deft, expert strokes. Then she opened a bottle of perfumed oil, heavy with coriander and cypress. She was just finishing her work when Iphis returned. 'The other officers have left. You should go to him now. Shall I take you over there?'

Achilles' quarters were barely a spear's throw away, across a rough track that had once led up to the citadel. Briseis shook her head. It would be better to do it alone.

It was dark when she stepped outside the women's tent, but the moon was out and she could see over to the light shining from Achilles' quarters. She did not move across to it straight away. She stood there, silent in the darkness, trying to prepare herself for what was to happen.

It would not do to think of Mynes. She could not bear it, if she did that. How could she bear it at all? She imagined herself bursting into tears in front of Achilles, and knew immediately that it would be shameful to do so. There had to be a way of enduring the inevitable honourably.

Honour. That was the word Iphis had used, walking down to the harbour. It had never been a word she connected with slavery. Honour was the business of kings and princes, not their underlings. Honour was Mynes going to his death with sword flashing. It was hard to associate it with her behaviour when Achilles reached out to paw her. The only honourable course of behaviour she had been able to think of had consisted in grabbing the man's dagger and stabbing him through the chest. She had been uneasily aware that she had not the courage to do that.

But there was honour, too, in something else: not in fighting, but in proud acceptance of a cruel fate. Go to him willingly, Iphis had said, as if you wanted it more than anything. She could not do that. That was not true, it was not right. She had no wish to lie to the world, to grow an armour as smooth and impenetrable as Iphis' own. But pride? Pride not in him, but in herself, for enduring what had to be endured? There was honour in that. For Mynes, for Ianeira, for her family, for herself, she must find that pride. She sent up a brief prayer to all the proud, cruel gods, and began the short walk to Achilles' quarters.

He did not have a tent, like most of the common soldiers' quarters. It was a low wooden hut, built in the Thessalian style with a deep colonnade around it and a courtyard surrounded by a heavy stockade. Grass was growing on the turf roof. In the yard a couple of goats were tethered, and there was a pen full of sheep. A pack of hunting dogs yapped around Briseis' ankles. The place looked foreign and yet settled, as if it had stood there for decades. There was nothing warlike about it.

Briseis had seen the hut, but she had never been inside before and she gaped as she entered it. She had not expected anything so luxurious.

The room was dark after the moonlight, though a lamp was

lit and there was a fire burning low. Achilles' officers had been feasting again after their return: a faint smell of cooked meat and of the wine they had spilt to honour the gods still hung in the air, and a pair of dogs were scuffling together by the fire, quarrelling over a bone.

At either end of the room were curtained alcoves. Behind the curtains Briseis could make out high beds, covered with a heap of skins: the topmost ones were not oxhide but lionskin, she thought. The boards of the floor were cut smoothly, and brushed clean; the walls were hung with rugs, patterned in deep reds and blues. In one corner, the mens' armour and their spears were stacked neatly; in another a harp had been set down on a small table. A carved sea-chest stood by the wall.

As Briseis closed the door behind her, the draught blew the smoke from the fire across the room. She closed her eyes against the fumes, and it was a moment after she opened them that she saw Achilles.

He was not alone; Patroclus was with him. They sat at a long trestle, leaning forward from the bench, elbows on the trestle and winecups in their hands. They had clearly been talking, though their conversation had been cut off as she entered. There was a warmth, not only in the room, but in the atmosphere that surrounded the two men. They had the ease of close companions.

To her surprise Achilles rose to his feet, and so did Patroclus a moment after. She hesitated, then dropped a rather awkward curtsy; she did not want to meet the men's eyes.

'Briseis.' There was an experimental note in Achilles' voice. His manner had been impersonal, even cold, in the square, but it was quite different now. She could think of nothing to say. A murmur between the two men, and Patroclus crossed to where she stood at the door. He smiled easily. The women were right: he did have plenty of charm. She found herself smiling back. They exchanged a long look, then with a swift 'Sleep well' he was gone into the night.

It was tactful of him to leave; Briseis knew from Iphis that the two men shared these quarters. She took a deep breath and moved forward into the room.

Achilles' presence seemed to fill it. Even in the dim light the angles of his face were sharp and straight, as if it had been cut from wood that split only along the grain. He gestured to the bench beside him. 'Sit. Take some wine.'

She had not expected that at all and she made no move to obey him. He watched her for a moment, then added, 'You speak Greek, don't you?'

'Yes, sir.' It came out in a whisper.

'Come on, sit down.'

Briseis sat, but she was too nervous to drink, or to match the conversation that flowed from Achilles. He was nothing like the man whose image she had kept in her head since Lyrnessus. She had been all ready to do battle with a dangerous animal, and here instead was the man the others had talked of, a man all his women seemed to love, a cultured man who did not leap on her, but offered her wine and talked of music. It disconcerted her. She had expected him to take her body, while remaining quite indifferent to her mind. His gentle assault upon it found her totally unprepared. It had never entered her head that he might want her to like him.

Of course she did not like him. How could she? He was the man who had killed Mynes, chief among the bloody pirates. Her resolve not to think about Mynes melted. His quiet, steady voice came back to her, and she felt herself softening. That would not do. She gripped the edge of the bench hard with her hands and fought to rekindle the anger that Achilles, maddeningly, showed no interest in fuelling.

Achilles' voice, raised slightly, cut into her thoughts. He had asked her something and she had not even heard him, let alone thought of an answer. 'I'm sorry, sir. Could you repeat that?'

'I asked if you played the harp. Or if you liked to sing.' His voice, naturally harsh-toned, was deliberately level.

'Yes, sir. That is, not well, sir.' It was a lie: she knew she played well. Panic was rising in her. Surely he would not ask her to play to him? It seemed suddenly a more awful prospect than to be seduced by him. She had an urge to jump up and run for the door.

Achilles watched her for a moment, then he stood up abruptly and snuffed out the wick of the lamp on the trestle.

'You must play for me; but not tonight.' He walked over to

the fire. It was burned almost to embers; he banked it up to last through the night. She stood up too, and waited uncertainly by the trestle. He crossed over to her and with surprising gentleness pulled her close. He spoke into her hair, in a quiet, firm voice. 'There is nothing to fear. I shall not hurt you. Relax.'

How could she, with the body of this unnerving stranger hard and unyielding against her own? But she made herself look up. He looked into her eyes for what seemed like an age, then he bent and kissed her. His mouth was warm and dry, his touch confident and oddly reassuring.

The curtain was half-pulled across his bed-alcove and he elbowed it aside as he led her over to the bed. All resolve seemed to have left her. She stood there in a daze as he carefully untied her belt and drew the cream dress over her head. He undressed himself, deliberately, unhurriedly. Then he pulled her down onto the lionskins and stretched his long body out against hers.

His mouth was on hers again, harder, demanding a response. He ran his hands over her body hungrily and possessively, then reached to take her hand. Her fist was clenched rigid. He uncurled the fingers gently, bent to kiss the inside of her wrist, circled the tip of his tongue around her palm. An involuntary tremor ran through her and unconsciously her body arched against his. Even before the movement was over she recognized it and with a surge of revulsion she moved to push him away from her and to turn her back to him.

She heard him draw breath sharply and for a moment felt the night air cool against her body. Then he was pulling her towards him again, his body warm against hers, his hands and mouth caressing her with agonizing skill.

She was alert to him now. He could not take her by surprise again. Hate him, her mind urged her body. He is a killer. A pirate. He has ripped your life to pieces. Hate him. Fight him with your pride and anger.

He showed no hatred towards her, no cruelty. There was no ruthlessness in him. He made no move to take her. It was as if she was not fighting him at all. She was fighting herself, the part of her that ached to respond to him.

Her endurance stretched, like damp leather pulled taut on a frame, and she felt it begin to fray. When he does take me, she realized with sudden clarity, I shall have no more resistance left to show him. The thought brought her a rush of desire that made her body relax suddenly, and she expected him to recognize it, to take the swift advantage of a fighter who sees his opponent's guard momentarily fall.

But even as her body softened he was drawing away from her. He sat up and swung his feet down from the high bed. Briseis turned to look at him. She was not quite sure what she felt; she hoped it was relief. He did not look back. He stood and walked over to the fire. The shape of him was black against the faint light that came from it. A sudden rush of pleasure shot through her. She could happily have lain there alone on the comfortable bed, watching him, for the rest of the night.

'You may go. Tell Diomede to come to me.' Briseis took in the coldness in his tone first. The words came afterwards. She hesitated for a moment. She had an urge to refuse, but that would not do at all. She rose quietly and picked up the cream dress from the floor.

Walking back into the women's tent with the message for Diomede seemed much more difficult than the walk in the opposite direction had been. The women were surprised to see her. She herself was surprised to see Diomede leap up, cast her a confused glance which held a hint of triumph, and rush out of the tent. Stupid of her – she had never stopped to wonder why Diomede disliked her so. Perhaps she would like her better now.

Indeed Diomede did. She hid her triumph more carefully the next morning, and life in the women's tent was more placid than it had been since Briseis had arrived.

The capture did not come as a surprise to Chryseis. It seemed to her as if she had known, ever since her conversation with Troilus in the storeroom, that it was all going to end in disaster. She had left for Chryse with her father in a mood of flat resignation, not expecting ever to return to Ilios. The journey, the attack, the capture, all seemed curiously distant, as if they were happening to someone else. There was blood, but it was not horrific. It was no worse than the sacrifices at the shrine. Everything went forward in exactly the appointed way. She had an impression that her father had escaped with some of the escort. The attackers did not seem to care, they were more interested in her; except that it was not really she who was there. The real Chryseis was gone, and she did not know where to look to find herself again.

Her prescience stopped at that point, with the crowd of soldiers in black tunics who surrounded her, not so much hostile as forceful and sure of themselves. She had not thought out the rest of the story in her mind, and had no idea what to expect as a captive. The soldiers did not rape her or beat her. They simply drove her, with a bunch of other captives, down to the harbour and onto a waiting ship.

It was not much like Andromache had imagined it, she thought to herself on the ship. Andromache had always lived in such a neat and tidy world. This one seemed to be cruder, rough-edged, rather dirty, and much more exciting. On the whole, it was more to her taste than Andromache's world. The guards had long hair and wore outlandish short tunics, but they looked at her in just the same way as the soldiers in Ilios had done. It did not occur to her to take offence. Their looks and remarks gave a link with reality that she badly needed. They still did not go beyond that, and by the time the ship beached she was beginning to feel perfectly safe.

The camp came as a shock, though. It was larger and more forbidding at close quarters than it had looked from the towers of Ilios, and it was humiliating to be herded onto the shingle and looked over by such a crowd of people. The rest of the captives bore it with empty dejection, and Chryseis felt a sudden surge of panic. They were almost all farm girls and serving girls, and she did not want to associate herself with them at all. Act proud, she told herself firmly. She pushed down the fear with all the force she could muster and tried to play the part of a beautiful captive with whom the king was about to fall desperately in love. It felt as if she was overacting appallingly, but the soldiers seemed appreciative, so she supposed it would do.

A good actress maintains the illusion by never quite looking into her audience's faces, and there was a blankness behind Chryseis' fine eyes as she followed the rest up to the square. She gathered only the vaguest impression of the Achaean leaders. It was a relief when a man stepped across to pick her out early from the group. He looked to be very important. Perhaps it was the High King, Agamemnon himself? He was obviously not going to say, and she could hardly ask him. Anyway he seemed reason enough to keep playing the part with redoubled conviction. She stood by his side, smiling demurely at the men who came to talk with him. You're doing all right, she told herself inwardly, as her face began to ache from the strain of keeping up the mask.

Then a servant led her away and washed her. That was good, she was filthy from the journey. It seemed reasonable to ask the servant. She was a youngish woman, but she looked tired and listless, as if she had given up caring about herself. Yes, she said without expression, Chryseis' captor was indeed Agamemnon, King of Mycenae and High King of all the Achaeans.

The evening passed by in a blur. There were a great many people, and there was more food than Chryseis had ever seen. Obviously the Achaeans were not on short rations. Were they winning the war? The possibility that the Trojans might be losing had never entered her mind before, and it was disconcerting to suspect it now. She drank goblet after goblet of sweet, thick wine and heard her voice grow higher and louder as the evening wore on. She ought to have drunk more slowly, she thought to herself, but it was too late now. It was a relief when Agamemnon rose to leave the company and a servant motioned to her to follow him. It seemed she had not disgraced herself.

He led her through wooden corridors to a small room containing a high bed, a small table of inlaid ivory with a lamp burning on it, and two chairs. The furniture was intricately carved, in a straight, precise style quite different from the ornate curves of Ilios. There were hangings on the walls, complex geometric designs in reds, blues and purples. She looked around, curious, and the High King stood watching her. His voice, when it came, was a surprise. 'Take your clothes off.'

Of course she had known what was to happen, but the command still gave her a shiver of embarrassed shock. She sobered, suddenly and totally. Then she pushed the shock down and brought back the girl she had been in the square. The beautiful captive slowly untied her belt. She released the buckles at her shoulders and carefully, deliberately, let her shift fall to the floor. She could feel the High King's gaze scanning her body, though she could not bring herself to look directly at him. She stood there, still and proud, for what seemed like a long time. Agamemnon made no move towards her, and at last it struck her that he expected her to move towards him. She took a deep breath and crossed the floor to where he stood. When she was less than a pace away she reached out and put her arms around his shoulders. He was no taller than she was. She moved still closer, pressed her naked body against him. She could no longer avoid his eyes. They seemed pale in the dim light and the flame from the lamp flickered somewhere inside them.

The High King held her gaze briefly and for an instant she expected him to kiss her. No. He reached out to take her arm, just above the elbow, in a firm grip, and twisting it brutally he flung her, face downwards, onto the bed. Before she could move he was on her, pulling her thighs apart and thrusting hard into her from behind.

Chryseis woke alone and a servant came to help her dress. The girlish tunic she had worn when she was captured would not do at all, it appeared. The servant brought with her three trunks and lifted the lids one by one to expose dresses, sashes and jewels.

Chryseis let out a low gasp as she reached out a tentative hand to run through the contents. There were necklets, bracelets and rings in gold and silver, set with rubies, diamonds and huge chunks of lapis lazuli. There were brooches of amber and jet, pins shaped as snakes and two-headed lions and tiny daggers. There were dresses of thick linen and thin soft wool, dresses of golden tissue and dresses sewn with pearls. There were sashes and ribbons of silk, veils of fine gauze, slippers of kidskin dyed deep blue and red. Everything in the trunks was fit for a queen to wear.

She hesitated to wear the jewels. It was too soon, she felt: the High King might think it presumptuous of her. She chose a silken dress, dyed the deep blue of a summer sky at sunset, and a wide red sash edged with tiny discs of gold. The dress had the full, layered skirt and close-fitting bodice that the palace women at Ilios favoured, so she knew it was fashionable. Helen herself could wear a dress like this, she thought as the servant fastened the sash and arranged the ends so that they fell down her back.

She still had only the haziest idea of Agamemnon's appearance, and as she explored the little jars of perfumed oil and the tubs of kohl and lip paint, the thought crossed her mind that she might not recognize him if he returned without the kingly robes he had worn the previous day. He entered the room just as she finished arranging her hair and it was a relief to find that she knew him after all. This time she looked more carefully.

He was ordinary enough, taken by himself, though there was no mistaking the air of power about him. He was not young: he had seen perhaps forty-five summers. He must once have been slim, but his body had filled out in middle age. His hair was thinning. He wore a trim beard on his chin, in the Achaean style. His features were regular, except for the wide, thin mouth. There was something mobile and sensuous about it. Involuntarily, the memory came back of the ways in which he had used it on her body the previous night. When she met his eyes they shared a knowing look. He sent the servant away and, pushing the tiered skirt casually up around her waist, had her again on the floor.

She lay still on the scrubbed boards for a few moments after he had gone. Then she stood up cautiously. She was shaking a little. She crossed to the bed, threw herself down upon it, and began to cry.

She did not stop crying until the servant returned. The woman did not seem at all surprised; indeed she was sympathetic, if careful not to ask any questions. But it embarrassed Chryseis to sob in front of her and she dried her tears quickly and accepted the drink the servant offered her, a bitter herbal tea.

It's just the shock of it, Chryseis told herself firmly. She was sore inside, and there was a livid bruise coming out on her arm. The pain was reassuring; it seemed a solid reason for her distress.

It was not because of the pain that she was crying, however, or even because of the stress of the previous days, though maybe she would have reacted less violently had she not already been close to exhaustion. It was out of plain fear of the man to whom she now belonged, and of the effect he had on her. It was as if the association with him had already marked her in a way that she could never erase.

It did not seem to Chryseis that she could have acted any differently. She could no more have avoided being chosen by Agamemnon than she could have resisted being sent away from Ilios. These things were in the hands of the gods, or at least in those of other people. The distinction had never been entirely clear to her, just as she was still not certain when one was supposed to fight, and when to give in gracefully. Apollo had certainly not spoken to her since her capture. But her conscience was clear as she played over in her mind the events of the previous day. Perhaps her act could have been different, but it could not have been better. She really had been trying hard, and it would have been less honourable, not more, to face up to the troops snivelling and downcast. Where had she gone wrong?

There were no answers, or at least none she was prepared to face. She composed herself as well as she could, and went out to join in the life of Agamemnon's household.

The household seemed to run itself. Even with a war to fight, the High King had a private army of servants. There was nothing for Chryseis to do, it seemed, but to make herself pleasant to Agamemnon and to the other commanders who came to talk with him. She saw them often, for Agamemnon kept her with him in his private quarters and had her eat with the men when they joined him.

His hut was really more of a small palace, built plainly but strongly out of heavy split logs, with floors of wood in his private rooms and beaten earth in the big open room that acted as a megaron, except that there was no porch and it gave straight onto the central square. The furnishings were rich and ostentatious: woven hangings bright with gold and silver thread, woollen rugs, some on the floors as well as the walls, finely wrought lamps of silver and bronze, golden cups and dishes for the King's table. There was a shrine to every major Achaean god. There were rooms where the High King could rest or talk alone with his advisers. Behind the palace was a maze of storerooms: still rooms of mudbrick to hold meat and cheese, firmly barred huts for storing the gold and silver that the High King had taken, wooden huts holding fabrics, musical instruments, jars of oil and perfume; and beyond these, the pens in which the cattle, sheep and goats were held ready for slaughter.

Every evening a group of Agamemnon's commanders came to dine with him. After they had gone he took Chryseis to bed. He had her every night, except when she was bleeding and unclean. He called one of his other women then, but she did not think he turned to them at any other time. Often he would come to her in the daytime as well; he took a pride in his manhood, she soon realized, and she was careful to praise his appetite. She did not tell him of the soreness, even when it was agonizing to her.

The fear she had felt that first morning never altogether left her, but it did change, into a kind of watchful awe. The High King was often rough with her, but he was not sadistic: when he hurt her it seemed to be more out of majestic indifference to her feelings than out of any inclination to take pleasure in her pain. Soon, to her surprise, she began to enjoy his visits. She had expected them to be something she would have to endure, act her way through. But there was something exhilarating about making a mighty king pant, and sweat, and cry out in passion. Agamemnon always seemed to her to abandon himself totally in the heat of desire, in a way that justified her doing the same. She did do the same. The very forcefulness of him came to arouse her intensely, and his sexual demands had a sophistication that she soon recognized to be quite different from Troilus' straightforward style. She never thought him beautiful, in the way that she had found Troilus beautiful, but that came to matter less than she had expected.

Chryseis watched the men who visited Agamemnon's quarters and picked out the most important ones quickly. Menelaus, Agamemnon's brother and Helen's erstwhile husband, came most often. He did not offer any advice; he told crude jokes, laughed a lot, though the laughter never reached his cold eyes, and drank heavily. Ulysses hardly drank at all: he generally put only enough wine into his water to kill the marsh spirits. He was a short man, shorter than Agamemnon, and extremely hairy. He looked like a peasant farmer, and ate like one, but he spoke with authority and, it seemed to Chryseis, a deal of sense. There was Nestor, elderly and calm, with a manner that hinted at ironies he never made apparent; Ajax, a big man with straightforward gestures and a loud voice; Idomeneus, quiet and rather sly. They spoke often of Achilles, but Achilles himself, stern and intense, rarely came. They all treated Agamemnon deferentially, a little cautiously, much as Chryseis did. Chryseis did not ask herself if she liked them; she simply watched them, and smiled at them all.

At first they flirted with her, in a casual way that she took to be more play-acting than a serious expression of desire. She did not dare to flirt back. When they discovered it they seemed to ignore her, as if to tell her that she would soon be packed off to the women's tents and lose her privileged position with the High King. She did not like that. She began to flirt herself then, watching Agamemnon more carefully than she watched the others. He liked it, she soon realized. It amused him to know that all the men present were aroused by her and only he would possess her. It aroused him, too, when she directed her attentions at the others. Afterwards he would take her harder, with even fewer preliminaries, and she found that she enjoyed that when she was excited herself. She flirted with Agamemnon himself sometimes, but that did not have quite the same effect.

'Who was he?' Agamemnon spoke as they lay together in the heavy carved bed in his private room. Chryseis had been in the camp for almost a full moon cycle. The High King rarely tried to converse with her when they were alone.

She turned to face him in surprise. 'Who do you mean?'

He spoke calmly and easily. 'You know very well who I mean. The man before me.'

The question was entirely unexpected to her. Was he jealous? It seemed ridiculous to her even as she thought it. Belatedly, it struck her that the High King must have expected her to be a virgin.

She did not think to answer him directly. Her mind tried to frame a suitable response that would seem modest but not quite apologetic. Perhaps he felt cheated. It was a little frightening to think that she might have offended him. 'Was it so obvious?'

He gave a short, contemptuous laugh. 'My dear, I have had enough girls to be able to tell the difference.' He called her 'my dear' and 'darling' and other such things often in front of the other men, but rarely in bed, where brief crude commands were more in his line. It did not strike her as affectionate now.

She did not reply, and after a pause he drawled, 'So there was more than one man?'

He meant it to wound, and it did. She sat up, pulling away from him in fury. 'Of course not. What do you think I am?'

'A whore.' He smiled as he said it, and tried to meet her eye. She sat rigid and did not look at him. He reached out lazily to run a hand slowly down her naked body. It did not occur to her to stop him. From the start he had done just what he liked with her. He lingered over her breasts, and then moved casually between her legs. Almost unconsciously, she opened them wider. 'And a very good one.'

'Well, if I am, you have made me one.'

He laughed again. 'Turn over. No, suck me harder first. Yes, like that.'

She had saved herself from one betrayal, and it felt for a moment as if she had won. Her sexual power over him seemed in no way weaker than his physical power over her. He wanted her body, just then, more than he wanted her reply. But he had not forgotten, and when he had finished and his breath had slowed to its normal pace he returned to his questioning. 'You have not answered me yet.'

Chryseis tried to think first. It would not do to wait too long before replying: but the humiliation he had subjected her to made her less, not more, inclined to reply. He might be able to control her body, she told herself, but he could not do the same with her mind. 'I do not want to tell you.' The words frightened her less when they were out in the open.

'But I want to know.' He still spoke easily, but his voice was firm.

She turned to look at him. She expected him to be annoyed

if she refused to tell him, but the prospect of angering him seemed less dreadful to her then. And she did not expect him to do anything; just to be angry. No man had ever hit her, and she was entirely innocent about the sanctions he might use.

All the same, she knew it would not do to cross him too directly. He was the High King and her master, and she did not want to stop being his favourite. She leaned over him, her long braids brushing against his chest, and kissed him lightly. 'You have never told me about the women you had before me. Tell me about the things you did with them.' She reckoned he would enjoy watching her get aroused by what he told her.

He reached out to take hold of her arm. His grasp was not hard, but it was enough to stop her moving away. 'Do you want to hear what I did to them when they made me angry?'

Her eyes widened as she took in the expression in his. There was something dark in it, something that seemed to reach well beyond her understanding. But she did not pull away. She looked straight back at him and whispered, 'Yes. Tell me.'

He did tell her. Not everything, but enough to make her shake and quiver. As he told her he maintained his firm grip and ran his free hand across her, lightly and expertly. It was exciting. The secret words in the dark room, mingled with the prying fingers, thrilled her to the core. Her arousal thrilled him in return. After a while their lust became unbearable and they both forgot why he was telling her these things.

He did not hurt her that night. And she did not tell him. But they both knew now that if he asked again she would not resist him.

■

From new moon to full moon had not been long enough for Briseis to mourn. When she found she was to be given longer she welcomed the respite. As the days went by, however, living in the past came to be increasingly difficult. She began to feel that she should have been getting over the grief, letting the present slowly push the past aside; but the present was completely empty.

It did little honour to Mynes and Ianeira to mourn them simply because there was nothing else to do. Her grief seemed to become diffuse, to dilute itself as it spread out to fill the vacant days. She found herself having to concentrate before she could even recall the details of Mynes' face.

Whatever she had hoped for from the future, it was not this emptiness. It was her twentieth summer and she had already made the decision not to die yet.

Briseis had expected Achilles' return to end the transition period and force her to come to terms with a new life. His return seemed to have changed things for everybody else she encountered. Everybody else was fully involved in the business of a summer of war. She alone stood on the sidelines, with no part to play. She had thought he would provide her with a part, just as the soldiers at Lyrnessus had done. He did not. There was nothing to accept, either reluctantly or enthusiastically; nothing to refuse.

She had taken it for granted after that first night that he would call her again: the next night, perhaps, or the one after. He did not. The moons waxed and waned, and no call came. When he did take a girl it was Diomede, usually; sometimes Doris, or one of the other girls. She watched as each one was selected and reselected, in an order that proved, after a while, to be perfectly predictable. It seemed she had no place in it at all.

As far as she could judge, being called to his bed was the central thing in Achilles' relationship with each one of the women. It was not just that the sexual act mattered: though it would have to her, and obviously did to some of the others. How often the women were called determined how often they were asked to wash him when he returned from his sorties, tidy his quarters or prepare honey cakes and mulled wine for visitors. It determined, Briseis now saw, the pattern of relationships inside the women's quarters. Take that away, and there was nothing left.

No; not nothing. There was a shape to the relationship, this business of being a master and a slave. There was the shared knowledge that he had absolute power over her. Its under-current ran through every casual encounter, even if there was nothing said or done to reinforce it.

Briseis was not just a slave, anyway. She was a prize of war. That gave her a symbolic value: it reflected Achilles' status as a warrior. He had chosen her because she had been the wife of a prince. He could not honourably have sold her, whether he wanted her or not. He should have slept with her at least occasionally, whether he desired to or not. It would have been an expression of his power, a symbolic reconquering of Lyrnessus.

Why did he not do it? The question occupied Briseis more and more. He was physically repelled by her? She could not believe that, though she did not feel beautiful any more. He would not risk a second humiliating encounter, when plenty of women were eager to make love to him? There was something in that, but he did not seem to her a man to shirk unpleasant but necessary tasks. He pitied her? That was humiliating. She did not want his pity. He was waiting for a cue from her, some sign that she wanted him? It had to be that. The memory of his touch told her so; and yet she was angered at the thought. It exposed him to too high a risk of failure. He should not have expected it of her. All the same, she knew that he did. It was as if he was too proud to take her against her will, just as he was too proud to make any further attempt to bring her to love him.

By midsummer, his not calling her had come to take on an inertia of its own. It no longer seemed strange: it was the way things were. Nobody, least of all herself, expected it to change. She went for days at a time without even glimpsing him.

Their rare encounters were both brief and guarded. Achilles' public contact with all his women was polite and formal. The only emotion he ever showed was an occasional flash of anger. He unbent, Briseis knew, in the privacy of his own hut. During the long evenings she would hear the sounds of music and laughter emanating from it. She herself had never returned to his hut, not even on a casual errand. There was no music or laughter in her own life.

Briseis began to drift into a deep depression. There were not even public altars in the camp at which she could have prayed

– if she had known what to pray for. She spent her days sunk in a stupor in the women's tents. The other women were not cruel to her, but they were contemptuous: she had no position among them, no friends. Doris and Iphis were occasionally sympathetic, but did not invite confidences.

Finally an answer came. Diomede suggested that she should go to tend the wounded.

It was not expected of concubines that they should do hard physical work, or have any contact with the common soldiers. Diomede made the suggestion cautiously, in a way which implied that she expected Briseis to reject it.

Briseis watched her face carefully. 'Achilles told you to ask me.'

'No. I doubt if he would have thought of it. It was Patroclus' idea. Achilles knows, of course.' Diomede hesitated. 'He said it was for you to decide.'

'I'll do it.'

'Think before you agree, Briseis. The work is hard, and you know many men die.' Diomede's face added, though her voice did not, that accepting the suggestion would destroy Briseis' last chance of taking her proper place among Achilles' women.

'It will be something to do. I like hard work. I have done the same sort of thing before.'

'Please yourself.' Diomede stood and stretched herself. 'I'll go and tell him.'

'Achilles?'

'No, Patroclus.' There was a slight smile on Diomede's face.

There was no fighting that day and Patroclus came across to the women's tents shortly afterwards.

It was just after midday and very hot. Patroclus was stripped to the waist, his body burned almost black by the sun, and his hair bleached fair. Briseis, confronting him outside the main tent, was uneasily conscious of him.

'I'll take you over to the hospital tent,' he offered.

'Is it far?'

'It's at the far end of our section. You know each contingent cares for their own wounded? Only the surgeons are common to the whole army.'

He told her more as they walked together, side by side.

He was vague about the work; Briseis supposed it would be straightforward enough: cleaning wounds, feeding the men and that kind of thing. But he was precise about the individual men, their characters and their injuries. It surprised her. Though the faces of the officers were clear in her mind, the common soldiers had been just a mass of humanity that milled around the camp. It was disconcerting to think of them as town boys and country boys, brave and cowardly, cheerful and morose, individuals whose names she would get to know.

'You know them all so well,' she said to Patroclus when he paused for breath.

'Of course. There are barely two thousand Myrmidons and I know them all, at least their faces and names. I've fought with them for eight years, some of them for much longer. And I see the injured every day. So do all our officers. Achilles insists – not that he needs to.'

'I thought most of them died.'

If he thought her words brutal he did not say so. 'Too many do: not just of the wounds, but of fever and dysentery. The camp is too low-lying: there is always sickness. But we lose less men than most other contingents. They have to want to recover, to know they are not forgotten or thrown on the midden. Our men do. Some of the other commanders – they don't take the trouble that Achilles does, and it shows.'

They turned a corner in the track then and came to the tent. It was a vast arrangement, sewn strips of canvas looped over half a dozen roof trees. A thick, rich stench of decayed flesh hung over it; clouds of flies circled the middens. By one side of the open doorway there was a row of stirrup jars, leaning askew on the uneven ground, their glaze cracked; by the other, a cart, roughly covered in a coarse canvas blanket. The flies told Briseis its contents: bodies, whole and dismembered, waiting to be carried to the pyres.

Patroclus glanced at her as if he expected her to flinch, or turn and run. Conscious of his look, she did neither. After a moment he moved forward through the open door and Briseis slowly followed him.

It was dim in the tent. As her eyes adjusted to the light she made out the rows of pallets, thin, blood-stained, each with its occupant; a wooden chest, opened and spilling a confusion of bandages; a mass of faces, all turned towards the two of them. The noise was astonishing. Every man not on the brink of death had begun to talk as soon as they entered.

Briseis never had liked mess. She had found a bowl and clean water and was washing the bloodiest of the men before Patroclus even left.

Briseis returned to the hospital tent every day. She enjoyed the routine; and she rapidly came to care for the men. After the women, they seemed friendly and unguarded. They chattered about the war, about their homes and families back in Trachis and Phthia. They joked with each other. It was almost enough to make her forget the squalor and the misery, the flies and the gore.

It was good, too, to have the feeling that many of them cared about her. It was something to live for: the smiles, the admiring looks, the thanks they gave her.

Achilles and his officers came daily. Briseis slowly grew to know his captains and his lieutenants, Menestheus, Eudorus, Peisander and Alcimedon. Phoenix, old and gentle, was kind to her. Automedon came sometimes and greeted her with a politeness which assured her that he would forget their encounter at Lyrnessus if she would do the same.

There was also Patroclus. He would always stop and talk to Briseis after he had seen the men. If it was late, and if Achilles was not with him, he would walk back with her to the women's tents.

They talked in the easy way he seemed to use with everyone. That too brought her pleasure, though she read nothing particular into his friendliness. It was his manner to make himself liked, and to enjoy being liked in return.

Achilles was liked by the men too. Briseis was slow to realize it because she found him to be abrasive with them. Even with the wounded he was brusque; with the rest of the Myrmidons he was harsh. But they thought him fair, and they enjoyed the reflected glory of his reputation. They were the best contingent in the Achaean force, with the best commander, and not one of them doubted it. They thought it unfair that Achilles was so disliked by the Mycenaeans and by some of the other contingents.

They also thought it unfair that Briseis disliked him – for so they interpreted the determined indifference which she showed whenever he appeared. One or two of them told her so, superficially joking but deadly serious underneath. She should be nicer to him they warned her gently: it was dangerous to acquire Achilles for an enemy. It annoyed her; but to please them and to avoid their ribbings, she did her best to treat him courteously in the tent.

It proved less difficult than she had expected. There had been so little to fuel her hatred of Achilles, and he never showed any sign of friendship to which she might have been obliged to respond. She had the impression sometimes that he was watching her, but if she turned towards him she would find him busied with his knife, or in conversation with one of the men. He was linked in her mind with the fall of Lyrnessus; but she felt no revulsion in her small contacts with him.

On the contrary, she found herself increasingly, and disturbingly, attracted to him. His lithe physical strength, his air of authority, the cool efficiency with which he approached everything he did – all this appealed deeply to her nature. She was drawn, more and more strongly, to watch him at work in the tent. The army was short of surgeons and he had enough skill himself to do most of the jobs the surgeons did, cutting out arrow- and spearheads, straightening broken bones and tying splints to help set them. He worked neatly and rapidly, with a steady concentration which he rarely broke; and on the rare occasions when he glanced towards Briseis she was careful to lower her gaze before he met it.

It was perhaps a moon before she admitted this attraction to herself; and some time after that before it occurred to her that she might do something about it: that she might now give him the sign she believed he had once been waiting for. She balked at that. Certainly she would have welcomed it if he had called her one night. It would have made things simple, put them right. She would have obeyed his orders without feeling any particular guilt. She would have taken pleasure from him, and the knowledge no longer worried her. It would have been

inconceivable to touch him again with the air of passive submission that she had attempted before.

But it was one thing to obey orders. In the abstract at least,
it sounded clean and straightforward. Maybe it would not have
been heroic, but women are not expected to be heroic. It would
not have been shameful. It was another thing entirely to exceed
the demands of duty, to make it clear that she wanted him.
That was not submission to an irresistible power, that was
collaboration with the enemy, Mynes' killer, the bloody pirate.

Briseis fixed on this as a sticking point, a point at which
the honourable ended and the dishonourable began. It was
honourable, she argued to herself, to use her skills in tending
sick and wounded men even if they were Myrmidons. It would
not have been honourable to succumb to her attraction to their
commander.

When Achilles did finally make demands upon her they
proved to be quite different. He had noticed her neat bandaging,
the calmness with which she soothed men in agony or in fear
of approaching death. She in turn had noticed his lack of an
assistant. Patroclus helped him sometimes, but clearly disliked
it; most of the other men were too clumsy. Once, when no
other helper was available to hold down a man while Achilles
extracted an arrow from his shoulder, he called on Briseis; and
finding her as steady and helpful as she had promised to be, he
continued afterwards to use her regularly.

There developed between them a cautious professional relationship. They talked, but only of the men and what needed
to be done for them, of healing herbs, cauterizing fires and
cleansing fumes. They measured, and valued, each other's com-
petence. He did not try to spare her the ghastly episodes, and
she respected him for it. After each occasion when she worked
with him he would thank her carefully. He never touched her,
except by accident.

Patroclus came to the tent without Achilles one evening and
stopped to wait for Briseis. A man had been brought in with his
leg crushed from the knee. A charioteer, he had been entangled
in the harness when his horses bolted. He had been conscious
when the orderlies carried him in but so badly wounded that

they had sent for Machaon, the best surgeon in the camp. The screams as Machaon had got to work with his knife still seemed to hang in the air, though the man's body now lay in the cart by the door.

Patroclus had heard of this from an orderly. As soon as they were clear of the tent he said, 'You should not stay in the tent when the surgeon comes. It is not fit for you.'

He did not mean it unkindly, but there was a curtness in his voice and Briseis, tired and upset, turned on him angrily. 'I help Achilles with that kind of work all the time. True, that was worse than most; but you cannot think I should have turned and walked out, so all the men knew that what was coming was too dreadful for me to watch. I would never be so cruel. It helps the men to have me stay. It keeps their mind off the knife.'

'It's you I was thinking of.'

'And it's them that I think of.'

There were lines of fatigue around her eyes and her dress was smeared with blood. But there was an energy in her walk that had been missing two moons before. The misery had been wiped away. Patroclus, assessing her, reckoned it had done her good to worry about somebody else for a change. He said, 'I am glad you have come to care about the men.'

Her face softened a little. 'It is difficult to think of them as enemies when you get to know them.'

The words shook him. He took a moment to absorb them, and then said quietly, 'Do you still see me as an enemy?'

She turned to look at him in surprise. It was as if she was taking him in for the first time. He was still in his armour, though his shield and spear had been left at Achilles' hut. His body was hard and muscular and he was covered in the dust and sweat of the battlefield. After the stench of the hospital tent he reeked of health and power.

They stood only a pace apart and he towered over her: she had to look upwards to catch his eyes. She did, briefly, and then looked downwards again. 'I don't know. I honestly don't know.' She shook her head. 'I feel I should, but it seems unreal, seeing you as an enemy now, when nobody around me does, and when you never treat me as one.'

'Do you think I should treat you as an enemy?'

'I cannot see why not. If you were taken prisoner, you'd not turn about and side with the enemy straight away. You would feel like a traitor if you did. So why do you expect it of us? I am still a Mysian, and the Mysians are your enemies. I still have kinsfolk in the Trojan armies. Did you honestly think I could watch you and Achilles set off for battle, hoping that you would kill someone I loved?'

She seemed to be finding more conviction as she spoke, Patroclus thought, alarmed. They were almost at the women's tents, but he did not want to leave her in this mood. He frowned. 'It is different for a woman, though. You talk as if you were a man.'

'Women should have self-respect too. They should try to act honourably. Maybe we cannot fight back, but we should expect something of ourselves. I do think it shameful when women happily go to bed with the men who killed their husbands and children. Maybe you expect it of us, but you despise us when we do it.'

'That's ridiculous. You have no choice.'

'I think we do.'

This was dangerous territory. Patroclus recognized it, but he pressed on all the same. 'So that is why you are cold with Achilles? To hold him off?'

Briseis flushed. The conversation seemed to be driving her towards an intimacy with Patroclus that she had not planned at all; but she replied honestly. 'I have nightmares about what happened at Lyrnessus: as if it will change the past if I watch it happen often enough. As if one time I will be quicker with my knife and stab it home hard into the first soldier who comes near me. If I had done that I would not be here worrying about how I behave with Achilles.'

Perhaps she would have been, Patroclus thought. It had rather pleased Achilles, the knowledge that she had fought like a tigress when cornered. He would not have held it against her if she had killed the man. 'But you did not. There are things we all think we should have done, that we did not do. You have to forgive yourself, and go on living.'

'I do. I try not to hate myself for it. But if I could not live up to that I have to set my goal somewhere else. Surely it is no answer to give in completely, and do whatever anyone asks of me.'

Patroclus had an urge to tell her he admired her. It was true. Though he had never asked what had happened that night when they returned from the raids, he had always thought Briseis' dislike of Achilles to be irrational, an awkward personal incompatibility. It set her in a different light, the realization that she was making a conscious stand against him. He could say none of this, though. 'You think it would be better if we lived together like enemies? I cannot accept that. Perhaps we ought to give you a while to get over it, but then you have to settle for changing sides. That's not dishonourable. Men do it. I did it myself in a way. I came to Phthia, to Achilles' father Peleus, because I had been exiled from my own country. I fight for him because there is no alternative, but I do not feel as if I am dishonouring myself when I do it. If I had to, I would fight for Achilles against my kinsmen.'

She looked him in the eye again. For a moment he thought she would try to stare him out, but she must have been satisfied by what she saw and she dropped her gaze. 'Honour is a funny business. It sometimes seems to me that men persuade themselves that whatever they want to do is honourable.'

'Not all of them. Some persuade themselves that it is honourable to do what they least want to do.' He was feeling his way through the argument as he spoke. 'I don't think they are always the better men for it. It's more that some people like life to be easy, and some like it hard and difficult.'

'You are an easy man yourself.'

'I suppose so. I'd not call myself a dishonourable man, though. I doubt if anyone thinks that of me. I hope if I were sure that it was right to do something I had no wish to do, I would find the strength to do it.'

'But you rarely think that.'

'No.' He was not at all certain that he was winning the argument. 'There are two things really. There is deciding what to do, and there is doing it. In a way, honour is more bound up with the second. People rarely ask themselves whether you have decided to do the right thing, but they always notice how you are doing it. If you do it with your head held high, and put all your heart and mind behind it, then they reckon you have behaved honourably.'

'So honour is what other people think about what you do?'

'Not only that. It is what you think about it yourself, too.'

She smiled at that, and there was a sudden lift in his heart. She was beautiful when she smiled. She spoke thoughtfully, but with less intensity. 'I think I can live with what I am doing at the moment. When I wake up in the morning it seems to me that I did little to be ashamed of the day before. There is something to be said for that, isn't there?'

'Yes. There is.'

They stood silent for a moment. Briseis had not felt so close to anyone since she had come to the camp, and she took a quiet pleasure from it. Then there was a stir behind them, as Iphis came out of the women's tent. She stood still, giving the two of them a long, cool look. Briseis blushed and hurried into the tent. Patroclus made himself stay and chat with Iphis for a few moments before he set off in search of Achilles.

Briseis slept better that night than she had for many moons. She had an uneasy feeling the next morning that she had dreamed of Patroclus. But dreams are easily forgotten and she tried not to dwell on the details.

Iphis was cold and snappy, and that was less easily argued away. Briseis briefly felt guilty; then her mood changed to anger. Why should the other girl be annoyed with her? She had done nothing wrong. She watched out for Patroclus' return that evening, but it was Achilles who came alone to the hospital tent. She swallowed hard and busied herself with the bandages. Achilles must have caught her mood because he did not come near her.

It was five or six days before Briseis had a chance to walk back with Patroclus again. It did not seem quite as casual as it had been before.

They talked about the fighting. Briseis said, 'Nothing is happening, is it? Oh, the casualties are real enough, but there are not that many. Or have more Trojans been killed and wounded?'

'Perhaps a few more, but not many.' Patroclus was surprised at her interest, but flattered by it, and he answered her seriously.

'Really, we are holding back. Agamemnon has no desire to pitch a full-scale battle yet. Priam has just enough troops to keep us from campaigning elsewhere in Troy, and we have enough here to persuade him that he will not be able to dislodge us.'

'Why do you fight at all?'

He stopped to think before replying. The war was sure to look very different to Briseis, seeing it from the camp and the hospital tent, from how it seemed to him out on the plain. He did not want to repel her. 'The horses need to be kept at it, and so do the men. We should lose our sharpness if we sat in the camp all summer doing nothing.'

'I can see that, but it seems a dangerous way of keeping in practice. Could you not settle for chariot races along the shore?'

'But that is a part of it: to get used to facing a little danger each day. Then when a big battle does come it will just seem like more of the same.'

'Do you want a battle to come?'

'Yes,' Patroclus said with a forcefulness that surprised Briseis. 'I dislike this halfway business. I would rather push forward, and so would Achilles. The High King is so half-hearted about hard fighting. He talks of starving out Ilios, or bankrupting Priam so his allies desert him, but that could take another eight years. It would be better to attack head on; and there will be no better time than this. The Trojan morale is bad now, you can sense it out there.'

'You are not afraid?'

'Of dying? Of course. But there are worse ways to die.'

'I suppose so.' Her voice was small, and he felt he ought to say more. 'You are thinking of your husband? It must be hard. But it was a good clean fight. He could have killed us, or we could have killed him. We did not hate him; there is no room for hate on a battlefield. You just get on with the job.'

'And you did it better than Mynes.'

Patroclus could not recall Mynes at all. There had been so many fights, so many men killed. He had heard enough of the Mysian, though, to say what needed saying with conviction. 'From what I heard, he was as good a fighter as anyone; except Achilles, of course. His men were less well trained than ours. That is why they lost.'

'It was not a job to him, or to them. They were fighting for us: their families, the people they loved.'

'That doesn't always make it easier. It doesn't help you to fight better.'

'Well, it should.'

They were silent for a few moments, then Patroclus added awkwardly, 'We fight for you now. You know that, don't you? We would risk everything to keep you safe: me, and Achilles, and all the Myrmidons.'

'It is not the same, being a slave. A possession.'

'I do not think of you as a slave.'

'I think of myself as one.' She looked up at him. 'That sounds ungrateful. I know you mean it. I suppose it should make me feel a little less lonely.'

It seemed to Patroclus then that however they started out, their talks veered across into intimacy. He was coming to care for her a great deal: more than he should, because she was Achilles' woman. But he had thought a lot about her attitude to Achilles and had begun to feel that that would never come right. Anyway, Achilles was going about it in completely the wrong way. He was starting to wonder how his friend would react if he asked for Briseis for himself.

He could not suggest anything like that to her; he would have to talk to Achilles first. He tried to turn the conversation to more neutral territory. 'There is no need to feel lonely. Do you not have friends among the girls? They all seem like-able.'

'They are, yes.' It was difficult to explain politely how competitive they were. She opted for bluntness. 'I doubt if any of them are really close, though. It is difficult, when we all belong to the same man.'

Not quite, he was tempted to retort. 'Do you see none of the other girls in the camp?'

'We hardly ever go beyond the Thessalian tents. I suppose we feel safe here.' It was true. Briseis never feared anything from the Myrmidons now, but it would have terrified her to brave the rest of the troops alone. A pause, and she added, 'There is a girl I know quite well, with Agamemnon. I had meant to ask if I could go to talk with her.' She had kept to her determination not to ask Achilles; but somehow she did not want Patroclus to think her grumpy and friendless.

Patroclus seized the opportunity. He reckoned it could only be a good thing for Briseis to talk to her friend. He knew of Chryseis – all the men in the camp did – and thought to himself that the girl might well help Briseis. It only needed a little nudge in the right direction now, surely, to encourage her to love an Achaean. Chryseis seemed content with her own master and might make her friend see sense about hers. And if she failed – then he could have a word with Achilles with a clear conscience.

It was settled before they parted. When he stopped to think about it afterwards it seemed to Patroclus that it might be difficult to mention the conversation to Achilles or to Agamemnon; but there were other ways of arranging things. He sent one of his own men to Chryseis with a private message, and – lest Chryseis be as curious as he knew she could be – orders not to make it clear who he came from.

■

Her new status was important to Chryseis. Agamemnon made her act the public Queen to his King, as well as the private whore to his rake. She played her part well, she knew. She also knew he had a real Queen back in Mycenae, but that was a long way away, and a long time ago by then.

Agamemnon was extravagantly generous to her. The jewels and the fine clothes in the trunks were all hers to keep, he had assured her.

It had disconcerted her with Troilus, the knowledge that it was she who was forcing the pace. There was none of that with Agamemnon. He fixed the rules. It was the limits of her character they pushed against, not the limits of his. If he had any limits himself, she had not discovered them yet. Though she disgusted herself at times, she knew that she always delighted him.

She managed quite well, on the whole, to keep the disgust locked away in that secret corner of her mind that she reserved for all those things best not thought about. There were many of them. She did her best never to think about Chryse or Ilios at all. Except sometimes on the rare nights when she slept alone, she never thought of her father, or of her friends from that other life. She had not let herself think of Troilus since the night earlier in the summer when Agamemnon had coolly tortured his name out of her. She never sacrificed to Apollo. She had had no sense of the God's presence since she came to the Achaean camp.

It would have been harder if there had been anyone who spoke to her of these things; but there was not. There was nobody in the camp, as far as she knew, who could have known about any of these private things.

When the messenger came from Patroclus it threw her into turmoil. Her first instinct was to refuse to see Briseis. She panicked; then pulled herself together. She decided she ought to see it as an opportunity to show off her success in her new life, and not to tremble at the prospect of being exposed as a fraud, as a fragile actress whose mask papers over a yawning chasm of misery. She would carry it off in a broad daylight; and on her own territory at that. She ordered one of Agamemnon's heralds to go and summon Briseis to Agamemnon's quarters with as much regal show as she could muster.

Briseis was duly impressed. She imagined that the rumours she had heard of Chryseis' power were exaggerated, but it seemed that they were not, if the girl could order the troops around. The hospital tent would have to do without her for a day. Shaking her head, she went to fetch the Cretan finery from the chest.

The herald escorted her formally across the camp and led her into a large room, furnished even more richly than Achilles' private quarters. There he handed her to a woman servant, a tired-looking girl in a rather grubby tunic, who removed her sandals, washed the dust of the camp from her feet, and led her through a warren of corridors until she stopped to knock at a closed door. Chryseis' voice called to them to enter.

The servant opened the door, then slipped back into the passage, leaving Briseis to walk in alone. She felt suddenly awkward in the Cretan dress, as she had not done walking across the camp. It was not an outfit that allowed one to creep into a room. As it demanded, she drew herself up straight, thrust her chest forward, and strode in proudly.

Chryseis was standing in the centre of a small room. It was furnished like a cave of treasure, with woven rugs on the floor as well as the walls, and a great bronze lamp hanging over a low table. There was no window to the outside, though an opening along one wall gave onto a narrow light well. The golden shaft of sunlight that it let into the room fell at Chryseis' feet.

Chryseis' dress was in the same style as Briseis' own, a warm yellow, less thickly embroidered, but of finer stuff. Her dark hair was clean and shining, braided and curled at the front, and hanging loose behind her. A thin line of kohl rimmed her eyes. A necklace of rubies and sapphires, caught in a mesh of gold, glowed at her throat, and there were more jewels in her hair, round her wrists and ankles. On her lips was the confident smile of a queen at home in her palace.

As Briseis watched, the smile drooped and disappeared. Chryseis' face folded, as if she was a baby about to bawl. In an instant, it smoothed again; but the voice that came from her was low and unsteady. 'But you were in the square, with the captives.'

Briseis looked around uncomfortably, as if she would have preferred to sit, but was not sure if she should, or had forgotten how. 'It is no wonder you did not know me. I feel so unlike myself in these clothes. The Achaeans have strange tastes, don't they?'

'There is nothing strange about these clothes. You know Helen wears the same kind of thing, and Cassandra, and the other women at the palace in Ilios.'

'You forget,' Briseis said gently, 'that I have never been to Ilios. I did not know that you had been there yourself.'

'I was there this last spring.'

'Oh.' It was not a very satisfactory reply, and there was a momentary silence, as if Chryseis was waiting for a longer one that did not come. Finally she spoke herself. 'Please sit. The servant will bring a drink in a moment.'

They sat almost simultaneously, on a large rug with a pattern of donkeys and eagles. Chryseis remained in the ray of sunlight, but she turned so that the light shone on her hair, and her face was in shadow.

If she was still shaken there was no sign of it. Briseis said politely, 'What a beautiful rug. Is this Agamemnon's room?'

Chryseis gave a slow, satisfied smile. 'I think I would call it my room. I spend most of my time during the day here, though not the nights, of course.'

Everyone knew where she spent them, and it seemed she was happy to boast of it. Briseis picked her words cautiously. 'I had heard that you were in favour with Agamemnon.'

'He's a very generous man. He treats me like a queen.' Chryseis' hand came up to finger her necklace, nervously.

'So I see.' That too would not do as a response. A small pause grew again, and Briseis, ending it, began to work through an inconsequential account of how she had encountered Agamemnon only in the square, and how rich his cloak had seemed to her. She was rescued by the servant, who brought two silver cups on a little silver tray. Drawing the table towards them, she set the cups down, gave a perfunctory curtsey, and withdrew.

Briseis half-expected them to hold mulled wine, though it was hardly what women drank in the afternoon. Instead it was a herbal drink, slightly bitter, and quite unfamiliar. It had a Greek name, which Chryseis gave her. She did not think Chryseis knew what it contained; if so, surely, she would have said.

'It's unusual. Different.'

'Like so many things here.'

'Neither of our lives have turned out as we expected.'

Chryseis felt a shaking begin inside her. It was difficult to hide such things in a light dress which showed every quiver. She did not trust herself to reply, and it was a relief when Briseis said gently, 'Do you miss the shrine? They rarely worship Apollo in the camp, do they? And Artemis not at all.'

Of course Briseis did not know, and she was thinking not of Troilus but of Chryses' plan to send his daughter to Artemis' sanctuary. Chryseis felt the tension leak out of her. 'I think very little about the gods. It was so important back in Chryse, but we have to leave the things from that life behind.'

'I'm not sure. I've thought about it a great deal, how we ought to behave. I know a lot of the girls think it is best to try and forget everything they used to care about, and start afresh. I can understand that; but I cannot make myself do it.'

'If you spent all your time thinking about the people you have lost, or about the terrible things the Achaeans did to the Trojans, you would go mad.'

'I suppose you would. I felt close to it myself when I came. But now I am beginning to think the opposite. When you do not think about the past at all you lose touch with who you really are. And that is where the real danger comes.'

Chryseis looked down at the floor. It seemed to them both that Briseis' words were too close to the truth. Briseis felt a sudden rush of sympathy. But the other girl's reply, when it finally came, dissolved it instantly. 'I heard that Achilles hates you.' There was a sneer in her voice, though whether it was that of the bully or of the terrified victim, Briseis could not have said.

Briseis sat for a moment, letting the anger mount to a peak and then subside, before saying carefully, 'It is not quite like that. He has been good to me. Not in the sort of way that Agamemnon has been to you: there have been no jewels, no presents. But I needed time to get over Mynes' death, and he has let me take it.'

She hesitated. Chryseis seemed brittle to her. Earlier in the conversation she had been tempted to try to crack her veneer, regain the intimacy they had known back in Lyrnessus. Now she was a little afraid of what she would uncover beneath it. If she pushed too hard, she felt, they might both find themselves saying things they could not take back. She added, 'I do not mean to crtiticize you. It is not as if you lost a husband you loved. If you felt that you could love Agamemnon straight away I am sure that was for the best.' She fumbled for words of praise that she could say with conviction. 'It suits you, being treated like a queen, but it is different for me. It is something, that Achilles and I should understand each other.'

'So do we. Agamemnon and I.' Chryseis' face, still in the shadow, gave no depth of meaning to her words.

They sipped the strange drink in silence for some time. Outside there was a clang as a servant dropped a cauldron on the baked earth. The women turned sharply, though there was nothing to be seen from the room; and turning back, their eyes met briefly.

'He struck me as hard, Achilles. A cold man.'

Briseis kept the anger down, like a snake curled low in a cooking pot. 'I think he is an honest and fair one.'

'But he gets angry, surely.'

'So do many people.'

'Does he hit you? In bed?'

Briseis did not try to hide her shock. Across from her, Chryseis' face turned red. Briseis did not look at it; she gazed into her cup, empty but for a jumble of leaves at the bottom. To them she said, in a tight, prim voice, 'Of course not. There has been nothing like that. He is always gentle with me. If you heard such a thing, then whoever said it to you was lying.'

Chryseis could not explain why she had asked. 'I expect they were,' she said in a thin voice. If there had been any hope of rebuilding their friendship it now lay shattered around them, devastating the elegant room. A sudden rush of panic, of loneliness, hit her in the stomach and brought bile to her throat. She tried to think of something to say that would wound the other girl, but misery seemed to slow her mind and she could not. She rose to call a servant to show Briseis the way out, and in the pause while the girl was coming they talked with the awkwardness of strangers about things that could not possibly matter to either of them.

Well, Briseis thought later, as she slipped off the Cretan dress and rubbed away the kohl before going back to the hospital tent, I shall not see her again. The little lie about Achilles hung heavily in her mind. It had only occurred to her on the way back that she might have told the truth to Chryseis.

My loyalties must have changed after all, she thought to herself. I would not betray Achilles to her even in a small way. I would not betray Patroclus. I would not even rat on the other girls in the tent. If I had to say which side I was on now I suppose it would be the Thessalian side.

It was not a comfortable thought. Was she being unfair to Chryseis? If she was it was too late to do anything about it. Anyway, she added cruelly to herself, Chryseis was lying somewhere, too. She could not tell where, but she was sure of it.

Her conclusions were a little too glib to satisfy her, and that night as she lay in bed Chryseis' face came back to hover in front of her. What a strange question to ask, she thought sleepily. Maybe Agamemnon beats her? If he does she is not going to tell me about it now. Briseis was too tired to make herself care very much.

■

In Agamemnon's hall, an ox turned slowly on a spit over a roaring fire, attended by three of the High King's cooks. More cooks were dismembering the two lambs that had already been roasted. Servants brought baskets of warm bread and flasks of Rhodian wine to the men seated around the trestle.

Nearly two dozen of them were there. Diomedes sat on the High King's left, Menelaus to his right. Ulysses and Nestor were joking with each other. Little Ajax had come, big Ajax, Menestheus and Meriones.

It might almost have been a council of war, Patroclus thought to himself; but it was not. Talthybius the herald had made that plain in inviting him and Achilles, and all round the trestle the conversation was of dogs and horses, food and wine. Menestheus was telling an old tale of a boar hunt in the hills outside Athens, Diomedes describing a fight outside the camp whorehouse.

At the far end of the trestle Achilles too was laughing, at a joke Agapenor had been telling. But his shoulders were set squarely and his eyes were cool. Achilles was rarely invited to Agamemnon's hall. He had no intention, Patroclus knew, of wasting this opportunity in drinking and joking and telling old tales.

Achilles waited until the ox had been carved and dished up, until the cooks had retreated to their quarters and the winebowls had been replenished. Then he calmly swept the remains of the meat and bread from his end of the trestle, set his elbows in the space he had cleared, and clapped his hands together for silence.

He began to speak immediately, before Agamemnon could intervene. He spoke of the war, quietly and lucidly. He discussed the impact of his own spring campaign in Mysia, and of Ajax's devastations to the north of Troy. He reviewed the progress of the summer skirmishes, the situation in the citadel, the strength of the Trojan forces, and the state of their morale. He considered the likely Trojan strategy. He assumed, Patroclus noticed, that the final decisions would be taken not by the ailing King Priam but by Hector, the field commander, and a man he greatly respected.

Hector, Achilles concluded with a hint of regret, would not be in a position to launch an offensive that summer. Therefore it was essential that there should be an Achaean offensive: one that would take the Trojans by surprise, at a time when their morale, he believed, was at a low ebb, and while there was enough of the fighting season left to follow it up. He made it clear he had no doubt that if his strategy was adopted the Achaeans could hope to be close to winning the war before the autumn.

There was a moment's silence when he finished speaking. Ulysses broke it, remarking that it was a pity Achilles did not have access to the High King's intelligence about affairs in Ilios. It was not clear from his words – at least to Patroclus – whether he had such access himself.

Achilles regarded him with a touch of annoyance; then swung round to confront Agamemnon. 'Perhaps the High King will continue by briefing us.'

Agamemnon stared back at him impassively. 'I was not aware that I had called a council of war.'

'You have not called a council of war all summer.'

'I see no need for one at the moment,' Agamemnon replied. He turned to Diomedes and launched back into an argument about hunting dogs.

Achilles' voice, loud and harsh, cut into the conversation. 'Are you refusing to brief us, Agamemnon?'

Agamemnon stopped in mid-sentence, turned deliberately, and surveyed the trestle. He looked into every face before bringing his eyes to rest on Achilles. 'Nobody else, it seems, is demanding a briefing.'

Achilles held his gaze a moment, then turned to Patroclus. Patroclus had been expecting it; but still his spirits sank.

It was more than a personal quarrel, he knew that. Achilles resented Agamemnon's high command. The Mycenaean leader had every right to it: he was High King, he had planned and financed the expedition to Troy, he led its largest contingent – well, joint largest, with that of Idomeneus who nominally shared the command, but had more sense than to push his counsel. Achilles recognized all that; and yet he resented it. It never came easily to him to submit to another man's orders. Perhaps he could have tolerated it if Agamemnon made a show of taking his advice, but the High King never did.

It was difficult enough counselling a king, even for a more tactful man than Achilles. There was always that fine line to be drawn between sycophancy on the one hand, failure to do one's full duty in telling the truth, and on the other, the over-presumption that suggested a man wanted to take more than his allotted role. Achilles always seemed to want more. It was not by chance that he sacrificed not to Apollo, the god of moderation, but to Zeus, the god of supreme power.

Patroclus said cautiously, 'I think the High King has a valid point. This was not called as a council of war, and Idomeneus for one is not here. Perhaps Agamemnon would undertake to call a council tomorrow.'

Agamemnon's eyes narrowed. 'I think I have already made it clear that I do not intend that.'

Achilles said sharply, 'But it is essential that we agree on an offensive. Ulysses, you agree with me?'

'I think,' said Ulysses, 'that you stated your case with admirable clarity. The High King now has all the information he requires to decide on our strategy.'

'He decides with the advice of his counsellors, damn it.' Achilles was close to losing his temper. Patroclus, seeing it, tried to cut in, but Achilles ignored him. 'Nestor, surely you agree?'

Nestor took his time in answering. Finally he said, 'I agree that we need a new offensive – on the winebowl.'

The table erupted in laughter. Achilles' cause was lost for the evening and he had, Patroclus recognized with relief, the sense to realize and accept it.

Chryseis rose to pour more wine. There were no other women present. Patroclus watched her as she moved from man to man, laughing and joking with each, brushing against some in a way that appeared quite deliberate, neatly avoiding the odd groping hand.

With the confrontation out of the way, Agamemnon seemed content to let her dominate the gathering. She held every gaze, switching them in and out of play like a weaver with her coloured threads. She did it skilfully, Patroclus realized, guiding the evening along the path Agamemnon intended it to take. He and Achilles were not ignored, but they received less than their fair share of her attention. She lingered the longest over Diomedes and Menestheus, who were both rather drunk and flirted shamelessly with her.

She flirted back, but it looked innocent enough to him. It is all calculated, he thought: she plans each glance for public effect. He could not imagine that she went further – or even as far – in private. Agamemnon appeared quite unconcerned. He was not a man to tolerate infidelity, and Patroclus did not believe that there was any. Chryseis seemed acutely conscious of every movement the High King made.

Beneath the brashness she is nervous, thought Patroclus. On edge. Is she frightened of him? It was no secret that Agamemnon used his women roughly. Patroclus had assumed that the High King would be more gentle with this young priest's daughter, but now he could not escape the uneasy suspicion that he might have been wrong. He could not see any marks of violence on Chryseis' bare arms and breasts. But there are ways of doing violence that do not leave any mark, a voice in his head told him. Though there was an unmistakable bond between the two of them, he did not think that it was love in any sense he recognized.

He suddenly recalled Briseis' words. Many of the men despise us, she had said. It seemed an apt summary of Agamemnon's habitual attitude towards women, captive or otherwise. He treated this one well enough in public. She was done up in fine clothes, and she wore regal jewels. He spoke to her politely, even deferentially. But Patroclus thought he recognized a faint undercurrent of contempt, as if it was all a game to Agamemnon. All the public show will come to an abrupt halt as soon as they are alone, he thought, and the High King will take her as crudely and brutally as if she were a harbour whore. Patroclus was not the kind of man to be aroused by the picture, or to tell himself that she probably enjoyed that. He felt a surge of pity for the young girl as she flashed and postured in front of the men. He caught her eye hoping to show his sympathy; but though Chryseis smiled brightly back at him, there seemed to be an emptiness behind her look.

I should not have sent Briseis to talk with her, he thought miserably. He and Briseis had not had a chance to talk alone since the encounter between the two women the previous day, but it had been obvious to him that Briseis was downcast. Had Chryseis confided anything to her friend? Perhaps he should have hoped that she had, for her sake. But he cared more for Briseis, and he did not want her thinking that all Achaean men were like Agamemnon. It struck him that Briseis might have encountered the High King on her visit to his quarters and he felt a chill deep inside him. Oh no, he thought. Agamemnon must not get his hands on her.

He would have to tell Achilles. He should have done so already. It might be a small enough matter on the surface, but he had a suspicion that it could be important to them both. With a heavy memory of some of Briseis' other words – the ones about honourable deeds coming easily – he followed his friend and leader back to their quarters.

It was late by the time they got back. The night was cloudless and cool after the heat of the day. Achilles was in a mood to send for Diomede and Iphis and make straight for bed.

'I'd like to talk about something first. Shall I pour us some more wine?'

'No. Agamemnon's is so strong, I doubt if I could take any more. Can it not wait till morning?'

'I'd rather we talked tonight.'

'Look, if it's about bloody Agamemnon and the offensive I really don't . . .' Achilles caught a hint of tension in his friend's face and cut himself short. 'All right, I can see it's not.' He threw himself into a low chair by the hearth. 'Come on then. Spill it out.' Patroclus hesitated a moment, and he added more gently, 'What can be so terrible that you cannot tell me straight out?'

'It is nothing terrible.' Patroclus frowned. This was going badly even before he had started. He crossed to pour a cup of wine for himself, then stopped to add a little water before coming to sit at Achilles' feet. 'It's about Briseis.'

'Don't tell me you're sleeping with Briseis.'

'No, of course not.'

'But you would like to.'

'Well, yes, but that was not . . .'

'No.'

Patroclus turned to look at Achilles. He had not moved at all, but there was something tense about his sprawl, as if he was a lion watching its prey. Achilles looked back. 'I'm sorry, Patroclus, but you cannot have her.'

The refusal mattered more to him than he had expected. He drew in a shallow breath before replying as evenly as he could, 'If it matters to you, then of course not. I'm sorry. I had the impression you might not have cared either way.'

Achilles stared down at his hand on the arm of the chair, as if he were willing the tension out of it. Then he gripped hard and stood up. He went over to pour some wine which he did not water, and stood by the trestle, his heavy hammered bronze cup in his hand. 'I would not refuse just to spite you. You know that.'

Patroclus was silent. He rarely resented his friend's authority over him, but at that moment it came hard. Achilles had always had more of everything; and Patroclus did not like to feel like a poor relation begging for leftovers. Still, it would be stupid to destroy a twenty-year friendship for the sake of one girl. And if it was not indifference that lay behind Achilles' pointed neglect of Briseis, was it perhaps too strong a desire for her? 'Would you like me to help to get her for you?' he asked Achilles.

'Would you mind doing that?'

'No. Yes.' By Zeus and Apollo, all Achilles had to do was send for her. Why did he not do it, if he wanted her so much? Patroclus took a gulp of his wine. It tasted weak and thin after

Agamemnon's rich brew. He went on in a rush, 'She needs a man. She's not the sort of girl to go without for moon after moon; and she has changed, she no longer hates us. I doubt she would turn you away, if you sent for her now.'

'But you think she would rather have you.'

Patroclus had an uneasy feeling that Achilles would never forgive him if he agreed. He was well aware that Achilles must envy his own popularity just as much as he envied Achilles' power and position. It took a great deal to keep a friendship like theirs alive. They could be at ease together, but only if they were careful never to say too much. And never to lie either, he added to himself. Nothing must be allowed to undermine their absolute trust in each other. He spoke slowly and carefully, his eyes on Achilles so that his friend would know he meant the words. 'I like her, we talk together often, and I know she likes me. There's no more than that, though. She's lonely, and she wants a man, and she likes me. If I were to hold back, I think you could make her come to love you.'

Achilles was still standing across the room. The glow from the lamp on the trestle caught the planes of his face, emphasizing its hard, clear lines. His red hair shone golden in the warm light. There was something magnificent about him, it seemed to Patroclus. He felt a hot rush of love for his friend. It was inconceivable to him that Briseis might be unable to feel the same. Oh yes, she will love you, he thought to himself. Even if she does not yet know it.

Both men were quiet for a moment, then Achilles' sudden smile broke the tension. They both relaxed.

'You'll send for her?'

'Not tonight.' Achilles came to sit down again and finish his wine. 'Was there something else?'

It seemed to Patroclus that everything had been said by then; but he had thought the business with Chryseis important earlier, and there would be no better opportunity to tell it. He went through the tale conscientiously, but he could not recover the sense of urgency and it seemed quite meaningless as he spoke. Achilles listened, but without concentration, and when Patroclus finished he drained his cup and rose without hesitating. 'Thank you for telling me. Come on, let's to bed.'

'Shall I call Diomede?'

Achilles shook his head. 'Not now. I would rather we were alone together.'

Patroclus' answering smile made it clear that it would suit them both very well.

■

The sun was just going down as Aeneas made his way along the streets of the upper town towards Hector's house. He hurried a little, as if to get there before the light disappeared. But in Troy the darkness came slowly, and there was no need to rush.

The streets were busy. Water carriers, orange sellers, palace servants, priests and serving boys from the shrines, soldiers, grooms, stray children and old men all jostled Aeneas as he pushed his way through the crowd. He glanced at them all, and at the streets on which they walked.

The place is cleaner than it was when I came, he thought to himself. Has there just been a garbage patrol? No, it is more consistent than that; and it is written on the faces, too. Ilios has pulled itself together. There is no sense of imminent disaster now, as there was in the spring. People have fallen back into their routine. They are working hard, and cleaning up after themselves. Perhaps there is hope for us yet.

Hector certainly seemed to think that there was. Was it Hector, Aeneas wondered, who had brought about the change in Ilios? Or had he simply responded to it and moved ahead of it? Whichever was the truth, it was obvious to Aeneas that Hector was now the focus of the rise in morale.

He could hear the buzz from the tall black and white house as he turned the corner and approached Palace Square. A low, distinctive noise, quite unlike the high-pitched note that emanated from Paris and Helen's house when they had company. Hector and Andromache did these things differently. There were no dark secrets, no *frissons* of surprise in their establishment. The wine was well watered, and nobody drank too much or made a fool of himself. The conversation was good, and the company civilized. Even the singer caught the atmosphere and kept to his less bawdy songs.

It was for the singer that he had been invited. There had been other evenings, quiet ones when nobody else came, and Andromache herself played the harp and sang. But this was to be a formal entertainment, with Priam's bard Amphius. The ailing King had been withdrawing from public life as Hector blossomed, and there was hardly any work for entertainers in the palace. That is a part of it too, Aeneas added to himself. Priam casts a heavy shadow over the citadel, and it is a relief to everybody when he keeps to his bedchamber. Paris was also away, leading the delegation to Hattusas, and taking from Ilios a different kind of darkness.

The courtyard was crowded and the great double doors to the megaron had been flung open. Glancing through them, Aeneas caught the bright flare of pitch-soaked torches. The servants were moving around the courtyard, lighting torches there as well.

He took in the scene rapidly. Every respectable woman in Ilios, it seemed, and none of the hetairas. Five times as many men. Barely a handful of palace officials. The family, of course. Most of the allied commanders. The southerners were bare to the waist, and their oiled skins gleamed. The Thracians had renewed their blue tattoos.

Deiphobus was draped against a pillar, waving his cup as he tried to make a point to Aeneas' fellow Dardanian, Acamas. Helenus and Ennomus were lounging together in a corner, watching the activity carefully and exchanging the odd cynical remark. Helenus waved to Aeneas, but the Dardanian shook his head: he wanted to talk first to Hector.

There was no sign of Hector in the courtyard, so Aeneas pushed his way through the crowded porch and into the megaron. The torches, bright after the sunset gloom outside, turned the carved ceiling into a marvel of gleams and shadows. It looked almost like the Ilios of old, the wonder of a continent, before Priam had begun to sell off the treasures and they had all grown pale and thin on the tight rations. Only at a second glance would anyone have seen the weariness on the faces, or told the burnished bronze of this occasion from the gold of ten years before.

Ten years before, there would have been an ox roasting over the hearth, and another, most likely, in the courtyard. Now the fireplace was empty. Again no sign of Hector; but looking across the room Aeneas saw Andromache, deep in conversation with Cassandra.

Andromache was in a blue dress, beautifully dyed but awkwardly cut and giving her a rather lumpish look. Her head and hands were weighted down with gold and sapphires. Cassandra's dress was grey, severe and stylish, enlivened only by a heavy silver necklet. Cassandra looked in Aeneas' direction first and gave him a flirtatious glance as he approached. He responded with an involuntary frown. She always made him a shade uncomfortable. Behind the flickering looks and light words, he had the impression that she did not like men. She had surely seen thirty summers and still she was unmarried, though she was beautiful and many men must have offered for her. He found it odd that she and Andromache seemed to get on together: they were such complete opposites. He turned with relief to Andromache's open, smiling face.

'I had begun to think you were not coming, Aeneas.'

'I was held up in the camp.'

'Still, you're in time for the singer. We have some tumblers, too. We should go out into the courtyard to see them.'

Aeneas could hear a small commotion in the courtyard over the sound of conversation, as if the tumblers were indeed about to begin their act. He began to say that he would prefer to stay in the megaron and talk, but Cassandra cut him off. 'Oh, we must see it. They are the first tumblers to come here for ages. Where did they come from, Andromache?'

'From Mysia.' Andromache said no more and turned to shepherd both of them towards the doors.

The courtyard was packed now, and rather than fight their way outside they stood just inside the porch as the tumblers, two lads and a girl, ran into the cleared space in the centre and made their opening bows.

As the tumblers circled round in a rapid succession of flips and somersaults, their painted legs and arms flying, Aeneas watched abstractedly. He had seen it so many times before, the leaps and catches, the bodies balanced on two hands or one, the clownish fumbles before a particularly audacious move was completed. They were second-rate. First-class performers no longer came to Ilios.

The audience began to stir and mutter a little, and the tumblers moved quickly into their finale, a neat sequence of moves which left them standing on each other's hands to make a tower.

As the girl wobbled her way to a perfect balance on her partner's hands, a scream pierced the silence. It came from a dark corner of the courtyard. Another cry followed it; then the crowd surged into noisy life, pushing away from the far wall. The tumblers were swept aside, and Aeneas was knocked backwards into the shadows of the porch.

'A lion!' somebody yelled. 'Zeus, it's a lion!'

Aeneas scrambled to his feet. There was a clash of bronze as some soldiers rushed to the spear rack. A couple more were trying to push the doors shut, but some people were still outside, pressing hard against them. He looked for, but could not see Andromache. Then his eyes were drawn by Cassandra.

Cassandra had positioned herself well. She had been watching the tumblers from just by the inside of the door, where the surge of people through it had missed her, and now she was standing with her hands pressed against the hinges of the half-closed central door and her eyes alight. Her face shone with excitement. Aeneas, caught up in spite of himself by her vivacity, watched it for a moment; and then revised his opinion. No, Cassandra was not excited by the danger. She was laughing.

He pushed forward to stand just behind her and craned his head until it was close to hers. He found that he could see out to the courtyard through the narrow gap between the doors. A torch, knocked to the ground, lay guttering on the stones. Just beyond the jagged circle of light, a dark shape prowled. Against the far wall a few frightened figures hovered.

Not a lion. Surely not a lion. Not in the centre of Ilios. Not drawn to torchlight. He took a deep breath and yelled, 'It's a joke. That's no lion. A joke.'

Cassandra turned, grey skirts brushing against Aeneas' bare

legs, and caught his eye. A flicker of annoyance crossed her face, followed by amusement. She laughed again, more openly. Behind them the word was spreading across the crowd, and the terror was slowly giving way to hilarity. In the yard the makeshift lion, finding the game was up, had risen to his feet and was peeling the mask from his face. A boisterous crowd was circling round him. Aeneas could not see the face, but he knew it was surely a boy from the palace who had been bribed to play the little scene. He had no doubt who had arranged it. 'That was a dangerous game,' he said in a low voice.

Cassandra regarded him, as if to judge whether he was seriously annoyed. She said coolly, 'The tumblers were not hurt. I saw the girl slip down safely. Though he should have come a moment later, as they were finishing.'

'Were you trying to upset Hector and Andromache?' Aeneas asked.

'Aeneas, we always do this kind of thing at parties. Hector knows that.'

'But does Andromache?'

'Of course she does. Not that she would do it herself, not yet. But she will see how much it livens things up, and in the end she will learn.'

As she had learned, Aeneas thought to himself, to make friends with Cassandra and her cronies. He was still framing his reply when Hector burst upon them.

'Cassandra, I need you. Come and see to Andromache.'

Seeing her brother's expression, Cassandra's own suddenly sobered. 'She's all right?'

'I think so. I hope so. But the shock, right now . . .' He grabbed Cassandra's arm and hauled her back into the megaron. Aeneas followed.

Andromache was sitting in one of the high-backed chairs that usually lined the walls, with a servant hovering beside her. She was pale, but she looked up at Hector with a brave smile. 'I'm fine now, honestly. It was just a surprise.'

'It won't hurt the –'

'The baby?' she finished for her husband. 'No, I don't think so. I don't feel as if it will.'

'But Andromache, I didn't know you were expecting again,' Cassandra said.

Andromache's smile widened. 'We haven't told anyone yet. We are hardly sure ourselves. I was going to let you and Polyxena know tomorrow.'

Hector was barely listening. 'Well,' he broke in, 'if I ever find out who planned that ridiculous charade I'll break their arms.'

Aeneas met his eye, expressionless. 'I doubt,' he said, 'if you will ever find out.'

Cassandra did not trouble to show him her thanks.

Hector went on, more calmly, 'Troilus, Aeneas. Help me settle people again, and we'll get Amphius to begin. Cassandra, will you stay with Andromache?'

Aeneas turned, surprised, to find Troilus by his side. His eyes narrowed as if he were about to say something; then he thought better of it, and followed Hector out to the courtyard. The crowd were already settling back into their places, and Amphius, elderly and imperturbable, was tuning his lyre.

Troilus came to find Aeneas after Amphius had finished, as people were beginning to make their way home. 'Am I forgiven now?' he asked with an easy smile.

'For loosing the lion?'

Troilus grinned. 'That lad looked amazing, didn't he? Did you see how it was done? A real skin, and a mask made out of clay. Must have taken days and days of planning.'

'It must. Pity they were not spent on something more worthy.'

'Oh, come on, Aeneas. People in Ilios need to laugh.'

Aeneas frowned. 'They need,' he said acidly, 'to learn a bit of discipline.'

'The family vice, recklessness. Maybe you're right. I'm not forgiven.'

'What use is forgiveness, Troilus? If you keep on hurling yourself into skirmishes without watching your back you will be dead before the winter. Would you like me to forgive you then?'

'It would hardly be generous to refuse. All right, I'm sorry. I was in the wrong today, and I do know I would have been in deep trouble if you had not brought your men across to help get me away.'

Aeneas let a moment's silence grow between them. Then he said brusquely, 'I need a stronger drink. You can set my wine down to your ration at the tavern.'

'Done. Anyway, I have some more news for you. I'll tell you on the way.'

Helenus came up as they reached the courtyard door and invited himself to join them. Aeneas saw annoyance, quickly smothered, on Troilus' face. The news, evidently, would have to wait.

Helenus was still at the tavern when Aeneas left, so the news waited till the next morning. Even then, Aeneas' hunt for Troilus was unsuccessful: he was off on guard duty. So Aeneas went back to Hector's house to make sure that Andromache had recovered.

She had, it seemed.

'I hope you enjoyed the party, she said with a welcoming smile.

'Very much. A little alarming, though, that episode with the lion.'

Andromache raised her eyebrows slightly. 'I would have thought you shared Cassandra's idea of fun.'

'As you do?'

She considered that as she was guiding him to a chair.

'I didn't enjoy it, exactly, but I think I am beginning to understand it.'

'You see a great deal of Cassandra these days.'

Andromache nodded. 'She has been very good to me, Aeneas. Helping me get over all the deaths.'

'She has never struck me as a sympathetic person.'

'Not at all, no. But I am not sure that sympathy was what I wanted. It was more a question of coming to terms with things. Cassandra is good at that. She's very honest, she sees things clearly.'

It struck Aeneas as an unlikely description of the elegant, elliptical Cassandra; and in any case, he was not certain if he rated that quality as highly as Andromache seemed to. He did not reply, and after a pause she went on, 'I had no chance to tell you my news last night.'

'About the baby? I did hear. Congratulations.'

Colouring, Andromache looked almost pretty. 'Thank you. That isn't what I meant, though. There's news of Chryseis, my cousin. Did you meet her in Ilios this spring?'

'Oh, Troilus' girl. No, I never did.'

'You would have liked her. She is very pretty, and very lively.'

And you, my dear Andromache, are no judge at all of these things, Aeneas thought to himself.

'But maybe you will get the chance, after all. Troilus heard yesterday from Chryseis' father, Chryses. You know he is the priest at Apollo's shrine in Chryse? We had thought he had been killed when the Achaeans attacked, but it appears that he escaped with a couple of his escort. What with all the confusion in Mysia, he couldn't send a messenger before.'

'Did Chryseis escape too?'

Andromache shook her head. 'The Achaeans took her. Chryses thinks she was unharmed. He has been making enquiries, and he's fairly sure she was taken back to the camp. The one here, down by the harbour.'

'Who is holding her?'

'We don't know yet, but I'm certain Hector will be able to find out. Anyway, it's marvellous, isn't it?'

'I would not exactly call it marvellous,' Aeneas replied carefully. 'Troilus will not think it is.'

An expression that Aeneas could not quite decipher flickered across Andromache's face. She said slowly, 'You've spoken to Troilus?'

Aeneas did not answer. He was recalling Troilus' words and actions the day before. He must have found out after their argument, when he had returned to the palace; or perhaps Hector had told him during the evening. And the news had . . . what? Excited him, yes. Pleased him? Aeneas thought not.

'Anyway,' Andromache went on with slightly forced cheerfulness, 'Troilus doesn't know half of it. We are going to ransom her.'

That did surprise Aeneas. He let the surprise show on his face before he said gently, 'Surely that will not be possible, Andromache. It is a lovely idea, but not at all practicable. I know it is done for royal prisoners. It was done for Hector's brother Lycaon, was it not? But he was a prince, and it is different for a girl.'

'I don't think it is. She was promised to Troilus, so that makes her one of the family, just like Lycaon. It is our duty to get her back, just as it was for him.'

There was a moment's silence. Aeneas did not like to suggest exactly how Chryseis' treatment in the Achaean camp would have differed from Lycaon's. Surely the Achaeans would not expect a ransom request, not for a priest's daughter? Surely the priest could not afford a ransom? Or Troilus, either? He fixed on this to ask.

Andromache listened, with slight impatience. 'Hector and I will arrange it. Not Troilus. You have to understand, Aeneas, Hector feels he must do it. He pressed her father to take her back to Chryse during the Achaean raids, so in a sense he was responsible for her capture. Troilus will be pleased, won't he?'

It was ironic that Andromache should need to ask him. Aeneas took the question seriously. Finally he said, 'I will talk to him about it.'

'I would be glad if you did.' Andromache hesitated, then added, 'You will not tell anyone else, will you? You know Priam did not know about the betrothal?'

'But you will tell him about the ransom, surely?'

Andromache frowned. It did make her a little uncomfortable, knowing that they were planning all this behind Priam's back. It made sense, though. There was no point in disturbing a sick man unnecessarily. There would be time enough for talking to him when Chryseis was back and the wedding fixed. And there was always the possibility that Priam might be dead by then. She said cautiously, 'That is up to Hector. I am sure he will do whatever seems best.'

'But he plans not to tell Priam.'

She nodded.

'And what do you think about that?'

Andromache's eyes widened, as if the question both surprised and annoyed her. 'I think what Hector thinks. Of course.'

Of course. Aeneas got to his feet abruptly. 'I'll go and find Troilus now.'

He had forgotten about the guard duty. It gave him a moment's irritation when he remembered, and then he went back to the camp and was absorbed in a dozen chores and problems. It was after supper before he recalled the promise to Andromache and returned to the palace.

Thinking about the morning's conversation on the way, he realized quite suddenly that Andromache disliked the girl. She had no desire to see her back in Ilios. If she was supporting this crazy scheme to ransom her it was from quite different motives. To please Hector, perhaps; to please Troilus; to ease a guilty conscience.

The realization brought Chryseis alive to Aeneas, as she had not been before. He was tempted to ask other people for their opinion of her, so that he might have a better feeling for whether this was a unique antipathy, or a symptom of a failing in Chryseis herself. He had once asked Paris what she was like, but Paris seemed barely to have noticed the girl. He looked around the megaron when he arrived to see if there were any likely candidates. But there was no sign of Helenus, or of Cassandra – it surprised him a little to realize how tempted he was to ask Cassandra – and he told himself firmly that it would do no good to pry at this stage. It would be better to talk to Troilus first.

Troilus, when he finally appeared, was as boisterous and edgy as ever.

Aeneas said, 'We cannot talk here. Let's go back to the tavern.'

'On you, tonight?'

'One cup each tonight. And we set down our own.'

Troilus did not seem offended. It was a fine, cool night, and he told a series of rather dirty and extremely bad jokes as they made their way down the hill to the tavern in the Street of the Fletchers, where they had gone the night before. He made no reference to the news. Finally Aeneas asked. Yes, Hector had told him about the ransom plan.

'You sound as though you are not pleased.'

'Pleased? No, it's not that. I just want to know who has got her so that I can get my revenge on him.'

The recklessness again, Aeneas thought momentarily. Then he remembered that it was what he had himself encouraged Troilus to aim at, back in the spring. It seemed to him that the boy's wild energies might still be channelled, transformed into determination, if Troilus knew who to look out for. He thought of pursuing the subject, and then recalled what he had come for. 'But you do want her back?'

They had not talked directly about Chryseis since the morning after the brawl with Hector, so it seemed to Aeneas a reasonable question. Troilus turned on him, though, with surprise and a hint of anger. 'What kind of question is that? Of course I do.'

'Hold your horses. I hadn't meant to be rude.'

'You were. Bloody rude.'

'Calm down, Troilus. It just seemed to me' – Aeneas picked his words carefully – 'that from spring to late summer is a long time when you are young, and that maybe it didn't matter so much to you by now. It is a lot to ask of Hector, you know. If you did have any doubts it would only be fair to let him know about them. You will have no chance once she is back.'

'I have none. None at all.'

Aeneas eyed him carefully. There was a full moon, and in its cold light Troilus' face looked young and strong. Aeneas would have preferred to see some mark of indecision in it. He reckoned the boy had answered too quickly. It would have done him good to think first. At least he would have a chance to think before Chryses came to Ilios and the ransom could be offered.

Troilus grew impatient under Aeneas' gaze. 'I thought you were my friend.'

'I am, Troilus. I am more of a friend than to let you make a fool of yourself. But Hector had thought you were uncertain about the girl before she left, and I wanted to make sure that you were certain now.'

'You don't think Hector will do that?'

Aeneas laughed shortly. 'No. He feels guilty about it.'

'So he damn well should. He should not have let her go. All right, don't say it. I shouldn't have done so either. I knew it as soon as she was gone, though. I shall not let her go a second time.'

'You love her.' It was halfway between a statement and a question.

'Yes. I do love her.' Troilus paused. They were standing in front of the tavern, a tall stone building near the Dardanian Gate, and Aeneas thought for a moment that he would turn to go in. But he kept his eyes on the other man, and added, 'I think I only realized after she was gone just what that means. When Chryseis was around I was so stunned just to be with her, to have her, that I had no time to think about it. I suppose I did feel trapped a little, agreeing to marry so young. But I do not feel trapped now. I am committed now, and that's different, isn't it?'

'I imagine so.' Aeneas felt momentarily at a loss. He was not prone to strong passions himself, and they made him uncomfortable in other people. Doubtless that was why he, who had seen ten summers more than Troilus, had not yet married. 'Perhaps I would understand better if I knew her. She seems to have quite an effect on men.'

Troilus laughed. 'Oh, she does. Quite an effect. But I am not so young and foolish that I would mistake that for love.'

Aeneas laughed too, though it did not come entirely naturally. It was a wise man, he thought, who really knew himself that well. But it was not as if Troilus was committing himself to anything dishonourable. It would have been a murky business if he had felt inclined to abandon the girl to the Achaeans.

He said something on these lines when they had been served with wine and were standing together by the narrow window of the upstairs room. It was less crowded there than on the ground floor.

Troilus thought this time before replying. 'What worries me is that whoever has her might not let her go, that he might want her too badly to send her back. Do you think a man could honourably do that? Hold onto her?'

Aeneas frowned. 'It will be difficult if you and Hector decide not to tell Priam. In that case you will not be able to go yourself and ask for her. It will have to be Chryses who does it. I don't honestly know. You are right there: it would help if we knew who we were dealing with. Some men might be more reluctant to send the girl back to a lover than to her father.'

'She will have told him, though. Her captor. About us.'

'Troilus. I don't see how she could have if it was a secret from the High King. Well, maybe. We neither of us know enough about how these things work.'

'I suppose not.'

Aeneas felt he ought to say a little more. 'You do realize, don't you, how he will have used her? You are not trying to persuade yourself that she will have escaped all that? Because she will not, you can be sure. However much she loves you, it will not have helped her fend off the Achaeans. It will have been rough for her. It might have changed her.'

Troilus' face seemed suddenly older and wiser, in the dim light of the upstairs room. 'War does that, doesn't it? It changes us all. I suppose I am quite different myself now from the boy who kissed her goodbye in the spring.' He caught Aeneas' look, and seemed to brighten. 'But she will still love me. And I will kill him for her.'

Will you? thought Aeneas. But he touched the boy gently on the shoulder and said quietly, 'You will try. I am sure of that. And if you want to badly enough then maybe you will do it.'

■

It took Briseis ten days to notice that Patroclus was avoiding her. If he had not meant her to notice it, perhaps she would have thought it an accident. But it was no accident. She was quite sure of that.

Why, why? She was worried, then upset, then angry. Of course it was sensible of him. A couple of the men had told her that she brightened up as he came into the hospital tent; perhaps more had mentioned it to him. It would not do, a friendship with any man but Achilles. Briseis was tired of being sensible, though, tired of being cautious. She longed for warmth, for love, to be able to talk to someone without watching every word. Only then did she realize how close she had come to getting that from Patroclus.

She wondered at first if the change had been a side effect of her meeting with Chryseis. Then she told herself it was just a coincidence; then she caught a glance between him and Achilles. She did not think she had been intended to see it; but it told her what she wanted to know. Achilles had warned him off.

Not obliquely, either. Patroclus had probably asked Achilles if he might have her, Briseis decided. Achilles, clearly, had said no.

The anger was for Achilles then. The very strength of it told her something else: that she could live with the disappointment if it brought her to Achilles.

However, it did not. She watched and waited, but Achilles made no move. He was involved, she knew, in an escalating confrontration with Agamemnon over the lack of progress with the siege. All the same, she reckoned he might have diverted himself by turning to her. It seemed that he was still waiting for a sign that he would be welcome.

It all made her furious, at both men, and even more so at herself. She was coming dangerously close to forgetting that they were bloody pirates. She owed it, not only to herself, but to Mynes and Ianeira, to remember that. Achilles did not get his sign. In the hospital tent he treated her abruptly. She forgot herself once and snapped at him in return. The men watched, those who were well enough to care. When he had gone one of them tackled her. He was a big, burly, easy-going man, who had joked with her every day when she tended the gaping wound in his side. He must have known it was festering, but he never mentioned it. 'Had a tiff with him?'

Her hand slipped, and she felt the man stiffen. She made herself smile and reply cheerfully, 'Must be the weather.'

'Too hot it is, today. Maybe thunder tomorrow.' The man watched her from under his lids as she fastened the bandage.

'Oh, I'm not afraid of storms.'

'You should be, love. Does you good to be a bit afraid of things that can hurt you.'

'I'll come and beg a cuddle of you, then, next time the lightning comes.'

The man on the next pallet roared with laughter. 'Try me, dear, I'll keep you warm. So long as Achilles is not around.'

The smile was fixed on her face. 'I'll ask him first. I wouldn't want to get you in any trouble.'

'I reckon Achilles doesn't know when he's well off.'

Briseis was inclined to think the reverse. Achilles had too much of everything. If he had needed her like these men did she might have found the same smile for him; but he did not.

She met the man's eyes. 'I know when I am. Don't worry about me.'

'Ah, but we do, love. We do.'

Briseis was not sure how much the other women had noticed. They had been intrigued by her visit to Chryseis. She had regaled them with the details of Chryseis' dress, and of Agamemnon's quarters, where none of the others had ever been. It had bought her a brief spell of popularity.

Iphis was particularly friendly. Patroclus was calling her more frequently than he had for some time and she glowed with happiness. It seemed clear that she did not know exactly what had happened. Perhaps Diomede did. Though Achilles took her just as often as before, she seemed edgy and irritable. She began to pick on Briseis, criticize her hair and complain about the time she spent with the wounded. Briseis, who was being doubly careful to behave irreproachably towards Achilles, could rarely resist the temptation to goad her in return. It worked best, she found, if she criticized the men. Diomede could ignore personal taunts, but she always rose to grumbles about Achilles.

'This surely cannot be the right place.'

The Thessalian women had come in a group, with a couple of Myrmidons to guard them, to wash their clothes in the river out near the camp stockade. It was a very hot day, and though they wore veils, the sun beating down on her was already making Briseis feel light-headed.

'Of course it's the place,' Diomede snapped. 'We always come here.'

Briseis scrambled down to the water's edge and ran her hand across the large yellowish stones that bordered it. 'These stones are much too rough,' she complained. 'We will not be able to rub the shifts on them at all.'

'Dear, dear. Would you like the guards to take you back to the washing place at Lyrnessus?'

Briseis had not meant the outing to be the occasion for another quarrel with Diomede. It was a break from their monotonous routine, a time for enjoyment. She tried to keep her temper down, but she was not prepared to concede her point. 'We could try to find out where the women from the harbour used to come. It could not have been here.'

'There is a place further upstream,' Iphis said, 'but it's no good when the river is so low. The soldiers must draw off more water than the harbour folk ever used. In summer the water goes nowhere near the rubbing stones.'

The water was barely a trickle, sluggish in the middle of the cracked riverbed.

'Well,' said Diomede, 'it was because of the bloodstains on your dress that we came. You'll not get them out unless you get started.' She glanced over to the guards, who had settled down with a pair of dice in the shadow of the cart at the top of the slope, and began to hitch up her skirt ready to wade into the river.

Briseis followed her, and tramped her fury into the tepid water. A moment later Iphis waded out to her and drew her a few paces away from the others.

'You must not get so angry, Briseis,' Iphis said.

'I am angry. I cannot help that.'

'Most of the marks will come out if you rub it well and then leave it to bleach in the sun.'

'Oh, it's not the washing. I quite enjoy that. It is the men who make me angry.' She threw a venomous look at the guards, as if they were to blame for everything.

'But the men are so nice to you. To all of us.'

'On the surface, maybe. It makes me furious, though, to think what they are really doing.' Iphis frowned, but Briseis plunged regardless into the familiar argument. 'It is all so wasteful. They never create anything: everything they have is plundered. And they say it has been the same in Hellas, and on the islands, for hundreds of years now. They take the best that other men have made, and use it for their own.'

'That isn't fair, Briseis,' Iphis said. 'It's not as if they chose to be Myrmidons. That is the proper thing for men to do where they come from. Men fight everywhere. You cannot complain because they do it better than most.'

'It's not the fighting I mind. It's the fact that there is nothing else. They don't fight to protect their wives and families, like the Trojans do. They don't seem to care a fig about them. It is all for gain, all piracy.'

Briseis' voice rose at the end of her speech, and Diomede, who had been moving towards the bank, heard her. She tossed back her neatly braided hair, picked up her sodden shifts and wrung them fiercely. Then she turned deliberately to Briscis. 'They do have something to fight for,' she said. 'They fight for Helen. That is why they all came to Troy. They are still here, fighting for her, eight, nearly nine years after they came. I think that is honourable of them.'

'You cannot really believe that Menelaus cares. He doesn't want her back. He just wants to avenge his honour. She is a symbol, an excuse.'

Iphis considered that as she too turned back to the bank, a bundle of washing in her arms. 'There is nothing wrong with honour. I am glad our masters are honourable men. Anyway, I shouldn't think it feels like that to Helen. Do you not believe in love?'

'Not when men mix it up with honour. I have no wish to be loved like that. I don't think men know how to love, in any case, when they have forgotten how to make things for themselves.'

'But honour is what they have made, Briseis. That is why it is so important to them.'

Briseis stopped to think, and to examine her dress. The bloodstains were nearly gone. She wrung it carefully and laid it out on the short grass on the river bank before saying, 'Perhaps you are right, Iphis. And if you are, then that is their tragedy. That when you take away the honour, there is nothing left at all. Especially not love.'

'I pity you, Briseis,' Diomede cut in crisply. 'You don't see the glory of it all. You belong to the greatest man of our time and you cannot see it. You would swap him, wouldn't you, for any farmer with a cow and a patch of beans growing? Except,' she added cruelly, 'that you cannot. Because his honour and power have ground your poor farmer into dust.'

'That,' Briseis said, 'is why I hate him. I hate them all, all these men who eat meat because they cannot be bothered to grow crops, who steal everything they possess. They have even stolen the honour that once belonged to good men like Mynes. In the end they will destroy us all. They will kill all the best men, all the ones with gentleness. What they call honour then will be more terrible than anything we have ever known. They will glean every last scrap from our world until nothing is left for any of us and it spirals down into chaos. And we are their prisoners, sitting here watching them do it.'

Diomede stood stock still by the river's edge, her face a mask of fury. She flung her bundle down onto the smooth dry stones with such force that the water splashed across them. 'Never say you hate Achilles, Briseis. Never say it. Do not even think it. You must be mad.'

'Perhaps I am.'

'Anyway, you cannot hate Patroclus,' Iphis said in a pleading voice. 'He is gentle, you would see that if you knew him better. So is Achilles in his way, when you get to know him. It's just that you don't know them, you don't give them a chance.'

'Iphis,' Diomede said, 'sometimes you are even more blind than Briseis. Ignore her. She is just jealous.'

Briseis could not make herself deny it. 'Doris,' she said quietly, 'can you put my clothes back on the cart for me? I'll not stay to wait for them to dry. I ought to go back to the hospital tent.'

'It pleases you, does it, to watch them die?'

That was too cruel to deserve an answer. She did not bother to give one as she stalked off, leaving one of the guards to scramble after her.

Privately, Ulysses endorsed Achilles' opinion that it was essential for the Achaeans to start an offensive before the summer wore on too far. He refused to express this opinion to Agamemnon, however, insisting that a confrontation with the High King could only damage the entire army.

Big Ajax agreed with Achilles, too, and he did tackle Agamemnon, perhaps ten days after the supper in the High King's hut.

Agamemnon heard out his views even more cursorily than he had listened to Achilles'. It seemed clear the High King had no intention of altering his tactics.

Nestor, who had waited to see the outcome of Ajax's endeavour, insisted that there was nothing more Achilles' supporters could do. Agamemnon had control of the army's tactics, and Idomeneus and many of the other commanders gave him wholehearted support. If Achilles had been in a position to challenge Agamemnon for the command matters might have been different. But he was not, and he knew it. He would have needed considerably more than private sympathy and half-hearted public protests from men like Nestor and Ajax and Ulysses if he were to make any headway against the High King.

Achilles pushed the Myrmidons as hard as he could during the interminable skirmishes on the plain. It was no compensation, however. Empty, ritualistic skirmishes did not win wars; an offensive at that stage just might have done.

The summer wore on. The Trojans harvested their crops, and the Achaeans raided their granaries. The leaves began to yellow. There was a day of rain, and the water level rose in the Simois and the Scamander.

Then Agamemnon unexpectedly called an assembly of the troops. He announced to them that he had decided to mount a full-scale attack on Ilios. There would be one full day for preparations, and the attack would be mounted the following day.

No hint of the announcement had reached Achilles and Patroclus beforehand. As far as Patroclus could judge, they were not the only ones who had been kept in the dark. Commander after commander rose to comment on the news. Most welcomed it, though several pointed out that there was no longer a realistic chance of defeating the Trojans outright before the war slowed to the usual winter pace. None made any reference to war councils, or even to informal soundings-out by Agamemnon.

Patroclus, who was standing next to Achilles, resisted the temptation to look to see how he had taken the news. He turned as if to walk back with Achilles as the assembly was breaking up, but Achilles shook his head. 'I want a word with Nestor. I'll see you back at the hut.'

Mildly annoyed, Patroclus stood watching him stalk off; then felt Diomedes' hand on his arm. 'Pleased?'

Patroclus frowned slightly as the Argive commander drew him away from the dispersing troops and into the quieter alleys behind Agamemnon's hut. 'I suppose so. It's more than time for us to make a move. I would be more pleased if I knew what Agamemnon was up to.'

'Spiting Achilles?' Diomedes enquired conversationally.

Before Patroclus could show his conventional exasperation at taunts of this kind he caught a hint of something else in Diomedes' face. He stopped, slowly and deliberately, and turned to face the other man. One of the grain stores was behind him; he leaned back against its rough wooden wall. 'So what will it cost me to find out?'

'Would you pay it?'

Diomedes' sly smile told him the answer. It was a price he had paid only once before, in an incident shortly after they had first arrived at the camp. He had not enjoyed the experience; but it had been a fair bargain, and Diomedes had stuck to it. And never, as far as Patroclus knew, told Achilles. 'You reckon it's worth it?'

Diomedes laughed. 'How flattering you are. What if I tell you first? Then you can decide.'

Patroclus did not move, and Diomedes took that for assent. 'He sent for a group of us yesterday. Meriones, Idomeneus, little Ajax – you can guess the rest of them. He wants someone killed in the battle. One of Priam's sons. Troilus, his name is.'

'Who?'

'We were asking that ourselves. Idomeneus reckons he knows him. He's been fighting mainly with Aeneas and the Dardanian charioteers. A sturdy kid with dark hair. Young, maybe nineteen summers, perhaps twenty. A good-looking lad. Not as if Agamemnon was ever that way inclined, though, is it?'

Patroclus ignored the jibe. 'Why?'

'You do price yourself high. You've seen many more than nineteen summers.' Diomedes' eyes narrowed, as if he were reconsidering his bargain. Then he went on more cheerfully, 'Damned if I know, anyway. Agamemnon didn't tell us that.'

'You must have some idea.'

'Oh, we all have bright ideas. Meriones' theory is that it's something to do with Chryseis. He's probably right. Agamemnon is obsessed with her. I don't suppose he would think it unacceptable to get rid of her old boyfriends.'

'And there were old boyfriends?'

Diomedes rolled his eyes. 'Does Achilles still like you to play the innocent little boy? You don't get away with it with me. You've made eyes at her too. How could there not be, with a girl like that?'

'That's hardly fair. She can't help the way she looks. She must have been a nice respectable girl before she was captured; and she's not exactly spreading her favours around now.'

'I wish she was. Agamemnon's wearing her out. He's not touched any of his other women since she came. To judge by his baggy eyes, he has her all night, every night. It's no wonder she reeks of sex. She might be a randy little piece, but with Agamemnon going at her as if every day was his last she'd hardly look for more on the side. Still, he'll tire of her before long. He always does.'

'Then you'll step in?'

Diomedes grinned at him. 'You bet.'

Patroclus barely noticed the response. He said thoughtfully, 'It seems a bloody thin reason for setting up an offensive.'

'The offensive makes sense anyway, as Achilles kept telling us. Agamemnon's no fool, he realizes that. But my guess is that that is why he's chosen to order it now.'

'It stinks.'

'Yes, it stinks. That's why I thought Achilles would be interested to hear it.'

'You don't mind if I tell him?'

Diomedes made a show of considering this, though Patroclus had the impression that he had already decided on his answer.

'If you tell him how you found out.'

'You bastard,' said Patroclus, moving away a little.

'Cool down. You'd be mad to tell him. What could he do about it if he knew?'

A good question. What could he do? Warn the lad not to fight? Stage the confrontation with Agamemnon that he had decided against earlier? Patroclus said slowly, 'It might be enough to tip him into challenging for the command.'

'Achilles as High Commander? Honourable Achilles, who never gets his hands dirty? No thank you.'

'You'd rather have Agamemnon?'

It was a stupid question, Patroclus realized as soon as he had asked it. Diomedes had always been in favour with the High King. Diomedes did take it seriously, however. 'Most of the men would, even now.'

'How did they take the order? Meriones and the rest?'

'What do you think? A few grumbles, but they'll do it. They've done some planning, asked around about the lad. Apparently he throws a straight spear, but he tends to rush in, so if a couple of us go for him at once he shouldn't stand much chance.'

'Have you fixed who'll do it?'

'You want me to promise it won't be me? Too bad. I have dirty hands too, you know that.'

Yes, he knew that. Yet Diomedes had chosen to tell him, and why? It was hardly unendurable lust that was driving him. It was not as if his reward would be Chryseis. Patroclus framed a few more questions, and deliberately threw them out, unspoken. He said instead, 'You always make yourself out to be more of a bastard than you are.'

Diomedes smiled. 'That way I get into everything that's going.'

'True. The storeroom suit you?'

Diomedes raised his eyebrows, as if the double-entendre had been unintentional after all. He gave Patroclus a long, hard look. 'Another time, maybe.'

He turned abruptly, and was gone before Patroclus had recovered his surprise.

Had Diomedes intended it as a trap? A way of coming between himself and Achilles? Patroclus considered this possibility, and then promptly dismissed it. There was no gain in that direction for Diomedes, and the man did not work like that. He had his own sense of honour, though he sometimes hid it well. If he had had a motive – and it might have been just a wild impulse that had led him to tell Patroclus – then it lay, surely, in his own distaste of the entire business.

It was not what war was about, singling out one man on the other side and deliberately murdering him. If Agamemnon had wanted to get some kind of revenge on the boy he should have done it himself, not foisted the job on a group of men with not enough scruples, or not enough courage, to turn him down.

It was the thought of this, the cold-blooded murder disguised as a clean fight, that made the conversation stick in Patroclus' mind. So he told himself. He had no particular qualms about the deal he had struck with Diomedes. He had been doing that kind of thing – not often, but when it seemed worth it – since he was a boy, and was hardly likely to get a guilty conscience about it now. What was more worrying was the awareness that once again he knew something, superficially trivial but potentially vital, that Achilles did not. He would have told Achilles, had he thought it necessary. It was just that Diomedes was right. Telling him could do no good, and might irreparably destroy Achilles' fragile coexistence with Agamemnon.

Pushing these less than comfortable thoughts to the back of his mind, Patroclus found himself coming back again and again to Chryseis. Her face swam before his eyes: one moment demure and pretty, the young girl waiting for her lover, and the next laughing and teasing, the practised whore tempting every man to do his worst. Behind her he felt he saw the shadowy image of the unknown boy, and he too changed as Patroclus watched, from a cheerful lad with his girl, to a corpse cut down on the battlefield.

Achilles eyed him with concern and Patroclus pulled himself up sharply. He would not have any man suspect him of the shakes at the prospect of the coming battle – not even Achilles, who had plenty of reason to know better.

Ironically, Agamemnon called Patroclus to dine that evening. He did not ask Achilles: they had not spoken for days. He must be sweetening the men he had kept out of the plot, Patroclus thought viciously to himself. Achilles shrugged and said he would rather plan his tactics with Ulysses, so Patroclus went along to Agamemnon's hall alone.

Chryseis was the first person he saw, and Diomedes with her. She held a winejar in one hand, as if Diomedes' empty cup had drawn her to him, and was caressing it with her free hand in a manner that was consciously lascivious, almost a parody of lechery, as she talked to him. Diomedes, frequently crude but rarely obvious, had his eyes fixed firmly on her face and not on her suggestive hand and bare breasts.

It was an act, her flirtation. Patroclus had always thought it, and watching her now it seemed to him to be a rather bad one. It crossed his mind, a shade uncomfortably, that it was the memory of his own careful flirtation that afternoon that allowed him to see through it so clearly. Was her overacting deliberate? Perhaps; yet though he was conscious of the artificiality of her gestures he was involuntarily aroused by her. He was turning away, determined to find someone else to talk to, when Diomedes caught sight of him and called him over. 'No Achilles tonight?'

'I fancied some different company for a change.' He met Diomedes' eyes as he said it, but found it impossible to interpret the other man's look.

Something in Patroclus' words, or his tone, drew Chryseis' attention to him. She broke into the conversation almost aggressively, as if she feared being excluded from it. 'Achilles always waters his wine too much from what I hear.'

And Agamemnon not enough, thought Patroclus. He replied instead, 'You must be confusing him with Ulysses.' He had an urge to cut her out, but he had no wish for another private conversation with Diomedes, so he smiled as he said it, and raised his cup for her to fill. She did so slowly and carefully. When the wine overflowed and spilled down his bare arm he had the impression that that was deliberate too. Chryseis mopped it with her hand flirtatiously, and Patroclus, shifting his attention back to Diomedes, saw open annoyance on the Argive's face. He was jealous, Patroclus suddenly realized. Of course, it was not himself that Diomedes wanted: he was well aware that it never had been, except casually, when it fitted in with other plans. Diomedes wanted Chryseis, badly enough to set carefully about getting her.

And he was welcome to her, Patroclus told himself firmly, ignoring his own inconvenient arousal. He left them to their flirtation as soon as he decently could, and crossed the room to talk to Nestor.

Nestor was cautiously cool towards him. Ignoring his manner, Patroclus said abruptly, 'What do you make of the offensive?'

'I will tell you when it's over,' the old man replied.

'Achilles told me of the plan you had for the charioteers.'

Nestor shook his head almost imperceptibly. 'Agamemnon has a sequence of meetings fixed tomorrow to decide on the campaign plan. Has he not told you of them?'

Of course not. As he had not told Achilles, and as Achilles and Nestor had not told Agamemnon of their own quite independent plans. Patroclus realized belatedly why Nestor was reluctant to be seen talking to him in front of Agamemnon. He assumed that the question did not require an answer. He took a deep draught of Agamemnon's unwatered wine and began to ask Nestor's advice about the best wood for making throwing spears.

The conversation was not engrossing, and despite his intentions to the contrary Patroclus remained acutely conscious of Chryseis as she smoothly abandoned Diomedes and made her way around the room, serving the men, teasing and flirting with all of them. He tried to avoid looking at her directly, but whenever he did so she seemed to return his look.

Did she desire him? He thought not, though she was perhaps intrigued by her earlier glimpse of a side of him that she had never encountered before. There were no more angry glances from Diomedes, so it could not be obvious to the rest of the company. She did the same with most of the men, he decided. She was finely tuned to respond to each glance and gesture that was directed towards her. Her response to Agamemnon himself was the finest of all. Watching them, Patroclus began to pick up the subtle hints from the High King that drove Chryseis to direct her attention to first this man, then that. She rarely spoke directly to Agamemnon.

What would Troilus have made of it? Patroclus wondered idly. Had Chryseis loved him once? Might she love him still, in spite of the performance she put on for her master? He left Agamemnon's quarters early, disturbed by the day's events and still in a curious state of arousal.

Walking back in the dark to his own quarters, the thought suddenly came to him that Briseis would surely know all about

Chryseis and Troilus – if there was anything to know. It might be a good thing to find out. Not that he could do anything about it, he supposed, any more than Achilles could. But there would be a cold consolation in fitting together the pieces of the puzzle.

Achilles was not in their quarters. Ulysses always kept late hours, and it was unlikely that he would be back for some time. The hut was empty, save for a couple of sleepy dogs. Patroclus took some more wine from the bowl on the trestle and flung himself restlessly into the chair.

It would be one thing to ask Briseis; it was quite another to ask her late at night. If he called her then she would hardly expect a conversation about Chryseis. Nor, he added to himself, would she welcome one. Would she welcome his making love to her? Yes. He had no doubt that she would. With that thought his desire came back, and it suddenly focussed, with alarming strength and clarity, not on Agamemnon's girl but on Achilles'.

And yet Briseis was not Achilles' girl. Patroclus had kept his word and not spoken to her since the conversation with Achilles; but Achilles had made no move to call her, and as more and more time had gone by he had become increasingly resentful. If Achilles really wanted her he should have done something about it, damn him.

It was not a sufficient excuse. Patroclus knew it, but in his sudden urgency he pushed the knowledge aside. He rose abruptly from the low chair, went to track down a messenger, and told him to send Briseis across.

Briseis was more than surprised when the messenger came to the women's tents. The other women exchanged glances, then stared at her in blatant curiosity to see how she was taking it. They had an unspoken agreement never to talk about these things, but there was no legislating for looks. Let them, she thought furiously. She went through the motions of combing her hair and changing her dress as coolly and deliberately as she could manage under their gaze.

She had not finished when Diomede spoke. 'Briseis. Has Achilles told you that you should obey Patroclus' orders?'

The question stung, and she spun round angrily. 'It's none of your business.'

'Calm down. I am not trying to get at you. You don't think I wanted to say anything, do you?'

'Why on earth did you, then?'

The other girls were watching, on edge. For all the tension that Briseis had fostered recently, there had never been an open fight amongst them. Diomede felt their hostility and turned to stare them down. She waited calmly until the temperature fell. Then she turned back to Briseis. 'To protect you.'

'I don't want your bloody protection.'

'You'll get it anyway. All Achilles' women do; and you're Achilles' woman, even if he never sends for you. It's his orders that you have to obey. Nobody else's.'

'Don't be ridiculous, Diomede,' Doris said. 'It's not as if Agamemnon has sent for her.'

'That's not the point.' Diomede flushed, but she was determined to finish. 'All right, they are good friends, but it could still be very nasty for Briseis if they fell out over it.'

'They don't normally share any of us,' one of the other girls said.

'Worse luck.' There was general laughter at that. Diomede did not join in, and nor did Briseis, nor Iphis, sitting rigid in a corner of the tent. Diomede's cool tones cut through the laughter before it had died down. 'So if Achilles wants her to go to Patroclus he ought to tell her so himself. Patroclus must know that perfectly well.'

Briseis was shaking. She had an urge to turn and walk straight out of the tent, but she would have to come back before morning and she knew she should try to get the situation under control before she left. She had to appease Diomede and stop her from making trouble over it. In the levellest voice she could manage, she said, 'It's all right, Diomede. Thank you for saying it. It was very thoughtful of you.'

'I couldn't let you walk into that kind of trouble. Achilles might kill you for it.'

A couple of the girls murmured at that; but it was true, and Briseis knew it. She could not think of a reply. It did not enter her head to submit to Diomede. She longed to be away from them all, and alone with Patroclus.

'I'll go across to tell Patroclus that you cannot come.' Diomede must have intended it to sound cool and decisive, but it came across as bitchily triumphant.

No. Briseis would not humiliate him like that. 'There is no need to do that.'

'One of us ought to go with you, then. That would make it all right if he just had some reason to talk with you.'

'No. Thank you.'

'So Achilles did tell you to obey him?'

She took a deep breath. 'He must have done, mustn't he?'

Briseis walked a few paces from the tent, then stopped. She would have to calm down a little before she faced him. Anyway, she tried to tell herself, he probably does just want to talk. Her body was not fooled. It seemed a very long time since she had touched a man, and she had always known that this one wanted her. A couple of soldiers walked by and she quivered at their glance. She rushed the rest of the way to the men's hut. The gate to the courtyard was open. She went through it, hardly noticing the dogs as they sniffed at her. And opened the door very, very slowly.

He was perhaps a man's length from the door. It was too far, and not far enough. They stood looking at each other for a long moment, and then she was in his arms and he was crushing the breath out of her with his kiss. It was some time before they even remembered to shut the door.

At first their lovemaking was hard and desperate. They had both been waiting too long. Later, it was slow, sweet and intense. Each move, each touch, was amazingly new and reassuringly familiar at the same time, as if they had always been like this together. Maybe Achilles came back at some point. They were too wrapped up in each other to care. If he did he must have left again without saying a word.

They did not speak at all until much later. She lay entwined with him in the shadows of the bed. The lamp was burning low, and it was black night outside. They were exhausted, at ease together, and too happy to sleep.

'Why did you send for me? Why tonight?'

He turned to her with a laugh. 'I thought I'd already told you.'

'Oh, I knew you wanted me. But you had already decided not to have me. What made you change your mind?' It did not cross hers that Achilles might really have given him permission. She was quite certain he had not.

Momentarily, he was grateful for the dark. There are some things it does not do to say, even to lovers. It seemed that any reason he gave would break the atmosphere of contentment. The guilt would have to come, but please, not that night. 'There was something I wanted to talk to you about. It can wait.'

She did not press to discover what it was. 'So you had not meant it to happen?'

'No. Well, I don't think so. But it was always going to, wasn't it?'

She smiled back lazily, and then reached to pull him closer. 'Yes. It always was.'

They were both drowsy. He wondered briefly if he should send her back to the women's tent. It might be awkward in the morning. But the morning was a long way off, and he did not want to lose her yet. He was not often cruel to Achilles. He would just have to hope it did not hurt too much this time. They kissed again and drifted to sleep in each other's arms.

Patroclus woke first. It was barely dawn. The air was cool, and the sky red. Perhaps there would be more rain. Not a good omen, with the battle tomorrow, he thought wearily to himself.

There was no sign of Achilles. He slid out of bed without waking Briseis, dressed in a rough tunic and sandals, tucked his dagger in his belt, and went in search of him.

He found him in the marshes by the seashore, out at the very edge of the camp. They kept the chariot horses tethered there, where the grass was still green at the end of the summer. Achilles must have been awake for some time. Perhaps he had slept with the horses. He often did before a battle, as if it would strengthen the bond between them and help to keep him safe.

Achilles had three horses. His father Peleus had given him a pair, Xanthus and Balius, which he had brought over from Thessaly. They were fast and sturdy, and he knew them even better than he knew Patroclus. He had taken a third horse, a big Trojan gelding he called Pedasus, as plunder from Thebe, and he and Patroclus had been working all summer to weld the three into a fighting team. It was the Hittite fashion to drive three horses in harness instead of two, and word had spread that it gave them an unassailable advantage.

There were few soldiers around, and they were giving him a wide berth. It was clear that Achilles was planning to take the team out. It would do them good to get a fast, easy run early in the day and then rest till the next morning. As Patroclus approached he was working steadily, setting the wheels on the axle of the war chariot, tightening the bolts, and harnessing the horses. It was not a task he normally did himself and he frowned slightly with concentration while he worked out the details of the harness. He did not look up as the other man came up to him.

'You cannot handle all three of them by yourself if you run into anyone. Shall I ride with you?'

Achilles turned very slowly to look at him. Patroclus braced himself. The look was even harder than a hit would have been, but he did not flinch.

Achilles turned away again as he spoke. 'We'll take them out past the boundary fence.' The heavy wooden stockade that marked out the limits of the Achaean camp was barely a bow-shoot away. 'I doubt if we shall meet anyone so early. Did you bring your spear?'

They kept light throwing spears in the chariot, but not their thrusting spears. It would be madness to risk going beyond the camp without them. 'No, it's back at the hut.'

'I have mine.' He handed it over, expressionless. Patroclus was not used to handling one so heavy, but he said nothing. 'I shall take the reins,' Achilles continued. 'You can take over if we meet anyone, and I will do the fighting.'

It was Patroclus who normally drove the horses, while Achilles fought. He watched Achilles whip them into a gallop with a blank face. Achilles drove fast, faster than Patroclus would have risked with the battle coming up. He did it carefully, though, knowing as well as the other man that it would not do to lame a horse on the rough ground.

Achilles did not drive out across the plain. He had no interest, it seemed, in checking out the terrain before the battle. Instead he kept close to the shoreline, just out of reach of the spray. The sea was rough, the waves hissing and squealing on the stony beaches.

They drove a long way. Past the tumuli that marked the graves of the war dead, past the great mound where Hercules was said to be buried. Past the ruins of Trojan villages, long since abandoned. Redshanks and sandpipers rose screeching from the scrub as the chariot came close to them; the gulls cawed above the waves. There were no other human beings in sight. Finally Achilles reined in the horses hard, pulled them round in a wide half circle, and set back for the camp.

The morning was quiet, and the wind seemed to blow away the emotions of the night. They did not speak at all until they were back within the fence and the horses had been unharnessed and rubbed down.

'You will want your spear back.' Patroclus held it out as he spoke.

'Yes.' Achilles paused. 'I shall not argue with you now. We'll talk about it after the battle.'

As they were walking back to the huts he added quietly, 'I'll tell Nestor that if anything happens to me, she is to go to you.'

Patroclus could not trust himself to reply.

■

Agamemnon is like a whirlpool, Chryseis thought to herself. His force reaches out to gather people in. And suck them, first close to the swirling centre, then faster, round and round, and down, down, under the surface, until they drown in the depths of the water.

She did not feel as if she was drowning now. It was as if she had found the still centre, way down inside. She could not escape from him, but she was still alive.

Indeed, she seemed to have caught the knack of power from him. She used it in her flirtation, playing with the men, growing bolder and more aggressive, watching the effect as her sexual force crackled across the room. It brought the two of them closer in a way. They both took such pleasure in controlling others.

Her weapons did not work against him, though. He always spun round a little too fast, and before she had had time to thrust them at him, he had turned them round and pointed them back at her. Even the sex – that most of all. It seemed a strange naivety now that had ever led her to think she might manipulate him in that way. He hit her less and less often, but it was always a battle. It was she, not he, who would lose it every time. However she fought it she would be driven beyond control first, and would beg him to take her harder, harder, as he watched her abandonment with a face that was contained and oh, so knowing. He would play with her like a cat with a mouse, making her wait until it pleased him to give her satisfaction. Only when she lay exhausted, at a point beyond both pleasure and pain, would he let himself become vulnerable. Then there was nothing she could do to stop him taking his own pleasure exactly as he chose.

She could not imagine how it would end. It would be terrible if he were to tire of her. She had no illusions about what would happen to her then. The looks of Diomedes and Meriones, hot and excited across the supper table, told her that the women's quarters would not be secure enough to protect her from their desires if Agamemnon himself decided not to. She believed he would not. His commitment to her lasted only as long as he desired her. Afterwards it would be too much trouble, and he was not a sentimental man. She could not protect herself. Too much of her present power came at second-hand from him.

Or perhaps their nemesis would come from within. At first, it had seemed to Chryseis that there were no limits to their relationship. Now she knew better. The limits were set far out, but they were real. He had never scarred her body, never lent her to another man, never insulted or humiliated her in public. She had done things for him against her better judgement, things which made her feel guilty and ashamed when she thought about them. But there were still some things, she said to herself, that she would not do, not let him do. Not that she had ever refused him anything yet. Except the business about Troilus, and then she had not held out for long. It had always been he who determined the limits. Still, if he ever stepped beyond the final limits . . . that would be the end, disaster, death perhaps for one or both of them. Well, if it was not she who thrust the dagger in his chest and pulled it out, dripping with blood, then it would be some other woman, that was for certain.

She thought all this as she lay waiting for him. It was late in the evening. Agamemnon had announced the offensive that afternoon, and he was still discussing its details with his closest advisers, Menelaus and Idomeneus and Meriones and the rest, long after the other men who had dined with them had departed and she had gone to bed.

Chryseis yawned. She was reluctant to go to sleep before he came. It would anger him. There had been something excited about him that day, as if he smelled triumph. He would be sure to want her: as she wanted him. She smiled to herself. It would be a poor thing to belong to a man who did not master her so completely. She should liven up, and think of something new that she could do to him that night. A little shiver of lust went through her. It had not quite subsided when Agamemnon came through the door.

He smiled at her. There was something brisk and businesslike about him, as if his thoughts were still on the campaign and his discussion with the others. 'I'm glad you are not asleep.'

Chryseis smiled too, and pulled the covers back, walking across the room to him. There was an ease about her nakedness, born of beauty and the absolute confidence that he desired her. She put her arms around his neck, and was about to whisper her suggestions into his ear, when to her surprise she felt him push her gently but firmly away. He held her at arms' length.

'Later. I want to talk to you first. Put on your shift, and come and sit down.'

He crossed to the little inlaid table, not looking at her, and lit a second lamp as she was dressing. She felt put down, like a small child whose favourite toy had been taken away.

Chryseis sat properly, and tried to look serious and sympathetic. It must be something about the war, she thought. She wished she had listened harder over supper. But he did not normally discuss that kind of thing with her, and she took no personal interest in it. It did not seem to her that anything that happened in the battles, barring Agamemnon's own death — which she rightly reckoned to be unlikely — would affect her situation at all. 'Is it something about the fighting?'

The serious expression came across to him as a slight frown. 'In a way. It is nothing to be alarmed about.' He carried straight on, keeping up the initiative. 'There are some things I want you to tell me. It will not take long, and then we can get to bed.'

The frown deepened a little. 'What kind of things? I know nothing about fighting. You know that, darling.'

'I never doubted that, my dear. I would hardly ask you to advise me how to set my shield or throw my spear.' He laughed: a hard, tinny sound. 'But you can help a little by telling me about the town. Where the main buildings are from the gates, how wide the streets are, where the sentries stand guard, that sort of thing.' The frown was growing deeper still, and he added quickly, 'Nothing complicated. I know you are tired, but it will be best if you tell me tonight. Then I can discuss it with the commanders in the morning.'

'The town? You mean Ilios?'

'Yes, of course.'

It struck her as suspicious that he had not mentioned the name. True, there was only one town he could mean, but it was as if he was trying to hide something from her. She did not answer for a moment, and Agamemnon spoke brusquely into the silence. 'Let's start with the palace. It's on the top of the hill, isn't it? The highest building we can see from the camp. And it faces south?' She still made no sound, and he repeated the question, trying to keep the impatience out of his voice. 'The palace. The main entrance is to the south?'

Chryseis looked down at the floor. The dim light of the oil lamps did not reach it, and its shadows could have told her nothing. But she seemed to come to some kind of decision, and she looked up, and across to the High King. 'I don't think I should tell you that kind of thing.'

'Don't be ridiculous. It's nothing so special. Any casual travel-ler to Ilios could tell me that.'

'But there are no casual travellers these days. No Achaean travellers, anyway. The Achaeans are enemies to Ilios.'

'That is why I am asking you, because you can help us in this little way.'

'Well, I would rather you asked somebody else.'

'I am not asking somebody else. I am asking you.' He said it like a parent faced with a stubborn child: hoping politeness will work, but quite prepared to enforce obedience if necessary.

'I'm sorry.' The voice quivered a little, as if she was expecting to be punished, but there was no hint in it that she was about to change her mind.

Agamemnon tried again. 'If it is the thought of the palace that worries you we can start with something else. Tell me about the road that leads up from the Dardanian Gate. How wide is it? Could you drive a cart up it? Or is it too steep for that?'

Chryseis shook her head. 'I am not going to tell you any of these things. I'm sorry, but I am not.' She stood up, as if she were about to go back to bed.

He stood almost at the same time, and caught hold of her wrist. 'Sit down. I have not yet finished with you.'

'I won't talk. Honestly I won't. Even if you beat me.'

'Yes you will.' Her resistance disconcerted him. She had sometimes made a pretence of refusing his sexual demands, but that was to excite him. This was not exciting him, it was annoying him, as she must realize. It was not how they usually played their games, and he did not like it.

'No. I don't think I should. I dare say you could find out that sort of thing from somebody else easily enough, but you will not get it from me. It isn't right. I was a guest in Ilios, and I think it would be very wrong to tell you all about the town. It's obvious why you want to know. It's in case you manage to break down the walls during the offensive, isn't it?'

In fact Agamemnon knew very well that there was almost no possibility of that happening. His motives were longer term, and more confused. It would not help him to reveal them to her, though. 'Do you not want us to win the war? I could take you back to Mycenae then. It is a much finer town than Ilios.'

Chryseis sat down again, abruptly. She twisted her hands together in her lap as she spoke. 'You treat me as a child, don't you? A cute little kid, who will do just as you ask if you bribe it with something pretty.'

'I treat you like a woman in bed.' He was beginning to think he should have fucked her first. It would have made her more submissive.

'That has nothing to do with it.' Her voice was growing harder. 'Whether or not I fancy an exciting trip to Mycenae has nothing to do with it. Really, it is about doing the right thing: not what I want, but what I think is right. And I do not think it is right to tell you about Ilios. Oh, the things you have asked so far are innocent enough, even I know that, but if I tell you about them you will ask more questions, and it will be harder to say no. In the end I might tell you things that I should not, things that could mean disaster for the people I know there.'

'You flatter yourself, my dear. I do not imagine you know many state secrets.'

She glared at him. 'I do not imagine you will ever find out if I do.'

'Do you feel no loyalty towards me?'

A pause, as she considered her answer. 'Yes. I suppose I do. So long as you treat me honourably. And for all the things you do to me in bed, I suppose you have done, so far. I agree to them, don't I?' She looked up at him, with a small, cruel smile. 'But I do not agree to this. And no, I will feel not a scrap of loyalty towards you if you make me a traitor to the Trojans. I should hate you for that, and I should hate myself even more.'

Her words did not seem to move him at all. He sat and looked at her for some time. He looked down and fiddled with the great sharp-cut ruby ring that adorned his middle finger. Then he spoke. His words hung in the air. 'I think I will call for Diomedes. I saw how he was eyeing you over dinner. He will come quickly. I shall watch you, and tell him exactly what to do to you.'

'Go ahead, if that is what you want.' She had hardly hesitated. The threat disappointed her slightly. It was sordid and unpleasant, but banal. I know him now, she thought to herself. He cannot catch me by surprise any more.

Agamemnon watched her for another moment, as if to give her time to change her mind. Then he strode to the door, and was gone. She thought briefly about running away. There was nowhere to run to, though. Instead she went back to bed. Some time later she got up to snuff out the lights. It was hard to sleep while they were burning.

She must have fallen asleep then, for when she woke it was morning, and she was still alone.

■

The women's megaron at the palace in Ilios was a great echoing room. Cool and light, it had white walls, red pillars, and a gypsum floor painted in a design of red squares and circles. There were no windows to the outside, but along one wall, above a low stone bench, there was an opening to a narrow inner light well.

The looms were always set ready for work. Hecuba often had two or three pieces in progress at once, moving from one loom to another as the fancy took her. Helen's yellow-gold fabric, Polyxena's red, sat half-finished as if those ladies would return to their work at any moment. A group of serving girls were spinning and carding wool in a corner, but only one shuttle was in motion: Cassandra's. Just then Andromache entered, and Cassandra, seeing her, set the shuttle down and waited as Andromache approached. Andromache nodded at her friend and turned to peer at the length of cloth that was taking shape within the heavy wooden frame.

'Say something polite,' Cassandra prompted.

'It's lovely even work, Cassandra. And good thread, too. Who does your spinning for you?'

'One of the palace girls. I'll send her to you if you're short. It's an acanthus design. I've already finished one piece. See?' She took the thin strip of cloth up from a stool, opened the folds, and smiled sharply at Andromache.

'And it will hide the dirt well.'

The cloth was dark-dyed, a sort of mud colour, and the leaves were worked in undyed stuff, bright against it.

'Won't it just. Perhaps I should use it for cleaning rags.'

'Oh dear me no, what a waste that would be. Why not give it to your mother? To make a dancing dress?'

Cassandra could not help laughing. Andromache could be so funny when you got to know her, though she did still jump like a startled sheep when anyone played a real joke on her. 'It would not look right in red, Andromache. Honestly it wouldn't.'

Andromache met her gaze, owlishly. 'I still don't know how you do it, Cassandra. You use the same yarns as everyone else, and the same patterns, and somehow it always looks so different.'

'And you think that is an accident. No, you're right, I suppose it is. I could not do your kind of work if I tried. Anyway, I like it.' Cassandra picked up her shuttle again with an apologetic glance. 'If I finish this strip this morning I can set it on my other dark dress and wear it for the battle tomorrow. Now it would suit that very nicely, don't you think?'

'Battle?'

Cassandra worked another few rows and bent to bite off a loose thread before replying. 'Hector really should have told you.'

'He's planning an attack for tomorrow?'

'No, Agamemnon is.'

The words sank in, and Andromache paled. 'How on earth do you know that, Cassandra?'

'From the shrine.' Looking up, she caught sight of Andromache's face. 'Not straight from Apollo, you turnip. Did you not know the chief priest is a master spy?'

Andromache quivered.

'Laugh, come on. I meant it as a joke.' Cassandra, with a pang of guilt, went to hug her sister-in-law. She led her to sit on the bench by the light well. Polyxena came in just then and joined them, sending one of the serving girls to fetch them a drink. Andromache, recovering, sipped at the hot mint tea and said, 'But there really is going to be a battle?'

Cassandra sighed under her breath. 'Yes, there really is going to be a battle. And I really did hear it from the shrine. I thought you knew. All the spies exchange messages at the shrine. It's the one place that is neutral territory, where the Achaeans can go openly. There is no secret about the battle. Priam knows. Hector has made all the preparations.'

'So the enemy are hoping to surprise us,' Andromache said slowly, 'and really we will be expecting them.'

'I doubt if Agamemnon is quite that woolly-headed. He will take it for granted the spies will have told us. He just gets the advantage of deciding when to attack.'

'I cannot see why he should attack right now.'

'Apollo,' said Cassandra, twisting her cup in her hands, 'did not tell me that.'

'Did he tell you anything? The God?'

Cassandra examined her sister-in-law carefully, as if she was not sure whether she in turn was being teased. Then she said, 'I would know if anything disastrous was about to happen. I always do feel it. You believe that, don't you?'

Andromache was still pale, and she did not look entirely convinced. Cassandra stood abruptly, spilling the dregs of her tea down the dark stuff of her dress. She paced across the room, oblivious to the stain, and announced dramatically, 'Hector will not die tomorrow. Or Troilus. Or Helenus, I am sure of that. Or Achilles.'

'I cannot say I care about Achilles.'

'Ah, but Polyxena does.' The sharp eyes turned to Polyxena, who flushed, and then grinned. She said in a light voice, 'Life would be a lot duller if Achilles were killed.'

'It would be a lot safer, I would have thought,' Andromache retorted.

'Who wants safety? No, don't tell me, you do.' Polyxena stood up with a similar gesture to Cassandra's, though she was careful to avoid the cups, and said deliberately, 'I am going to talk to Troilus. He needs calming down.'

Andromache watched her leave the room, then turned to Cassandra and said, 'She's not serious, is she? Caring about Achilles?'

Cassandra smiled, cuttingly. 'It suits her to make a joke of it. Then it doesn't hurt so much when Helen and I tease her.'

'You mean it's true.'

'Maybe half true. If Achilles were a Trojan, every woman in

Ilios would fancy herself in love with him. As it is, he just has Polyxena as a devoted admirer.'

'She sees him?'

'Don't be ridiculous. How could she? Maybe she has seen him once or twice at the shrine. It's not an affair, just a . . . fascination. And face it, how many fascinating men are there in Ilios?'

'Hector,' Andromache said loyally. Then she could not stop herself laughing as Cassandra did. She sobered down, and added, 'Or Aeneas, maybe?'

'Oh, Andromache. Not even you could manage to fall in love with Aeneas. Anyway, he's too short for Polyxena. Achilles is nice and tall, though I never cared for red hair myself. Did you know that Achilles has Briseis?'

'Has her?'

'As a slave. A captive. I heard that from the shrine too.'

Andromache thought. 'Did you hear who has Chryseis as well?'

'Naturally.'

'And?'

'And?'

'Who has her, Cassandra?'

Cassandra smiled. 'Can you not guess?'

Andromache frowned. 'Achilles, you mean?'

'No, of course not. Agamemnon, I mean. Girls like Chryseis go to men like Agamemnon. Don't worry. She will survive it.'

'Chryseis,' said Andromache with a sharpness of her own, 'would survive most things.'

Cassandra came to sit by her again. 'The problem,' she said, 'would come if Troilus managed to kill Agamemnon. I am not sure what would happen to Chryseis then, but it probably wouldn't be pleasant.'

'Would he have any chance?'

'He means to try. Aeneas is worried. He reckons Troilus is a mite too reckless. But I told you, Troilus is not going to die yet.'

'The God told you.'

'Yes, The God told me. Anyway, he doesn't want to die.'

Andromache considered that. She was not sure if it was a valid argument. Then she thought, and said, 'Cassandra, I thought you told me you were not fascinated by Aeneas?'

'Did I really say that?' Cassandra enquired to the air with a deliberately vague expression.

■

The petty war with Chryseis distracted Agamemnon more than he liked to admit from preparations for the real battle with the Trojans. He tried to tell himself that the two were linked, that it was essential to get her co-operation before the attack began. It was not true, though. It was just that he could not come to terms with his defeat.

How stupid he had been to make a threat and not carry it out. That was the trouble. When he had said the words he had been quite certain that he would go through with it if necessary. He had made much nastier threats to women in the past, and stuck to them without qualms. He had felt just the same way when he had left her. He had even sent for Diomedes; but while he was waiting for the man he had begun to have doubts. He had not expected her to turn stubborn after she had taken so much from him. It had been exciting, the prospect of defeating her, but the threat had seemed poorly matched to the challenge. If it had worked, he had had an uneasy feeling it might have knocked the spirit out of her, and stopped her from playing their little games so enthusiastically in future. That had not been his intention at all. He had not liked to dwell on the possibility that it might have failed.

It would not have done to send Diomedes away unsatisfied after he had been called from his bed. Agamemnon had taken him in search of a couple of other slave girls, ones he had tired of the year before, who had reacted with predictable apathy to his demands. The whole appeal of Chryseis was in her lack of apathy. It was not as easy to despise her. Indeed, she tended to despise the other girls herself. Somehow it had never occurred to her, Agamemnon suspected, to class herself with them.

He had told himself that Chryseis would just have to wait till the morning. That had made perfect sense in the night. If Diomedes had been disappointed he had not shown it. He had probably enjoyed what he was offered, the girls had been all right in their way, and he had taken his several times, and in some positions that had surprised even Agamemnon. Agamemnon had stirred himself to emulate the Argive, though it had been hard to work up the right amount of enthusiasm. The little orgy had left him briefly satisfied; but it had all been even more difficult in the morning. Agamemnon would not have stooped to make the same threat again. He had not trusted himself to make a stronger one along the same lines. And what else was there to threaten?

Yes, he had thought seriously of telling her of the order to kill Troilus. He had not wanted to do that, however. It was tempting fate too far to tell her before the boy was dead; and he had thought she might take it badly. He had ordered it done for his private satisfaction, not with any intention of telling her about it.

The problem occupied him all morning. It left him with only half a mind to put to the final campaign plans and the first of the talks to the troops. This will not do, Agamemnon said to himself. I do not want the offensive to be handed to Achilles on a silver dish. I shall have to put some effort into it if I am to keep control. I shall just have to go to see her, and drive some sense into her head. By midday, he was hurrying back to his private quarters.

Chryseis was sitting in the inner room where she had met Briseis. It was cool after the heat of the sun outside, and there was a scent of roses in the air. She had been mending the torn ruffles of a dress. She set down the needle when he entered and greeted him quite unconcernedly, as if they had parted on the best of terms. That was disconcerting too. It would have been easy if she had given some sign of repentance.

He did not take her to bed. He called the servant to bring chairs – he would not sit on the floor, as she had done – and when they were seated she asked politely about the preparations. He told her a little, nothing too technical. She asked if she could do anything for him. He did not think she meant the questions about Ilios. No, he said. Yes. Go and sacrifice for me.

He always felt a coward when a battle approached. He envied Achilles, and the others to whom it seemed to come so easily. He even told her that. She came across, sat on his knee, and held him like a lover. He felt like a lover. He kissed her. It was not exactly their usual style, but it seemed right at the time.

And he went away, with things between them changed irrevocably. It seemed he had given in gracefully.

He did not think about her again all afternoon. He ate with his commanders that evening, and she did not appear. There was no call for her to: they were still arguing tactics, drawing maps of the plain in the spilt wine on the trestle, and planning out the troop dispositions. When the meeting broke up he went in search of her before going to sleep with the troops in the open, as they expected of him.

She smiled when he entered the room, an open, friendly smile with nothing of the whore in it, and came across to be kissed, like a child about to go to bed. 'I made the sacrifice to Apollo. Do you mind? You sacrificed to Zeus yourself?'

'Should I mind?' The words meant little to him, it was the tone that mattered. Loving, eager to please.

'No, of course not.' She reached up to pull him towards her, and he kissed her again. 'Sleep tight.'

'And you.' She slipped away from him and studied his face with apparent contentment. He felt her eyes still on him as he shut the door.

Later, on the hard ground with his shield for a pillow, he found himself mulling over the business. It really was not possible to treat somebody like a slave, he concluded, unless they agreed to it. Certainly he could have treated her badly; but she just did not seem to think like a slave.

It did not bother him particularly to think about the power he had given her over him. He did not expect her to use it against him. Loyalty? Was that the word? Strangely, he felt it too. When he slept it was heavily, with no dreams that he remembered in the morning. He woke to a rosy dawn, and as his groom tied on his breastplate and greaves he felt more fervour than he had known since he was young and innocent. It would not be too bad, he thought, to be killed that day:

provided it was quick, and not too painful. It would be even better to stay alive.

It would have been too much to hope for a surprise. Of course the Trojans had spies, as well as guards on watch. The sun was high by the time the Achaeans had lined up on the ground they chose, backing onto the dry bed of the Scamander, and by then the Trojans were forming up their troops on the other edge of the plain, near the course of the little river Simois.

The heralds went through the usual preliminaries. Talthybius, for the Achaeans, demanded Helen back and received the conventional refusal. The Trojans proposed a formal single combat instead of a full-scale battle. Agamemnon occasionally accepted this suggestion – while ensuring that not too much would depend on the outcome – but this time he had given Talthybius orders to refuse it. Both parties confirmed the signals for a surrender, the arrangements for concluding a truce.

While these negotiations dragged on Agamemnon looked at the foot soldiers. The best spearmen were lined up in front, in three solid rows, with the rabble of stone-throwers behind them, straggling back to the river bank, and a flanking guard of archers.

The Mycenaeans were formed solidly, their front line as straight as a spear-cast. Next to them, Diomedes' Argive troops were stirring restlessly. Agamemnon paused when his eye came to the Myrmidons, on the far flank. Was Achilles slipping? Or was it his wishfulness that saw something ragged about their line?

'Hot for action?' Diomedes' chariot was next to his own, and the Argive seemed packed with excitement. Agamemnon smiled back exultantly. For once, he was impatient for the battle to begin.

The heralds returned to the commanders. Agamemnon called out the orders for the advance, and the heralds echoed them. The soldiers lifted their spears, all along the line, as each contingent acknowledged the order. The trumpets blared, and the lines slowly moved forward.

The first spearmen clashed with their Trojan counterparts. The archers tensed their bows and loosed their first arrows. In a flurry of dust, the chariots launched forward across the plain.

Agamemnon's sudden confidence seemed to have gone to his

head. His charioteer took his exhortations rather too literally and drove almost up to the Trojan chariots before pulling the horses back and waiting for him to dismount. Agamemnon threw his javelins, a little wildly, at the nearest Trojan, and jumped from the car.

His landing on the hard ground jarred him and he had scarcely regained his balance before a sturdy young Trojan, with a good bronze breastplate and helmet and an air of absorption about him, was at him with spear poised. Agamemnon brought his shield up, falling to one knee. The Trojan thrust at the same moment, and the sharp bronze point of his spear, glancing off the bronze surface of the shield, dragged along Agamemnon's upper arm, cutting right through the thick linen. Agamemnon faltered, his knees seeming to give way beneath him. The Trojan moved forward, exultant, and his battle cry echoed in Agamemnon's ears.

The world went black for a moment. When Agamemnon was able to focus again he found himself sprawling on the dusty ground, behind a solid row of Achaean fighters: Meriones, Diomedes and half a dozen members of his own guard. Their weight of numbers was pushing back the Trojans, and a small space had cleared in front of the High King.

He stumbled to his feet, leaning heavily on the shaft of the thrusting spear he had not yet used. Blood was welling out of the wound and down his arm. A soldier crossed to give him a hand, and turning at a cry close by, he saw that his driver and chariot were there. The driver reached to pull him back into the chariot and immediately set the whip to the horses. Agamemnon, pale and panting, did not notice what had happened to the Trojan.

The charioteer drew up the horses close to the river bank. They were well out of range of the Trojans, and he slipped the reins around a branch of a low tamarisk tree before coming to check Agamemnon's wound. He had a thin strip of linen bandage in a pocket at the side of the car; he tore off part of this and used it to bind the High King's arm.

Agamemnon slipped down to sit on the narrow back rail of the car. He looked vacantly at his bandaged arm. It was years since he had last suffered an injury.

The wound did not hurt him. His main emotion was a dull astonishment that he should have retreated so quickly, and without killing his man. It was the charioteer's fault. He turned on the man, his anger surging to a peak, and shouted curses at him. The charioteer bore it indifferently, and by the time a few of his guard reached them, Agamemnon's fury had subsided.

The guard had brought with them one of the scavengers whose job it was to retrieve javelins. The man had a couple of Trojan spears, fine and straight, and Agamemnon thought momentarily of returning to the fray and loosing them. The thought made his arm begin to ache. He had forgotten how unpleasant injuries could be.

It would be more prudent, the soldiers hastily reassured him, to watch the battle from a good vantage point. Talthybius and the other heralds would carry his orders to the other commanders. Agamemnon looked around. The river bank was not a good vantage point. He could see something of the fighting, but he was not high enough to make any sense of it.

He told the charioteer to drive on, and the soldiers ran after them. They stopped at the foot of one of the tumuli near the shore, and Agamemnon, dismounting, slowly climbed the little hill. From its summit he could see the shape of the battle.

The Mycenaean and Athenian troops in the centre were holding their ground well against the core of Ilian and Dardanian troops. Diomedes' Argives had advanced against a contingent of Carians, and little Ajax's Locrians were doing well against a Thracian division. The charioteers were evenly matched. The Trojan archers were always the stronger, but the wind was not in their favour, and Agamemnon reckoned they were unlikely to turn the course of the battle.

The Myrmidons should have done that. Set against the Lydians and Lycians, they should have been able to push forward, outflank their opponents and attack the rear of the main Trojan army. As it was, they had barely advanced a spearthrow. It was not enough.

'Where is Achilles?' he asked the heralds.

Achilles was fighting, they replied. He was fighting hard, though not brilliantly: had already killed a Ciconian and his charioteer, had wounded one of Priam's bastards. He was taking no interest, though, in the progress of the Myrmidon spearmen. He had delegated command of them to Automedon before the battle began.

Agamemnon offered a fervent curse to Zeus under his breath. Exasperating of Achilles. Though it would make little difference, he told himself, in the long run. The battle already had all the marks of an indecisive action. It would not bring the Achaeans to the walls of Ilios – not that he had ever expected that – but it would give the Trojans no advantage either. Perhaps it would be as well if Achilles' men had nothing to boast about afterwards.

The neat plan of the battle had disintegrated by then. The foot soldiers were milling around the chariots, the heralds complained, completely blocking off the line of retreat of some of the champions. The archers were useless now: in the mêlée it was impossible for them to tell Achaeans from Trojans. The spearmen's arms were aching, their thrusts losing power, and their spear points battered where they were not broken.

Agamemnon thought of ordering a retreat. It would blunt Achilles' arguments more effectively though, he reckoned, if the men fought on to exhaustion. He sent Talthybius with orders to Idomeneus to command a final thrust forward.

Before the chief herald had even reached Idomeneus the rain came. It pattered gently on Agamemnon's bronze helmet, splashed on his face, soaked slowly into his linen tunic. He found it pleasing. It would refresh the soldiers, he told himself.

Perhaps it did, for a moment. The fighting seemed to intensify. Then Agamemnon, moving a pace forward, found himself slithering on the damp grass of the tumulus; and he realized that the whole plain was becoming slippery and treacherous.

Talthybius returned. 'Idomeneus advises a withdrawal,' he said. 'The Trojan heralds have signalled that they want to pull back.'

Agamemnon made a show of reluctance before giving Talthybius orders to confirm the withdrawal. Slowly, the noise of the battle faded. The rain was falling more heavily; it cut down visibility, and Agamemnon had to rely on the heralds to tell him when the army had reformed. His charioteer took him to its head, where Idomeneus, Diomedes and the rest greeted him exhaustedly. Slowly – for the ground had become even more slippery, and the plain was littered with corpses – the ragged ranks of the Achaean army moved back towards the gate in the great stockade.

It had rather pleased Agamemnon to envisage Chryseis as a nurse: washing the cut, clotting the blood with yarrow powder, and bandaging the arm with loving care. She was genuinely concerned when he got back to his quarters, but protested that she had no idea about that sort of thing. He called another girl to do it, and took Chryseis to bed, uncharacteristically subdued.

He did not remember until some days later about the business of Troilus. Nobody had told him that the boy had been killed. He still hoped he had – things were back to normal by then, though Chryseis had kept her advantage – but he did not want to ask. If it had been done, he thought to himself, one of those jackals would have been quick enough to claim the credit. He was not in the mood to look for a disappointment.

There is always something depressing about the aftermath of a battle, even if it has been a great victory. This one had not been.

It was almost dark by the time the soldiers reckoned it safe to go out onto the plain and check over the bodies. The rain was coming down in sheets then, and they could not light torches to make the task easier. A few of the men were still alive and were carried, groaning, to the hospital tents in the Achaean and Trojan camps. Most had been dead for some time and their bodies were beginning to stiffen. The living soldiers turned over the corpses and checked for the badges which told if they had been friend or foe. They washed off the worst of the blood and gore with buckets of rainwater and straightened the limbs as well as they could before heaping them onto the piles in the carts. It was too late to build the funeral pyres that night, but they had done enough to keep the bodies from the kites and wild dogs that scavenged on the plain.

Every lamp in the Thessalian section had been taken to their

hospital tent; almost all the old casualties had been moved out
to make room for the new. Briseis had gone there in the late
morning and was waiting when the first injured men returned.
She wished one of the surgeons could be there too, but they
had been commandeered by the Mycenaeans and Cretans and
there was no prospect of getting one for her injured. There
were men in the camp willing to do what they could – cooks,
helmsmen and quartermasters – and she sent back to the
women's tents to see if any of them would come. Doris did,
Iphis – to her surprise – and a couple of the others. There was
no time for malicious looks or words. They set to work, washing
and bandaging the men who looked as if they had a chance of
surviving.

Late in the day, Achilles and Patroclus returned together. As
far as she could see, they were unhurt. They were unwashed,
still in their armour, their helmets in their hands. Iphis went to
unfasten Patroclus' breastplate and greaves; Briseis hesitated,
then went to Achilles. He nodded to her, saying nothing; and
when she had finished he went to stack his armour in the corner
of the tent. Then he turned back to her. 'Where do I start?'

'Over here, I think. That man has an arrow in his thighbone;
he is maybe better left for Machaon, when we can get him. This
one needs an arrow point cutting from his shoulder. Can you
do that yourself?'

'Patroclus can, or Eudorus. And the next man?'

'That one is messier. In the stomach. I doubt if Patroclus
would know how.'

'I'll start with him. Where is my knife?'

'Here'. She had kept it for him, tucked into her belt.

'Good girl.' A faint smile crossed his tired face, and he set to
work.

It was a long night, following a long day. The sky was growing
light again before they made their way back to their tents to
snatch a little sleep.

The heralds arranged a truce for ten days, to give time for the
funeral rites on both sides. If the rain continued it would last
longer because the Scamander would flood across the plain.
Neither side kept to the inland fashion of ending all hostilities
in the winter, and there was no prospect of the Achaeans going

home, for the storms on the Aegean would continue till the spring. But the pace of fighting always slowed as the days shortened, and there would be no new offensive that year.

In the morning the soldiers were out scavenging for timber to build the pyres and making preparations for the funeral feasts. Machaon came briefly to see to the wounded, but Achilles did not. Most of the men were not interested in the living casualties: they were left to the women.

Briseis kept at the work with blank despair. She had thought she was inured to the men's pain, but she had never known casualties on this scale before, not even at Lyrnessus before the end came. There was so little she could do. Even the few things she had learned about medicine were useless because most of the healing herbs were not to be had in the camp. There was poppy to dull the worst of the pain, but she knew she must not give that to the men too freely. It killed their spirit, and if they took too much they would find it difficult ever to do without. It was mainly a business of dressing wounds, binding them tight to try and staunch the flow of blood. At least the wounds were clean then. In ten days or less, many of them would be black or green with decay.

It was early evening before Achilles came. The flames from the pyres had died down, though the smell of burning flesh still hung heavily all across the plain. He was the first officer she had seen in the tent that day. He did not call her over, or fetch his knife. He just went quietly from man to man, talking to them, holding their hands, listening to what they had to tell him. Briseis did not let herself watch him. She kept on with her work as the other officers followed him in, Eudorus, Menestheus, Phoenix and the rest. There was no sign of Patroclus.

It seemed a long time before Achilles came across to her. He stood waiting as she finished changing the dressings on a man's arm. When it was done she stood up and faced him.

'The men can take over now. Let's go.'

She followed him outside the tent. The dregs of a red sunset hung in the sky. The camp was still busy, and there were men all around them. They walked together in silence back to Achilles' hut.

He shut the door behind them. The hut was empty, though

a servant had retrieved a lamp and lit it. There was no fire: all the wood had been used for the pyres. Achilles crossed to the trestle to pour two cups of wine. Then he turned to look at her. She was still standing by the door.

'You look tired out.' He said it gently, and the words and the tone were so unexpected that Briseis burst out crying. She *was* tired out. It had been a very long three days since the night with Patroclus, and she had barely slept at all.

Achilles came over to her and put his arms around her. She sobbed, clinging to him, with her head on his shoulder. He held her, stroking her hair, until the sobs died down, and then he led her over to sit on the edge of the bed. She told him about the men. What still needed doing for them, how she had been trying to arrange things. The little worries of getting food they could eat easily, enough wood to heat the water; and the big worries: the mangled limbs that would never be straightened, the men she cared for and knew were dying. He knew them all, at least as well as she did; he knew of the difficulties. He listened patiently to her, adding names and facts sometimes where she forgot them in her exhaustion.

When she had finished Achilles said quietly, 'I do what I can for them. You know that, don't you?'

Briseis turned to face him. He was staring away from her, into the shadows of the hut. There was a drawn look to him. She was conscious that the last few days would have been even worse for him than they had been for her.

'Yes, I know you do. Much more than most of the commanders. But it is never enough.'

Achilles gave a small smile. 'There is never enough of anything in wartime.' He moved the arm that had been around her shoulders and stood up abruptly. He walked a few paces away, towards the door, and still without looking at her, said, 'You can sleep here tonight. Patroclus will be back soon, he has been seeing to the horses. I shall be going over to talk with Ulysses. I shall not be back until late.'

It was a moment before Briseis grasped his meaning. It shook her. 'Must you go?'

Achilles was silent. He did not turn towards her, and Briseis was not sure enough of his thoughts to walk across and touch him. He made a step towards the door, hesitated, and then walked out, rapidly, and without saying another word.

Briseis still sat on the edge of his bed. She felt at a loss. She was too tired to think straight. If only he had stayed and kept on holding her until she had fallen asleep in his arms. Now she felt as if she had been abandoned, though he must have meant it to be kind, even loving. Perhaps Patroclus would make it all come right again. But she was so tired, and Patroclus was not there. Across the room she could see his bed. But it was Achilles' bed she was sitting on just then, Achilles whom she longed to see come back through the door. She swung her legs up onto the bed, nestled down among the lionskins, and was asleep before Patroclus returned.

Achilles and Patroclus had not spoken about Briseis at all since the battle. There had been so many friends lost, so much work to be done. Several moments passed after his return before Patroclus even realized that the girl was there. He saw the cups of wine first, untouched on the table, and then he heard her breathing and crossed over to the bed. She was still fully dressed, her limbs flung out across the covers. He reached out to touch her cheek, but she did not respond and he could not bring himself to wake her. He went to drink the wine instead, leaning against the trestle, and looked at her as he did so.

He had seen the streaks of tears on her cheeks when he was close to her, but she seemed peaceful then. However he put the pieces together, there were not enough of them to tell him what had happened between her and Achilles, or what they intended him to do. What did he want to do? Perhaps he was not sure of that either, because he stood there for a long time in the dim light, gazing at Briseis as she stirred in her sleep.

He had drunk all the wine, but his hand was still clenched around the stem of the cup. Unthinkingly, he had picked up Achilles' own cup, a heavy–hammered bronze one from which nobody else ever drank. He looked down at it, shaking his head. Then he picked up the second cup and carefully poured the wine from it into Achilles' cup. He set the two cups down, hesitated a moment, and switched them around. Then he went to the door to shout for a messenger and told him to go to the women's tent and send Iphis to him.

Iphis came in a rush that died to a standstill before she reached the door. Patroclus reached out a hand to draw her into the hut. In the light, her eyes were round and shiny with unshed tears. When he bent to kiss her they spilled over and flowed unchecked down her cheeks.

If Iphis noticed Briseis she had more sense than to mention her; and anyway, there were things she cared about more. She slept, a smile on the wet face, as soon as Patroclus loosed his grip on her; and he gazed down at her with an expression that, if it did not show happiness, at least suggested acceptance. The lamp was still burning. He left it for Achilles and drew across the curtain to shut out its light without glancing again at the other bed.

It was almost midnight when Achilles returned. The clouds had cleared away and it was a bright starry night. The evening had not improved his mood. Ulysses' cronies had drunk too much and grown loud and cynical about the war. He had, he supposed, grown loud and cynical too: certainly he had drank more than Ulysses. His head spun and Briseis' parting words still rang in his ears.

There was barely a trace of oil left in the bottom of the lamp, and its tiny flicker of flame did little more than show him where to reach to snuff it out. He did, without looking into the depths of the hut, and undressed in darkness. It came as a surprise to find a girl in his bed. He thought at first it was Diomede, whom Patroclus must have called to dull his misery. He was tempted to throw her out, but that would have been unfairly cruel. Instead he made love to her, roughly, without bothering to wake her fully first. It was only afterwards, when she was awake and whispered his name, that he realized it was Briseis.

Somewhere among the mixture of emotions there was joy, and love. His arms tightened round her, and she reached up to pull his head down to her and kiss him in the dark. He kissed her back, his fervour growing with his joy. He would have made love to her again, in a way that somehow told her all he felt, but she grew heavy in his arms and he realized that she was asleep. No matter. It was enough to hold her, and know that he had her now. And would never, ever let her go.

Chryses returned to Ilios on a wet and windy day. The last leaves were drifting from the trees; the midden scraps had turned to mush in the streets of the lower town. The priest shivered and wrapped his wolfskin cloak tighter around him.

He told the guards at the Dardanian Gate that he wished to speak to the High King, but they directed him instead to Prince Hector. Chryses was not a man to argue and he left his escort to go to the camp while he dutifully followed the soldier who led him up the hill to Palace Square, and Hector's house.

It was early afternoon, and Hector was not there. Andromache came to the gate to greet him and led him across the courtyard and into the megaron. The house was warm and comforting, and Chryses settled down gratefully to mulled wine and a rather skimpy meal. He had forgotten how tight the rations were in Ilios. Andromache had not; she apologized, in a way that suggested it was Hector's fault rather than her own that the rationing extended to her household.

They talked, a little awkwardly, of the forthcoming baby. Chryses had never been good at that kind of conversation, though Andromache seemed happy to do most of the talking. It was a relief to him when she turned to more serious matters. 'Hector will tell you the details, of course, but I think he intends you to go tomorrow to petition for the ransom. It will be the last day of the truce we negotiated, though he says there is unlikely to be more fighting when it ends.'

'Not the weather for it, I suppose.'

'No. There are to be two ransom demands – had you heard? My mother is alive, and a prisoner of Achilles. We found out a few days ago when he sent a messenger with the offer to ransom her. Hector and I thought it would be best if you handled both negotiations. The price is fixed for my mother, but nothing has been arranged yet for Chryseis.'

'That is good news. About your mother.'

'Wonderful news.' Andromache's wide smile lit up her face. 'I hadn't expected to see any of my family again. The ransom is high, but it will be worth it to have her back with us.'

'Achilles has acted well, it seems. You know he buried your father with full military honours at Thebe?'

'So the messengers told us. It will be a comfort to my mother.' She hesitated. 'I only hope Agamemnon will behave as honourably.'

'Is there reason to doubt it?' Chryses frowned. He was not at home with this kind of diplomatic haggling and all the way from Chryse he had been worrying about the task of arranging the ransom.

'Not really. There has been no offer from Agamemnon, but there was no reason to expect one. He would not have taken Chryseis with a ransom in mind, as Achilles took my mother. And Hector thought it best to wait till you came, and not send messengers in advance.'

'Is Hector to come with me? Or Troilus?'

Andromache shook her head. 'Hector thought it should be a Mysian delegation. There will be an escort, of course, from the Mysian troops in the camp.'

Chryses nodded abstractedly. 'Apollo will be with us too. And I shall do my best for her.'

'Of course.' Andromache stood up, with a touch of fussiness. She knew all about Hector's arrangements, and she knew that he would have liked her to pass them all on to Chryses. He had not looked forward to a reunion with the priest himself. But she felt embarrassed about telling Chryses of the need for secrecy in front of the High King. Priam knew only of the planned ransom for Queen Astynome. Andromache was also not entirely happy about the decision not to mention Chryseis' relationship with Troilus to the Achaeans. Those were Hector's decisions, and she planned to leave any discussion about them to him.

Her orders from Hector were to keep Chryses in the house, and it did not prove difficult, for he was tired from the journey. He went upstairs to rest and was still resting when Hector returned from the camp. Troilus was with him, and Ennomus.

'Is Chryses here?' Hector asked.

'Yes, upstairs.'

'Helike, will you go and call the priest? Then tell the other servants to leave us alone here.'

Chryses came down, bleary-eyed, to find the three soldiers aggressively in occupation of the megaron. He felt at a loss already. Their kind of power was so different from his, and though they showed proper respect to the gods, they seemed to hold him personally in a kind of casual contempt. Still, perhaps it would help to inure him to what he might expect from the Achaeans.

Hector outlined the remaining details with a speed and brevity that made him seem dismissive of their importance. Troilus did not speak. Ennomus, the Mysian, was already well known to Chryses. He had the favour of the gods and was a good man to take on such a mission. He smiled at Chryses, as if to dissipate the frown that was knitting together the priest's forehead.

Chryses did not smile back. He had not expected there to be anything underhand about the business. It was not to his liking to do anything behind Priam's back. If he had been a man to anger easily he would have been furious.

'Do you have any questions?' Hector asked curtly.

Chryses blinked. 'Not yet.' He looked at Andromache, who smiled encouragingly, and at Troilus, who looked worried. Maybe he should protest a little, he thought. It would not do to upset Hector, though, when he was providing the bulk of the ransom. It was handsome. Chryses had expected it to be around the cost of a slave girl – half a dozen oxen, or a tripod, something on those lines – but Hector had provided for almost ten times that much. He had made it clear that he hoped Chryses would negotiate a lower amount, but his manner suggested that he had limited faith in the priest's ability.

'That's settled. Ennomus and his men will come to you in the morning.' It was evident from Hector's tone that the discussion was over.

'I would like a short word with Troilus, if I might.'

Hector nodded and ushered Ennomus across to the other side of the room, out of earshot.

Chryses crossed to take the boy's arm and they sat down together, close to the hearth, in the chairs he and Andromache had used earlier.

'There is something troubling you?' Chryses put on his confessional manner, almost as if Troilus was a supplicant at the shrine.

Troilus looked at him with a blank face. Then a lazy smile came to it. 'Of course not. I'm very glad everything has been arranged so well.'

Chryses examined him doubtfully. Troilus had stretched out in the high-backed chair in a pose that seemed almost a parody of ease.

'You can talk to me, my son. Remember I am a priest. I can call down Apollo's forgiveness, as well as his wrath.'

The sturdy legs propping up the hearth did not move, nor did the expression change on Troilus' face. 'There is no problem about Chryseis. None at all. I do want her back, if that's what is worrying you, and I shall marry her as soon as she returns.'

'I am glad to hear it. But I still think it would help you to call upon Apollo to ease your mind.'

Troilus shook his head slowly, his eyes on the fire. Chryses was about to give up the initiative and move away, but then the boy began to talk, seriously, in a quiet and thoughtful tone, as if he were talking to himself. 'It was just the battle. I had the strangest feeling in the battle, as if the Achaeans had singled me out and were trying to kill me. Not in the general way of battles, but something specific, as if they knew me. I went out there wanting to kill him – Agamemnon – for what he might have done to her, and I thought for a moment I might manage it. I got close, and I think I wounded him. But then it was as if the gods deserted me, and I knew that it would not happen like that. I know it was all understandable, his guard rallying round and getting him back to safety, but it felt like more than that. A foreboding. And now it is hard to think she might be back tomorrow. Some god must have stayed with me then, I suppose, or I would not have come back from the battle alive. But I do not expect to have the support of the gods any longer. I do not really expect her to come back. Or if she does, it will be when I am not here any more.'

Chryses said gently, 'You should trust Apollo more than that. Have you sacrificed to him?'

Troilus looked around, as if he was surprised to find the priest still there. In a more conversational tone he replied, 'Before the battle, of course, but not since. Not to ask for success in this. Perhaps I should.'

'I think you should, and so should I, and Ennomus. If Hector agrees we will do it first thing in the morning.'

'I am sure he will. Thank you.'

Chryses hesitated, and then went on. 'You have never been to my shrine at Chryse, have you? It is dedicated to Apollo, but to Apollo as God of the Mice, as well as God of the Rising Sun. Chryseis always cared particularly for the mice. It worried her, when she was small, that they were too weak to be worthy of Apollo. But they are not. Given the right opportunity, the weak can triumph over the strong.

'The mice won a battle once. At Hamaxitus, not so far from Ilios. They swarmed out of the ground at night and attacked the Teucrians by biting through the leather in their armour and the straps of their weapons. They left strong men helpless. A mouse can sometimes take a bite out of the sun itself. The mice are a reminder that there is no need to fear your weakness. If you set about things in the right way it can become your strength as well.'

Troilus smiled. 'Yes, she told me that story. And it always seemed true of Chryseis, that her strengths and her weaknesses were so closely bound together there was no telling which was which.'

'But that is true of all of us. There is no real distinction between the promptings that make men brave and those that make them reckless, between the love that makes us strong and the love that makes us foolish. It is the support of the gods that makes us use our talents in the right way, and triumph.'

'Do you think you will triumph tomorrow, and get her back?'

'I wish I knew. Apollo did not make me all-seeing, unfortunately. But I shall do my best to carry out the will of the gods, and I shall ask him for the strength to accept whatever happens.'

'I would rather fight against it if the wrong thing happens.'

Chryses smiled at that. He was touched, and amused. He had not liked Troilus at first, and not only because he had felt Artemis' anger at Chryseis' choice of him. Now, though, it seemed to the priest that the young couple were well matched.

They were so similar. It seemed natural that he should hear Chryseis' words and ideas coming from her lover. Perhaps he should have told the boy not to fight what must be. But he had not the heart to do it, and he rose to break the conversation before Troilus could say something that made him like the lad less.

They made the sacrifice – an ox, for it was a big undertaking – in the morning. There were no good signs, but no bad ones either, and Chryses set off across the plain with the escort in a cautious good humour. He had always thought Ennomus distant and dreamy, but the Mysian came across more forcefully in front of his men and organized the soldiers, the carts and the goods for the ransom efficiently. Chryses wore his priestly robes and carried high in the air his golden staff with the garland of white ribbons fluttering at its top.

The plain was wide, and they moved slowly, so the journey took much of the morning. It was not cheering. The ground, so dry and dusty in the summer, had been turned into a sea of mud by the rains. The river was high, with brown water running fast and scouring the sides of its bed, and the dogs were still along its banks scavenging for the forgotten victims of the battle. There was a sickening sweet smell of rot in the air.

The stockade around the Achaean camp was heavily guarded. The soldiers at the gate searched them all, then held back Ennomus' men, telling Chryses that he was to go alone to the High King. He left Ennomus to guard the ransom goods.

Chryses was escorted to what was, he supposed, a kind of campaign tent. There were more guards outside it. When the priest was ushered in he found Agamemnon sitting in state, surrounded by several priests and a dozen or more of his commanders.

The High King had evidently taken Chryses to be a delegate from Priam himself, for he was dressed in his state robes. Beneath the rich purple cloak, his arm was heavily bandaged. Chryses knelt politely before him.

'The Trojan priest, sir.' The herald seemed to think his name unimportant. There was no offer of food or drink, no suggestion that he might make any offering to the gods.

'King Priam wished to ask something of me?' The voice was powerful, with a note of harshness in it. Chryses looked up at Agamemnon. He sat impassively. He seemed not unlike Priam, though he was a younger and stronger man. They both had the air of absolute power, the priest thought: and the inevitable hint of corruption that goes with it.

'No, sir. I am not an envoy from the High King. I am a Mysian, and I lead a Mysian delegation. We hope to ransom two Mysian ladies. I understand that you yourself hold my daughter Chryseis, and that Lord Achilles holds Astynome, Queen of Thebe. Lord Achilles is here?' He looked around, uncertain which of the other men might prove to be the famous Achilles.

When Chryses turned to look at Agamemnon's face again it told him that he had asked the wrong question. One of the soldiers broke the silence. 'You will be escorted to Prince Achilles later.'

Agamemnon's scowl slowly faded, and he said, 'So you are Chryseis' father.'

'Yes, sir, and a priest of Apollo, as you see. I have come to take her back home to Chryse.'

'No.' Agamemnon rose as he spoke, and appeared about to end the audience. Chryses drew in his breath sharply. He had been prepared for a tough reception, but not for that kind of rudeness. He said hurriedly, 'My Lord, wait to hear the terms I have to offer. I can assure you they are generous.'

Agamemnon turned to look at him. His face now was hard and contemptuous, the face of a despot. 'I have no wish to return the girl. She will stay with me. There is nothing more to be said.'

Chryses stared him out doggedly. 'It is Apollo's wish that she be returned. I am sure you would not slight the God.'

'It is my wish that she remain with me, and I do not care a fig for Apollo's wishes.'

The priests shivered, and there was a murmur among the soldiers around Agamemnon. Chryses tried to catch the eyes of the priests and he succeeded in attracting the attention of the one who appeared to be the Achaean High Priest. A short round man with rolls of fat around his neck, his beady eyes darted from the Trojan priest to the High King.

'My Lord,' the priest said to Agamemnon in a deep, rich voice, 'you must consider the will of the gods.'

'I do not learn the will of the gods from a Trojan priest.'

'Then let me interrogate this priest myself, and discover the signs that he has followed.'

'That is not necessary, Calchas. Your request is refused.'

A soldier broke into the exchange, a big beefy man who towered over the High King. 'Sir, I think you should listen to the priest if he has a fair ransom to offer.'

'I did not ask your opinion, Ajax.'

'I am giving it to you anyway. I do not think it right to slight Apollo for the sake of a girl. You have plenty of girls. Why not give this one back if her father can offer a decent ransom for her?'

'Do not make me angry, Ajax.'

Ajax seemed unabashed. 'It is you who are making us angry, Agamemnon. Stay and listen to what the priest has to say.'

Agamemnon glared round at the other men. As far as Chryses could judge, he found little comfort in their faces. A second soldier spoke up, a short, hairy man with a low echoing voice. 'Listen to the priest, at least.'

The High King stood unmoving, fury rising high like thunder clouds in his face. Chryses expected a storm of anger to burst over the assembled men, but then the danger passed and Agamemnon sat down, subdued. He examined his hand, as if he had detected a splinter in his finger, then looked up. He spoke in a casual tone. 'I will listen.'

Chryses stumbled through the details of the ransom. He did not trust himself to better this hard-faced man in a bargaining match, and he listed everything that he had brought with him. Agamemnon's face told him that it would not be enough. Only his pride made him carry on to the end of the list. He wanted the High King to know how much his daughter meant to the Trojans.

He had no doubt about the reply, but Agamemnon took his time in giving it. Finally he said, 'You are remarkably generous in your offer, but the girl is worth more than that to me. I shall not return her.'

Chryses had only one more offer to make. 'If my daughter is

returned to me I shall call upon Apollo to bring you victory over Ilios, and a fair wind home.'

Agamemnon looked as contemptuous as ever. 'And if she is not?'

'Then I shall pray to the God to send his curses down upon you and your men.'

The High King smiled cruelly. 'Perhaps I should ask your daughter to counter your prayers. I think she will, if I tell her to.'

'I am sure she knows the will of the gods better than that.'

'I am sure she would not be a traitor to Troy for the sake of getting back to your shrine.'

Chryses' blood ran cold. He knew he had gone too far; but there was no taking back the words. Agamemnon sat, coolly watching the priest's distress. Then he said, 'The girl has been well treated, and she will continue to be. There is no need to fear for her.'

Chryses looked down at the floor of the tent. The beaten earth was a strange contrast to the richness of the High King's clothes. Then he looked up again. 'May I see my daughter?'

There was a long silence. Chryses had expected to be refused, but instead Agamemnon said, 'Why not? She will tell you that you have been wasting your time, and that she prefers to stay with me.'

'I may talk with her alone?'

This time the High King replied quickly, as if he were afraid of raising doubts in his confidence, 'She will tell you just the same alone.'

He stood as he spoke, and began to walk towards the door of the tent. Then he turned, in the same casual manner he had kept throughout most of the encounter, and said, 'Ajax, I shall leave you to arrange it. The priest may see Chryseis.' He smiled slightly. 'Alone.'

Ajax walked the priest across to Agamemnon's quarters. He was silent most of the way, but just before they reached the hut he said, 'You should believe the High King. He will not change his mind, he never does. He treats your daughter well. Be prepared, though: you will find her changed.'

'You know her yourself?'

The big man smiled. 'Every soldier in the camp knows her. Agamemnon makes quite sure of that.'

Chryses frowned. He had no idea what to expect.

It was a relief to find the same Chryseis standing in a large room waiting for him, though her dress and hair were different. It crossed his mind that she looked like a Trojan princess: there was something of Helen's air of sophistication about her. But she had the same liveliness he remembered, and beneath it, she seemed as self-contained as she had always been, even as a child.

His daughter hesitated for a moment, as if she expected her father to find her more strange than he evidently did. Then she turned to the servants. They disappeared through a doorway at the back of the room: clearly they already had their orders. Chryseis relaxed and came across to hug him. 'Father. I am glad to see you safe.'

There was a trestle table, with benches alongside it. By the hearth, there were a couple of low chairs. Chryses sat down, heavily, on the nearest one. 'I came to ransom you, my dear: to bring you back to Ilios. But it seems that the High King will not let you go.'

She came to sit next to him. He could not tell from her silence if she had been warned why he had come, or if it came as a surprise. Then she replied, in a level voice, 'I do not think I could go, Father.'

'That is a ridiculous thing to say, child. We all want you back in Troy. Prince Hector arranged the ransom, and Princess Andromache, and Prince Troilus, of course. I had hoped to see you married to Troilus on your return. He is a sensible lad, and he will not blame you for anything that has happened here. He loves you, and he misses you.'

She frowned. 'I am sorry. I had thought he might have forgotten me.'

'As you have forgotten him.' There was a tinge of sharpness in Chryses' tone, and his daughter looked across at him quickly. 'Of course I have not forgotten him.'

'But.'

She hesitated. 'It has been a long time, Father. Things have happened here that have changed me. I doubt if I could feel the same way about Troilus now.'

'Are you trying to tell me that you love this godless Achaean?'

She smiled slightly at that. 'Father, he is not godless. Perhaps he does not worship the gods in quite the same way that you do. He tempts fate a little more, but I do not think he underrates the power of Apollo, or Zeus, or any of the other gods. He fears them. He prays to them, and sacrifices to them, and so do I.'

'And you think this is what the gods intended for you? To be a slave to an Achaean king?'

'You never really believed that they intended me to be a princess in Ilios, did you?'

Chryses clenched his fist under the folds of his robe. She had always been so quick to turn his arguments against him. He said quietly, 'You have not answered me.'

'Told you if I loved Agamemnon? Yes, I do. At first I did not, at first it was horrible, but I have come to know him. We understand each other. There is much that is frightening about him. He showed me things about myself that I had not known were there. He can be cruel, and so can I, it seems. We are well matched. I know he loves me, and I love him.'

Chryses' fist bunched tighter. He had never understood men like Agamemnon, men who dealt in power and cruelty. Any sort of love they could feel was surely a totally different emotion from the gentle warmth he had felt towards Chryseis' mother. But he could see that there was a grandeur about it: being loved by one of the most powerful men in the world. 'It is not as if you were his wife.'

'I know. It is not so very different, though, Father. He does treat me like a wife, not like a slave. He is as committed to me, in his way, as I am to him.'

'It was useless, then, my coming.'

She smiled at him. 'It is not like you, Father, to talk of uselessness. I thought you believed the gods gave a purpose to everything we did. Perhaps there was a use to it, even if it is not clear to us now.'

'Perhaps so.' Chryses stood up. He had intended to ask Chryseis to pray with him, but the prayers he must now invoke, the ones he had brought upon himself in the meeting with

Agamemnon, were not prayers that he dared to involve her in. 'I must go, child. Ennomus is waiting, and I have to see Achilles before I leave the camp.'

She stood, too. 'I may not see you again.'

Chryses could not tell her of the curse that he would be forced to call Apollo to bring upon Troy if ever she were to be returned to him. 'It is in the God's hands, my dear. He will protect you.'

'I believe he does, Father. I believe he does.'

Chryses had hoped to return to talk with Ennomus before he sought out Achilles, but the guards firmly prevented him. It seemed they wanted him out of the camp as quickly as possible. They marched him across to Achilles' lodge at a pace which left him breathless. It was muddy in the camp, though reeds from the river had been strewn across the worst patches. He arrived dishevelled, with his white robe black around the hem and his face red from unaccustomed effort.

He was not expecting courtesy by this time, but Achilles greeted him respectfully. He dismissed Agamemnon's guards and set his own Myrmidons to watch at the door. He gave the priest a chair and told his girl to prepare a hot posset. She looked familiar, Chryses thought vaguely, but he could not recall her name, if he had ever known it, and she did not speak to him before her master smiled at her and gently ordered her out.

Achilles came to sit by the priest. A taller man than Agamemnon, and a stern-faced one, but with a warmth about him somewhere. 'I understand you have spoken to Agamemnon,' he said.

Chryses nodded. The numbness that the earlier meetings had brought on him was beginning to wear off, to be replaced by misery and despair. 'I had hoped to ransom my daughter, but he refused.'

Achilles considered. 'Agamemnon does not like to ransom prisoners. Few of the commanders from the south do. I was not aware that he had taken any for ransom.'

Chryses shook his head. 'He was not expecting it, but we offered a good ransom for her, and I had hoped he would take it.'

'He must have had his reasons for refusing. Perhaps he felt

she had learned too much in the camp, or that it would upset the other servants.'

'But you do not feel the same about the Queen of Thebe.'

'I have always intended to ransom her, and she has been kept apart from the other prisoners. There is little that she can tell you. And I would not wish Briseis, for instance, to know that another woman is to be ransomed from me. She might feel that her father should have offered to pay the price for her.'

Briseis, that was the girl. Briseus' daughter, from Lyrnessus. A bad business. 'But Briseis' father is dead. You did not know?'

Achilles shook his head slowly. Chryses told him the tale briefly, and he listened in silence, his face an expressionless mask. There was a further silence when it ended. It crossed Chryses' mind that he ought to offer to speak to the girl, break it gently to her. He had had enough difficult meetings for one day, though, and he said nothing. Instead he sipped the drink she had made for him, and waited till Achilles roused himself and spoke. 'Thank you for telling me. When you are rested I will take you to Astynome. You will find her in poor spirits. We have treated her kindly, but she is not young, and it has all been too much for her.'

Chryses nodded. 'Have you told her she is to be ransomed?'

'She knows, yes, and is expecting you.'

'Let us go, then.' He drained his cup and stood up.

As they walked to Astynome's tent, Achilles said, 'I am sorry about your daughter. It must be a great disappointment to you.'

'Evidently it is not to Chryseis.'

At the name, Achilles started a little and turned to look at the priest. He had spoken not with bitterness, but with pained resignation. It was a shock to discover that this faded, thoughtful man was Chryseis' father. He had none of her energy about him. Perhaps, Achilles thought, like so many priests he came fully to life only during the rituals. 'It must be for the best if she has accepted it well.'

Chryses shook his head. 'It is not what the gods intended for her. Apollo will be angry. And I will call on his anger, I swore that to Agamemnon.'

Achilles frowned. Was Agamemnon risking the wrath of the gods to keep the girl? The High King took too much on himself, the war was not won yet. He would have to discover what had taken place, from Ajax perhaps, or Ulysses, or even from Calchas. Perhaps he could turn the incident against Agamemnon, and to his own advantage. Later. For now, there was business to be done.

When Astynome had been delivered to Ennomus at the gate, and the ransom handed over in return, Chryses told the escort to wait, and made to go back into the camp. The guard reached out to stop him, but Achilles came to his rescue. 'The man is a priest. Let him do what he has to. Give him an escort through the camp, and show him back to the gate when he is ready.'

The priest set off immediately towards the harbour. There was a new energy about him that drove speed into his weary legs and made men look at his rapt face, not at the mud spattering his robes. He did not stop until he reached the shingle. The sea was rough, even in the bay, and he had to shout to make his voice carry above the roar of the waves.

He stood among the black ships and held out his golden staff with its white bands as if he felt it would touch the sky if he reached far enough. He called out the words of the invocations. Hear me, Apollo. Hear me, Master of the Sun and Lord of the Silver Bow. Hear me, God of the Mice, the meek and the defenceless. Hear me, who reveres you, and let my wish come true against those who dishonour you. Let your arrows rain down on the Achaeans, and bring your force to do what my tears cannot. Make them return the girl to me. And if they do this thing, then hear my second prayer, and grant them plunder of Priam's town, and a fair wind home.

Chryses repeated the prayers again and again, as if the God were certain to reply if he persisted for long enough. The sky darkened; the storm clouds which had been massing again on the horizon came up to cover it and hide the sun. The thunder roared, first distant, and then closer at hand. The lightning that followed made Ilios, high on its hill, loom suddenly, deceptively close. Then the rain came, first in heavy drops, and then in a downpour that turned the day as dark as night and made the white ribbons cling translucent round the staff. Chryses did not make for shelter. He stood there in the full force of the rain, shouting out the words as if he was still not sure that Apollo had heard him. But there was a fervour in his eyes, as if he had no doubt now that he was speaking direct to the gods.

He did not notice the troop of soldiers who pushed his escort aside and moved forward to grab him by the elbows. There was no fervour about them, merely the determination of men told their orders too plainly to dare to dispute them. 'Come on, old man. You must be gone. The High King's orders. He'll not have you loitering around the ships any more. If you do, he says, your ribbons and staff will make no difference. Never mind the truce, he'll hurl you in the sea.'

They bundled him unceremoniously back through the camp and tossed him into Ennomus' waiting arms as the rain began to die down and a weak sun pushed its way through the mass of clouds. If that had been Apollo's answer it had not been enough. They would go back to Ilios without the girl.

Briseis was surprised and shaken to see Chryses at the hut. The priest had none of his usual composure, and she found it strange that he should not recognize her, or attempt to speak. Surely he did not think Achilles would forbid it? Achilles did, however, make it clear that their talk was not for her to hear, and she went back to the women's tents to see if any of them knew more.

The women's grapevine in the camp was never strong, and gossip spread only slowly, when the men deigned to tell them anything. Diomede thought it was to do with the Queen of Thebe.

'But why should the priest come?' Briseis persisted. 'It cannot be he who plans to ransom her. Surely Andromache, her daughter, and Hector would do that.'

'Hector would not come.' Diomede had been in the camp when earlier prisoners had been ransomed, so she could be presumed to know. 'There has to be some intermediary.'

Briseis shook her head. 'Chryses makes a strange intermediary. He would be no good at negotiating a ransom.'

'You know him well?' Diomede used her sarcastic tone, and Briseis flushed.

'Quite well. He is Chryseis' father.'

'Perhaps he is ransoming her too.'

'Maybe. I could ask Achilles.'

Diomede glared at her. She had taken Briseis' unexpected rise to favour as gracefully as she could, but it was galling to have Briseis draw attention to their closeness. 'It would be dangerous, asking him about something like that.'

Briseis knew that Diomede was probably right. Though Achilles showed her both passion and consideration in bed, he treated her outside it with a formality that she found difficult to break down. He was still the man whose women loved him and did not dare to ask him questions. All that had changed was that she was now one of them. 'Perhaps. I doubt if he will call for me again this afternoon. I'll go over to the hospital tent. Are you coming?'

Diomede hated to come, and Briseis was not surprised to have only Doris walk over with her. She was grateful for her company. The men teased her about Achilles when she was alone – more gently than they had ribbed her about disliking him earlier, but it still embarrassed her. It was alarming to realize how quickly news of their conciliation had spread. I wonder what Chryseis is making of it, she thought to herself. Can her father really have ransomed her? She had not thought Chryses would have the resources to do it. What did women like Chryseis cost? Five oxen at least, surely. If the priest had anything of such value it would belong to the God, and not be his to offer to the Achaeans.

When Patroclus came into the tent it seemed to Briseis that he would know; and she could ask *him*, surely. Conscious of her eyes following him, he crossed over as soon as he had finished with the men. 'There's a storm on the way. You should get back before it breaks, and Doris, too.'

'Will you walk back with us? I'll see if Doris is ready.'

Briseis made her way between the pallets to where Doris was chattering away to the soldier whose leg she was binding. Doris turned to nod and grin at Patroclus, and he waited, leaning back against the timbers of the tent, till she had finished.

'Did the priest come to ransom Astynome?' Briseis asked as they were leaving the tent.

Patroclus was taken aback by her directness. 'The Queen of Thebe? Yes, he did.'

'You sound surprised that I knew.'

'Guessed,' he corrected. 'I am, a little. Achilles kept her apart so it would not upset you.'

'Upset us?'

'Knowing that someone else was to be ransomed.'

Looking up, she met his eyes. He held hers for a moment before turning away. 'There was a time,' he said, 'when you would have longed for it to be you.'

Doris said quickly, 'I doubt if any of us let ourselves think of that.'

Her caution was not needed, for Patroclus had struck wide. Briseis said, 'I still cannot understand why the priest should have come. Was it something to do with Chryseis?'

'Chryseis? Why should it be?'

'He is her father.'

'I knew nothing of that. I could ask, if you really want to know.' He looked sideways at Briseis and added, 'Or you could ask Achilles.'

The challenge annoyed her. 'Yes, I will,' she retorted, with a touch of anger.

Doris broke the silence that followed and talked with Patroclus about the injured men until they arrived at the women's tents. When he had left the women she turned to Briseis and said quietly, 'You are too blunt with Patroclus.'

'He knows me.' Briseis realized how tactless that was as soon as she had said it. She glanced at Doris' face and caught an expression – not of contempt, though that would not have surprised her, but of concern. 'I'll talk to him tonight,' she added in an undertone as they made their way into the outer tent.

In retrospect, the little exchange with Patroclus worried Briseis more than the matter of the priest. The memory lingered of Achilles' implicit offer on the evening of the funerals. Even had she been in a state to consider it more rationally, she doubted if she would have accepted it. The sheer force of Achilles had attracted her so intensely. But she wished her decision had been taken more cleanly; and she wished she knew whether Patroclus was aware that the choice had been hers, and not Achilles'.

She had seen Patroclus only rarely, and in Achilles' company, since their night together. On the surface he had treated her with his usual easy friendliness, but there had been an edge to his remarks that afternoon, and she began to wonder, for the first time, whether he had been more deeply hurt by her sudden defection than he had shown.

She did not fear his anger, or expect him to hate her. But she realized then that he was, in a way, as essential to her happiness as was Achilles; and that they might never regain their earlier intimacy.

Achilles called for her early that evening. Patroclus was there when she went to the hut, and so were Automedon, Phoenix and some of the others. Briseis was awkwardly conscious of Patroclus, particularly when Achilles came across and took her in his arms. She could feel his eyes on her as they kissed. She felt as if she should have kissed him as well. Breaking free from Achilles and crossing the room seemed emphatic enough, though, and she contented herself with standing in front of him and saying quietly, 'I upset you this afternoon.'

He met her eyes, and the look told her that Doris had been right. He said evenly, 'It was nothing.'

At least, Briseis told herself, it was better than the denial she had half expected.

She could not have asked Achilles anything then. It would have risked upsetting both men. She was conscious, too, that the friendship between the two of them was still beyond her comprehension, and that she herself feared being shut out by them both if she proved to be too great a threat to it.

The other officers went early, and the three of them were left alone together. They moved over to the fire, sending the dogs outside into the yard.

'You'll send for Iphis?' Achilles asked.

Patroclus silently shook his head.

Achilles settled down in his low chair and motioned to Briseis to come and sit at his feet. She leaned back against him and he began to play with her hair, twisting and untwisting the heavy brown braids. After a minute he unfastened the ribbons at their ends and began to work her hair loose with his fingers. Briseis glanced up at him and he smiled back at her, his face softening.

Patroclus' voice, from the other side of the hearth, had a taut edge to it. 'Briseis told me the priest was Chryseis' father.'

Achilles' hands paused, and his leg tensed against Briseis' back. It was no secret, he reminded himself: it would be round the camp by morning. 'He came to ransom her, but Agamemnon refused to let her go.'

'He didn't offer enough?'

Achilles shook his head. 'It was as much as we got for Astynome.' He looked down at Briseis, but her touch told him she had known about that. 'According to Ulysses, Agamemnon just set himself against it. He goaded her father in front of Calchas and a dozen of the commanders until the priest threatened to bring Apollo's curse upon us. He went down to the seashore and made the invocations before he left the camp. It frightened the men who heard it. Ulysses is arranging a sacrifice in the morning to appease Apollo.'

'That did not concern Agamemnon?'

'He has shown no concern, no contrition, no willingness to change his mind, though Ajax and Ulysses have pressed him to. He refused to speak to Calchas. I have no idea what he thinks he is doing. Perhaps he is so mad for love of her that he cares nothing for the wrath of the gods. Perhaps he has some elaborate scheme that he's hiding from the rest of us. The priest promised to call on Apollo to bring us victory if he does send the girl back.'

'Maybe he will tire of her in a moon or two, and send her back then.'

'Maybe.' Achilles hesitated. 'Her father had talked to her. He told me she had no wish to return to Ilios.'

Briseis turned at that and looked up at Achilles. 'You disagree?' he asked.

'I saw Chryseis earlier in the summer. I had the impression then that she was unhappy.'

Patroclus said, 'She was, then. I think she is much happier now.'

Briseis smiled. 'Perhaps she loves him now.'

'It happens.' Achilles said it, and Briseis, meeting his eyes, found herself forgetting Patroclus and joining in his quiet laughter.

Patroclus watched in silence for a moment, then said abruptly,

'I heard she might have had a lover in Ilios. Troilus, one of Priam's sons.'

Briseis turned to him, surprised. 'Her father had intended her to go to Artemis, to the sanctuary up above Thebe. She never wanted that, she was always hoping to find a husband before it happened, and he never did send her. I didn't know there was anyone, though.'

'You think it isn't true?'

Briseis thought. 'No. I think it probably is true. She had been to Ilios before she was captured, so she could have met him then. I had thought there must have been someone for a ransom to have been offered, especially a large one. Chryses is not rich. And when we talked I had the feeling that there was something she was not telling me, or something she lied about. Perhaps that was it.'

'The priest cannot have mentioned it if there was,' Achilles said with a note of annoyance. 'Agamemnon would have had to send her back if he had. Who told you, Patroclus?'

Patroclus did not want to explain. In any case, they had not killed the boy, as far as he knew. 'Oh, Diomedes. I've no idea where he got it from. Agamemnon should have sent her back anyway, to pacify the gods.'

'We don't always do what we should do, any of us.' There was a hardness in Achilles' voice. Patroclus rose slowly to his feet. 'True. I'll leave you for a while.' It was a fine night now that the storm had passed; he would walk across and talk to someone. Ulysses, maybe, or Ajax.

Briseis relaxed when he had left, but she sensed that Achilles did not. Was he still jealous? she wondered. He could be so edgy and proud, and yet she felt that the generosity which could have made things easy between the three of them should really have come from him. He was their master, he should have been the strongest. At the same time his weakness, his vulnerability made her love him even more. She moved to hold him closer.

After a while she said quietly, 'I would not want to go either. You do know that?'

Achilles looked at her for a moment and bent to kiss her lightly. 'Yes, I know.' He rose to pour some more wine and turned to her from the trestle. 'But I would have sent you back if my honour had obliged me to.'

She looked into the fire. The wood was not seasoned: it had been cut only a couple of days before and was damp from the rains. It hissed and crackled as it burned. 'Is that what you are frightened of? That someone will come to ask for me?'

There was a long silence, and finally she turned to look at Achilles. He met her eyes. His were dark and troubled in the firelight. He came to sit by her again.

'I was.' He spoke clumsily. 'Chryses told me that your father is dead.'

'I took it for granted that he was. That he died with the rest in the spring.'

He had still not relaxed.

'Was that not it? Was it something else? Please tell me, if it was. I don't want you keeping things from me.'

'I had not meant to tell you.' Achilles took a deep breath. 'He survived the attack and went back to Lyrnessus afterwards. He killed himself there, in the ruins.'

'How?' She was not looking at him now, and her voice was hollow and expressionless.

'He hanged himself.' They were both silent, and the words seemed to repeat themselves in the crackling of the fire. He reached down and pulled her up to sit in his lap. She came like a child, all arms and legs, as if her body was not fully under her control.

She let him give her what comfort he could, and then pulled away and sat up on his knee. 'Poor Father. He told me he would kill himself if it came to that. I never thought he would really do it.'

'It must have been what he thought was right.'

'In a way,' she shivered, 'he was a priest too. Of Dionysus. Oh, he was a merchant first and always, but they got into him, the ways of the Dionysia. A little part of it all seemed to stay with him each year, when the festival was over. The wildness that can drive men even to death. Perhaps that was how it was: a wildness. His God told him to do it.'

'If that is so, then there is no shame in it.'

'It still feels shameful to me.' She shivered again, and when Achilles reached to touch her cheek it was chill against his hand. 'You're cold. Here, have some of my wine.'

She turned to him and smiled, unsteadily. It was ironic that the wine of Dionysus should be the only remedy he thought to offer. 'No. Not now. Take me to bed, please?'

He did. When they had made love the tears came, and he held her until she cried herself to sleep.

Part Three

HEROES AND SURVIVORS

'I THINK YOU SHOULD talk to Chryses.'

Hector spoke. It was early evening, and he was sitting with Andromache in her private room.

'What about?' Andromache had hoped to go to bed early. Seven days had gone by since her mother had been brought back to Ilios. Instead of the joyful reunion she had anticipated, she hardly recognized the mother she had known in the weepy, querulous old lady who moped around the house and demanded little tasks of her all day long.

'He's keeping something back, something that happened in the Achaean camp.'

'Something about Chryseis?'

'I suppose so. I'll leave you to find out.'

'Has he not told Troilus everything?'

'I don't think so.' Hector sighed. Andromache had been so much more obliging during this pregnancy than during the last, but perhaps she was now working herself into an obstinate phase. Could she not just do as he requested, without asking a dozen questions, and come back with some sensible answers? 'Maybe it's something he feels he cannot tell Troilus.'

Andromache repressed the temptation to tell Hector to do it himself. 'If we cannot ransom her, it makes no difference what is wrong, surely?'

'It does to Troilus.' Troilus and Chryses had both seemed edgy and awkward. It was Troilus who had insisted that Chryses was not telling him everything, and Hector had no wish to see him launch into a mad scheme of his own to retrieve the girl. 'We need to know for his sake: so we can avenge her if anything dreadful has happened, or tell him to forget her if it is her own fault in some way.'

Andromache shifted on the high bed and looked at the ceiling. Its painted clouds failed to lift her spirits. She thoroughly disliked the prospect of asking Chryses intimate questions about his daughter's behaviour. 'If it is anything embarrassing, I doubt if Chryses would want to talk to a woman. Could we not ask Aeneas?'

'No.'

Andromache did not answer. Presumably he would have to take that for a refusal. Hector rose, grumpily, from the low carved chair. 'I shall ask Helenus. Perhaps Chryses will talk to him.'

Andromache turned to look across at him. He had made no move to leave the room, and she did not want him to leave in this mood. Though he was rarely demonstratively affectionate, Hector was friendly these days, and she wanted to keep his friendship. She could certainly do without his lingering annoyance. 'Shall I talk to Helenus for you?'

Hector brightened. It was the first helpful remark she had made all day. In retrospect, though, he supposed she had been right earlier. It would not do for her to be involved if there was something unpleasant to be uncovered.

He left Andromache to sleep and set out across Palace Square. The sun was setting behind heavy clouds. He found Helenus in the megaron, squatting in a corner and playing at dice with Troilus. They were extremely merry, though not drunk, he decided after a few moments, and the game was very complicated and not at all familiar to him. When they finished it they embarked upon a second. Hector, leaning against the wall where his shadow loomed over them, declined their invitation to join in. Finally Troilus, edgy under his older brother's gaze, excused himself, and Helenus pocketed the bone dice and turned to Hector. 'Does it embarrass you to suggest a private conversation with me? Surely I am not that disreputable?'

Hector looked at him with slight annoyance. He had reckoned he appeared more diplomatic than that. 'Of course not. It's just something I cannot discuss in front of Troilus.'

'Poor Troilus. He's in danger of turning into the baby everyone wants to pat on the head.' Helenus smiled archly. Hector's annoyance grew.

'Troilus told me he felt that Chryses was keeping something back from him. I thought perhaps you might talk to him about it.'

'To Chryses?'

'Obviously. Troilus doesn't know what it is.'

Helenus looked up at his brother more soberly. 'There is a lot that Troilus doesn't know.'

'Are you trying to tell me that there are things you do know?'

'A few, yes.' Helenus hesitated, as if he was reluctant to tell Hector what he knew, and then decided that there was no real alternative. Hector encouraged him by slipping down to sit on the floor. 'Not direct from Chryses, but I did talk to Ennomus. Chryses told him most of what happened, and he talked to the Achaean guards while he was waiting at the camp. You know Ennomus: he can put a few hints together and make a convincing story out of it.'

As could Helenus himself, Hector thought. With all his access to Priam's private information, he sometimes felt less well informed than his brother or the Mysian leaders. 'And?'

Helenus shrugged. 'Chryseis is well, no doubt about that, and in favour with Agamemnon. The guards told Ennomus he parades her around so the whole camp knows her.'

'So it might have been a humiliation if he had agreed to ransom her?'

'Ennomus had the impression that Agamemnon was obsessed with her and simply didn't want to lose her.'

'That's ridiculous. Kings don't behave like that.'

Helenus laughed. 'You mean you don't, Hector. Men do. Paris did, and does. Troilus does in his modest way. Evidently Agamemnon does as well.'

Hector took in this judgement slowly. 'So you see Chryseis as a kind of Trojan Helen, causing Agamemnon to risk all for love, and bring about the downfall of the Achaeans?'

'I prefer Helen myself, though I can see that Chryseis could have the same effect on the right man.' Helenus paused. It was unlike Hector, he thought, to play such a passive role. He was slow to respond, as if this was alien territory to him. Hector had never really thought of the war as being about Helen. But then, he seemed to be immune to her charms, and Helenus was not. Helenus had always seen the war in terms of intrigue and passion, among both men and gods. He pitied Hector's blindness on this front, and continued carefully. 'Chryseis will not bring about our downfall, Hector. That is already determined. Chryses knows it, and Ennomus knows it, and in your pragmatic way you know it too, don't you? It was determined long before the Achaeans took her, long before the fall of Lyrnessus, perhaps long before the war even began. Chryseis has already brought about Troilus' downfall, but there is nothing to be done about that now.'

'You don't think we should wait a couple of moons until Agamemnon has tired of her, and then try again to ransom her?'

It was unlike Hector to ask Helenus' advice, too, especially when his brother verged on the prophetic. Helenus had learned as a child that nobody took his prophecies quite seriously, any more than they took his twin Cassandra's. He had taken refuge in a silence on the subject which he was rarely tempted to break. He was not tempted now; instead he gave a diplomatic answer. 'I don't think so, no. It would be humiliating to leave the ransom offer open, and I think it would be a disaster if Chryseis came back.'

'You mean Troilus would not accept her?'

'He would want to. But you saw how the captivity changed Astynome, and Lycaon before he was killed. It will have been harder for her.'

'I cannot see why. She is young and tough.'

'Ah, but they expected to be ransomed, and Chryseis did not.' Helenus surveyed his brother. Hector was frowning, as if the distraction was not entirely clear to him. 'I think she will have changed sides. She might find it difficult to change back again.'

'She can hardly want to stay with Agamemnon.'

'According to Ennomus, she does. Chryses told Ennomus he had talked with her, and Ennomus had the impression that she was reluctant to be ransomed.'

'The deceptive little bitch!'

'No, Hector, not deceptive. Realistic. You cannot blame her for that. I think we should respect her, if she has done her best with what the gods sent her, and won Agamemnon's favour. Oh, he will tire of her, but so would Troilus in a year or two.'

'I cannot understand you, Helenus. One moment you speak of passions strong enough to make men risk wars, and the next you reckon they will tire of it all in a year or two. You can hardly have it both ways.'

Helenus' smile had become cynical again. 'Men do, I think. The passion makes them start on a cause, then honour keeps them to it when the passion wears off.'

'Well, if the passion has worn off for Paris we might as well send Helen back and have the war over with.'

'No.' Helenus hesitated, then expanded his denial. 'The war is not about that any more. Helen is different, anyway, and Paris has not tired of her.'

'Perhaps Chryseis is different for Agamemnon. Or for Troilus, come to that.'

'For Troilus she is; but there is honour bound up in that. She's his cause, and he manages to love her much more now than he ever did when she was around.'

Hector gave a half smile. 'True. What do I do, though?'

'Do?' Helenus grinned lazily back. 'Nothing at all. Tell him to get out there and kill Agamemnon as soon as the floods are over.'

'Perhaps he would fight harder if I told him she was unfaithful.'

'He has to kill Agamemnon, not her. He'll do his best as it is.' Helenus paused. 'Don't imagine he will marry someone else, whether she has been faithful or not. He will never do that. He has chosen to be doomed by it. Leave him to his fate.'

Hector sighed. 'It would make the fighting so much easier if we felt it would change our fate.' Perhaps, he thought to himself, that is why Helenus has never shone as a figher. He has always been so convinced that it will not.

'We do it anyway.'

Hector's look this time was sharp and exasperated. He clambered to his feet.

Helenus watched him, only slightly abashed by the thoughts that were obviously going through his brother's mind. Why, he wondered, did Hector always want to change him? He was a watcher and listener, not a doer, and Hector should have recognized it. Chryses should have been the same. 'Will you talk to Chryses now?' Hector was already making for the doors.

'No point, is there?' And Hector was gone.

*

The conversation disturbed Hector more when he reached home and had a chance to think about it. It seemed it had solved nothing. What had he expected to discover, other than the things Helenus had told him? Nothing, he supposed. He had always thought Chryseis a light little miss, who would change allegiances as soon as a new man looked her way. He could see the difficulty of explaining that to Troilus, though.

There had to be some way of calming Troilus, of making him more careful. Aeneas had warned Hector several times that he feared Troilus' recklessness would kill him. Hector had repeated to Aeneas Troilus' fantasies about the Achaeans singling him out in battle and had been disturbed to find that the Dardanian did not think them fantasies at all. Aeneas had seen what happened in the battle before the truce and had endorsed Troilus' own interpretation; except that in his version of events, the boy would have been killed had Aeneas and a couple of other Dardanians not moved in to rescue him.

But why should the Achaeans go for Troilus? Was this, too, a part of the madness that Chryseis was casting over the men who tangled with her?

Was Troilus doomed? Everyone else seemed to think it, but Hector could not persuade himself that it was honourable to give up on the boy. Perhaps Priam could be induced to send him away on the next diplomatic mission. When he came back he might be ready to set his eyes on some other girl. Hector had little difficulty in persuading Priam to do as he chose at that time: the High King was too sick to concern himself with any but major issues. It was not the season for diplomacy, however. Priam had intended to seek support from the Thracian King Rhesus, but he would send no one to Thrace in midwinter.

The lines on Hector's face deepened. Before the battle he had been full of enthusiasm, with the prospect of the child coming and the new spirit in Ilios to buoy him up. All that seemed to be gone now. It had been enough to get them through the Achaean offensive, but there would be another offensive, and another, until the enemy finally won through. Helenus was right, he supposed. They were all doomed.

And there was no way out. It had been stupid even to suggest that Helen might be sent back. There were now too many other wrongs for the Achaeans to avenge. The war was growing dirty, with messy vendettas and broken promises on all sides. It hardly seemed honourable to fight on in a mean and defeatist spirit. Still, honour was all that Hector had left. He would stick to it, he hoped, to the end. In that, he sympathized with Troilus. He reckoned the boy might as well go down fighting, so long as he took a few Achaeans with him to the underworld.

Hector was still in the deserted megaron. He had been leaning against a pillar, in the half darkness broken only by the single lamp the servants had left for his return. He brought his hands behind his back and pushed away, as if he planned to go somewhere; then hesitated, unsure where to go, what to do.

There was nobody else he could face talking to. He might have talked over a different worry to Andromache, but she disliked this kind of thing, and she was asleep anyway. A pity he could not go to sleep with her. There would be five, perhaps six more moons before the baby came: it was a long time to endure a cold bed. He had never risked upsetting her by laying the servant girls, and it was a long walk to the lower town in the dark. If only he had some enduring passion to drive him on, like Paris and Troilus – and, perhaps, like Agamemnon. That was not something you chose, though. It was something the gods gave you.

The servants were nowhere to be seen. It was late; presumably they too were all in bed. Hector rummaged around for a cup and some wine to fill it. He drank standing, close to the fire. It was banked high; they must have left it for the night.

A shuffling noise on the hard floor made him turn abruptly. It was difficult to see in the shadows. He thought for a moment that it was just a mouse. Then Astynome moved out into the centre of the room.

A new flicker of annoyance crossed Hector's face. Maybe he had been missing company, but he had no wish to make polite conversation with his mother-in-law. She too had doom hanging heavy about her head.

'Couldn't sleep. I thought I heard someone moving around downstairs.' Astynome moved closer to the hearth and looked around vaguely. Hector fetched a chair for her. She sat, but kept looking, as if she expected him to fetch a second one and sit with her. He did; it seemed he had little choice. She hunched towards the flames.

'Are you cold? Shall I fetch a blanket for you?'

'Thank you, Hector.' He stifled his exasperation and set off to find one. When he returned to the megaron, Astynome seemed not to have moved at all. She did not watch him as he walked across and arranged the blanket round her shoulders.

'I was thinking about the priest.' She spoke as if to herself. 'Chryses, the man of Apollo. Such a lot of disappointments we both have had. A terrible thing it is, to anger the gods.'

'I cannot see that Chryses has angered anyone, except perhaps Agamemnon.'

'Oh, not Chryses; his daughter. She turned her back on Artemis first, and then on Apollo.' Astynome's voice took a firmer pitch, as if Chryseis had angered her too. 'And to drive her father to make curses like those . . .'

'Curses?'

Astynome looked at him. Her face did not seem to contain quite enough energy to register surprise. 'Did he not tell you? He called down Apollo's curse on the Achaeans if they keep the girl. And if they give her back, then they will get Apollo's blessing, and his curse will be on us.'

'They will never give her back.'

'He thinks they will.' She gave a faint, faint smile. 'And then the girl will be the downfall of Troy.'

The doom-laden words exasperated Hector. It was not that he took Apollo's curse lightly: no sane man did. But as he had agreed with Helenus, Troy's downfall had been determined long before Chryseis had come to Ilios. Whatever dire curses Chryses had employed, he could not see that they would make a scrap of difference in the end. 'You sound as if you want her to be.'

'Oh, but I do. She refused my son. My favourite, Maris. Now he is dead, it pleases me to think she will never marry another man.'

Hector lost his patience at this. The woman might be Andromache's mother, but her captivity seemed to have addled her brains. He wished they could be rid of her and enjoy each other's company in peace for the winter. Was there anywhere else he might honourably send her?

'You had not thought of marrying the priest yourself?' The idea rather pleased him: the two of them grumbling away together in Chryse. It was many moons now since Eetion had been killed, and it would not be too bad a match. It even seemed she liked the man.

'Marry the priest? My dear boy!' In her voice now, there was a touch of the old Astynome, the forthright queen with seven sons and a royal household to run. Her eyes narrowed and she seemed to size up Hector. He was not sure whether he looked large or small to her. 'You want me gone, don't you? And Andromache does too. Oh, I don't blame her, she wants to enjoy the baby coming, and I am a drag and a misery. So I shall oblige you. But I shall not marry Chryses, oh dear no. I shall go to my father. You will arrange it, won't you, Hector?' As he did not reply, she added, 'Of course you will,' and stood up with a sudden air of confidence, as if the decision had lightened her spirits. 'And now I shall go back to bed.'

Troilus raised his spear and sighted along it. It was not perfectly straight; it was so difficult to get good pieces of ash. The rough straw target was thirty long paces away. His body measured the wind, his hand assessed the weight of the spear. He shifted his balance a little, took a two paces' run – no more, there was often not time or space even for that on the battlefield – and loosed it.

The point flashed through the air and buried itself in the ground a pace short. Troilus sighed as he went forward to retrieve it. It was not just the warped shaft that was making him throw poorly. There was the uncomfortable sensation that he was almost the only soldier in the camp who was training hard at the end of the fighting season; and there was the lowering, lingering knowledge that he no longer knew what he was fighting for.

To learn that Chryseis was not coming had been such an anticlimax. That, and his narrow escape in the battle, seemed to have killed in him even the urge for vengeance. She was distant from him, more distant in thought than the quarter-day journey which separated them in reality. He could recall her as she had been before she left Ilios, but it was a strain trying to imagine changes that might or might not have taken place in her. He had prepared himself mentally for the task of welcoming back a girl who might barely be recognizable as the Chryseis he had loved. It was different, and harder, to keep that uncertain person in his head, as a symbol of his fate, the object of his desire.

Chryses' manner had been disturbing, too. The priest had been vague and distant, as if his head was up in the clouds with the gods. Hector had apparently taken Troilus' worries seriously, but his response when it came had been equally unsatisfactory. It was not even clear to Troilus whether he had actually spoken to the priest. To be told she was well was one thing; he had gathered that much from Chryses. But there had to be something wrong, something that had wrecked the ransom negotiations, something that had been putting the priest on edge and sending him to the temple daily for long communions with Apollo.

Troilus had not slept well since Chryseis had left Ilios. He had not slept at all for days after the ransom negotiations failed. Now, forcing himself back into training, he was beginning to sleep. But the thoughts still came, and more insistently.

He ran his hand along the smooth wood as he paced back to his throwing position, then let his fingers linger on the bronze speartip. It had to be something she had done, or not done. Was she neglecting the gods? Surely she would not have told her father if she was. No; it had to be Agamemnon. Something about her relationship with the Achaean High King had upset her father. It was not just that she was sharing his bed; she would have had no choice about that. Had she fallen in love with him? Had she perhaps not wanted to come back at all? Had it been not Agamemnon, but she, who had refused the ransom?

He had reached this point a dozen times before; and each time, had turned his mind away. It was hateful, the very thought: not only the prospect of Chryseis' unfaithfulness, but the suspicion that he might be thinking it wrongly. He was being unfaithful to her, in his willingness to believe as much.

This fear of having his doubts exposed as unworthy had kept him from going to ask Chryses outright if it was true. Aeneas might have asked Troilus what was wrong, but he was back in Dardania, comforting his elderly father and doing what he could to put his lands to rights. So Troilus had kept his fears to himself; and now Chryses had returned to his sanctuary and was no longer there to ask.

Wrapped up in his thoughts, Troilus paced on too far. Looking up he exclaimed in annoyance and began to retrace his steps to the muddy line scratched into the soil. He weighed the spear in his hand once more. I could ask Hector again, he thought, flexing his arm muscles experimentally. I could ask Ennomus. I could ask Helenus. One throw for each? And one throw for another sacrifice to Apollo? Not that he appreciated the priests and their cryptic advice. They would only tell him what he knew already, wrapped up in mystic confusion so that it took him days to decipher the message.

That would be four more throws. Five would be enough for this session; he ought to be getting back to the citadel in time for the council meeting that afternoon. Hector, Ennomus, Helenus, Apollo — and one throw for silence.

The trivial little contest that was not really so trivial focussed his mind. His next spearthrow grazed the top edge of the target. The next grazed the bottom. And the next landed plumb in the centre.

He could hardly ask for a clearer sign. He would ask Helenus that evening. Abandoning the last two throws, he set off back to the citadel.

The prospect pleased Troilus when he considered it in the afternoon. Helenus would listen, and not laugh or condemn him. Helenus always seemed to have secrets of his own, and respected other people's. Helenus would not give him sympathy, but sympathy was not what Troilus wanted.

Ironically, Helenus suggested that they go to the tavern in the Street of the Basketmakers, the one where Troilus and Hector had fought. Had he forgotten, Troilus wondered, or was he doing it on purpose? Troilus tagged along with him, his tension growing. A litter of broken jars and midden scraps lined the passageway through to the tavern. In the courtyard, a mush of dead leaves half covered the mud. Most of the drinking booths were dark, and a sour stench of vomit and stale beer drifted from the storeroom.

Helenus led them to an inner room, windowless, with a small fire hissing in the open hearth and a solitary lamp hanging from the rafters. A group of drinkers, hunched in the shadows, paid no attention as the two men entered. A listless girl brought them cups of wine. It did not seem as strong as Troilus remembered it.

They settled in a corner across from the drinkers and Troilus outlined his thoughts in a low voice.

'Why choose me to ask?' Helenus was not aggressive, just curious.

'Who else? If Ennomus knows then you will know too, and I wanted to keep it in the family.'

'Just in case you were wrong.'

'But I'm not wrong, am I?' Helenus' face told him that, and the way his brother was setting about the conversation.

'No.' Helenus ran his hands through his fair hair. 'At least, I don't think so. Hector asked me about it a few days ago. I told him not to tell you. That made me go to ask Chryses.'

'He told you she had no wish to come back.'

'Oh, it was Agamemnon who refused the ransom; but I gather she accepted it easily. She must have been facing up to the prospect of a lifetime with him ever since she was captured, and I suppose she felt she had gone too far to turn back.'

'She must have known I would try to rescue her. To ransom her.'

Helenus refused to share his brother's agitation. He took a deep draught of wine before replying. 'Be fair, she couldn't have. You were lukewarm enough. I knew nothing about the betrothal until after her capture, and Priam doesn't know even now, does he?'

Troilus was silent, and then drank too, as if to cover the pause in the conversation. Finally he said, 'You think I should forget her?'

'Is that what you want to do?'

Troilus cursed under his breath. How maddening Helenus could be, never giving an opinion if he could avoid it. 'I'm not sure what I want to do; or even what I ought to do. I'd been telling myself it might have been like that, but I can't really make myself believe it. I was so sure she loved me.'

'Maybe she did.'

'It's not what I call love, settling so quickly for another man.'

'You don't know she loves him. Troilus, she's a survivor. She plays the odds, treats life like a game of dice. She loved you in her way, but she made damn sure she picked a suitable prince to love. When she was captured she will have worked her hardest at loving Agamemnon. It's not as if she chose him. She was given to him.'

The calm voice, with its hint of cynicism, was infuriating. 'You make it sound so controllable.'

'I think for some people it is.' Helenus turned cool blue eyes on his brother. 'I thought maybe you were one of them.' It was not what he had thought at the time he had discussed it with Hector, but the Troilus in front of him now seemed more like the old Troilus, sometimes emotional on the surface, but always calculating beneath.

'Like you.' Troilus' voice was hard and angry, as if Helenus had insulted him.

'No, not like me: I've loved the wrong woman for years. Like Aeneas, say, or Hector.'

It was a deliberate confession and Helenus fully expected Troilus to take advantage of the opening. It seemed he would not. Helenus gave him a moment, then said, 'You might find it easier to control if you looked around for another woman.'

'Where would I find one? There are no suitable women in Ilios.'

It was true, there were not many, Helenus thought ruefully. So many men, with all the allied troops, and a handful of women they might marry. There was no looking to Thebe or Lyrnessus for brides any more, or further afield. Everyone between Hellas and the Hittite kingdoms knew that Troy was on the verge of disaster. He could not see Troilus marrying, unless Chryseis did return after all, and he could not see it for himself. Priam and Hecuba had not pressed him; there had been nobody for them to suggest. 'Not to marry, true. You can get a warm bed without marrying, though. There are plenty of girls in the lower town who will forgive your ignoring them for the last year. Pretty slave girls. It seems one suited Agamemnon well enough.'

Troilus was not in a mood to get any angrier, nor had he drunk enough. 'Maybe. Let's go and find a couple.'

Helenus grinned and downed the rest of his wine. 'Now you come to mention it, I had one in mind for you. A little fair girl I met last night, in the tavern with the rose bush. A giggler, but cuddly.'

'Don't tell me, she has a friend.'

'Who suits me very nicely. But of course.'

Troilus laughed. It was a warmer sound than his brother had expected. He stood up abruptly. 'Lead the way, sir.'

'My pleasure.'

Troilus did not mention this conversation to Aeneas when the Dardanian returned. It was not only because he did not want Aeneas to know about Chryseis; it did not seem to do him much honour, either. It still rankled that Aeneas had doubted his constancy before, and it would have hurt to admit that he was right, even partially. And in a strange way the discovery had rekindled his taste for revenge, so his outward actions would be much as they would have been had he believed Chryseis to be pining for love of him: except that now he had no hope of a happy ending. Though he and Helenus had worked their way enjoyably through a succession of pretty whores, it was not as if they were any compensation.

He did not want revenge on Chryseis. It felt as if he did not know her any more, as if the Chryseis who loved Agamemnon – or appeared to, at least – was nothing to do with the Chryseis who had loved him. She was a stranger who happened by some odd chance to bear the same name. Instead, he would take vengeance on Agamemnon. Or if the Achaean leader was not to be had, on any of his men who were.

*

In the yard of the camp stables Aeneas' war chariot stood, its wheels fixed, its bronze burnished and its wood polished. The whip was fixed to the side rail; from the front rail hung two twine bags filled with stones for throwing. In the stalls Troilus rummaged through the spears while Aeneas gentled the youngest of his bays, a bridle in the hand behind his back.

Aeneas had brought back a wagon full of spearshafts, light and heavy, cut from the ash and elm on his father's estates. He and Troilus had spent several wet days checking them over for warping and faults in the grain, and fastening the sharp bronze points to them. They generally took six, sometimes eight in the chariot with them.

Troilus had let a crust of blood dry on the handle of his sword, though the design of leopards chased down the blade was spotless. The thin film of oil on his breastplate, the suppleness of the leather straps on his armour, the groove on his forehead where his helmet rested, all told how frequently he had been fighting. He and Aeneas rode out daily, except when the rain came.

The bay, pacified, was being led out to join its partner in the traces, and Troilus finished his selection. Two of Aeneas' light throwing spears, two heavier spears, and two captured Achaean spears, with broad squat heads and alien markings on their shafts. He stowed them carefully and glanced across at Aeneas as the other man finished fastening the harnesses. 'To the plain, today?'

'Maybe towards the mountains. We might find woodcutters; it's a fine day. Or hunters, even.'

Only a few men rode out on winter mornings. Priam's inland allies, used to truces in the cold weather, were reluctant to stir their troops at all, and many of the local men had returned to their towns and villages. There was no danger of a full-scale Achaean attack: the plain was too muddy, and many of the Achaeans were wintering offshore on Tenedos. Some days it was difficult to find prey at all on the plain, or Troilus and Aeneas would have ridden invariably in that direction. There was less sport in attacking woodcutters or boar hunters. Earlier in the war it would have been reckoned contrary to their honour for charioteers to hunt such prey, lightly armed, sometimes without horses. But the time for matched contests was over. Now, it was open season.

It was a killing season. Aeneas had soon discovered, on his return, that Troilus had lost the reckless abandon of the summer. He had become a hard-headed lad, every bit Priam's son, ready to fight carefully and press home any advantage he could gain. Aeneas too had been more than ready to do some killing. What he had found in Dardania had not made his feelings towards the Achaeans any warmer.

Between them they had already killed a dozen men, and wounded as many again. They went with a single chariot, and one man would step down to fight while the other held back the horses, ready for a quick getaway if necessary.

'You drive today?' Troilus asked. Aeneas still disliked seeing any other man controlling his own team. He would usually drive to their destination before yielding up the reins. When it came to fighting it was different. Aeneas had assured Troilus that he was now as good a spearman as any in Ilios, and a better swordsman even than himself. The boy despatched his prey neatly, without a qualm or moment's hesitation.

Aeneas nodded. 'I was thinking,' he said, 'that we could maybe take out two chariots. Mine and yours. Gyrtius would drive me, and I could find you a Dardanian driver too, if Helenus will not come with you.'

That would enable them to challenge teams of Achaean fighters from whom they had previously been forced to turn away. It would mean bigger and better prey, more and harder fights. 'We'll do that tomorrow,' Troilus said.

Aeneas pulled the reins, and the horses drew the chariot in a wide circle towards the stable gate.

They could not take the chariot up into the further foothills; it was difficult enough driving over the rough ground of the far fields. The skill was in finding cover from which they might surprise woodcutters or hunters too far from the mountains to escape back towards them. They had marked out half a dozen places which they used randomly: clumps of trees, low outcrops of rock, an abandoned barn. That day they waited in the lee of a little oak grove. It was nearly midday when they caught sight of a group of Achaean hunters, perhaps eight of them, with dogs but no horses, and a dark shape slung on a pole. A buck, perhaps, or even a boar: they were too distant to be certain.

They did not break cover until the dogs scented them, when the hunters were perhaps two hundred paces away. Aeneas whipped the bays into a near-gallop and the chariot bounced and jumped over the furrows and clumps of the far fields. The hunters, dropping their burden, turned and scattered towards the hills.

They chased one at random, a short man with the long, lank, black hair of an Achaean islander: a Rhodian, perhaps, or a Cretan. A thick sheepskin hung over his shoulders and Troilus aimed one of his light spears at this. He caught the man full between the shoulderblades. By the time Aeneas had pulled up the horses the Achaean had choked out his blood onto the mud and was still.

Troilus kicked away the dogs and turned the corpse contemptuously. The sheepskin had been torn where the spearhead had ripped through it and was soaked in blood. There was a copper bracelet on the man's arm: he could take that as a trophy.

He pulled the spear free and wiped it on the man's tunic. The point was dented; it would have to be hammered out. He took the bracelet and slipped it onto his own arm, muttered an invocation and jumped back into the car.

The dark shape proved to be a young boar. They lashed it to the back rail of the chariot and made their way slowly back to the camp.

'Not a bad day,' said Aeneas.

His men had just finished dismembering the boar and skewering it for cooking. Troilus had left for the palace, but Hector had come down to the camp and agreed to stay for the feast. He glanced around as Aeneas spoke: at the soldiers, exultant, at the glowing fire, the hide spread out for tanning, the discarded bones and entrails, the portions set aside for the priests. The blood everywhere.

'We could use more meat in the stores,' he said. 'You should hunt boar more often.'

'We were not boar hunting today.' Aeneas' eyes narrowed as

he tried to assess Hector's mood. 'It does not displease you, surely, when Troilus kills Achaeans.'

Hector shrugged. 'I've no objection to you taking Troilus to fight, so long as he does nothing too reckless.'

They had talked of Troilus often before, and Aeneas believed he understood – understood even the things of which Hector would not speak directly. It had been a source of annoyance to Hector, surely, that most of his brothers did not shine in warfare as he did. Paris and Helenus were poor fighters, Deiphobus an indifferent one, Lycaon had been killed only days after he had been ransomed, and few of Priam's bastards had made more than a passing impression. For Troilus to emerge as a champion would help to restore the family honour. It was equally true, though, that Ilios could not afford to lose the boy. A prince's death just then could destroy all that remained of the Trojans' morale.

'I am the boy's friend, not his keeper,' Aeneas said curtly.

'You are his elder. I look to you to watch him.'

A quiet fury grew in Aeneas. He would gain no credit, he suspected, for Troilus' achievements; and he would lose all the ground he had made with Hector if anything did happen to the boy. 'I reckon,' he said, 'that Troilus is looking to kill, not to be killed.'

Hector made as if to disagree, and then he curbed himself. 'I hope you are right,' he said, in a quiet, cold voice.

'You're carrying, aren't you?'

Iphis did not respond at all, and Doris wondered briefly if she had used a phrase the other girl did not recognize. 'A baby,' she added.

'Why? Can you tell from my hair?' Doris had been combing it through as they sat together in the outer tent.

Doris appeared to consider this. 'You know, I think that was how I noticed. It gets glossier at first; it's only after a baby is born that it starts to thin and coarsen. Then when I thought about it I could see that you had all the other signs too.'

Iphis said nothing, and Doris kept on combing for a few moments before she asked, 'Have you told him yet?'

'I'll tell him tonight,' Iphis said. Her voice was cool and expressionless. 'Or at least, when he next calls me.'

Doris did not reply to that. They all knew how rarely Patroclus had been calling Iphis. She supposed that the others, like her, all had a fair idea why; but they did not talk about that.

'It's a bad time of year for it.' Iphis spoke quite impersonally. 'With the tent being so damp.'

The pallets they were sitting on were decidedly wet to the touch. 'If we both sat on my pallet,' Doris remarked, 'we could hang yours up to air. We really should air the tent better, too. Perhaps we could pull the sides up in the daytime.'

'I'll talk to Diomede,' Iphis said. 'She might not be pleased if we mess with the tent without warning her.'

It was, Doris supposed, Briseis who they should have talked to those days. Briseis hardly ever came into the women's tents, though. She divided her time between the hospital tent and Achilles' hut, which was perfectly dry, even in the autumn rains. And nobody mentioned Briseis to either Iphis or Diomede.

Patroclus did not call Iphis that night. He did call her the following evening. The hut was crowded when she walked in. Most of the officers seemed to be there, and so was Briseis, by Achilles' side.

Iphis told him straight away, in front of all the others, in the same low, level voice she had used with Doris. Achilles heard her too, and Briseis, and Phoenix.

A flicker of an emotion that might have been annoyance, or surprise, appeared on Patroclus' handsome face; and then it was swallowed by his charming smile. He stood and hugged her. 'But that's marvellous,' he said.

Iphis smiled, without quite looking at him. Then Briseis was on her feet too, and the word spread, and everybody was moving to congratulate her.

Patroclus found her a place to sit by him on the bench, and Achilles crossed the room to fetch his harp. He smiled at Iphis. 'This is for the baby.'

He sang a Thessalian lullaby, short, with a simple tune. The notes fell one by one from the harp strings and echoed in the silence of the hut. His voice was low and true, and he sang the words plainly, without lingering on them. Iphis found that she was crying. Patroclus turned to look at her and put his arm around her shoulders.

Achilles did not pause when the song had ended, but moved straight into another, a lament for a fisher boy, pulled beneath the waves by a great fish and never seen again. Then his hands moved faster, and his voice rose, and he moved into a marching song, one all the men knew. Automedon's strong voice joined in, and Patroclus', and the hut vibrated to the chorus. Iphis sat in the circle of Patroclus' arm, her body cold, and her voice silent.

'I could give you Doris,' Achilles said. There was only half a questioning note in his voice.

Patroclus looked up at him, surprised. A spoke had broken on a chariot wheel and they had been working together, replacing it. 'There is no need for that.'

'You will need a girl to see to you. Iphis has been quite sick, Diomede told me.'

'Not too sick to unfasten my armour or wash me down.' He hesitated. 'I doubt if she would like it if I called on Doris instead.'

Achilles' face was expressionless. 'Well, you know you can call on Doris if you want her. I'll tell her I've told you so.'

Patroclus frowned. He said carefully, 'I'd rather you didn't tell her you were giving her to me.'

Achilles turned deliberately and met his friend's gaze. He held it for a long moment, then dropped his eyes and moved away. He rummaged in the store hut and emerged with a piece of elm. 'There's a weak spot on this back rail. We don't want it snapping when we're in action. I thought maybe I could splice this piece in.'

Patroclus came across to inspect the rail. 'I doubt if that would work; it's not long enough. There would be weakness here, and here. We really ought to replace the rail. I think Ulysses had some figwood that would do. I'll go and ask him.'

'Do. And try Nestor if he has already used it. I'll start to unfasten this rail while you are getting it.' He was setting to work on the woven leather thongs that made up the floor of the car as he spoke.

Patroclus did not move immediately, and after a moment Achilles turned to look at him. 'You don't want me to offer you any of the other girls.' It was not a question at all, this time. And it did not need an answer.

The following night Patroclus rose to leave the hut as Automedon and the rest were going. He caught Achilles' glance.

'I've already done the horses,' Achilles said.

'I know. Don't leave the light for me.'

'I will if you plan to be back. There's hardly any moon tonight.'

'I won't be back. I'll see you in the morning.'

When the door had shut behind him Briseis said, 'Where is he going?'

Achilles sat down on the bed and began to unfasten his sandals. 'I imagine,' he said, 'he means us to assume that he is going to the whorehouse.' He threw a sandal across the hut, accurately, so that it skidded to a halt by his shield. 'Or possibly to Diomedes, who has a new girl he has been boasting about and is happy to share.' He threw the second sandal, not quite hard enough, and looked at Briseis. 'I am not planning to ask him about it.'

Briseis was frowning and did not move across to him. Achilles stood and untied his belt. 'I am not,' he said, 'going to discuss it with you either.' He shrugged off his tunic. 'Are you coming to bed? Or are you thinking of going out yourself?'

She seemed not to have heard him. Then she roused herself and stood up. 'Of course I am coming to bed.'

■

The sheep had been trussed, front legs together and back legs together, so that it lay splayed out across the stone altar, with its belly exposed. Calchas raised his double-headed axe and brought it down upon the animal's throat. He set the golden cup beneath the end of the channel cut in the stone, so that the blood would run into it. Then he took his bronze knife to the sheep's belly. He made a long, straight cut and reached in, drawing out a shining mass of entrails which he spread across the top of the altar. The other priests crowded round and began to pull the entrails apart, searching for the omens that would provide them with their prophecies, while the altar boys started to wail the sacred songs.

In front of the altar Agamemnon kneeled, his head bowed almost to the floor. Menelaus was a step behind him. Behind Menelaus, in rows, kneeled Chryseis and the rest of their household servants.

The same as it was in Troy, thought Chryseis; and yet so different. The Achaeans worshipped the same gods. They called many of them by the same names. They made sacrifices in the same way, and looked for similar signs when they cut them up. But in Ilios, it would have been Priam who stood behind the altar, presiding over the rite. Agamemnon was not High Priest of the Achaeans as his Trojan counterpart was of the Trojans. He was merely their temporal King. Calchas, as High Priest, had his own sphere of power, quite separate from Agamemnon's.

Separate – and yet intersecting. The High Priest was very sparing in his demands of the High King. He would let pass almost unnoticed incidents as grave as Agamemnon's refusal to return Chryseis. But when he did make demands they were great and terrible, and not to be refused. When the Achaeans had set out for Troy he had demanded that Agamemnon sacrifice his own daughter in order to ensure favourable winds. Agamemnon had done so. He had been scarred by the act for life.

For that alone, Chryseis would have hated and feared the High Priest. Nothing was necessary, however, to fuel her hatred. Every line of Calchas' piggy little face, every spark from his beady eyes, almost invisible among the rolls of fat, every gesture of his plump body, drew her detestation.

She participated in these rites, a regular occurrence at each half moon, as a matter of course. It was demanded of every member of the High King's household. But she was always conscious that this offering, to Zeus and the lesser gods, was entirely separate from her personal worship of Apollo. Apollo she worshipped in private, going to his altar at times when she knew nobody else would be there, and preparing her own offerings: a golden chain for her forehead that Agamemnon had given her, a little statue she had fashioned out of the mud of the estuary, a perfect peach or a few ears of corn. She asked Apollo for nothing in return: except that he renew her trust in him, and that he speak to her occasionally.

The golden cup below the altar filled, and the blood began to overflow. A junior priest reached down to take it and wiped the sides with a linen cloth. He handed the cup to the High King, who lifted his head and, with a deep obeisance to the altar, began to drink.

Two serving boys lifted the body of the sheep from the altar, leaving the entrails laid out in full view of the assembly. Taking it to a corner of the square, they began to dismember it and to thread the chunks of meat onto skewers, ready for roasting above the sacrificial fire.

■

Aeneas was restless. For days it had been cloudy, with winds roaring across the plain and sudden squally showers. There had been only two fine days in the previous ten. On one of those, he had arranged a meeting with Paris; on the other, there had been a council meeting.

He woke up one morning to find that the clouds had cleared. The sky was pale and bright, the wind low. He went immediately to the palace. Troilus was already armed when he reached there, and before the red had faded from the horizon the two of them were out on the plain with their charioteers.

They always took two chariots now, with Gyrtius and Archel-ochus to drive them. They always rode to the plain, even when they were unlikely to find Achaeans there. Both Aeneas' and Troilus' bloodlust had been blunted by the repeated kills they had made. They looked only for Achaean chariots now, not for wood-gatherers or huntsmen. They had been trying to live down the reputation they had acquired for fighting hard and dirtily, and would observe every protocol. But the reputation had not faded: often the Achaeans turned away before they were within spearshot. When they did not, Aeneas himself frequently turned back at the last moment. He sensed a recklessness in the Achaeans who stood up to them. They were men who might kill one of them. Aeneas had not forgotten Hector's warning, and he had no wish to risk lives unnecessarily.

Troilus generally followed him when he withdrew, but under protest. Aeneas had been quietly insistent that the choice to withdraw must always be his. Occasionally he had an uncomfortable sense that Troilus was waiting for something: a chance for a purer revenge, a chance for glory, perhaps. This was not a matter he wished to discuss. He knew it was always possible that the boy would refuse to come when called. A part of his mind knew that they should have stopped fighting together, that he had served his purpose for Troilus, and that their sorties were now a private indulgence of his own. He needed them, though: he did not want to stop.

It was too early, Aeneas thought to himself. They could ride hard down almost to the stockade, and along the shoreline, but they would be unlikely to find any opponents. Still, they had been shut in the citadel for too long. They had missed the feeling of the wind in their faces, the sound of the horses panting and the chariot creaking. They were neither of them inclined to wait any longer.

Halfway to the stockade, as they were skirting the banks of the Simois, Troilus saw a couple of charioteers, Myrmidons, riding in their direction. Aeneas watched as the Myrmidons sighted them. He saw the leading fighter lean over to give his charioteer an order. It was not an order to withdraw.

'Turn back,' Aeneas shouted.

Troilus gave him a mutinous look. He wrenched the reins from Archelochus, and pulled a few paces closer to Aeneas, so he could dispute the order. 'There are only two chariots. Four men, the same as us.'

'Troilus, how many Myrmidon charioteers are there? There's perhaps a one in three chance that one of the fighters is Achilles.'

Troilus gave a sudden, ferocious grin. 'I should like to kill Achilles.'

It had been the wrong thing to say. A chance for glory. For this, Aeneas realized, Troilus might well rebel against him. He decided to reason with the boy, rather than repeat his order directly. 'So should we all. Unfortunately he will kill you first.'

'Maybe not. You told me I was as good a spearman as any in Ilios.'

'I reckon Achilles is better.' The memory of that morning in Dardania was still clear in Aeneas' mind. Men who had escaped Achilles once and valued their lives did not give him a second chance.

'We shall soon find out.'

The Myrmidons were closing fast. Aeneas looked again. One of the chariots was drawn by three horses. Only one Myrmidon charioteer drove three horses like those. Aeneas' resolve strengthened. 'We withdraw now, Troilus. That is an order.'

'You withdraw. I'm fighting.' Troilus turned stubbornly away and urged Archelochus forward. With an apologetic glance at Aeneas, the Dardanian whipped the horses. Cursing, Aeneas told Gyrtius to follow.

Troilus had leaped down, his thrusting spear poised, before Aeneas' own chariot drew level. The leading Achaean was down too, ready to engage him. Aeneas did not bother with a second look. He turned to the other man. It did not enter his head to observe the rules of combat: desperation was uppermost in his mind. He threw his javelins, hard and straight, at the horses. Then he jumped to the ground, dodging a cast that went wide, and taking his position with shield fixed and spear ready.

The Myrmidon was a good head taller, but that was no problem: if anything, it was better to thrust upwards. They circled round, warily assessing each other's stance, then the Myrmidon thrust, firmly but wildly. The spearhead stuck fast in Aeneas' shield, cutting through the outer layer but not breaching it. A bad move, which gave Aeneas an advantage.

His opponent was, he thought, Patroclus. Achilles' charioteer in the main battles, he would doubtless take the chance to do some straight fighting himself in the winter. But if it was Patroclus he was not fighting as well as he was reputed to.

Something seemed to have distracted him. Aeneas' quick thrust caught his spear arm, not deeply, but well enough to stop the man.

Before he could move in for the kill he heard a cry to his side. A glance told him that Troilus was down and Achilles was moving to his friend's aid. Above the shouts from the Myrmidons there came a yell from Gyrtius. He leaped for the chariot, and they were away.

They pulled the horses up a couple of hundred paces off. Aeneas did not expect pursuit, with one of Patroclus' horses rearing in agony and his driver fighting to keep control. He had no wish to fight on single-handed, but he knew it would not be honourable to return without Troilus' body. He watched silently with the two Dardanian drivers as the Myrmidon drivers set about the task of despatching the wounded horse and replacing it with Achilles' third.

Achilles went first to his friend, and then when the blood had been stanched with a strip from his tunic, to the body that lay in the mud. Troilus did not move as Achilles' foot reached out. Aeneas knew that he was dead. He felt, though he could not see, Troilus' unseeing eyes gaze up at the sky. There was no indication that Achilles recognized Troilus, though he surely knew from the entwined dragons on his shield and breastplate that he was one of Priam's sons. Perhaps Patroclus knew him. They talked, and it seemed they agreed that the boy deserved his honour. Achilles took his sword, but did not touch the armour. He looked across at Aeneas, who did not doubt that he was recognized. Then the Myrmidons were back at their chariots, and away across the plain.

Aeneas did what he had to do. There was a look of anger on Troilus' face. Aeneas did not think he was angry at Achilles. He was angry with himself for not fighting quite as well as the other man.

It had been a clean death, a thrust below his shield and then a sword sliced across the throat. And an honourable one. There was no shame in losing to Achilles. He could hardly have hoped for a better end, but that knowledge did not ease Aeneas' grief. He held back the tears till they were at the gates, and then he made for his quarters, and let them wash over him.

Troilus' death frightened Andromache. It also made her feel guilty. She felt she should have done more when he was alive, offered him sympathy when the ransom demand failed, talked to Chryses when Hector asked her to. She had not loved him – he had always made her uncomfortable: she had found him unpredictable – but she missed him. It had been so unexpected, too. People prepared themselves to face deaths before the big battles, but nobody expected princes to die in the middle of winter, in little skirmishes.

Hector might console her, she thought briefly. He had done that after she had lost the baby; but she was pregnant now, and the sort of consolation he had provided before was out of the question. Hugging a man, in her limited experience, always led to more. If she wanted a shoulder to cry on she supposed it would have to be Polyxena's, or Cassandra's.

It surprised her when Hector came to her looking for consolation. It had always been she who was weepy and distraught, he who played the strong, steady part. He was not weeping now, but his broad face was ashen and his shoulders drooped. She reached out her arms and he came into them, as well as he could with the bulge of her belly in the way. He did not seem to find the embrace arousing. They went to her room and lay on the bed together, on top of the washed Cretan blanket with its faint stains.

Andromache held her husband tight, then loosed her arms as if the scene rather embarrassed her. She said, 'It surprised you too, didn't it?'

Hector rolled onto his back. 'I should never have believed Aeneas. He said Troilus was safe with him, that he'd not do anything stupid. But to let him fight Achilles – absolute idiocy. And then to come back himself without a scratch. I nearly killed him myself.'

His fists clenched and Andromache could feel his body tense next to hers.

'I don't understand it either,' she said in a small voice. 'He always seemed so fond of Troilus.'

'You'd think it now, to see the way he's wailing over him.' The misery in Hector's voice had gone, to be replaced by a cold, hard anger. 'A bloody insult it is, in the circumstances. It's we who really mourn him, not Aeneas.'

'I don't think he means it like that, Hector. He honestly is sorry. You said he had worked so hard with Troilus, teaching him how to fight better.'

Hector lay there for a moment, then sat up heavily and swung his feet to the floor. 'The pity of it all is he was doing such a good job. Troilus really was a damn good fighter. Another year or so and he might have got the better of Achilles. He was only a boy, though. It's no competition, a lad against a man like Achilles.'

'So you are angry with Achilles too.'

He stood up and crossed to the window, as if he were planning to look out and send his fury across the plain. He did look out, for a long moment. When he turned back to Andromache his face was calm again. 'I suppose I should be. But Achilles is a long way away. And that rat Aeneas is right here.'

Troilus' funeral procession was led by King Priam. It was the first time in months that Priam had stirred outside the palace. He had taken a dose of poppy large enough to kill a mule, the soldiers whispered; and he moved slowly, with Hector supporting his left arm and Paris his right.

The priests followed: priests of Apollo, of Zeus, of Dionysus, Poseidon and all the other gods, and then the priestesses of Athena and Artemis and the other goddesses. It was whispered that Priam had been inclined to send for Chryses to lead the priests, but that Hector had dissuaded him.

The other princes and princesses of Ilios came next, then the subsidiary kings, the lower-ranking commanders of the allied forces, and the common soldiers and townsfolk. They walked, wailing, from the Scaean Gate, along the path that led to the shrine of Apollo, to the flat piece of land where the pyre had been built. The procession slowly formed itself into a wide circle around the pyre. Altar boys led Troilus' hunting dogs and his team into the clear space. Priam had not the strength to kill them: the Chief Priest of Apollo did it for him. The blood was offered up to the gods, then the carcases were arrayed around the edges of the pyre.

In the centre, Troilus' body lay on a bier draped with a golden cloth, patterned with entwined dragons. He wore the armour that Achilles had left him, burnished bright. Hector had set his own sword in the boy's hand.

These were honours given only to heroes. It was by Hector's orders, Aeneas knew, that Troilus was being given a hero's funeral. If Achilles had seen fit to do the boy some honour, Hector had argued, then the Trojans must show him far more.

The priests drenched the corpse once more with oil, then poured oil on the other carcases.

The flame had been kindled at Apollo's altar. It was a still day: the torch burned steadily. The Chief Priest set it in Priam's hand, and the High King lowered himself, slowly and painfully, and touched it to the lowest branches of the bier.

Aeneas turned away as the flames licked hungrily upwards. He had seen it too often, and it never ceased to be terrible. Instead he looked at Andromache. Her face pale but composed behind the mourning stripes, she stood between Hecuba and Helen. The child was surely due very soon, he thought to himself.

He saw Priam turn to Hector, the light extinguished in his eyes, as if that son were the only one he had left now, and Paris, Deiphobus and the rest were nothing to him. He heard Cassandra wail with grief, her eyes black and unseeing, as if her mind had cracked like an egg and the inner madness were oozing from it. Aeneas felt a sudden warmth towards her. There was nothing feigned in her misery.

Had anyone told Troilus' own fragile love? Aeneas wondered. Never having seen Chryseis for himself, he envisaged her as somewhere between Helen and Cassandra in looks. Younger, of course, but with the same kind of cool – and breakable – sophistication. Perhaps with the same blend of passion and calculation that Troilus himself had always shown. There had been a rumour that she had forgotten Troilus and wanted to stay with Agamemnon, but he and Troilus had never discussed it.

Into Aeneas' mind then came Troilus' conviction that the Achaeans knew him and had sought him out. He remembered Patroclus' face in that moment when his attention had turned from Aeneas and towards the boy. Patroclus had not been seeking him out. It was more as if he had felt that some other Achaean, not himself or Achilles, should have been destined to do the deed. Perhaps Patroclus would tell Chryseis, Aeneas thought. He might do it gently, and not laugh at her if she cried.

There had been a strange destiny about it, it seemed to Aeneas. He had no doubt, now, that it had been the death Troilus had wanted for himself. Clearly it had not been the death Hector had wanted for him. Hector's opinion had been repeated over and over in the taverns.

That had angered the allied commanders almost as much as it had angered Aeneas. They all agreed that there was nothing Aeneas could have done. He would have if he could, of course he would. He had loved the boy.

So much promise, and so much work, all thrown to waste in a moment of madness. So much work on Hector too. Hector, though, was the greater loser, Aeneas reminded himself. All Priam's family were. They were all so careless of the allies, as if gold alone would buy their loyalty. It did not. They mourned Troilus in the camp, but there had been little sympathy for his family. Even Helenus had found the Mysians beginning to close ranks against him.

The flames burned fiercely, almost silently, accompanied by the rhythmic, tuneless chants of the priests. The cloying smell of burning flesh and sweet oil blanketed the ground. As the flames reached the corpse Aeneas saw Hector look up and bring his hands to his face. His expression was blind as the nails raked down his cheeks, again and again, and the blood sprang brightly to the surface. Andromache moved forward then, and Hecuba, and Helenus and the rest, and Priam's family huddled together in their public grief, while the allied kings and the soldiers and the townsfolk stood unmoving, a dozen paces away from them.

*

Aeneas was, he told himself, unmoved by the rites. Perhaps it was not entirely true, because he did not leave Ilios as he had intended. He stayed in the camp, waiting to see what would happen next, and fighting to kill as he had done with Troilus. He needed a new partner to ride out with and he turned to Acamas, another Dardanian leader. Acamas was young and could be daring, but he was a solid fighter: perhaps better than Troilus had been, even if he did not get the same credit from Hector. More important, Acamas had no death wish and could be relied upon to pull back when he had to. Aeneas pulled back too, but only when it was strictly necessary. He began to keep a tally of his kills, notching the front rail of his chariot every time he finished off an Achaean.

As always, news from outside Ilios came to the camp first. It was just after the full moon following Troilus' death, when the winter was almost over, that Aeneas heard of Andromache's mother Astynome. A good strong woman, he had always thought, with more that was Amazon than her name about her. He had not seen her in Ilios after she was ransomed and had been surprised to hear that she had chosen to leave Andromache and return to her father's estates, far to the east. It shocked him to learn that she was dead.

It was not clear how she had died. The messenger was inclined to blame it on Artemis. Sharp pains of some kind, then, as if the goddess had shot her. She expected to die, the messenger added. It could have been poison she gave herself, but perhaps it was kinder to blame it on her heart. However it happened, the goddess had not been angry with her. She had done it as a favour.

Aeneas went away thoughtfully from his interview with the messenger, to make sacrifice. Men did not sacrifice to Artemis, or he would have done. He chose her brother Apollo instead.

It seemed to be expected in the camp that he would carry the news to Hector and Andromache. Aeneas had not had a real conversation with Hector since before Troilus' death. Still, somebody had to do it, and he did not think Hector would hold it against him. He went up the hill to the house on Palace Square with a heavy heart.

Hector could have the job of telling Andromache, he said to

himself as he asked the housekeeper if he might see her master alone. She moved him to a plain, almost empty room. Glancing around while he was waiting – he had to wait some time – Aeneas recognized Hector's armour stacked in the corner, and a sheaf of the heavy spears that only Hector used. There was a small clothes chest, but nothing more personal in the room.

Hector appeared at last and greeted Aeneas coolly but not rudely. He did not invite Aeneas to sit, and Aeneas did not take either of the two small stools that the room offered. Instead he crossed to the window and gazed out at the view down across the citadel to the smiths' quarter and the East Gate while he related his news.

Hector took it calmly.

'You knew she was sick?' Aeneas asked.

'She was not all that sick. Unwell, but not desperately sick like Priam. All the same, I am not surprised. I suppose she went home to die.'

It was chilly in the small room, which received no direct sunlight in the afternoon. Aeneas repressed a slight shiver. 'I always thought of her as a tough woman. One who would take everything the gods handed out, and keep on going.'

Hector shook his head. 'I think Andromache would. I might have thought it of her mother a winter ago. It changed her, though, the captivity. She said Achilles treated her well, but it drew the spirit out of her. She had no wish to go on, not even till the baby came.'

'Perhaps she expected this one to die too.'

'Everybody dies in the end. We cannot stop loving people because we know the end might come at any time.' Hector clenched his fist and then released it slowly. He is letting the losses get to him again, Aeneas thought.

'Did you love Astynome?' He asked it lightly, conversationally. Hector gave him a sideways glance, then shook his head once more.

'No. I respected her, until she came here. Then it seemed there was nothing left to respect. Andromache loved her. I think perhaps I will keep it from her until after the baby is born. She wanted her mother gone, she was driving us all to distraction, but it may worry her now, thinking she might have sent her to her death.' He looked up. 'I am more angry. Not at the ransom, though that was a waste, but at the hopelessness of it all.'

'Men do it too, in a different way. Choose to die.' Aeneas did not like to mention Troilus, but he was thinking of him.

'I don't,' Hector said sharply. 'Not yet. And you don't either, do you, Aeneas?'

'No. I feel I am a survivor.' And like all survivors, he added to himself, I shall see many more deaths before my own.

It was not difficult to keep the news from Andromache. There was scant interest in the woman who had once been Queen of Thebe. The palace women discussed it a little in the women's megaron, but Andromache did not hear them, since she was keeping to her room. She had a grim determination that this time nothing would go wrong with the child. She prayed daily herself to Artemis, not for death but for an easy delivery. Her prayers were answered. Eight days later her son was born.

There was joy, though it was not unclouded. Priam came to see the child as soon as the birth rites were over. Hector held him proudly. He was a big baby and looked to be strong. The High King wanted him named Scamandrius, after the river, but his parents decided that though this would be his formal name, they would use one that had no echo of his dead grandmother's. To them he would be Astyanax, Lord of the Lower Town, as his father was lord of the citadel.

Hector sat in the shadow of the fig tree that grew, stubbornly, in a corner of Palace Square. The square, exposed and windy, had no other trees, and the fig was warped and bent over, as if its life were a permanent battle.

It was dark under the fig tree. Across the square, on every wall, and carried by slaves where there were no walls, torches flared. Under their light a crowd of people drifted and clumped, chattered and drank. In a far corner of the square the dark mass of an ox slowly rotated over a roaring fire. In a starry sky a limpid full moon shone. It was the full moon festival, the festival for the presentation of Hector's son to the moon.

Hector himself had no part in the festival. It was the women's task to celebrate a birth. Artemis' moon maidens had traced out the crescents and circles of their sacred dance. Hecuba and Cassandra had led the priestesses in their bloodless sacrifices. Andromache still sat in state on the steps to the palace, holding the baby in her arms and showing it to the women of the citadel as they approached, one by one, to offer it something very close to worship.

Some of the men came too, for the festival was not forbidden to men, but their part in it was strictly subsidiary: as was Hector's part in his household, he was inclined to think, now that the baby was there. Andromache, Helike, the little slave girl who tended the fire – all of them seemed to see him only as Astyanax's father.

That was one of the nagging grumbles in his mind. The other was Astynome. He was still conscious that he had not told Andromache of her mother's death. But there was no hurry: he did not expect her to hear of it from anyone else.

Nobody else in Ilios, it seemed to Hector, had any troubles at all; or if they did, they did not mention them. The momentary depression at Troilus' death had given way, in everybody but him, to a boundless optimism. Priam's cough was not so hoarse, and he stood up straighter, though Cassandra said he could never leave off taking the poppy again. The missions had gone well. All the old allies would be back in the spring, and some new ones as well. Word had come at last from Rhesus, the Thracian king, and when the sea had calmed and the last of the Thracian snows had melted he would bring a thousand men to Ilios. It did not look as if the Trojans would lose the war just yet, and for the first time in years men were beginning to speculate out loud that they might win it.

Hector was not one of them. Even if the miracle happened, he thought to himself, Troilus, Eetion, Maris, Mynes, Lycaon and a host of others would not be there to see it. And Astynome. He really ought to tell Andromache about Astynome.

*

It was another two moons before Hector told Andromache about her mother. His delay was due partly to his reluctance; partly to the simple fact that he had seen so little of her. Though there were plenty of nursemaids, she seemed to be absorbed permanently in the baby, feeding it and dressing it and doing the other strange things that mothers do. He continued to resent that. The baby pleased him well enough, but he had expected to get Andromache back after its birth, and now it seemed that he would not. Not yet; perhaps, he was beginning to think, not at all.

He supposed he had never been prepared to take from her the kind of overwhelming affection that she lavished on the child. He did think she might have arranged it better, though: kept things as they were with him and given the baby the overflow. He wondered if he ought to demand more attention from her, more love, but he was not used to acting like that and he was afraid of being repulsed.

Even when he asked to talk privately with her, and she should have realized that it was important, he had to wait while the baby was fed and settled to sleep. It made him grumpy, pacing around while the maid eyed him disapprovingly, as if his very footsteps were an insult to the child. Though he had taken care in waiting for a suitable time to break the news, he felt increasingly disinclined to tell Andromache gently. He did not expect her to care particularly. It did not seem as if she would have any feelings to spare for her mother when she had few enough for him. He had expected her to mourn Troilus because he did, but Astynome's death had not touched him deeply.

At last Andromache emerged from the nursery, pink-cheeked, with her hair mussed around her face and her dress crumpled. The baby was asleep at last and she seemed ready to deluge Hector with a flood of tiny details about its every gurgle and gesture. He cut her off abruptly, in mid-flow. 'You can tell me later. I have to see Priam before midday.'

She stopped short and looked at him as if he were unexpectedly strange to her. He was in a way. She had been expecting the proud father, not the irritable husband. 'I am sorry. Did I keep you waiting long?'

'Longer than I would have liked.' Hector frowned. He should

have been more gracious in the circumstances. 'Let's go to your room.'

Andromache led the way along the corridor, suddenly apprehensive. She had no idea what Hector might want with her. Surely he did not expect to make love to her? It was much too soon, that ought to wait until she had finished feeding the baby. Possibly it was something to do with the fighting. She had barely listened to the recent news of it.

She waited awkwardly while Hector sat down in the only chair. They had talked in her room several times during her pregnancies, but she had always been lying on the bed. That did not seem quite appropriate now, but she could not stand in front of him like a naughty child waiting to be punished, so she went to perch on the edge of it. Hector must have thought it awkward too, because he stood and came to sit next to her.

He put an arm round her, clumsily, and she tensed a little. Feeling her tension, Hector tightened his arm slightly. 'I have some painful news to tell you. About your mother.'

Andromache turned to him, but did not look at him. It was suddenly clear what he was going to say. Important things always happened on this bed. All her biggest griefs and joys seemed to be centred on it. She should have expected a grief to come next, her happiness had been too intense to last. She said in a small voice, 'She's dead.'

'Yes. I'm sorry, darling.'

Endearments always came easiest to Hector at this kind of time, Andromache thought vaguely to herself. 'How? When?'

He told her, clearly but quickly. She said nothing else, and he added after a moment, 'You expected it, surely?'

'No. Perhaps I should have, I can see that now.' Hector's arm felt heavy across her shoulders and she stood up and walked over to the window. His presence seemed to join with the painted ladies in the fresco, crowding the room. They were all beings from Ilios, all essentially alien to her, however hard she tried to belong to them. She wanted to shut him out and yet she had the urge to keep .talking. 'I know Mother was so unhappy when she was here, she couldn't come to terms with all the deaths, my father and my brothers. I thought it would be better, though, when she got away from Ilios. I imagined her up at her father's house, turning back into the mother I used to know. I had thought of taking the baby up to see her, not this summer, but perhaps next, when he was stronger, and she had had time to get over it. I never thought about her dying. She had died once to me, at Thebe, and when I found out that it was not true then, it seemed to me as if she were immortal, that it would never really happen.'

'Perhaps it would help you to pretend that it never did. That she is still up there in the hills, though you will not be going to see her, this summer or next.'

It was a kind thought of Hector's. It warmed Andromache towards him a little to realize that he was trying to sympathize and help her. She did not think she could do what he suggested, but she said quietly, 'Perhaps it would.' Then she turned from the window and came across to him. They were used to mourning together, it was the thing that had brought them closest. Closer than the baby had brought them, it seemed to Andromache. The baby had no part in this; she did not want grief to touch its tiny life. It had to be between her and Hector, and their ghosts. So many ghosts filling the room. When she reached out and Hector pulled her down to him it felt as if she were taking all the ghosts in her arms, and crying with them all.

'Priam's device.'

Achilles stood over the body of the dead Trojan. He had turned it face upwards and the Trojan's face stared up at him with blank eyes and a look of anger. A good expression for a dying fighter. He had not shown fear, even at that moment when he had known the fight was lost. It had not lasted long, but the man had known what he was about. Boy, rather. He could barely have seen twenty summers.

Patroclus scarcely glanced at the entwined dragons on the shield and breastplate. 'He's one of Priam's sons.'

'Do you know which?' Achilles did not expect him to. It was

not Hector or Paris: anyone could have recognized them.

'Troilus.' Patroclus was quiet and sounded perfectly sure. 'And it was Aeneas who cut me.'

'We all know him.' Achilles glanced over to where the Trojan horses and their survivors waited just beyond chasing distance. He could not have recognized the Dardanian from so far off and had barely glanced at him during the fight, but he could tell the horses. Aeneas had the best pair of any Trojan. He thought briefly that it was a pity he had not taken the time to raid Anchises' stables when he was in Dardania. There were reputed to be four more there, just as good.

'You'll not go after him?'

'Not with two horses and your arm cut to shreds. I never did feel I was destined to kill Aeneas. I suppose I should leave him the body.' If the dead Trojan was a prince it could have fetched a ransom, but Achilles was inclined to be generous. Perhaps Patroclus would not be, since Aeneas had speared his horse. Achilles glanced across, half expecting to be contradicted.

'Leave the armour too.' Patroclus saw Achilles hesitate and added, 'I'll tell you why when we are back at the camp.'

'If you say so. He deserves it, he fought well. I'll take the sword, though. It was a clean fight, at least on our side, so I reckon I have a right to it.' He bent to pull it from the Trojan's scabbard. It was a good heavy one, with a silver hilt, blood-encrusted, and a design of leopards chased down the blade. A prince's sword, but workmanlike. Evidently this son of Priam's had been more on the lines of Hector than of Paris. 'Let's get back.'

Patroclus seemed edgy. He had not fought well, Achilles thought to himself. Aeneas was a brilliant spearman, true, but Patroclus should have been more than a match for him. Perhaps there was something up. It was no use discussing it then, with the Trojans watching them and the body stiffening at their feet.

'Ride with me. Give your spear to Automedon. He can go in the other chariot. Automedon, will you carry this sword too?' Achilles handed over the Trojan sword.

The news of the encounter preceded them as they reached the gates of the camp, and before they had left Automedon to take the horses and made their way to their own hut a swarm of men had gathered. Achilles dismissed them, a little abruptly. 'I'll tell you later. Let me see to Patroclus. Epeigeus, can you send Briseis to us?'

When they reached the hut Briseis was already there. She unbound the strip of cloth that covered the cut and looked it over. 'It's not so bad. If I wash it and bind it again it should mend before the new moon.'

She spoke to Achilles. He smiled. He had never known such a woman for washing wounds; he had always been more inclined to let the blood dry around them, but the men had been mending under her care and he trusted her.

'I'll leave you and go and talk to the men. Stay with him, Briseis. I'll be back when I can.' He caught a glance from Patroclus. 'Don't try to tell me now. I'll give nothing away. You can talk this evening if you feel up to it.'

Achilles left before Patroclus had had a chance to protest. Briseis looked after him, and then at Patroclus, confused. Then Iphis came through the open door with hot water, and she bit back her questions and set to work.

Patroclus said nothing to her until the wound was salved and dressed and Iphis, who had returned repeatedly with water, drinks and everything else she thought Patroclus might need, had been gently but firmly dismissed. Achilles had not returned and they were alone together. 'Shut the door.'

She did it and came back to where he lay on the bed. He looked up at her for a moment, then closed his eyes.

'Do you want to sleep?'

He shook his head. 'Come and lie next to me.' It did not sound like an order, but Briseis was not inclined to refuse. She slipped off her sandals and clambered across him to lie on the side away from his injured arm. He turned to look at her again and she looked back and brought her own arm round him. It was the first time they had touched since their night together and they lay silent and still, savouring the touch, for a long time.

'Thank you.' Patroclus shifted a little and Briseis sat up, leaning over him. Then she bent and kissed him softly. 'You know I love you.'

'Yes.' He managed a smile. 'But you love Achilles more.'

'So do you.' It had needed saying for a long time. She slid down in the bed again to hold him tighter. 'Am I hurting you?'

'No.'

'Did you want to talk?'

'It can wait until Achilles is back.' After a moment he added, 'I think perhaps I will sleep now.'

'Shall I go?'

'He told you to stay.'

Briseis returned his smile and moved to sit up again. She did not want to let go of him, but at the same time she did not want Achilles to find her in his arms. It had to be deliberate, planned, so that Achilles would know it all without being told.

He did, Briseis thought, when he returned. It was much later: he must have talked to the men and then seen to the horses for himself. The light was fading outside, and Achilles crossed to the bed. She looked into his eyes from across the sleeping man. Achilles met her gaze, nodded briefly and turned to light a lamp.

'Shall I wake him?'

'Does he need to sleep?'

'Because of the arm? No. He will want some supper. And I want to come and kiss you.'

Achilles gave a sudden grin that lit up his face. 'Do that first, and then we'll wake him.' He reached out his arms and lifted her high out of the bed and down to the floor. Patroclus did not stir and they stood there, locked together in a long and passionate embrace. When he released her she leaned against him, with her arms still round him and her head against his shoulder. He looked down at her and then across at Patroclus sleeping. 'You love him, don't you?'

'Almost as much as I love you.' Briseis turned her face upwards. Achilles was serious, even stern, but there was no anger in his look or his touch.

'Do you want to sleep with him tonight?'

She had not expected it, and for a moment she searched Achilles' face as if for a clue to the answer he wanted from her. It seemed he was not going to give her one. 'Will you make love to me first?'

He smiled. 'That's greedy.'

'I know. But I want you both to be happy.'

'I am.' She thought from his face that he meant it. Then he turned away and said over his shoulder, 'I'll send for some food. Wake him gently.'

'You told me about Troilus, I remembered afterwards. He was Chryseis' lover.'

They had just finished supper and were sitting together round the trestle in the light of a single lamp. Achilles spoke to Patroclus, but it was Briseis who replied. 'Troilus? Why Troilus?'

'I killed him this morning.'

Her surprise showed on her face: not that he should have killed a man, of course they killed men all the time, but that he should choose to talk about it afterwards. Seeing it, Patroclus said quickly, 'I'm fairly sure it was Troilus. I'd heard he fought with Aeneas and he looked to be the man.'

'Who told you what he looked like?'

Patroclus frowned. There was no suspicion in Achilles' tone, but he knew it would all have to come out, and it would break their happy mood. He glanced across at Briseis as if he would have preferred her not to be there, and took a drink before replying. 'Diomedes. It was back before the summer offensive. Agamemnon wanted Troilus killed and he asked Diomedes and a bunch of others to make sure of it. It seems they made a muck of it and they failed to get the boy.'

'Were you one of them?' There was a dangerous look on Achilles' face.

'Agamemnon would never pick me for that. I told you, Diomedes told me.'

'And you did not tell me.'

Had Briseis not been there Patroclus might have been tempted to show contrition. 'He asked me not to. He told me as a favour, so I could hardly refuse him that.'

Achilles rose and paced away to the end of the hut. He stood there in darkness for some time and then he said carefully, 'Let me get this straight. Are you telling me that Agamemnon ordered the offensive as a cover for the killing of this boy?'

'It made sense to hold the offensive then. Damn it, you had argued for it hard enough.'

'But Agamemnon had refused to consider it.'

'True. But he must have seen the sense in it, and when he wanted this lad killed it swayed his judgement.'

'I'll accept that.' Achilles' voice was cool and hard-edged. 'So what was his justification for having the boy killed?'

'He gave no reason, apparently. All Diomedes could suggest was that it might have had something to do with Chryseis.'

'Agamemnon wanted to avenge something Troilus had done to her?'

'That would be the kindest explanation.'

'But you do not believe it.'

Patroclus considered. 'Frankly, no. I was inclined to put it down to jealousy or spite.'

'Briseis?'

Briseis jumped at the sound of her name. She said quietly, 'I have never heard anything against Troilus.'

'And there is plenty to set against Agamemnon.' Achilles' voice remained cool, his tone logical. He moved suddenly, swiftly out of the shadows and back into the light of the lamp. He sat and with a familiar gesture he swept away the crusts and discarded bones and set his elbows on the trestle. 'Agamemnon must have known that the boy had been involved with Chryseis. He knew that back in the summer, before the offensive. He ordered the offensive unexpectedly, and it seems that a major motive was to have the boy killed, to see him murdered under cover of the fighting. The plan failed. After the offensive he made no attempt to inform the girl's family that he was holding her, or to suggest a ransom. They evidently found out her whereabouts by other means and Chryseis' father came to offer a large ransom for her. Agamemnon refused to consider it – in spite of the threat of Apollo's curse.'

'Which has had no effect,' Patroclus said slowly.

'What form does the Mouse God's curse take? Plague. Plague, always and inevitably. When do plagues come? In the summer. Tell me that next autumn and I shall believe you.'

Patroclus and Briseis were both silent. Achilles said, 'Am I making any unwarranted assumptions?'

'I don't think so,' Patroclus said. 'Though there is a great deal that we don't know.'

'Some of it I can find out; but what we do know is surely damning enough. In his private dealings Agamemnon has acted dishonourably and shamefully. As High Commander he has always been incompetent and now we can begin to glimpse why. The summer campaign was clearly planned for his personal convenience. He has no respect for the gods, little for his commanders, and no real interest, it seems to me, in defeating the Trojans.'

Patroclus made no immediate reply. He was tempted to copy Achilles' earlier gesture and stalk into the shadows. But he stayed put, and finally Achilles said, 'Is it not clear to you what I must do?'

Patroclus frowned. 'You intend to challenge for the High Command.' Achilles gave a short nod and Patroclus went on, 'I don't think this makes a suitable excuse to do it. I didn't think so when Diomedes told me of the plot back in the summer, and I don't think so now. If you make it public that you know of the plot you will lose any support you might have had from the men who were involved in it.'

'You think I want Diomedes' support?'

Achilles' voice had acquired an angry edge. Patroclus' own anger began to rise to match it. 'Damn it, Achilles. You'll never win the command by being the best man for the job. You will only win it by gaining supporters. This way you get open hostility – not support, not indifference, positive hostility – from a dozen influential men who will be made to look incompetent and unscrupulous. You think Diomedes is the worst of them? Zeus! I would have said he was the best of the bunch.'

'Since when were you an admirer of Diomedes?'

Patroclus flushed. 'Achilles, he told me of this. I'm damned if I'll abuse his confidence.'

Achilles' knuckles whitened on the edge of the trestle. The silence grew. Then he said in a low, level voice, 'But I will have your support if I choose to make the challenge now.'

Patroclus took his time replying. At last he said, 'If you agree to keep this private: to hide the fact that you know. Half of the men you must canvass know it anyway, it will make no impression on them. You have other grounds for challenging. I'll do all I can to help you to gather support. Then as soon as

Agamemnon gives you some other excuse you can make the challenge openly.'

The silence grew again. Finally Achilles said, in the same low voice, 'Done.'

The other two did not reply and he moved to fetch his harp and dissolve their unease in music.

Briseis did spend the night with Patroclus. The looks she shared with Achilles told him that they must have discussed it and he was not inclined to refuse. He needed the reassurance of her love. It grated on him that he had fought so poorly, though he knew Achilles would never mention it and Briseis not even think it. He was lucky, he supposed, to be alive.

Patroclus did not pretend to himself that the night would change things. She was Achilles' woman, on loan to him. He said as much to her the following day when they were alone again and she was checking the wound.

'It's not that you mind so much about us, is it? More that you feel left out?'

He stared at the smooth brown head bent beside him, then made himself smile. 'How did you know? Have you felt like that?'

'Sometimes. He loves you too.'

'Not more than he loves you.'

Briseis stopped to consider that. 'Perhaps not. Not now. But at first he loved you more.'

'Not enough to give you to me.'

She looked up at him and for a moment he regretted saying it; though she had known, surely, that he had asked? Then she said, 'You're wrong, Patroclus. I know he said no to you once, though we've never talked of it. But later – after the battle – he let me choose. He would have accepted it if I had gone to you then.'

'But you did not.'

'No, I chose Achilles. I want you to know that, so that things are honest between us. That I feel I had the choice, and I chose him.'

He remembered that night. And he remembered a part of it that she had not known because she had been sleeping. He was tempted for a moment not to tell her; but then he found himself speaking. 'You went to sleep on his bed. You were sleeping when I came back. I had no way of knowing what had happened between the two of you, but it felt to me then as if it were my choice. To let you go to Achilles, or to fight for you.'

'And you chose not to fight.' She said it in a whisper.

'Are you sorry?'

There was a long pause before she answered. A pause long enough to let him know that things might have worked out differently if he had made the other choice. Then she spoke, in the same whisper that he had to strain to catch. 'No. No, I'm not sorry.' She met his gaze. 'Though I'm glad we've had what we have of each other. And I'm glad you told me.'

There was silence for a moment, then Briseis said, 'May I ask you something else?'

'I doubt if there is anything that I would not answer.'

'Were you and he lovers once?'

It was not what he had expected. She must have known that. But he answered straight away, 'Of course we were.'

'Who ended it?'

'It never ended. It changed.' She did not respond and he asked her gently, 'Do you mind?'

'No. I suppose I should have known without asking.'

'You never asked Achilles?'

She started at that. 'Perhaps I should have,' she said slowly. 'But it would have been more difficult. It always is, in a way, to talk to him. Now that you have told me I shall tell him that I know.'

It would have been disloyal, Patroclus told himself firmly, even to admit to himself that he was disappointed.

The conversation stayed with Briseis for days. It pleased her, the knowledge that they had trusted each other enough to be so open. At the same time it was unnerving to have uncovered the choices they each had made, and seen the fallibility of the path that had led them to where they were. It was not that she had lied. She did love Achilles with an intensity that was quite different from her feeling for Patroclus. She also knew, though, that she would find it difficult to say the same kind of thing to him.

She felt she should: partly because she had told Patroclus that she would, and partly because it seemed to be a failing in their relationship if she could not. But it had to be at the right time, when they were alone and at ease together. She waited for several days, never feeling that the time was right. Then Achilles forced the choice upon her.

They were together in the hut one afternoon. Achilles had returned alone and taken her to bed. They lay there naked, their desire temporarily sated. Achilles reached out to pull the lionskin over them. 'I'll be going on a raid tomorrow, with Ulysses and some of his men. We'll be away three, maybe four days.'

'Be careful.'

'Of course.' He had been working at his friendship with Ulysses, she knew, in the hope of getting his support when it came to a showdown with Agamemnon. Ulysses had been cautious in committing himself and there was plenty of need for care, not only when the Trojans were around.

Achilles was silent for a moment, tracing circles on the skin of her shoulder. His touch did not change as he said quietly, 'Sleep with Patroclus, if you want to, while I am away.'

She turned to look at him. He was not looking at her face, but he felt her waiting for him to return the look, and he did. It told her very little.

'No.'

'I'd not tell you to if I minded. I hadn't meant it as a test.'

'I never imagined that you had. I think it would be better, though, if I did not.'

'If that is what you want.'

'We have never talked about it.'

Achilles lifted his fingers from her shoulder and turned away from her slightly. 'I think some things are better not talked about.'

'Are you afraid I love him best?' He did not answer and she went on, 'I had thought you knew by now that I do not, but you are afraid a little, aren't you? I have talked about it with him. He knows I chose you and he accepts it.'

'So do I.'

'But you still find it hard to discuss?'

'I am not Patroclus. It's no good trying to make me act like him.'

She was chastened for a moment. 'I hadn't meant to. It worries me to think that there are things I can say to him, though, that I cannot say to you.'

'Tell me what you said to him.' Achilles' voice was hard, challenging. Briseis propped herself up on an elbow and reached out her own hand. His chest and arm were scored across, again and again, with the scars of old wounds. She did not trace the lines; she stroked him, steadily and firmly. Under her hand she could feel the tension in him. She kept touching him, as if she needed the sheet-anchor of it, as she told him as plainly as she could what she and Patroclus had said to each other.

Most of the tension had gone by the time she finished. Achilles looked back at her. 'Are you trying to tell me that you would mind if he and I slept together now?'

'No. I just want to feel that you knew everything that we knew. I would mind, though.'

'There has been no one else. You know that.'

'Yes.' He had not called Diomede for many moons. 'If there were to be I would rather it were Patroclus. But I would rather still there were nobody.'

'So would I. But I would not stop you loving him if that was what you wanted.'

'I don't think it is.' Briseis was curiously dissatisfied with the conversation. It was not as if she felt Achilles were holding anything back, or being dishonest with her, but somehow it had not given them the intimacy that she and Patroclus had shared. Perhaps he was right, he simply was not Patroclus, and she was asking the wrong things from him.

'You are not happy about it?' Briseis had sat up, almost unthinkingly, and was starting to dress. Achilles' voice surprised her.

'I suppose not.'

'Do you want to tell me why?'

'I would if I knew.'

'Try.' He meant it, but he was not helping her. He never did with this kind of thing. She clenched the side of the bed and let her own body tense with all the thoughts that she tried to keep to one side when she and Achilles were together.

'I think it is harder with you because you are my master.' She took a deep breath before going on. 'Because you can tell me what to do. All right, you never do, but you are still my master and I am still your slave, and it is not even between us, as it can be with Patroclus. It is not as if I were your wife, even if you treat me like one. And I know it is you who killed my husband.'

'I doubt if it was.' Achilles' voice was steady. 'If any leaders are killed in a battle when I am there it tends to be credited to me. Maybe I did kill Mynes. I have killed many men, you know that. But I don't recall doing it.'

Briseis was silent.

'Did you love him more than you love me?'

'I loved him differently.'

'Because he was your husband? And I am not?'

She nodded, wordlessly.

'Would it be easier for you if we married?'

Her hands clenched harder on the bedframe. 'I do love you. I don't pretend any of it because I am your slave.'

'I never thought you had. But it would be different for us both if we were married.'

She did not answer and after a while he said quietly, 'Is that not what you want?'

She turned to look at him. 'I had not thought you meant it.'

'I do mean it. It is no reason for us not to marry, that I captured you: if it is what we both want.'

'I suppose it is.'

'I have no other wife, if that worries you. I have a son, but his mother died when he was born. You will not come second to any other woman when we go back to Phthia.'

'No, it wasn't that.' She shivered slightly and then moved forward to hold him. 'It is just difficult to believe.'

'You trust me, don't you? You love me?'

'Yes.' She smiled. 'Yes.'

Later he said, 'We must marry properly when we get home. I don't know what the rites are in Mysia. But I am married to you now, in my own eyes, and in those of the Myrmidons. I will tell them so. We shall tell everybody in the camp.'

'Would you like me to tell Patroclus?'

He smiled at her. 'I thought you said he loved me best?'

She reached to hit him, but before her hand had even touched him the blow turned into a caress.

◼

Diomedes told Chryseis about Briseis' marriage to Achilles. She might not have learned of it otherwise because Agamemnon's other slave women rarely spoke to her unless they had to, and it was not the kind of thing Agamemnon would have mentioned. Diomedes realized as much and took a malicious pleasure in passing on the news. The memory still rankled with him of the night when he had expected to have her and Agamemnon had changed his mind. He wanted to annoy her, and he wanted to remind her that he still expected to enjoy her eventually, when Agamemnon tired of her.

He told her in Agamemnon's hall one afternoon. He had come to talk with the High King, but Agamemnon had not yet returned and Chryseis was left to entertain him.

There were a couple of servants in the room. Chryseis thought of sending them out: she said plenty of things, those days, that she did not trust the servants to keep to themselves. But it would not do: she needed them for propriety's sake and for her own safety. She settled for despatching them to the far end of the room.

As he related his news Chryseis inspected Diomedes, her eyes narrowing. He was a slightly built man, tall and rather sleek. He reminded her of a weasel. She knew exactly what thoughts were passing through his head. He disgusted her and at the same time she was involuntarily aroused by him. He did not physically resemble Agamemnon, but she reckoned he would be rather similar in bed, taking the same voyeuristic pleasure in her excitement. She did not want him to know any of this, and she did not want either him or the servants to see that the news affected her. So she did not let it affect her. She gave an arch smile and said in a light voice, 'What an extraordinary thing to do.'

Diomedes smiled back. 'You're jealous,' he said cheerfully. He knew she could not afford to show anger towards him. Agamemnon needed his support too much.

'Of Briseis? Why should I be? Achilles doesn't attract me at all.'

'Come on, Chryseis. Not of her having Achilles. Of the marriage.'

'Oh, the marraige.' She shrugged. 'It doesn't sound much of a marriage to me. No ceremonies, no prayers and sacrifices, no feast, no wedding dress even. What is there to be jealous of?'

'He means it as a public commitment. He made that plain. And he has no other wife.'

'She is still his slave, though. He can go back on it any time.'

Diomedes was tempted to remark that Achilles was an honourable man who would never do anything of the kind. But it was not what he had come for: to praise Achilles to Agamemnon's woman. He had a little too much pride to play at changing sides every other day. Instead he said, 'Any man who marries can do that in Achaea. Agamemnon could turn his back on his queen if he wished, and take a new wife instead.'

'He has done, hasn't he?' Chryseis answered fast, then walked across to the door, as if she were looking out for Agamemnon. It would give her time, she hoped, to think up a second comment and stop Diomedes from replying to the first.

She did not really expect it to work, Diomedes was too quick-witted. He said to her back, 'I have heard no public announcements from the High King.'

She turned, quickly, to show a flash of anger that was only half intentional. 'Private commitments are just as binding to honourable men.'

Diomedes smiled slowly. 'So we can expect an announcement from Agamemnon any day?'

'You do not imagine that he would demean himself by imitating Achilles? Or that I would expect him to?'

'My pretty little Chryseis, you are turning pink. Am I annoying you? I never suggested that I expected anything of the kind.'

Chryseis was on the verge of real anger. It felt as if she would be exposing something dishonourable about both herself and Agamemnon if she let Diomedes win. Not that they had done anything to be ashamed of, she reminded herself furiously. Their relationship was fine by any standards – except perhaps Achilles'. Damn Achilles. Well, she could afford to be angry with Achilles. It would be an improvement on getting angry with Diomedes, or with Agamemnon. At all costs she must avoid that. She paced across the room, letting a self-righteous anger at Agamemnon's rival wash over her, then sat down and pushed the fury to one side. When she looked up again at Diomedes her face was perfectly composed. 'I am inclined to think that it is you who are jealous, Diomedes.'

'Oh no. Why should I be? I shall have you in the end.'

Chryseis was not looking at him any longer and when Diomedes turned to follow her gaze he saw Agamemnon at the threshold. He must have heard. He did not look at Diomedes, though. Instead he crossed to Chryseis, who stood to greet him, and kissed her formally. 'I am sorry to be late, darling. I trust Diomedes has been entertaining you?'

She smiled sweetly at him. 'Of course. He has been telling me of Achilles' marriage.'

'Oh, nobody takes that nonsense seriously, my dear.'

'So we were agreeing. As I told him, it is no different from our relationship, yours and mine.'

Agamemnon met her eyes. She had not expected to find sympathy in his face, and there was no sign of it; she was looking for complicity, and that was there.

'No different at all, my love. No different at all.' He turned to Diomedes and continued smoothly, 'Has Chryseis poured you some wine? She will leave us now and we can talk.'

For once, her carpet-hung room brought Chryseis no pleasure. She slid to the floor and sat, pulling her legs tight against her body with her arms and rubbing her face against her knees like a baby in search of consolation.

Marriage. She had never seriously considered the possibility that Agamemnon might marry her. Achaeans did not marry their captives; at least, that was what she had thought until then. She had told herself that no man's commitment to a slave woman could be greater than Agamemnon's to her. She had told herself, as she had told her father, that they loved each other. It was unnerving to catch this glimpse of someone else's love, a love that seemed to belittle the one she herself enjoyed.

It was a long time since Chryseis had permitted herself to envy Briseis. The old envy came back now with redoubled force. Everything that she had to work so hard for seemed to come perfectly easily to Briseis. Now Briseis had gained something so far beyond her own expectations that she had not even thought to covet it.

She coveted it then. Nothing would have been more welcome to her than Agamemnon's walking into the room and announcing his intention to marry her. Even as she thought it she knew that there was no prospect of that ever happening.

Chryseis felt the tears come welling up. They filled her eyes and threatened to overflow. Before they did so the anger came. She had not let herself cry since the day after they arrived at the camp. It would be an admission of defeat to do so now. It was no good, she reminded herself fiercely, looking sideways at what the gods gave other people. Her task was to make the best of what the gods gave her.

After all, the gods had not been unkind to her. Agamemnon had shown no signs of tiring of her over the winter. He asked a great deal of her; but never again had he asked for anything that she was not willing to give. She gave that much with plenty of enthusiasm. He certainly gave something back. Ajax had told her exactly what the offered ransom had been, and how quickly he had refused it. A dozen people had told her of her father's threats and promises. Agamemnon had not kept her lightly.

Just as he had learned not to ask for what she would not give, she had always been careful to ask only for what he was likely to give her. Indeed she rarely asked him for anything, she just accepted what he gave. That way she was never refused, and it was a pleasing thought that Agamemnon had never said no to her. It was a consolation she needed. She would never have dared to ask him for marriage, for fear of losing it.

Maybe he would never publicly marry her, she went on to

herself with forced cheerfulness, but he had never shamed her in public. She had trusted him to back her up against Diomedes, and been proved right. Maybe that was not a sign of love, but it was still worth having.

Of course, Agamemnon had more sense than to do otherwise for the sake of giving Diomedes a moment's cheap amusement. He needed her almost as much as he needed the Argive. She was his confidant, his fellow plotter in the escalating, though still covert, battle with Achilles.

He took the battle seriously, though he was only slightly afraid. He and Chryseis were both convinced that Achilles was not influential enough to topple him from the command. The Myrmidon leader might be a better fighter, but that did not mean he was preferable as high commander. Still, the challenge was upsetting. Agamemnon wanted it over, and Achilles defeated, before the summer. He had been mustering his supporters, just as Achilles had, and was waiting till the time was right to force a confrontation.

Chryseis managed a smile. She could see that it was a mistake of Achilles' to announce his commitment to Briseis at this stage. It would not help his popularity. Maybe she herself had more pride than to go whining to her lover that she wanted to get married too, but some of the other concubines in the camp would, no doubt about that. She must work on that line, she thought to herself. Encourage the women to nag their men, encourage the men to blame it all on Achilles.

Agamemnon would laugh at that strategy. She thought she had the self-control to outline it to him. She had done well enough in the scene with Diomedes. A pity about its ending, though. They still needed to do all they could to bind Diomedes to their side. He was cunning and influential. Win him and they would win half a dozen other commanders with him.

What could she do to put things right? She had always flirted with him, but flirtatious smiles were not what he wanted. Chryseis knew precisely what he wanted. She wondered idly what it would be like to give it to him. Agamemnon would have to be there. In fact, it would be exactly what he had threatened her with the previous autumn. Agamemnon would watch, perhaps make a few suggestions, as Diomedes' smooth sleek body clambered all over hers. And thrust into hers. Then he would grow too excited to keep watching and he would join in and the two men would overwhelm her with their demands.

Would it please Agamemnon if she suggested it? She was not sure. In some ways it would. He would be grateful that she was willing to do such a thing for him. He would enjoy it, no doubt about that. But it was not what a wife did. Perhaps that was why it tempted her. If she suggested it, it would be she who sabotaged the suggestion of marriage. In a bizarre way, it would restore the balance of power between the two of them.

Chryseis was still playing with the idea when Agamemnon returned. Her first enthusiasm for it was beginning to pall. She could see the disadvantages more clearly, and the advantages seemed too measured, too calculated. It was something she should have offered without forethought, if at all. But she felt she might still suggest it if their conversation went in that kind of way.

It did. 'You were angry with Diomedes,' Agamemnon said as he came into the room.

'Yes. Though he will be more angry with me now.'

'For making a fool of him?'

'We came close to that, yes.'

Agamemnon gave her a long cool look and walked past her. He unlaced his sandals and lay back on the donkey-patterned carpet, his hands behind his head. 'A pity, that. I need him to work on Ulysses for me and he is dragging his feet.'

'I thought that might have happened.' Chryseis paused a moment, then came to sit close to him. 'Maybe I can help you there.'

He examined her carefully, as if that would tell him what she had in mind. She wished it did, or that her voice had when she had said it. Apparently not, because at length he said, 'How?' in a calm, neutral voice.

Chryseis outlined her plan. Agamemnon watched her, expressionless. When she had finished he said, 'Do you think you would enjoy that?'

'I am not sure. The thought of it is exciting. Maybe I would not like it so much when it really happened. Perhaps I would, though, if I knew you were enjoying it.' She gave a sly, almost catlike smile. 'You would enjoy it, wouldn't you?'

His returning smile was almost identical to hers. 'I would. And Diomedes certainly would.' He was watching her still and she expected him to reach out to touch her, to arouse her. He might even call for Diomedes straight away, before she changed her mind. Instead he said, in the same cool voice, 'No.'

'No?'

His smile this time had a dangerous edge to it, like a leopard's. 'Are you disappointed?'

'I don't think so.'

He laughed. 'We are too alike, you and I.' He did reach out now. 'I don't leave you dissatisfied, do I?'

'You know you don't. I just thought that maybe it was something I could do for you.'

'Not for those reasons. Not to win him round.' His smile was different this time. 'I will have to be in much deeper trouble before I ask my wife to act like a whore.'

It was enough. She did not dare to ask him to expand on it. Instead she bent to kiss him and he kissed her back.

Much later he said, 'I should enjoy it, you know, watching you with another man. I shall have you do it some time. But not with Diomedes.' He paused. 'Or did you particularly want Diomedes?'

Did she? She was not sure herself. But she smiled and said, 'Of course not. I will leave you to choose.'

'You are lying, my dear. It excited you, the thought of him.' His voice was not cruel, or at least no more so than usual. 'You had been thinking about it, hadn't you, before I came? Tell me what you were thinking. What you wanted him to do to you.'

She smiled back. To tell Agamemnon would be almost as good as doing it, and much safer. She did, at length, with a few newly invented touches that would please him particularly. She did please him. It still surprised her to discover how well she did.

At the full moon after the incident with Diomedes, Chryseis began to suspect that she was pregnant. She should have anticipated it, she supposed, but it came as a complete surprise to her. It was just as well, she thought, that things with Diomedes had not turned out differently. She felt no pleasure. A child had not come into her scheme of things at all.

She did not think seriously about what she should do until she was quite certain. The alternatives were both frightening. She could go to a woman, she assumed, and get rid of it. Her knowledge of the camp women who did such things was not very precise, but she had no doubt that they existed, and that the other women would direct her to them if she asked. They might not even tell Agamemnon. Chryseis did not think any of them would be able to judge whether he would be more pleased or angry to be told.

Or she could tell Agamemnon herself, and let him decide what to do. He would be angry, she was quite sure. It was not a good time for it. Achilles still had more supporters than was comfortable, and the remaining ones were remarkably resistant to Agamemnon's powers of persuasion. He needed no more problems. He would not blame her; these things happened; but he would still be annoyed.

All the same, she felt inclined to tell him. It would be difficult if he heard from someone else. There was a possibility he would like her to have the child. And she was squeamish at the thought of what the woman would do to her: it hurt, she knew that much.

So she told him. They were sitting over supper one evening when they had, unusually, been eating alone. She normally told him things in bed, but that would not have been suitable. It was wrong to go to bed with a man once you were sure about a baby coming.

Agamemnon listened calmly. Evidently he was not as surprised as she was. That was not so odd, she realized afterwards. Many women must have told him the same thing before her, and Chryseis had never had to tell any other man.

'I shall have a bed of your own made up.'

It seemed she had been mistaken about the anger. She was so disconcerted that she said nothing at all in response.

'Is something wrong? Are you upset? Has there been another man?'

'No, of course not. I suppose I am a little upset, but there has been no one else, no one at all.' She paused. 'I thought maybe you would want me to get rid of it.'

'Why should I? If you get rid of this one there will be another in a few more moons. And I am perfectly happy for you to have a son by me.' After a short pause he added, 'Or a daughter.'

She had no intention of producing a daughter. If you were determined, she had always been inclined to think, it would turn out to be a boy. 'I shall be sorry not to lie with you.'

Agamemnon was amused. 'I am glad to hear it. So shall I. But I shall enjoy you all the more afterwards.'

Chryseis gave a wan smile and he went on, 'I shall not put you aside, my dear. You shall still see me. I value your advice, you know that.'

'So all will be well?' She spoke with determined cheerfulness.

'Naturally.' Agamemnon privately wondered if she had expected him to suggest marriage. It had been annoying, that business of Achilles and his girl. Gave them all ideas if their masters were at all kind to them. But he had no intention of imitating Achilles. Chryseis was a good girl, and he enjoyed her considerably more than he had ever enjoyed his wife Clytaemnestra, but she was only a priest's daughter. There was no need to stir up future trouble in Mycenae by making her a queen. He had to admit, however, that she had played the part very prettily in the camp. Perhaps he would think again if the child turned out to be a boy.

Chryseis herself had not seriously considered the possibility of marriage. If Agamemnon had wanted that, she thought, he would have offered earlier. What did upset her was the prospect of watching him take other women to his bed. She was quite certain that he would, he was not the kind of man to do without.

She knew she was fortunate that there had not been more over the previous year, but all the same the thought made her deeply, and unexpectedly, jealous. That, however, she did not tell him. It was not as if telling him would make him act any differently.

It was a pleasure, though, to realize that once again he had given her more than she had expected. In some ways at least she was more like a wife to him than a whore. She went to move her things to the other end of his hut with more composure than she had expected to achieve.

'Ajax? No.' Ulysses paused to take another bite from the leg of lamb he held in his hands. He wiped the fat from his chin onto the back of his arm and went on, 'He reckons he could do the job better himself.'

Agamemnon hid his disgust. He took a delicate sip from his winecup and set it down precisely on the trestle. 'There he is mistaken.'

Ulysses grinned. 'Diomedes thinks the same.'

'And Idomeneus,' added Menelaus. 'While Meriones and Menestheus and Gouneus and most of the rest have always been your men.'

'Who do you reckon would support Achilles right now?' Chryseis asked.

'Patroclus,' Ulysses said. Menelaus roared with laughter and Ulysses joined him. Agamemnon smiled thinly. He was not in the mood for laughter. Ulysses sobered down and added more seriously, 'And I think Nestor, though he will not declare himself while it is so obvious that Achilles has not enough support to defeat you.'

'I think,' said Agamemnon, 'that I can afford to be generous. I shall not hold it against him.'

Ulysses' directness was a façade, Chryseis knew that. He had been campaigning himself for Achilles at one stage. His agreeing to dine with the three of them might have been no more than a ruse, a tactical feint designed to gather information. If only Ulysses had been a drinker, she could have judged his openness by his consumption. For all his riotous laughter, though, barely a half-cupful of wine had found its way into his water. Precisely his usual ration. It was Menelaus who was drunk, as usual.

She rose to offer Ulysses more bread and then paused behind him, where she could signal to Agamemnon without his seeing her. Only a slight narrowing of the eyes showed that Agamemnon had taken in her sign.

Evidently he agreed with her diagnosis. He said, with well-feigned casualness, 'You have not mentioned Diomedes.'

Ulysses raised his eyebrows. 'You know precisely where Diomedes stands.'

'But do you?'

Ulysses was too skilful to be taken aback. He gave Agamemnon a level look before taking his next bite. Then he set down his meat on the trestle and produced a dry smile. 'He told me yesterday what your offer was.'

The casual manner disappeared. Agamemnon leaned forward across the trestle. 'And you expect me to match it in return for your own guarantee?'

'Oh no, Agamemnon. I expect you to better it.'

Until she felt herself exhaling Chryseis did not realize that she had been holding her breath. She dared not catch Agamemnon's eye. Agamemnon saw no need to look at her as he leaned still further forward and began to bargain for Ulysses' commitment. They both knew it was the turning point. If they could win Ulysses then Achilles would certainly not have enough men to sustain his challenge.

The only men who could defeat Agamemnon now were the Trojans. It would be inconvenient if they were to launch an offensive at this delicate stage. But the Trojans were still being held off, and Agamemnon had no intention of calling an offensive himself. Somehow, he intended to find a chance to destroy Achilles' pride and end his ambitions for good. Then when the offensive did take place, and the war was won, the credit would be his alone.

Or so he would see it. Agamemnon never had been a man to give credit to the gods. He might blame them for his failures, but when he thanked them for his successes there was no conviction behind the conventional gestures.

The only men who could defeat him were the Trojans. But what of the gods? It worried Chryseis at times, the knowledge of the curse that her father had brought down upon the Achaeans.

Plague, that was the form it always took. The sickness had come early to the camp that year, and already it seemed more virulent than usual. Agamemnon had surely noticed that, as clearly as she had herself. It was one issue, though, which she would never be able to discuss with him. It was upsetting to find herself thinking of it now, in the midst of this minor triumph. She must enjoy the successes as they came, she told herself firmly, and not cast her mind forward to what might follow.

'It seems there is nobody to be trusted at all in this bloody camp.'

Achilles said it to Patroclus, as he paced up and down the hut. Patroclus pulled a scrap of meat off the leg he was eating and fed it abstractedly to the dog at his side. Another dog trotted up and he fed that one too. Then he looked up, brought a smile to his face and raised his cup. 'Wrong. You can trust me, and Briseis. Any of my Myrmidons, come to that.'

Briseis was not with them. She was tending Iphis, who had lost her baby, and a great deal of blood, the previous night. It did not occur to Patroclus to add Iphis to his list.

'Anybody else?'

Patroclus regarded him. Was he expecting to be contradicted? 'I can think of no one else. No, that is unfair. There are honourable men: Nestor is honourable, and Ajax, and Ulysses, for all his scheming. And a few of the others. But they give you no promises.'

Achilles sighed and came to sit at the trestle. He had not eaten and showed no inclination to. 'Every sensible commander in the camp knows how woeful Agamemnon's tactics have been. The war has dragged on far too long. There is no heart left in the siege, and raids now bring miserable rewards. The High King and his favourites sit and sit and gain too much, while men dare and risk their lives for nothing. Zeus, what a way to make a war.'

Patroclus barely listened to the familiar argument. 'The commanders do agree with you there. The ones who fight, anyway.'

'I suppose so. Oh, they say they do. Men like Ulysses and Ajax, the ones who have always been my good friends. But then they start to talk about something else. Ajax even asked me if I would support his claim to the high command. The other ones, the Cretans and the Rhodians, go along with everything I say, and make promises, and then Agamemnon has a quiet word with them and they take it all back again. It is as if I were always a step behind Agamemnon. Either the men I talk to say they promised themselves to him the day before, or they turn round and make promises to him the day after. Why, Patroclus? Why? Can they not see that I would make a better commander than Agamemnon with his bribes and dirty tricks?'

Patroclus looked down at the boards. His urge was to offer sympathy, add anger to Achilles' own well-hidden fury, but that would not do. It would only store up problems for the future.

What else could he say? In spite of the determinedly rational words and manner, he did not think Achilles really wanted or needed honesty. His honest answer would have been that Achilles might not be the better commander. Bribes and dirty tricks were necessary in war. Achilles would get blood on his hands readily enough, but not mud. He would let honour and pride get in the way of crude advantage. He was an innocent abroad when it came to backbiting and deception. And though he was universally admired as a fighter, that did not necessarily make for popularity.

It had been a great mistake, Patroclus now realized, to encourage Achilles' bid. No, that was not quite true: he had always realized it, but at the time he had seen no alternative. He could not honourably withdraw his support now. He said cautiously, 'Have you not thought of supporting some other man's claims? Not Ajax's, necessarily. Diomede's, say, or Ulysses'?'

'Zeus!' The iron self-control snapped. Achilles leaped up from the table, his face rigid with anger, and began to pace again. 'I have waited nine years, Patroclus. Nine years, before I tried for the command. And now you tell me to throw it all away.'

Patroclus fought to keep his own patience. 'Not to throw it away. To take the best advantage of the goodwill you have gained. To recognize that there is no honour in being seen to knock on a closed door.'

Achilles halted and slammed his fist down on the trestle, shaking it from end to end. Then he said in a calmer voice, 'Diomedes would be no better than Agamemnon. He's braver, perhaps, but he is no good at leading men, and he's as twisted as they come. The army would never take Ulysses. He would be a good choice in himself, but what is his contingent? Half a dozen ships?'

'A dozen. But then the Myrmidons are not as many as the Mycenaeans. You have to recognize that his power and wealth make up much of Agamemnon's appeal.'

Achilles' face was hard-set with fury in the dim light of the hut. 'I may not have as many troops, but mine are the best. The Achaeans would be lost without us.'

'I think that's true. A lot of the leaders deny you the credit you deserve as a commander. They think of you as a hero, and you are more than that. You and I know that there is nothing god-given about the Myrmidons' superiority. They are just better led and better trained than the rest. You can hardly pull your troops out of the campaign to prove your point, though.'

Achilles managed a thin smile. 'It would be tempting. You remember Calchas' prophecy that the Achaeans will only take Troy with my assistance? No; I cannot do that. But what can I do?'

'Accept defeat gracefully. That comes hard to you, doesn't it?'

Had another man said it he might have been hit for his pains. Achilles glared at Patroclus; then moved away abruptly and began to pace the floor again. He marched up and down the hut, repeatedly, for a long time. Then he stopped. He looked across at Patroclus and said quietly, 'Very hard.'

For once Patroclus pitied him. Achilles disciplined himself so tightly, worked constantly at containing his fierce emotions, and yet he remained so transparent, so vulnerable to anyone who knew him at all. It was deception that armoured a man against this kind of thing, and Achilles had never been any good at that. And he had such pride, he would never admit to being less than the best at anything.

Patroclus rose and went across the room to where Achilles stood. He reached out his arms, pulled him close and held him tightly, like the lover he had once been and was no more. For once it did not seem incongruous that Patroclus should be the taller, the older, and perhaps the wiser of the two.

Achilles stood there unresisting for a moment. Then he gently pushed his friend away, holding him at arms' length and looking intently at him. 'You have never lied to me, have you?'

'No. No, I never have.' Patroclus watched Achilles stride across the room and fling himself onto his bed. He set his hands behind his head and looked up at the logs of the roof. To a casual observer he might have appeared perfectly at ease. 'At least I still have you. And Briseis.'

'And two thousand troops, who will do exactly as you say, even if Agamemnon orders them otherwise.'

'Agamemnon would not dare. He would not dare to touch any of you.'

I hope not, Patroclus thought to himself. I hope not. If Agamemnon did it would probably finish them all.

Andromache was surprised when the servant announced Cassandra. It was midday and Cassandra rarely came then. It was not a polite time to visit, and that was when she fed the baby.

So she sent word downstairs that she was busy and calmly carried on seeing to Astyanax. She watched the maid change the soiled cloths around his bottom and sat down to feed him. As she was urging the baby to manage one final burp Helike entered and reminded her cautiously that Cassandra was still waiting.

'You told her I could not see her now?'

'She said she would wait. Now she says she will come up to the nursery if you are not finished soon.'

From Cassandra that was a threat to be taken seriously. Cassandra seemed to upset the baby even more than the baby upset her. Annoyed, his mother handed him over to the nursemaid and set off down the stairs.

Her visitor was not alone. Two of the palace guards were standing just in the shadow of the porch, evidently waiting for her.

'You were ages,' Cassandra said unnecessarily. 'Come with me to the shrine.'

Andromache frowned. It was an unusual request. She rarely went at all to Apollo's shrine – the one Cassandra must mean – and had never been there with her friend. She felt uncomfortable there and she was very dubious about the prospect of witnessing Cassandra indulging in her peculiar trances and prophecies.

'It cannot be that urgent,' she complained.

'Oh, don't be horrid, Andromache. You know how I get upset over these things. I feel I ought to go straight away; and I need someone with me to calm me down afterwards. Helenus can't come, there's a council meeting.'

Cassandra was visibly agitated, now that Andromache cooled down and looked at her. Her hair was straggling loose and her plain grey dress was rather crumpled. She was barefoot, too. Andromache brought back her motherly manner. 'Come and sit down, and tell me what's upsetting you. You cannot go anywhere in such a state.'

'I need to be in a state to talk with the God.'

'That's silly. The priests never get themselves in a state. Take Chryses. He is the calmest person I know.'

'It's different for him.'

Andromache sighed under her breath. 'Give me just a moment to tidy up.'

Cassandra waited. When Andromache was ready she set off briskly, leaving Andromache and the guards to tag after her in the midday heat. She did not even slow down when they reached the plain, where the ground was rough and uneven. Andromache sighed again. Cassandra's head was bare and Andromache reckoned she would be dizzy from sunstroke even before the trance came over her.

She did not seem dizzy, though. Her eyes brightened as they reached the wall around the sacred grove, and she greeted the priest on duty like a lover. The priest seemed to expect her and he had the cup of herbs ready prepared. She drank it rapidly, without wincing at the heat or the bitterness, and let the priest lead her up the paved way to the shrine at the top of the hill.

Andromache followed, feeling superfluous. Cassandra and the priest paid no attention to her. She hovered with the guards on the edge of the clearing, her little beribboned staff in her hand, as the two of them approached the altar. The snakes terrified her, but it seemed less dreadful to keep her eyes on them than to turn away in ignorance. The priest had disturbed them and the vast slimy creatures were slithering and hissing around the hole beneath the altar stone. Above the altar the stone figure of Apollo brooded, a blank-eyed embodiment of knowledge.

There was a sense of power. Andromache could feel it now, in the cool sunlit grove. It seemed to centre on the slim figure of Cassandra as she stood, unmoving, before the altar while the priest began the prayers and invocations. Andromache had no idea what would happen. She expected Cassandra to do something dramatic, scream at the very least, caress the snakes, even disappear in a haze of smoke. The priest finished speaking. In the silence the power grew until Andromache could sense its weight pressing heavily upon her. The snakes were now coiled, motionless, on the short grass. The white ribbons hung limply on the staffs. The sunlight played on the cold features of the stone god.

Finally Cassandra seemed to relax and she turned and walked away from the altar.

'It's all right now,' she said to Andromache in a very ordinary voice. 'I must just talk to the priests, then we can go back.'

Andromache gulped. 'Yes, of course.'

They went back more slowly to the women's megaron at the palace. Cassandra called for mint tea and they sat together to drink it.

'Is it always like that?' Andromache asked.

Cassandra said, 'What did you see? What did you feel?'

'Nothing much. I could feel a sort of aura about the place.' It had rather pleased her that she had been able to sense that.

'It's very strong at the moment,' Cassandra said. 'No, it is not always like that. The God did not speak with me. You did not think he had?'

'I was not sure.' Andromache felt vaguely cheated.

Cassandra paid no attention to her frown. 'The omens are

very confused at the moment. Even Ennomus could not read the signs in the birdflight. I can sense Apollo at work. There is plague in the Achaean camp, you know that? That is the God's doing. But as for what will happen next . . . none of it is clear to me. Except that it will be terrible.'

'It was not frightening, though, at the shrine.'

'Did you expect it to be?' Cassandra was recovering a touch of her sharpness. 'Apollo is not frightening. He brings knowledge. There is no fear in knowledge, only in ignorance. And even without sharing the God's knowledge I found that the shrine calmed me. You saw that, surely? It is like the eye of a storm. The storm itself, the wrath of the God, is raging all around us. In the Achaean camp; and in Ilios.'

'You do fear Apollo's wrath?'

'Oh yes, I fear that,' said Cassandra in a matter-of-fact voice. She went on, just as prosaically, 'Can you stay for a while? I promised to help trim Polyxena's red dress this afternoon.'

Andromache was inclined to think that there was a great comfort in ignorance. Still, there would be a small comfort to be gained from trimming Polyxena's dress. She gave a brave little smile and said that yes, of course she would stay and help.

There was always sickness in the camp. There was sickness everywhere; but especially in the camp, lying low in the marshes where the two rivers fed into the great bay. In Ilios a wind washed across the heights day and night; in the camp there was rarely as much as a shiver in the air, and every smell lingered for days.

In winter the sicknesses went as quickly as they came, but in the heavy heat of midsummer, when the middens bubbled like winejars and the flies hung thick around the store tents, they did not.

That year the sickness grew worse than it had ever been. It was a kind of plague. It started with the animals, the horses, the mules and the dogs, and spread to the men who handled them. Little bumps appeared on their skin, as if they had been pricked by an arrowhead. The redness grew in a great circle around each one, and then the centre broke and evil-smelling pus oozed from the open sore. Once the sores had appeared hardly a man or beast recovered.

At first there were patches of the plague, contingents which had it hardest. Then its spread quickened, suddenly and alarmingly, until there were sick men all across the camp and the stench of burning corpses never quite evaporated.

With the plague came a wave of terror. It was the work of a god, surely, this nameless, invisible enemy which seemed to strike men down at random. The soldiers wanted it gone. Knowing that there was no way to make it go, they wanted to be gone themselves. There was talk, first scattered and then spreading even faster than the plague had done, of lifting the siege and setting out in the long black ships for home. No matter that nine years and more had been invested in the enterprise if the gods were now against it.

If the talk reached Agamemnon he gave no sign of it. Daily the men expected him to call an assembly to discuss the disaster; daily they were disappointed. He did not even call his counsellors together. The High King kept the fighting at its steady summer pitch, calling out more men from the healthy contingents and cutting the quota from the worst hit. He seemed to know precisely the pattern in which the sickness was spreading, but nobody ever saw him discussing it with his commanders. He had not even consulted the priests, men whispered, in order to discover which god was offended, and why. The reason was not hard to find. Which Achaean leader had caused grave offence to a god, which god's curse had been called down upon the army? There was not a man in the camp who could not give a ready answer. There was not a man, either, who was willing to say as much to Agamemnon.

Finally the leaders turned to Achilles. As the pretender to the high command, Ulysses, Ajax and Diomedes told him sweetly, it was his task to make Agamemnon see reason. He had the privilege they all nominally possessed of calling an assembly, a muster of the entire army, to discuss any issue that was of general concern. He must use it, or his last shreds of credibility would be lost.

Achilles could see the trap they offered him, and could see no way of escape. He had no doubt what Calchas and the other priests would say. If Agamemnon obeyed them then the High King would keep the high command, gain Apollo's blessing and win the war. If he did not then the command might go to Achilles, but with it the certainty of defeat. Perhaps he should ignore the priests and simply call for a withdrawal? He knew as soon as he thought it that the army would not stand for that. With a heavy heart he did as he was invited to and called a muster for the following day.

It was midday by the time the troops had assembled. The square outside Agamemnon's hut was like a furnace. Achilles left Patroclus to head the Myrmidons and strode to the place at the front where the commander always stood. Agamemnon, in a plain tunic, black-bordered, was there before him. He moved a step sideways, blank-faced, to acknowledge that this assembly was not of his calling. Achilles turned to the heralds and took the speaker's staff, a great branch studded with gold nails, into his hand. Then in front of the entire army he called on Calchas, High Priest of the Achaeans, the man who had promised success in the enterprise and caused so many to come to Troy, to tell them what the gods had said to him.

Calchas in his sacrificial robes looked more than ever like a fatted pig. He fixed his dark, deep-set little eyes on Agamemnon and his face crinkled up around them, as if he were staring straight at the sun and it hurt him.

It was a trap for him too. He could give only one reply that the men would believe. He could recommend only one remedy. If Agamemnon obeyed him then the High King would keep his position, and sooner or later he would take his revenge. Achilles had given the army's promise of protection, but in those circumstances it was not his to give. If Agamemnon refused him . . . that was not to be thought of.

Calchas' neat little mouth opened and shut again. Achilles held his breath. Then Calchas turned towards the troops. He raised his hands and opened his mouth again. He made no move to take the staff and Achilles, suddenly conscious that he was still holding it, handed it back to Agamemnon's herald Talthybius.

The priest's unexpectedly deep, unexpectedly beautiful voice spoke the familiar words of the invocations to the gods. His body trembled and his eyes closed, as if a trance were coming upon him. He spoke again, this time unfamiliar words that emerged in awkward jerks and stops. Their message was cryptic, but even the slowest-witted man could disentangle its strands: that it was Apollo's bow that had struck the army, Apollo whose wrath threatened the entire enterprise. It was no lack of diligence in the prayers and sacrifices that had brought this about. It was Agamemnon himself. He had refused the Trojan priest's pleas for his daughter's return and in response had heard Apollo's curse brought upon them all.

'The curse . . . of Apollo.' Calchas' voice rose to thunder pitch and his hands reached out to the heavens, as if the lightning and the downpour would follow. The air was as charged as in the moment before a storm breaks. Then the plump body seemed to shrink and crumple and Achilles reached to catch the priest as he tumbled headlong towards the ground.

The rustling and whispering of the army sounded like the steady pattern of raindrops on parched land. It was not an angry sound. Why should it be? If it was not what Agamemnon wanted to hear it was what everybody else did. It meant there would be no need to abandon the siege, no need to do anything disagreeable. No blame attached to any of them, no sacrifices would be demanded of them. It would all be up to Agamemnon.

Calchas was already recovering and wiping the dust off his robes. Agamemnon had not moved at all. The priest turned to him. In the little eyes was a look that hinted at terror and at a malicious pleasure. He was like a spider that can see a great bumblebee coming to blunder into its web, shattering the pattern, and emerging blinded, bound head to foot by sticky threads, but with its sting still intact.

'What is to be done?' Agamemnon did not wait for Achilles to ask. It seemed he and the priest had both forgotten Achilles.

'A sacrifice. The sacrifice the God demanded. You will return the girl Chryseis to Apollo's priest, her father.' Calchas' eyes did not blink and Agamemnon did not move, though the blood seemed to drain, drip by drip, from his face. 'He will pay no ransom.' The little mouth twitched and the blood rushed back into the High King's face, turning it purple. 'And you will send thirteen bullocks with her to the Mouse God's altar at Chryse for a thanks-offering.'

Agamemnon was silent. The priest turned back to the crowd of men, their mutterings stilled. 'The Trojan priest promised Apollo's aid if this were to be done. He will make those prayers to Apollo, and I will make them too. Apollo will speed our arrows and sharpen our spears. He will give us courage and strength. And we shall destroy Ilios.'

He reached a crescendo, as if he expected his last words to be drowned by a roar from the crowd. No roar came. Every eye but his own was still on Agamemnon.

His own, and Achilles'. Achilles was watching the priest. His lip curled down. Calchas had always had a malicious streak in his divinations. This time the will of the gods was clear enough. The irony came in the echo of that time when the will of the gods was not so clear and the priest, in interpreting it as he chose, had demanded almost the same thing, of the same man.

The sacrifice of Agamemnon's daughter Iphigenia, at Aulis immediately before the expedition set off, had surely been the most terrible penalty ever demanded of a king. No man could have recovered completely from it; no man, surely, could have had total faith that the priest had been correct in demanding it, or that he himself had been right to submit. Now it fell to Calchas to demand a second sacrifice, perhaps equally terrible, from the same man. And in those extremities the gods still gave the priest the urge to prick and goad. He was a man who could steal your soul, and tell a dirty joke as he chopped it into tiny pieces.

A trap. A trap for himself. A trap for Calchas. And – he must not let himself forget it – the tightest trap of all for Agamemnon. It would have been too great a sacrifice for Agamemnon to surrender Chryseis when it was first demanded. It must be an even greater one now. There had never been any way out for the High King. He had not bought himself the girl for good when he told his men to toss her father out of the camp. He had just bought himself a few moons of passion at the price of five thousand lives. And in the strange way in which the gods work it seemed he would win himself his victory as part of the same deal.

He deserved – what did he deserve? Sympathy? Jealousy? The contempt a strong man cannot help feeling for a weaker one, put into a situation that demands more of him than he can give? His eyes on the priest, Achilles savoured all those emotions one by one. With an effort of will he forced the sympathy to the fore and turned to look at Agamemnon.

The High King still had not moved at all. The silence lengthened. Agamemnon held it in his hands, crushed it in his grip; then flung it, shattered, to the ground. He let rip. He turned to Calchas and roared. He called the priest a knave, a seer of hell. When at last the little mouth trembled and the piggy eyes looked down to the ground he turned again, to the crowd. He gave his anger a long leash and let it whip across the whole assembly. He luxuriated in his fury. He shouted, he wept. He broke down, and rose up again. He screamed, a long thin animal sound of anguish.

Then he turned to Achilles; who saw, with sudden clarity, that set in the mask of fury the light-brown eyes were as flat and cold as frozen pondwater.

The mask changed and the High King's face settled into lines of fixed determination. 'I shall do it. I shall not let the army be destroyed for the sake of my own pleasure. Though I love her with all my heart I shall give her up. But there must be a price. She was my prize of war and if I am to lose her I must have another prize. It is not fitting for me, as High King, to go without.'

He was hardly going without, Achilles thought viciously to himself. There were surely a score of women in the High King's quarters. His own voice sounded hard and unnatural to him, as if, watching the other two, he had forgotten how to speak. 'We have no common store of booty, Agamemnon. You know that as well as I. There have been few raids this spring. There have been no major campaigns since last year and every last trophy that we took then was shared out among the men many moons ago. You cannot ask any man to turn in his share now. If you do what the gods require of you your victory must be assured.

We will make it up to you, two or three times over, when Ilios is ours.'

The High King held his gaze for a long moment. He was a head shorter and he thrust his chin in the air as he looked up. Achilles met the cold eyes steadily.

'You are trying to cheat me, Achilles.' Agamemnon's voice was quiet, but the words carried across the silent square to every man watching. There was a rumble from the mass of men. Agamemnon turned suddenly, outwards to them. 'And I will not be cheated. Do you expect to keep your own winnings while I lose mine? Must every sacrifice be mine?' He paused for a moment. His voice rose again, with an actor's perfect pitch and timing. 'I tell you now, this one will not be. If I must give up my girl I will take another to set in her place. From Ajax, or Ulysses, or . . .' He turned again, and the voice dropped – 'from Achilles.'

The face still told of anguish and anger. But deep in the eyes a cold flame suddenly burned bright.

Achilles had never thought of himself as an actor; but anger he knew all about. If this was to be the season for fury he could outfury the High King any day. He locked onto the cold flame and fed on its power as he embarked upon an explosion of his own.

It was the time to air every grievance, every meanness, every act of cowardice that could be blamed on Agamemnon. It was the time to empty his store of invective. He called the High King the son of a whore, a dogface, a greedy fool, a godless donkey, an insolent boor. He thundered, he crashed, he hissed, he swore. Agamemnon blinked, and turned to examine the crowd.

Achilles paused. He felt, suddenly, what Agamemnon had already sensed: the excitement, and the detachment, of the men in front of them. They watched the spectacle like men who gather to watch an execution. They were caught in a trance, lifted up by the madness the gods bring, to a place in which men are beyond sympathy, beyond appeals to reason or justice.

Agamemnon could afford to smile now. He did, and there was an answering ripple from the crowd. He could afford to turn to Achilles and say, in a cool, level voice that did not need to carry any further, 'It seems you are appointed to share my sacrifice. You will surrender Briseis to me.'

'That,' Achilles said in a loud voice, 'is unjust. If you demand it of me I will withdraw from the campaign. I shall take my troops in the morning and set sail for Phthia.'

'Do that.' The other man's voice was equally loud now. It fought against a background of yells, jeers and cheers, mixed as indiscriminately as the cries a drunken audience utter at a pair of clowns, making fools of themselves on purpose. 'I shall be glad to see you gone. You have been scheming behind my back for many moons.'

Agamemnon paused again, to take breath and ensure that his next words won their battle and carried right to the farthest men. 'But I shall take my prize first. My own men will man the ship to return Chryseis. They will set sail today. As soon as they leave harbour I will send for Briseis. I will take her this afternoon. And that will show you who is High Commander of this army.'

He was not part of the crowd, drunk on excitement. He was not acting any more. The fury washed over him, drowning every other thought and feeling. Achilles' sword was half out of its scabbard even before the words had died in the air.

And Calchas, who was not part of the crowd either, stepped suddenly and nimbly between the two men. He stood there, the little deep-set eyes fixed on Achilles, and not on the sword which blazed in the sunlight. It flashed through the hot air and stopped, a finger's breadth from his throat.

The light that came from the blade rippled and then stilled. Set apart from the roars and cheers, Calchas' voice carried, quiet and firm, to Achilles. 'Would you too defy the gods?'

Achilles stood still as a statue. There was total silence for a long moment. Then he lifted the sword. He sheathed it, slowly and deliberately. He turned to Talthybius, who gazed at him blindly for a moment before coming to his senses and returning the speaker's staff.

'I do not think I shall kill you. Not over this. I would kill you if you took gold, or horses from me. It is not a fit punishment to kill you for taking my wife. I shall not defy the gods. Instead, I will do just as they did' – he paused, and went on more quietly – 'and take revenge on the army. My troops shall not sail and leave her behind. We will stay here and watch you fight without us. If you cry out for the Myrmidons to save you they will not do it. Even if the Trojans push you back to the shore, even if Hector kills a thousand men, we will not fight. We will no more come to your aid than this dry wood shall flourish.' At that he raised high the staff and hurled it to the ground with a thud that reverberated through the dry earth.

It would have made a good end to the assembly, and Achilles would have strode from the square then; but Calchas held him back. No man unleashed a mob. The men must be guided back, turned once more into an army.

Calchas did that himself. And Agamemnon. And Nestor, old and dry, and seemingly untouched by the madness. They made sure that the men heard it all again, but this time with understanding. Agamemnon made sure that Achilles heard, and understood, their refusal to pity him.

They did fear his threat. Nestor pleaded for both men to relent. So did Ulysses, and Ajax, and half a score of others. It was too late to relent, though. Too much had been said, there was too much honour to be lost. The assembly broke up, not in a tumult, but with the smell of disaster hanging heavily over it.

Just in case there should be revolution brewing later, Agamemnon sent his marshals to set the troops to work, patrolling and cleaning the camp, throwing the rubbish into the sea, and banishing with it the mice that scrabbled around the middens.

Achilles went to tell Briseis himself. He found her in the hospital tent and waited for her to finish wiping the sweat from a sick man and empty her water before she came to walk back with him to his hut. She did not say anything on the way: she could see the set of his mouth, and the looks on the faces of the men they passed.

Inside the hut it was comparatively cool. The dogs looked up and flopped back on the boards, sensing themselves unwanted.

She listened in silence while he told her what had happened. When he came to Agamemnon's threat she found that she began to shake. By the time he had finished the tale she had the shaking under control. 'Can you resist them? Fight when they come for me?'

Achilles met her gaze. 'No.' He dropped his eyes and began to pace up and down the hut. Then he stopped again, close by her, as if he felt he must give more of an explanation. 'It would not be honourable. You can see that, surely? I chose not to kill Agamemnon for you. It is what I would have done if you were a slave girl, and not my wife. I cannot attack his envoys when I decided not to kill him, in front of every man in the camp. There has to be another way. There is another way. I have chosen this way of taking my revenge and I will have to keep to it.'

'So you give me to him? And you fight back by withdrawing your men.'

He nodded impatiently, almost abstractedly.

'But you lose me that way.'

She saw his face cloud, the way it sometimes did before he lost his temper and shouted at his men. He said, in an exaggeratedly patient voice, 'There is no other way. That is the way it has to be.'

She had been leaning against the trestle. She bent to pull out the bench from under it and sat abruptly. She set her head in her hands and said to the scrubbed boards, 'Are you sure that this is revenge for Agamemnon's taking me? It sounds to me like revenge for losing the command, for not getting the support you had hoped for.'

The explosion did not come. He sat next to her, without touching her. 'Briseis. You have to understand. This is how Agamemnon is taking his revenge on me. And this is how I have to take my revenge on him.'

'By treating me like a prize in a game of dice, and doubling the stake with every throw.'

He touched her then. Caught her shoulder and dragged her round to face him. 'Of course you are the stake. What could he take that would hurt me more? Do you not think he knows that?'

She stared at him, wide-eyed. Finally she said, 'Yes, he knows. But do you know how to hurt him in the same kind of way?'

'He is not the same kind of man. Different things hurt him. I would not do it, not like that. He is not acting honourably, and I am. I will; and you shall too.'

Briseis said slowly, 'You are paying a heavy price for your honour.'

He was quiet for a long time. As if, she thought, they both had to be sure that the reply he gave was the right one.

'If I have to,' Achilles said at last, 'I will pay everything I have for it. I will surrender you. I will keep my men from fighting. I will die, if necessary. The only thing I will not do is ask you, or Patroclus, or anyone else I love to do anything that I would not do myself. Because there would be no honour in that, for me or for them. Is that what you wanted to know?'

She did not look at him as she answered, in a very small voice, 'Yes.' And then, 'When will they come?'

'This afternoon sometime.' He paused. 'We should say good-bye now. I cannot do it in front of them. I will send Patroclus to fetch you when they come.'

She hesitated, then moved to put her arms round him. He held her for a long time, his face buried in her hair. Then he drew back, kissed her and released her. 'You must not expect to come back. I could not take you back now, even if he offered. I must go through with it, whatever he offers me. You understand that?'

She did not understand at all, but she nodded, her eyes on him. Then he turned and walked out of the hut.

She waited, afterwards, for Patroclus to come. The first time he came, she told herself, would be to say goodbye; not till the second time would she have to go. She expected him to come as soon as Achilles left, but time went by and there was no sign of him, and a chill hand began to grip her heart. Then he was there, with her, and she was in his arms.

She did not expect him to speak at all, but at length he did, still holding her tightly and looking down at her. 'Dry the tears now. Achilles will not want you crying when they come.'

She nodded and wiped her face with the hem of her tunic.

'And put on a different dress.'

She had only one other dress in Achilles' hut, the creamy woollen one she had worn on that first night with him. She hesitated, then went to the trunk to fetch it. Patroclus watched her steadily as she changed. It did not occur to him to leave, or to her to ask him to. Then she turned and looked across at him.

Patroclus said, 'You must not blame Achilles. He had no choice.'

'Who should I blame? Apollo? Agamemnon?'

'You could blame me. I should not have encouraged him to challenge for the command.'

'I could blame you.' She repeated his words expressionlessly, as if they were unreal to her. There was a silence, still and heavy. She walked slowly across the room to him and stood close, not touching him. 'But you would not let me go if you were in his place.'

He met her eyes; then turned abruptly away from her, and was gone.

She fought the temptation to cry again. Instead she sat down and waited, silent and motionless, until the door opened once more and Patroclus was back. He said nothing this time. Without looking at him she stood up and walked past him and out of the hut.

Achilles stood in the courtyard. There were two men with him, men she did not recognize, dressed in Agamemnon's livery. His face was cold and still. His eyes when she met them were alive though, the storm rising high in them and ready to break. She turned away quickly and gave the envoys a little nod. They came forward to take her hand.

'There is no need to touch her.' Achilles' voice, too level, came from behind her. 'She will come with you willingly.'

Not willingly, no. But proudly, honourably. Briseis set her chin a little higher and without a backward glance set off after the men.

Achilles waited until she was out of sight. Then he turned and walked rapidly down to the shore.

There was no need for Agamemnon to tell Chryseis. His hall looked onto the meeting ground and she had watched it all. She was too far away to catch many of the words, but the meaning was easy to read. She had known ever since the plague came that he would have to send her back. It was not just Apollo's curse. It was a particular revenge of the Mouse God, this sickening disease that the mice and rats brought with them, this gift of the weak that brought the strong low. She had needed no diviner to tell her that. And she had known that Agamemnon knew it too, from the way in which he had steadily withdrawn from her as the plague mounted.

It was not that she wanted to return. There was no sense in either hoping for or dreading it. Apollo would decide; and the girl who had once chosen to challenge Artemis would never question the workings of Apollo.

She tried not to dwell on what awaited her in Chryse. The God would tell her what to do, once she was back at the shrine. And when it was clear to her what Apollo wanted she would do it. It crossed her mind, with cruel irony, that the God might tell her to marry Troilus. She pushed the thought fiercely aside. There could be no question of that, with Agamemnon's child in her belly.

Diomedes came across before the meeting finished and stood in front of her, sleek and arrogant, deliberately blocking her view. She did not think he could have known of her conversation with Agamemnon, but curiously its aftermath had left them with a hard-edged friendship. Perhaps he sensed that now her arousal was stronger than her disgust in him; and knowing it, no longer wanted her quite so much. Perhaps it was simply the taboo that her pregnancy placed on her.

'It seems you will not get me after all, Diomedes.'

'You never know. Chryse is not so far away. You need a man, and now you will never marry Agamemnon.'

Chryseis' eyes widened slightly, but they remained firmly fixed on his face. It would be a curious revenge of the gods, that one. She resisted the temptation to bite back at him and said smoothly, 'Are you to take me there?'

'I doubt it, my dear.' He lingered just a fraction on the endearment. 'He may still give the job to Achilles. If not, I think it will be Ulysses.'

'I would hardly expect him to choose Achilles.'

Diomedes smiled a slow, sly smile that never touched his eyes. 'You have not understood as well as you think, my sweet.

Our dear High King does not intend to suffer an empty bed. He has decided to confiscate Achilles' wife and take her for his own.'

The pregnancy had heightened her reactions, and Diomedes knew her too well. She made no attempt to keep her astonishment from him. When her first surprise had died down she said calmly, 'What a very neat revenge.'

'I thought it would amuse you.'

'Amuse me. Yes. Well, my dear' – she smiled icily back at him – 'I had better go to prepare for the journey.'

'You had. I think he will send you today, before there is time for any backlash from the Myrmidons.'

'Has Achilles said what he intends to do?'

'Withdraw his troops. He will not leave without the girl, but he will stop them fighting. That is rather neat too, isn't it?'

'Of course, the other prophecy Calchas once made: that only with Achilles' help can Troy be taken.'

'Ah, but Achilles will not stick to it, and Apollo will. Never fear, you will end up on the losing side.'

'No, my dear Diomedes. The winning side. Apollo's side.' She held his gaze for a moment longer, then turned and swept into the room.

It surprised her when he moved into the room after her and caught her arm. 'Kiss me goodbye,' His voice was low, firm, with an edge of cruelty to it.

Her eyes moved swiftly round the room. None of the servants were in sight. Nobody standing outside would be able to see them clearly. She met his eyes again momentarily, then reached to pull his head down. His mouth on hers was hot and wet, like and yet unlike the way she had expected it to feel. He broke off the kiss, looked at her curiously, and then kissed her again, snaking his tongue into her mouth and moving his hand to knead her bare breast. If it had not been for the baby, she knew that he would have taken her right there, where anyone could have come upon them. And that she would have welcomed him.

It came as no surprise to either of them when they heard footsteps. They lingered over the end of the kiss before turning to face Agamemnon.

Menelaus and Ulysses were with him. The High King slashed his hand across Diomedes' face. The sharp-cut ruby set in his state ring scored open the Argive's cheek, leaving a thin line of red behind it.

'It is me you should hit, sir. I encouraged him.' Agamemnon turned to her, his lips pulled thin and tight. She met his eyes too, full on, and saw them narrow. She believed she saw a hint of cold amusement in them. He said nothing, but turned from her to send Diomedes away. Then he looked back at her casually. 'Ulysses will take you back to Chryse. He will wait here while you get your things together.'

'May I say goodbye to you in private?'

'There is no need for that.'

It was, she told herself firmly, how she had expected him to react. 'If you say so. Goodbye.'

'Goodbye.' He paused for a moment and she was tempted to say something about the child. It would be humiliating, though: he should have mentioned it. Not that she was surprised that he had not. She turned away before he could beat her to it.

There was little to pack. She would look ridiculous wearing court dresses in Chryse. She did not think she would ever wear them in Ilios. She ignored Agamemnon's jewels. She took a couple of shifts and chattered lightly to Ulysses as she wrapped up the bundle. Then she picked it up. 'I am ready now.'

'Let me take that.'

'How kind.' What a good choice he was. Always the diplomat, always unruffled. She followed a step behind him as they made their way to the harbour, where a ship had already been launched. It was a small ship, a Mycenaean one — that was a surprise — with a high prow and twenty oarsmen. The men were hoisting cattle into the hold for the sacrifices and the sails were being unfurled as they approached. A white standard was flying from the top of the mast. She walked faster, as if she were afraid it would leave without her, and made straight for the boat that was waiting to ferry them out to it. Ulysses reached out a hand to slow her and she saw that Agamemnon was there, standing on the shingle.

So there would be a farewell, in spite of her sabotage. She stopped in her tracks and left him to approach her. She was out of breath from the walk to the harbour, but had regained it by the time he was by her side, and she looked steadily at him. 'Thank you for coming.'

There was no amusement in his eyes, now. 'I wanted to give you this. For the baby.'

It was a small package, wrapped up in linen. 'You are too kind, sir.' She made no attempt to look at it. 'I will give your respects to my father.'

His mouth twitched slightly. 'Of course.' He turned to Ulysses and started to give him directions for the journey and the sacrifices.

It was calm: the sails hung limply. Chryseis settled down in the stern, where she could watch the men strain at the oars and the sun strike the water as it splashed around the ship. She had never been seasick before, but almost before the camp had faded behind them she began to feel queasy. It was humiliating, and so was Ulysses' polite attention as she hung, her face green, over the edge of the ship. There was nothing personal in it: he simply wanted to ensure that his cargo was delivered safely.

It was close to evening before they were deep enough into the estuary to be able to make out both shores clearly. Ulysses made the oarsmen pause. They set about furling the sails and lowering the mast. Chryseis wiped the sweat off her face and smoothed her dress. Then they moved forward again, towards the harbour at Chryse.

It crossed her mind, as they were approaching it, that the villagers would see the ship and send word to her father. They would know the ship was Achaean, but it was past the raiding season, and they should be able to tell from the standard that it was coming to the shrine. There was nobody to be seen onshore, though. When they got closer Chryseis saw that the fishermen's huts were in ruins, most of their roofs caved in. As the first sailors waded ashore a couple of cranes rose lazily from the nearest hut, stretched their long necks, flapped their wings and flew off inland. There were no boats tied to the jetty, either. Instead she was handed down to a couple of the sailors who stood in the shallows, ready to carry her to the shore.

Chryseis shivered. Ulysses came across, his tunic still tucked into his belt and his sandals in his hand. 'Is the shrine far? It's not in the village?'

There was nothing in the village now, was there? She pulled herself together. 'No. There is a dip at the other side of the village, and then a little hill. Our house is at the bottom, and the shrine is at the top. I will show you the path.'

'Can you walk? The men could carry you.'

'No.' She turned towards the path as she said it.

Ulysses reached out and grabbed her arm. 'Wait. I'll not split the men. We'll get the cattle unloaded first.'

It took a long time forcing the bullocks out of the ship and into the water. The sky reddened and then darkened. Pragmatic, Ulysses. Obviously he planned to make the sacrifice just as Agamemnon had ordered it whether there was anyone at the shrine or not. What would he do with her if her father and Rhene were not there? Leave her there alone, or put her too to the knife? She felt the sickness rising again and willed herself to keep it down.

Eventually they were ready. Ulysses lit a torch and at his side Chryeis led the procession through the village and along the path.

They reached the house first. The roof was still on it, but there was no smoke, and nobody came out to greet them. Chryseis unlatched the gate and went into the courtyard. The mice were there, just as she remembered them. They squeaked as she came close. Their water was clean, there was food in the cages.

'Could the priest be anywhere else?' Ulysses' voice in her ear made her jump.

'There is a hut higher up the hill, where he works. May I go up there alone?'

He thought for a moment. 'No. I cannot allow that. I'll get the men to wait here and I'll come with you.'

She nodded and set off across the yard and out of the far gate. The path was narrow and Ulysses had to tag behind her in the gloom. There was no sign of life. If her father was there he clearly did not trouble to listen out for supplicants any more. She knocked on the door of the hut and called out.

Somewhere a dog barked. Then the door was open and Chryses was there, looking just as he always had, and hugging her, as he rarely had. She forgot for a moment that Ulysses was behind her. When she turned he was a few paces away, studying the bushes intently. She smiled and crossed to him, the dog nuzzling her legs. 'The plants are rare ones. We use them in making the incense. My father brought them from Babylon. Come and say hello to him.'

The sacrifices and the feasting took till past midnight. She was tired and the sickness had made her weak. She stayed awake until Chryses' prayers were finished and then fell asleep against a tree. Ulysses carried her down to the house. When she woke it was very dark. In the house it was still, but when she looked out of the window she could see the torches flaring at the top of the hill and hear the soldiers singing in drunken celebration. Celebrating what? she wondered vaguely, and stumbled back to bed.

It struck her in the morning that Chryses had said nothing to her all evening. The whole sanctuary seemed to be full of soldiers. They kept out of the house, and she stayed indoors until it was quiet. Then she walked to the harbour. The dog came with her. It was a new dog, but it seemed to like her. Her father was there, standing at the water's edge, in earnest conversation with Ulysses. The Ithacan was the last to board the ship. She leaned against one of the tumbledown huts and watched Chryses watching the ship as it pulled away and faded to a spot on the horizon.

Chryses shook his head thoughtfully and turned towards the path. He walked surprisingly fast and she had to run to catch up with him. He did not notice her until she was barely three paces away. Then he stopped and waited for her to get her breath back, nodded, and carried on, only marginally more slowly.

He will go straight back to his hut, she thought to herself, unless I say something. 'You have not had breakfast yet. Come back to the house.'

'I do not think I need breakfast today, my dear.'

'Come and drink while I eat, in that case.'

He considered that. 'If you want me to, Chryseis.'

There was thick dust on the trestle. The store cupboard was almost empty and the sink dirty, the ashes were overflowing from the firebox below the oven and the knives caked hard with the debris of old meals. It would all have to wait. So would breakfast. She found two cups and went to fill a jar with water from the spring. It took most of the water to wash them, but there was a little left to drink. Then she crossed to where her father had sat down, on the bench by the hearth. 'No Rhene.'

'She died last winter.' He said it as if last winter had been a very long time ago.

'You did not think to get another servant?'

Her voice was sharp and her father looked up and frowned. 'There is nobody to take. Perhaps in time the God will send us one.'

'Are there any women at all in the village? On the farms?'

'No, nobody.'

'And in Thebe?'

Chryses was still frowning, but his voice was calm. 'My work is here, child. I am not going to Thebe.'

His daughter fought to keep her patience. 'I must find a woman to help me before the baby is due. You did notice that I was carrying?' She could not tell from his expression if he had. 'It will be in the autumn. Perhaps four moons from now.'

'Yes.' He appeared to be thinking. 'Maybe you had rather stay in Thebe until then.'

'The palace? Is the Queen back there now?'

Chryses looked mildly surprised. 'I thought you knew, child. King Eetion is dead. He was killed in the battle. And the Queen died this last winter.'

'No,' she said slowly. 'I knew there had been a battle, but not that the King had died. And Maris? Is he dead too? And his brothers?' She stood up, seeing her father's face, and went abruptly to the doorway. A little while later she managed a reply. 'Not Thebe, then. Not to stay in, anyway. Do you think you could go there and find a woman for us? Someone who would come back here?'

'That would mean leaving you here alone.' It was a more rational response than she had expected. 'Perhaps I should. I ought to find a messenger to take the news to Ilios.'

Surely he did not think that she would marry Troilus now?

She did not ask. Instead she said, 'I would not mind being here alone for a while. Will you leave the dog with me?'

'Of course, my dear.'

'And now you would like to get back to your work.'

'If you do not mind.'

'No. There are a few things I have to do here.'

He nodded, stood up, and was gone.

Briseis assumed she would be taken to Agamemnon's private quarters: to the big hall, or perhaps to the room where she had met Chryseis the year before. But a woman servant came up, took her from the envoys while they were still in the assembly ground, and led her instead to a tent. It was maybe fifty paces from the High King's hut.

It was a small tent, made of thick canvas, with a birch roof tree. A canvas flap covered the entrance. Inside it was clean and bare. There was a single pallet and a wooden chest, finely carved. Fresh rushes had been strewn on the ground.

'Agamemnon will not see me yet?'

The servant had been backing out again. She jumped, as if she were surprised to be spoken to. She was a youngish woman, who must once have been pretty. Now she was just faded, as if she had been worked too hard for too long. She said listlessly, 'We never know what he plans till he gives us orders, miss. He sent word you were to be brought here. There's a guard outside, and you stay here until he sends for you.'

'Do I share this? With any of his other women?'

'Two of them used to sleep here, but he had it cleared out this afternoon.'

'Can you stay and talk to me?' Fear flashed across the woman's face and Briseis added quickly, 'I have no wish to make difficulties for you. If you had something else to do.'

'I doubt if he would like it.'

'You had better go, then. But tell me your name, at least.'

The woman seemed to think before she replied. 'It's Helen, miss.'

'Goodbye, Helen. Maybe I shall see you later.'

The woman paused, then fairly dashed out of the tent.

Briseis could hear the guard now, clanking as he walked about. Evidently he wore his breastplate and sword, even in the heat. There were shouts from further off, where the men were throwing mounds of rubbish into the bay. Inside the tent it was hot and still, with a faint smell of perfume in the air. A woman's smell. They would probably hate her, the two women who had been thrown out of the tent to make way for her. Maybe Helen was one of them.

She sat down on the pallet and looked over at the chest. She did not like to open it. It would be embarrassing, somehow, if anyone caught her rifling through it.

He would call her later, surely. At nightfall, if not before. She could not try to kill him, not when Achilles had chosen not to do it for her. What should she do? It might please him if she acted outraged. She supposed she should try to be haughty and indifferent. She reckoned she could manage to stick to that, unless he hurt her too badly. Best not to think too much about it. Think about Achilles. Achilles was her husband. She loved Achilles.

The guard called in to her as it grew dark, to ask if she wanted a lamp lit. She did not answer straight away, so he repeated the question, louder. Then she called back 'No thank you', so that he would not come in. She lay in the darkness for what seemed a long time, until there were different voices outside and a woman came in, a lamp in her hand. Not Helen, but a taller, flashier woman, with a heavily painted face and eyes that were weary underneath the kohl. She set the lamp down on the floor, and said, 'I've come to get you ready, my dear.'

'Thank you.' Briseis stood up and the woman nodded, as if in approval.

'My name is Zeleia.' She gave a slight smile as she said it. 'Have you looked through the dresses? Is there one you would particularly like to wear?'

Briseis shook her head. 'I'll leave it to you.'

'If you like.' The woman crossed to the chest and began to

rummage through it. 'They're all much of a muchness, Cretan style, you know the sort of thing.'

'Yes.'

Zeleia drew out a tiered skirt, dark-dyed — it was impossible to tell the colour in the lamplight — with flashes of gold coming from it. 'This will do if I can find the top. There's a sash somewhere that goes with it.'

She smiled as she unearthed the top and a wide golden sash. It seemed a friendly smile. She dressed Briseis confidently, with a mass of gold bracelets and anklets, and jewelled twists in her hair. She plastered on rouge and kohl with the same heavy hand she had used on herself, and stood back to admire the effect. 'I don't think there is a mirror. Shall I find one for you?'

'No thank you. I am sure it is very suitable.'

Zeleia nodded. 'That's how he likes his women to look.' Briseis was silent and after a moment the other woman went on, 'Would it help if I told you what to expect? What he will do to you?'

'I think I already know.'

'You are not expecting him to be like Achilles?'

'No. Shall I go now?'

'Not yet. He will send for you when he wants you.' Zeleia paused. 'Treat him gently. He will be missing Chryseis. He won't beat you tonight if you handle him right.'

'I'll remember. Thank you. There is no need to wait with me.'

'I'll tell the guards you're ready.' Zeleia nodded once more, then she was gone into the night.

Briseis was made to wait longer than she had expected. The wait made it harder: perhaps Agamemnon had planned that. After a short while she sat down again on the pallet. Do not think about it, she told herself repeatedly. Think about Achilles. Let his strength sustain you. Act as he wants you to. She fought to retain her earlier calm and after a while fell into a mood that was not exactly calmness, more a stupor of numb misery.

She did not notice at first when the flap of the tent opened. One of the envoys of the afternoon was there, with the guard just behind him. 'You are to come with me now.'

'I am ready.' She stood up, avoiding the men's eyes, though

she could feel them looking her over. They escorted her between them back up the track towards Agamemnon's hut.

They pushed her a little roughly into the main hall and shut the door behind her.

The room was brightly lit after the darkness of the tent and the path. Four heavy bronze lamps hung on long chains from the rafters and more lamps had been set on the trestle.

Agamemnon stood in the centre of the room, a winecup in his hand, as if he had been striding about declaiming his thoughts to his brother. He wore a purple tunic and rings flashed on his hands. Menelaus sat on a bench, listening to him. Zeleia was there too, sitting in a corner.

The High King turned to Briseis and appeared to inspect her. She turned her eyes to his face, but he did not meet them. His swept downwards, as if he were mentally pulling off the long skirt, and then moved up to linger on her bare breasts. He stood there, staring at her, until the flush that he must have been waiting for came across her chest and face. Then he walked forward until he was less than a pace from her. He was barely taller than she was, but he kept his gaze down, fixed on her breasts, until he stopped. Then he looked into her eyes. His were pale, but they did not reflect any light. His hand reached out and very deliberately, with his thumb and forefinger, he flicked her painted nipple.

'Very nice.'

The voice, cool and amused, came from Menelaus. Agamemnon turned for a moment to his brother. 'Adequate, I agree, but not exciting. I shall endure the disappointment of not taking her.'

Briseis could not keep her breath from drawing in sharply and Agamemnon turned back to her with a cold smile. 'I am sorry if I disappoint you too, my dear. Zeleia has prepared you so carefully. But it will not be in vain, you need not return to a cold bed. I shall give you to Menelaus.'

Menelaus' laugh rang out in the quiet room. 'Ah, that is excellent, Agamemnon. Then if you ever need to return her you can swear to Achilles that you have not touched her.'

'Hardly at all.' The smile twisted the corners of Agamemnon's mouth even higher as he reached out to her breast again. He rolled the nipple between his fingers, watching all the time, until it stood out hard under his touch. 'Take your clothes off, my dear.'

'Here?' Briseis' eyes flickered over to Zeleia, but the other woman kept her eyes fixed firmly on the floor.

'Would you prefer a bedroom? I fear it would be a little cramped for the four of us. I require two witnesses, of course, to swear that I have not enjoyed you myself. Though I shall enjoy watching you, naturally.' She stood there, frozen, as Agamemnon lifted his cup, held it out as if to toast her coming performance, sipped carefully at his wine, then turned and walked across to sit in a low carved chair near the door. Her eyes on him, she hardly noticed as Menelaus approached from behind her and began to unfasten the golden sash. She did not look at him again until Menelaus had finished with her. Agamemnon had not moved at all, and she stood up and dressed in silence.

'Yes, you may leave now.' His voice was as smooth as ever. 'Unless you would prefer to stay and watch me take Zeleia.' She did not reply and walked as carefully as she could across to the door. Agamemnon's voice came to her again as she was fumbling with the latch. 'I fear my brother is not a very imaginative lover. Tomorrow night I think I will invite Diomedes. He should give a more interesting performance.' Then the latch was free and she stumbled out of the hut and into the arms of the soldier who stood on guard outside it.

'Spies.' Priam hissed the word at Hector, leaning forward and gripping the arms of his throne. From a different man it might have sounded melodramatic.

The two of them were not alone. The usual heralds and guards stood in the shadows of the throne room, the priestess lingered in the doorway, and a messenger from the Achaean camp — from the Trojan spies in the Achaean camp — stood beside them, waiting for Priam's orders. However, Priam was not talking of *his* spies.

'I dare say there are spies working for the Achaeans as well as for us, sir.' Hector kept his voice level.

'Or should we say . . . traitors?' Priam sat back, his expression angry and yet satisfied, as if the anger helped to quell his interminable pain. 'It is too long since we found one. We should find another, and make an example of him.'

Hector frowned. The news from the messenger had not affected him in quite the same way; and he had no wish to spend his time rooting out traitors. 'Then I shall make some enquiries.'

'Do that.' Priam's arm lifted a fraction to dismiss both his general and the messenger. They both made appropriate bows and went – to a meeting of their own, for there was more that Hector wanted to know.

The messenger's news had been of the fateful assembly and of Achilles' withdrawal of his troops, which had taken place a few days earlier. It was Achilles who interested Priam. He found the Myrmidon leader more fascinating than Agamemnon, whose motives, however byzantine, he could invariably understand. Achilles, in contrast, was a puzzle. That a stronger leader, a born fighter, should take such a step for a mere woman was totally inexplicable. There had to be more to it, but the messenger knew no more, and Priam's thoughts had turned, in a tangle of their own, to secrets and treacheries.

There had also been a mention – skimmed over by the messenger, and barely noticed by Priam – that Chryseis had been returned to her father. Hector had a suspicion that that might ultimately prove more important to the Trojans.

The trouble was, its importance was not yet clear to him. He interrogated the messenger intensively, but the messenger and his informants had had no access to Chryseis and all he could learn was that Ulysses had taken the girl to Chryse.

Hector dismissed the man and threw an exasperated glance around the small room where they had been talking. A bare room that led off the porch to the throne room, it was used by the priestess and her assistants. A clutter of incense burners, jars of oil, dishes and cloths spread along the shelf on the wall. 'he priestess' spare robes hung from a hook, and on the floor was the wicker basket she used to transport the snakes. There was a smell of age: of rancid oil, of dust and decay. An Ilian smell.

It was a long time since Hector had thought about Mysia. Little news had come from that direction, none of it encouraging. He could not recall if Chryses had even been told of Troilus' death. His thoughts raced ahead of him as he made arrangements for a messenger to go down to the Mouse God's sanctuary, to make sure that the priest did know.

The girl had been in favour with Agamemnon, it seemed, right up to the time when he was forced to send her back. There was surely information that she could give them. She was a bright child and must have kept her eyes and ears open. Hector had a strong reluctance to interrogate her, though; and he had a suspicion that she might not tell him anything if he did. Still, it was a chance not to be missed. Somebody would have to talk to her, somebody with status and understanding. He could not leave it to the messenger.

Hector did not even consider entrusting the task to Ennomus or Chromis. He did think of asking Aeneas, but he decided that the Dardanian could not be spared from Ilios.

Perhaps the girl should be called back to Ilios, he thought. Andromache might be able to help, if Chryseis were brought to the citadel. He decided to ask her opinion when he returned home.

The business of Achilles was more encouraging. It was a pity they could not take better advantage of it, but Achilles' troops were not so numerous and the Trojans were probably still outnumbered. Rhesus' Thracian troops, so long promised, had been delayed. They might reach Ilios any day, but it would not do to risk an offensive before they arrived.

Hector sighed. It would just have to be more of the same. Casual skirmishes on the surface; and beneath, the same dirty war of infiltrations and treacheries. The war that made Priam hiss with indignation while at the same time his eyes lit up and his fingers gripped tighter.

What a job. Hector cringed at the prospect of nosing around Ilios, questioning every man's actions until he found a word or a gesture out of place.

Priam did not understand, he thought, how precarious relations were between the Ilians and the allies. Hector could see, in retrospect, how damaging his aggressive reaction to Troilus' death had been. It had opened a chasm where before there had been no more than a fault-line in the earth. Both he and Aeneas had belatedly tried to repair the situation, but things would never again be as they had once been. There would always remain a lingering distrust between the two sections of the Trojan forces. Only he and Aeneas ever bridged the chasm. Paris and Deiphobus rarely went to the allied camp; men like Chromis and Antiphus never entered the palace. Helenus moved freely among both parties, admittedly, but Hector was never certain that Helenus' endeavours improved the situation.

True, there were sure to be traitors. There always were. Hector could see that it was necessary to stop them if the war was to be won. But if he personally uncovered a spy among the allied forces he could see that such an action might bring the Trojans to the pitch of open warfare amongst themselves that the Achaeans appeared to have reached already. Nor could he delegate the task to an allied commander, not even to Aeneas. None of them would be likely to denounce any of their own men to the Ilians.

There was only one man who could conceivably undertake the task. Helenus would be able to do it. Helenus would be good at such a job. He always seemed to know everything, he habitually asked questions everywhere. Helenus the cynic, with no apparent scruples, could see through other men's disguises and uncover their basic natures. Helenus probably knew already who the spies were, Hector thought uneasily to himself; it was just that, habitually inactive, he had chosen not to share the information with anyone else.

Helenus had the access to the allied forces that such a job demanded. He only had it, Hector was conscious, because of his detachment, because men knew that he never took advantage of it. Helenus' equivocal position would be destroyed if it ever became clear that he had played a role in uncovering a spy in politically unacceptable quarters; but that was a risk Hector was prepared to take. In the last resort, Helenus was expendable.

Hector packed off another servant to tell Helenus to come and dine with him that night. It would do, he had made a start at least. He nodded to the priestess – still lingering, cautious yet curious – and set off for home.

It was good news on the whole, he supposed, but it had not pleased him. The war did not any more, particularly when its darker and less honourable side came to the fore. Priam was right. That summer the spies seemed to be more active than ever before.

His steps quickened as he reached the other side of Palace Square, and his face lifted. A smile hovered around his mouth. It broke out as he crossed the courtyard and pushed through the half-open door into the megaron.

Andromache was at her loom, waving her shuttle distractedly as she tried to explain something to Cassandra, and oblivious of the dog which was worrying a spindle of red yarn across the floor. Hector bent to cuff the dog away gently and handed the spindle back to her with a little bow. She grinned and wiped a stray strand of hair away from her face.

'Any news?' Cassandra asked.

'You mean, any news you are not yet likely to know? You've probably told it all to Andromache already, and spoiled our suppertime.'

Cassandra gave a mock groan. 'Hector, Hector. Did Priam's spies really tell you what Helen said to Paris the day before yesterday?'

'On the whole,' said Hector, 'I'm glad I missed it.' He sat down. 'No, they told me about Chryseis.'

'Now that is interesting. Chryseis is always interesting. Do go on.'

'Chryseis', he began slowly, 'is back in Chryse.'

Helenus appeared before the women had finished their questions. Hector's face fell slightly. Helenus had his distant look, as if he had not brought all his thoughts with him.

'Oh Helenus,' Andromache said. 'Now Hector will have to start all over again.'

'If it is about Chryseis, I already know.'

Cassandra started to say something, then bit it off sharply. 'I'll tell you later. Helen will be waiting for me. I'll see you in the morning, Andromache?' She was gone in a whirl of dark skirts.

'I'll go and fetch the baby,' Andromache said into the sudden silence. She had left him upstairs during Cassandra's visit. Hector normally expected to see his son, though, as soon as he got home. There was no reply, so she bustled off in search of the nursemaid.

'You wanted to talk to me?' Helenus was always inclined to be direct, but just then it was as if he were anxious to have the meeting over, and escape. Hector turned to look at him, nettled. Whether he did it then or later, he thought, the talk would destroy his pleasure in the evening. And Helenus, whose fair hair was dishevelled and tunic crumpled, he now saw, would do nothing to make it easier. 'It could wait until after supper.'

'I would prefer to talk now. I had other plans for this evening.' Helenus did not volunteer to describe them.

'Wait to see the baby first. It will upset Andromache if we don't.'

'I would hate to upset Andromache.'

Hector turned to him sharply, but there was no expression that he could read on Helenus' face. Then Andromache was back, with the maid behind her holding the baby.

'And how is my son today?' Hector reached out to take him, planted a big kiss on the little face, and tossed Astyanax high up in the air.

'Not so high, Hector. Please.'

Hector grinned. 'He loves it. You can see he loves it.' Astyanax was gurgling and giving every sign of loving it. 'Here, Helenus.'

Helenus just caught the baby, a handspan from the floor. He lifted him at arms' length and inspected him. 'He is going to have your nose, Andromache,' he said thoughtfully.

Andromache snatched him back. 'You're as bad as Cassandra,' she said with a tinge of annoyance.

Helenus smiled lazily and reached out to tickle Astyanax under the chin. He was rewarded by a smile from the baby, and a frown from its mother, which slowly dissolved into a surprisingly affectionate look.

'Fine. Shall we go to your room, Hector?'

Hector's room was cheerless in the early evening light. He propped himself against the wall, leaning on the windowsill, and motioned Helenus to one of the low stools that were among its few furnishings. Helenus hesitated and then sat down. 'Don't tell me. You have a rotten job for me.'

'True. Not a very enjoyable one. But I think you would do it well.'

Helenus considered his brother carefully and then flung his legs forward, balancing himself with hands behind him on the rim of the stool, and turned his eyes up to the ceiling. 'If it is spying, you can ask Deiphobus. Or Paris.'

'I am not asking Deiphobus. I am asking you.' After a moment Hector added, 'It's not exactly spying, anyway.'

'Spycatching, then.' Helenus said it confidently and did not bother to look at Hector again.

'It has to be done, and you would do it better than Deiphobus. You are sharper than he is, and you have better sources.'

Helenus looked across now, slowly and deliberately. 'So you do plan an offensive while Achilles is out of action?'

Hector cursed under his breath and said, 'No, not yet. I doubt if it would succeed right now. Or do you think otherwise?'

Helenus did appear to think. Finally he said, 'Yes, I do think otherwise. I think it is necessary for morale: for yours, and for all the troops. We spend too much time hanging around waiting for the Achaeans.'

'And as a result there is treachery in the camp.'

'Treachery? What do you mean by treachery?'

'You know perfectly well what I mean by treachery, Helenus. What do you mean by a question like that?'

'No, Hector. I do not know. The more I think about it, the less I know. What I do know is that I have no wish to use my own gifts in the cause of spying and setting one man against another, however good a reason you reckon there is for it. I think that would be treachery, of a sort.'

'Are you refusing me?'

Helenus smiled. 'Would that be treachery?' Hector did not answer and he continued, 'Until I saw you tonight I thought you would ask me something else. Maybe that is why I was on edge.'

Hector could see no way to avoid a direct question. Slowly he said, 'What did you expect me to ask?'

'You cannot guess? I reckoned you would tell me to get down to Chryse and interrogate Chryseis – who you might also think of as a traitor, perhaps. Though to which side, it might be difficult to say. Or did you think I would draw the line at that?'

'I had not thought of asking it.'

'Oh, Hector. You said that much too quickly.' Helenus rose as he spoke, as if to prevent a reply. He walked to the door, then turned, leaning on the door jamb. 'If I see any Achaeans strolling around Ilios I'll let you know.'

'It is not Achaeans who are traitors to Troy. It is Trojans. And it is Trojan names I want from you, Helenus.'

Helenus' face was in the shadow of the door as he replied. 'Perhaps you should begin with mine. Then you could try Aeneas.' He waited just long enough to be able to absorb Hector's expression, which hovered between perturbation and fury, then turned and walked out of the room.

Hector stood motionless by the window for a long time. At last he slowly roused himself and returned to the megaron.

Helenus was there, the baby on his knee, and Andromache giggling at some joke he had made, or something the child had done. He looked up, his face bland. 'The invitation was for supper? Or would you prefer me to set about your little task right away?'

'No, stay to supper.' Hector said it curtly and crossed to pour some wine before either of them looked too closely at his face.

Andromache watched him apprehensively. She generally asked Hector, these days, when she saw that something was upsetting him. But she thought he must have had a quarrel with Helenus and she did not think she wanted to know about it. Perhaps Hector would tell her without being asked?

Hector thought about it, over supper, but decided that he would not. He said nothing about Achilles either, and instead took her to bed early. She was surprised. He rarely did that for comfort. When she reached out to hug him he made love to her with an impersonal anger that left her shaken and curiously aroused.

He woke again in the early hours of the morning. There had been a dream which had upset him and left him disoriented. He had had the strange illusion that Troilus was still alive. He lay in the high bed for some time, unable to sleep, and slowly the ghost of Troilus that haunted his mind acquired Helenus' wry smile. Helenus? And Aeneas? They were neither of them men he should ever have doubted. He could think of no Trojans to whom he was closer those days; and yet he had had the feeling that Helenus had not intended the remark to be entirely ironic. Still, no man could fight a war while waiting for his brother and his friend to thrust a dagger in his back. It would have to be forgotten.

Ten days later the messenger was back with news that the Achaeans planned an offensive for the following day. Hector was glad, on the whole. Though he could not have forced the issue himself, his men had a pretty good chance, he reckoned; and he hoped Rhesus' Thracians would arrive in time to make Agamemnon extremely sorry for his decision.

Would the Myrmidons fight? No, the spies had told the messenger. Of course they will, said Priam, with an angry look as if Hector were talking rubbish. No, Hector said to himself when he was alone. Paris and Aeneas agreed with him; he did not ask Helenus. He chose to stick at that and planned the battle lines on the assumption that there would be no black tunics massed on the enemy flank.

When the sun rose high enough the next morning he saw that he had been right. The rest were all there. It hardly changed from one battle to the next. The central force of foot soldiers with their spears, slings and stones; the archers, poised to take the higher ground; and at the forefront, the charioteers. Agamemnon gave the order to advance before it was fully light. The dust swirled up from the midsummer plain as the soldiers and horses pressed forward, and then the plan was lost in the confusion of a full-scale attack.

They were fighting hard, harder than in any battle for years. By midday the bodies were thick on the ground. The living kicked a few aside, the orderlies carried a few back to the camps. The warriors fought on around and above the rest. There were casualties among the officers, a lot of them, on both sides. Paris was hit by a swordstroke, Menelaus by an arrow in the stomach, Aeneas was wounded in the thigh. Agamemnon took his man, aiming his spearthrust from behind at a tall Halizonian who was turning to retreat.

Those who were not injured fought on, the sweat darkening

the leather and linen of their battledress, the dust filming even the feathers of their crests, the blood crusting the tips of their spears and the blades of their swords. They withdrew to snatch breath and then returned to fight again, and again, and again. It was growing dark before the last soldiers limped away from the skirmishes, leaving the bodies behind them.

Hector had fought well, he reckoned afterwards. He had blunted or broken seven thrusting spears, and lost count of the javelins he had thrown. He was certain of three kills, and suspected he had made a fourth. He had taken a chariot and two fine horses, two swords, helmets, greaves, breastplates and shields large and small. He managed a weary smile as his servant spread out the trophies before him on the rough ground. There was still nobody to rival him among the Trojans. Nobody among the Achaeans either, with the Myrmidons kicking their heels in the camp; though he reckoned Diomedes might have given him a tough time had they come up against each other. Half a dozen Trojans blamed their wounds on Diomedes, and plenty of men were in no state to speak up any more.

They had held the enemy, that was all; and they were exhausted. Hector sent his heralds to barter a day's truce. Agamemnon would have to agree. They both needed time to gather and burn their dead, and to sacrifice again to the gods who had not yet given them a victory.

The day of truce dawned leaden-skied, and by nightfall thunder was rumbling above the plain. It seemed as if the offensive would end as had the previous year's, in a deluge that sent red rivers pouring off the plain. But the rain did not come and the following morning was bright and hot, the sun yellow in the dawn sky. So it all began again.

That day the Thracians arrived. Hector laughed exultantly when they told him and pulled back out of the line to go and greet Rhesus. When he came closer the laughter died on his face. Priam had been promised a thousand men, maybe two thousand: there were only five hundred.

It would have to do. No, they could not take a day to recover from the march. Zeus, what a suggestion! He set them to reinforce the centre, where the line was sagging back towards the citadel.

Then he forced out the laugh again and made sure that the messengers sent word from contingent to contingent, so that every man would know that they were going to win.

They did. Considering how little extra they had gained, they really did. The line pushed forward steadily, strung out from river bank to river bank, towards the harbour and the Achaean camp. Oh, but it was slow. How slow. A man could walk from Ilios to the sea and back in a morning, and by the time the light was gone they had covered maybe three quarters of the distance. In the last quarter came the ditch with its sharpened stakes, the stockade, the tents and huts, and the black rows of Achaean ships.

It was too much territory to give up. It was the best advantage Hector could recall. Starting from that position the next day, they might hope to bring the fighting right up to the enemy camp. Hector had his troops make their camp there, on the plain, amid the bodies, with the cries of wolves and jackals echoing in the night air. He sent for supplies from the town: beef and mutton, wine and bread, and wood. They would have to light campfires to keep the men safe. No truce, this time. The kites could have their feast.

A man came up as he was finishing the orders for the sentries: a dark man, with an air of excitement, and a reckless laugh on his face. Dragons breathed fire through the grime crusting his breastplate. Hector blinked, to exorcize the ghost; and saw Deiphobus. Deiphobus alive, and at first glance unharmed. No, with a rag tied around his forearm.

'Nothing much. It doesn't hurt yet. I reckon it won't, until we have won.'

'You have it looked at by the surgeons — with me watching. I'm not losing anyone through stupidity or over-confidence.'

Deiphobus narrowed his eyes. 'Yes sir.'

Hector managed a smile. 'You fought damn well. We all did. Come and get some supper.'

On their way to join the line leading up to the cooking fires Deiphobus said, 'You have put Rhesus right on the edge of the camp.'

'He'll not be going back to Thrace tonight. Not in the dark, with the wolves.' Hector's voice lowered. 'And I am not having anyone count his men.'

'If the Thracians think we are losing,' Deiphobus answered him slowly, 'then I think they are mistaken.'

'We have not won yet; and Agamemnon still has the Myrmidons. Fresh men, and pushing two thousand of them.'

Deiphobus considered. 'A night attack?'

'I doubt it. But I have ordered a double watch tonight, and a watch in Ilios too.'

'I didn't think there was a man left in Ilios who could carry a spear for more than a moment.'

'There's not. There are old men, and women, and lads. They have their orders. Do you blame me?'

'No. I reckon we will all sleep well enough tomorrow.'

Hector did not smile at that. He had not yet worked out how he was going to bridge the ditch.

Agamemnon was not smiling either, not with the Trojan campfires lit barely a couple of spearthrows from the stockade, like a thousand stars fallen on the dark plain.

He had had to do it: call the battle. He had given Achilles from new moon to full moon to climb down. The plague had peaked at about the time of the assembly and there had been barely a dozen new cases in the previous few days. The troops had been growing restive. It could not have gone on any longer.

The trouble was, this battle mattered so much. He was confident that the stockade was impregnable; but he was fighting Achilles as well as the Trojans, and he knew it would be enough to bring Achilles his victory if the Trojans pushed right up to the ditch and Achilles stood there on the high prow of his ship watching the Mycenaeans and the rest lose the entire plain and half their men. At all costs, Agamemnon could not let that happen. Achilles would only have to lift his little finger then and the entire army would be his.

Agamemnon stalked back to his hall. He threw out the servants, sent Diomedes and Menelaus packing a trifle more politely, and sat there alone in the gloom for a long time. At length he roused himself and had lamps lit, and the fire, and messengers sent to gather his counsellors.

They all came: Menelaus, Idomeneus, Nestor, Ajax, Diomedes, Ulysses and a dozen more. The High King had even demanded a Myrmidon. Not Achilles, the messenger told Patroclus. Achilles sent Phoenix. He was old, steady, and had more sense than to make concessions in Achilles' name, or to lose his temper. Agamemnon avoided their sullen eyes and they stood around muttering as the lambs and pigs were set on the spits and the wine poured. They ate in silence. Then the servants wiped the worst of the mess from the trestle, set out more wine, and withdrew.

Nestor began it. He said what they all knew had to be said: what Agamemnon must have been prepared to hear, or he would not have called them. He said it at length, in an old man's way, with digressions and anecdotes and occasional touches of forgetfulness. Agamemnon, his eyes cold and his face an impassive mask, listened politely to it all. Then he replied.

He blamed it on Zeus, his anger, as men will when their actions have turned out badly. The God had led him astray. That was apparent now. Since he was a long way from victory it was obvious that he had misread Zeus' will. So reparations would have to be made, to the God – and to the man who, it seemed, still had Zeus' favour.

It would be demeaning to bargain with Achilles, unendurable to be refused by him. The reparations would have to be on a scale that Achilles could not fail to accept. The High King, everyone would say, had been astonishingly generous. Right away there would be bronze and gold, horses and women. Once Troy was taken with the help of the perfidious Myrmidons there would be more than a fair share of her spoils. Back in Hellas there could be a marriage – a real marriage, none of the camp trumpery – to whichever of Agamemnon's daughters Achilles felt disposed to prefer. No bride gifts would be demanded. Instead the girl would be given a dowry on a regal scale: the overlordship of seven strongholds. Agamemnon enumerated them carefully: Cardamyle, Enope, Hire, Pherae, Antheia, Aepeia and Pedasus. They were all in Nestor's territory, not his own, and his eyes slid slyly across to the King of Pylos, making quite sure that Nestor took in his little revenge, and suffered for it. Oh, and the girl. She was, it seemed, no more than an afterthought. But she would be returned, of course, and with his solemn oath that he had not slept with her.

Diomedes choked on this and caught Menelaus' eye. Nestor, too, showed an unaccustomed anger by the time Agamemnon came to the end. The glances wove across the trestle like a spiderweb. Nobody said a word.

Agamemnon broke the silence. 'The emissaries will go now, to tell Achilles what has been decided.'

Ulysses lifted his cup and drank: deeply, noisily, and without a trace of self-consciousness. Putting it down again, he said, 'Of course you will go yourself. With the heralds.'

Agamemnon contemplated him frostily. 'No. Thank you, Ulysses, for volunteering.'

'You misunderstood me. If you will not go then why not ask Nestor?'

'I have a feeling,' Nestor said calmly, 'that that too might be misunderstood.'

'Select a party to go, then,' the High King said.

Nestor did not argue. He looked around the table. 'Ulysses. You will go, please. Phoenix. Not you, Menelaus. Diomedes?'

Diomedes silently shook his head. So, exchanging glances with him, did Idomeneus and Menestheus. Ajax agreed to go, after a look round at the rest. There was nobody else who was likely to be acceptable to Achilles. It was an ill-assorted delegation.

Agamemnon stood up and went to call in the servants. They brought water and the men washed the grease from their hands. The cups were filled again and the libations splashed onto the boards. Then Ulysses and his temporary companions hurried out of Agamemnon's hut.

Ulysses stopped them as soon as they were out of earshot of the High King's guards and told Agamemnon's escort to wait a few paces away. 'Phoenix, perhaps you had better tell us what to expect.'

Phoenix frowned. 'He might accept. If we put it tactfully.'

'Are the men ready to fight?'

'For him? Of course.'

'For Agamemnon.'

'For Agamemnon? Oh, I see what you mean. They are in pretty good shape. Patroclus has been seeing to them.'

'They are,' Ajax put in, 'in very good shape. Races and javelin contests every day, even when we were fighting. The horses exercised. The spears sharpened. No problems there.'

'And Achilles?'

'Achilles has not been talking at all. A wall of grief as high as the walls of Ilios, that's what Eudorus called it.'

Phoenix smiled slightly in the dark. 'You are out of date, Ajax. He cheered up immensely when the battle started.'

Certainly the Myrmidon section was not much like the rest of the camp. There was an awesome calm hanging over it, as if nobody had thought to tell them about the battle. The paths between the huts and tents were deserted. The strains of a harp drifted from the open door of Achilles' hut. The little group of emissaries stood and listened in the darkness. The strong, true voice was singing of Hercules, who had come to Troy once, the singer said, with just six ships full of men; and had razed Ilios to the ground, without a siege at all.

The dogs did not bark as Phoenix walked across the yard and through the door. Achilles nodded at him; so did Patroclus, who sat by the hearth. Achilles did not break his song. As Ulysses and Ajax followed he paused, then stopped singing and rose from the bench to greet them, the harp still in his hand. 'Ulysses and Ajax. What a surprise. My two great friends.'

Ulysses smiled and settled down comfortably in the chair that Patroclus had vacated. 'We ate,' he said, 'with Agamemnon.'

'Did you? Then you will eat again, with me.'

They did. Achilles called Automedon and the rest of his officers. A sheep, and a goat, and a pig were selected from the yard by torchlight, and slaughtered, and carved, and spitted, and roasted, and salted, and turned. And served to the gods and men. Patroclus mixed the wine, and mixed it strong. They ate slowly, as if the night were young, and they were old.

When the meal was over Ulysses made his speech: tactful Ulysses, who loved to talk. He held forth on battles general and particular; on tactics, and on the impact that fresh troops, trained to perfection, could have upon weary ones. He reminisced about a boy he had gone to fetch himself once, from Scyros ten summers before. A boy who had become a man, who fought like a god. Then he turned to meetings, and to a meeting that Achilles knew of. Achilles knew of the outcome too, except for the precise proposals that Agamemnon had come up with. Ulysses kept to Agamemnon's own words as he enumerated the tripods, the cauldrons, the slave women and the strongholds. And, of course, the brides – Briseus' daughter or Agamemnon's own. Or indeed both of them, if Achilles so chose.

Achilles listened. The firelight, flickering across his face, played tricks with his expression and it was not clear to Ulysses at first how he would respond.

'Thank you, Ulysses. You have made it very plain and I shall try to give you a plain answer.' He shifted slightly on the bench. 'You knew, perhaps, of one prophecy concerning me. There is another, of which perhaps you do not know. It seems there are two destinies awaiting me. I do not know, and maybe neither do the gods, which one will be realized. In one, I sail away from Troy. I go back home, to Phthia. I marry, possibly; and grow old in my own home, with the glory of my fighting days dimmed in men's memories.'

The hard face was softened by the firelight. Achilles smiled. 'In the other, I stay. I fight. I help to win Troy. My glory shines in men's minds for ever. But I die in the attempt and never see my home again.'

He paused, and the pause lengthened and thickened in the air. When he spoke again his voice was harsher. 'I have chosen now. I shall take the first. Tomorrow at dawn we shall make sacrifice to Zeus, and to Poseidon, and to all the gods who govern the winds and the waves. Then I and my men will launch our ships. If we get a following wind, perhaps three days from then we will see our homes again.'

Is it really up to you, Ulysses asked himself silently, to make the choice? He said levelly, 'And Agamemnon's offer?'

'Agamemnon has cheated me once, that sack of wine with a dog's heart and the courage of a deer. He has not come to look me in the eyes now. He is offering me the overflow from his ships' holds, a bride I am not free to take, and a set of overlord-ships that are in Nestor's gift anyway. Can you honestly swear to me, Ulysses, that he is not cheating me again?'

He did not wait for an answer, but added, 'I will not stop to find out. If he offered me as many gifts as there are grains of sand on the seashore I would not take them from him. We sail. Phoenix, will you stay here tonight, and come with us in the morning?'

Phoenix looked down. He had no sons of his own and he had loved Achilles better than he could have loved any son since he was a young man at Peleus' court and Achilles a tiny child.

'I think,' Ulysses said, not unkindly, 'that you should say your piece too.'

Phoenix frowned. Achilles regarded him. He said, 'I shall not hold it against you.'

So Phoenix spoke. He said what he had to say, coming on Agamemnon's business, with the heralds lingering in the doorway ready to report it all back. He talked at even greater length than Ulysses, rambling on as if he meant his message to be confused in the tedium of his tales. Achilles sat silent and it was not clear to his watchers whether he listened or not. When Phoenix had finished he stood up abruptly. 'Agamemnon should not have sent you. It is a bad thing to use men with divided loyalties. I will not have you dividing them any more. Ulysses and Ajax can take my answer back to Agamemnon. Stay here with us tonight and show him which side you are on.'

He made it sound like an order and turned immediately to Patroclus with a slight nod. Patroclus went to the door and called the guard to help make up a bed for Phoenix.

'I had better say something,' Ajax said.

'It's very late. Can you keep it short?'

'Yes, if you pretend to listen. The heralds are watching.'

It was short; and Achilles did appear to listen. There was nothing new in it. He replied levelly, without any more impatience. 'Enough. You have my message for the High King. I shall not fight the Trojans again unless I have my own cause for anger with them, not Agamemnon's. The wine is poured. Make the libations before you go.'

To Ulysses at least, the offering seemed for once no more than an empty ritual.

At the doorway, Achilles turned once more to the envoys. He looked up, to meet Ajax's glance; and then down, to meet

Ulysses'. He said quietly, 'We sometimes forget, do we not, why this war is being fought. But it began for a woman. For Helen. Because of Menelaus' lost love, and wounded pride. Well, the sons of Atreus are not the only ones who love their wives. I love mine too – yes, even though she came to me as a captive. I shall not forget what Agamemnon has done to her, and to me. This is my war now: my battle with him, not the war with the Trojans. He cannot end it by offering gifts. I shall never fight for Agamemnon again, and I want him to know it. I fight for my own now.'

They did not reply. Achilles stood watching them disappear into the dark. Then he turned back into the hut, where Patroclus and Phoenix were waiting for him.

Patroclus was angry. Achilles had expected that, after the decision to leave without her, but he had not known how angry until he saw his face.

'Don't say it.' It was an order, harsh and aggressive. He repeated it, in the same tone. 'Don't say it to me.'

There was a brief, charged silence. In a hard voice, Patroclus said instead, 'Shall I send for Diomede?'

Achilles did not look at him again, but crossed to the fire and bent to rake its ashes. 'Yes. And for Iphis. Phoenix? Shall I call your girl?' Phoenix shook his head, uncomprehending, and Achilles stood abruptly and made for his bed.

It was no way to spend the night between two days of heavy fighting. Ulysses thought as much, and then pushed aside the thought, as he stood listening to Agamemnon ordering his messengers out to wake the rest of the counsellors. Agamemnon went to fetch Menelaus himself. They would rendezvous, he said, at the gates to the camp.

Ajax walked slowly towards the stockade. Ulysses went on ahead. He was not yet sure why.

Diomedes arrived a moment after him. He had a lionskin

wrapped around his shoulders, from his bed presumably. True, it was cold in the night air. The Argive dug the point of his spear into the ground and leaned on it heavily, in the shadow of the stockade. A loud, theatrical snore came from the general direction of the dead lion's mouth. Ulysses gave a curt laugh and Diomedes straightened up.

There was a thick line of sentries along the top of the stockade. In its shadow there was nobody else to be seen.

'Achilles refused.'

'Naturally.'

'And now? Are we being called out to check on the sentries?'

'I think he has some scheme in hand.'

'Is there any scheme you would go along with now?'

'Perhaps.' Ulysses' voice was cold. Then Agamemnon arrived and he did not reply to any of Diomedes' whispers.

Agamemnon made no mention of Achilles. As soon as the last man was within earshot he said shortly, 'Nestor, can you advise us?'

Ulysses frowned. He thought that was too much, waking up an old man like Nestor. Not that Nestor seemed upset. He gazed back serenely. 'I cannot see that there is anything we can spring in the battle tomorrow. You are right, Agamemnon. We do it now.'

It was against all the rules of war; but there were no rules to this war any more. At least, Agamemnon seemed to think not. He said, 'An attack?'

'Not a full-scale attack. I think perhaps a small-scale foray. To gather intelligence, at least. To do some damage if we can. Not many men, they will have guards and scouts out themselves. Perhaps one man' — Nestor's eye lingered on Agamemnon — 'or two . . .' — he turned to Menelaus — 'would have the best chance of getting through the sentries. I would volunteer, but I doubt if my old bones would stand it.'

'An excellent suggestion. Everyone agrees? I suggest all the commanders should combine to offer a reward to the men who undertake it.'

'To say nothing of the honour,' Diomedes said, ostensibly to Ulysses, but in a half-tone that carried across the group.

'Not, of course, that any man needs a reward. Honour is

always uppermost in your minds. My dear Diomedes, I take it you volunteer.'

Diomedes hardly paused. 'Do I need to? I thought you had done it for me.'

'But you are the ideal choice.'

'True. May I choose my own partner?'

'If you wish.'

Diomedes' eyes lingered on the High King, as if he were hoping to disconcert him. Ulysses was not fooled. Diomedes would not risk his own skin like that. 'Then I shall take Ulysses. Agreed, Ulysses?'

Ulysses said in a firm tone, 'Agreed.'

'I left my armour back at my hut. I'm not going back for it, it's nearly dawn now. Anyone got a shield handy?'

Thrasymedes was wearing his gear, and Meriones, and a couple of the others. They handed over an assortment. Diomedes seemed to find it a great joke. He hooted over Meriones' helmet, set with rows of boars' teeth. 'Zeus, what a relic. Been raiding tombs again, Meriones?'

Meriones scowled. 'Watch it, Diomedes. It was my great grandfather's. You look after it.'

'I'll take it,' Ulysses said quickly. He turned to Diomedes. 'Go and tip a jar of cold water over your head, for heaven's sake, before you fall asleep again.'

Diomedes smiled sweetly. 'Do you think I am drunk, Ulysses? I wouldn't be such a bloody fool. Let's get going.'

They set off fast, in a loping crawl, following the line of a ditch that led, Ulysses hoped, into the bed of the Scamander. Sooner than they had expected they stumbled over the first corpses.

'Over there.' Diomedes had seen him first: a man running along the seaward path, away from the Trojan camp. A spy, if they were lucky. If not, a stray soldier set on robbing the bodies. They waited, flattened in the ditch, till he had passed them and was cut off from the Trojans, and then took after him.

The first spear cast stopped the man dead in his tracks. Before he could gather his wits and run he was flat on his back, with Ulysses' sword – or rather Meriones' borrowed sword – at his throat.

'Not so hard, Ulysses. He's trying to tell you something.'

Ulysses moved his knee and the man spluttered something about a ransom.

'We'll think about it. Now tell us about the camp.'

If he was a spy he was an amateur. He told them everything. Yes, there were sentries, lots of them. Changed three times during the night. Had Hector checked on them? Yes, and Deiphobus. And Aeneas, with his thigh all bandaged up. Except for the new Thracians. They were right at the end and Hector had turned back at the start of their section. He could not be sure if they had posted sentries like the rest.

Ulysses' teeth gleamed in the dark. 'Tell us more. About the Thracians.' He loosed his grip a little more and moved his sword. Behind the man's back, Diomedes drew his.

He told them more. There were horses: good horses, especially the King's.

'Which side of the camp are they?'

'The seaward side. Back towards Ilios, behind the Phrygians.'

Diomedes smiled. 'Well done. Very well done.' The man swung round to face him. 'Traitor,' he added, in a conversational tone, and his sword came across and sliced neatly through the man's throat. He turned the body over, contemptuous. 'Not much of a trophy. The cap feels like weasel. And a cloak. Wolfskin. Coming, Ulysses?'

Ulysses was not to be hurried. He stripped the corpse methodically and bundled the gear into the cleft of a tamarisk tree, breaking some lower branches so that they shone white in the dim light. He said, 'We should have asked him more. How to make out the Thracians. It will have more impact if we take the latest reinforcements.'

He could not see Diomedes' expression as the other man replied, 'We look for sleeping sentries, and a king with white horses.'

Ulysses snorted. All kings drove white horses.

Nearer the campfires they found another ditch. A damp one. They crawled stealthily along it.

'Sunflowers.'

'You're drunk. Shut up. The sentries.'

Diomedes' voice lowered. 'The Thracian symbol. They grow a lot of sunflowers in Thrace.'

Ulysses snorted again.

It was true. In the silver light of the stars the Thracians slept, arrayed in neat rows with their shields beneath their heads and their spears at their sides. A sunflower standard flapped lazily in the night air. The chariot teams were tethered side by side. Rhesus' horses were massive, and a snowy white.

'You kill, while I free the horses?'

'No, I'll take the horses.'

Ulysses went from pair to pair, freeing them, hitching their reins together and sending them off into the darkness with a whack from his bow. He took the farthest chariot that had its wheels still set on and, working coolly and efficiently, harnessed a team to it. Meanwhile Diomedes moved from man to man. Ulysses bent to drag a couple of the bodies out of the way. He did not want the horses to shy at them. Then Diomedes was there, nudging him, and they were up and away.

The Thracians seemed to have weird chariots. The whip was not where Ulysses expected it to be, so he used his bow again.

They heard the commotion behind them as they drove up to the broken tamarisk tree.

'Are they far behind?'

'A long way. Don't slow down.'

Diomedes vaulted down, grabbed the bundle and ran to catch up again. Then they were back at the gates of the camp, shouting and whooping with laughter.

Nestor was there at the gates, with the guards. There was no sign of Agamemnon.

'Quite a team you have there.'

'Thracians. The Trojans had been waiting for them since spring. They arrived yesterday. We made our presence felt.'

'Enough to shake the Trojans?'

'It should. Let's go and wash off this blood before it hardens.'

The sky was red, over to the east. So were Diomedes' arms, to the elbow. He tossed the spy's gear to Ulysses, who threw it high to catch the prow of his ship as they raced each other down to the harbour. They rushed into the cool water, splashing through the debris, and threw themselves into the depths of the bay.

'You were drunk.'

'Very. Not as drunk as you.'

Ulysses, who barely drank wine at all, had not realized it was true until he sobered, suddenly and totally. 'Maybe not.' Diomedes' face was red too, and there was sweat still glistening under the seawater. He added, 'An honourable victory.'

'A victory. Who needs honour?'

Ulysses' face hardened. In the camp they could hear the troops forming up. Diomedes answered for him. 'Achilles?'

The Ithacan shook his head. 'That man has given up. He is going to die here, and he damn well knows it. While you and I, Diomedes, are going to live.'

When Achilles woke a cold dawn light was filtering through the window into his hut. He rose quietly, without waking Diomede. Patroclus stirred, but Achilles did not cross to him; he tied the thongs of his sandals and retrieved the tunic he had worn the evening before.

By the wall of the hut Phoenix slept, in a heavy tangle of blankets. Achilles skirted him carefully; as he opened the door the light washed across the old man's bed. Achilles pulled the door shut behind him and made his way across the courtyard.

Most of the Myrmidons were already awake and on edge. Their commander avoided their eyes and none of them spoke to him as he strode out of their section of the camp and towards the harbour. He stopped at the ships.

'The wind is onshore.'

Patroclus' voice did not appear to surprise him. 'True.'

'Shall I have the men ready the ships?'

'Yes.'

'And we sail?'

'That depends.'

Maybe he meant only the wind. Patroclus did not ask him. Achilles turned and moved rapidly forward towards the water's edge. A moment later, Patroclus saw the movement that had caught his eye: two men splashing and shouting well out in the bay, the water as high as their chests. They gave off a holiday spirit, as if the fighting were over, the victory already won. One raised his arm and it glistened with streaks of red in the morning light.

Achilles stood, stock-still, watching them. 'Shall I go and ask?' Patroclus said.

'If you like. Get the men to work first.' He turned abruptly and made his way back towards the hut.

Patroclus did ask. One of Ulysses' lieutenants told him about the night raid. He did not feel inclined to relay to his commander what he had been told. If the Achaeans had their ways of winning the war without Achilles they were not, it seemed to him, ways of which any sane man could speak with pride. He moved away from the Ithacans who were waiting at the water's edge to dress and arm their king, and hesitated. On the prow of the ship by which he stood somebody had hung out the Trojan spy's miserable gear as if it were an honourable trophy of war. The flies were thick around the clotted fur of the cloak. Patroclus was still looking up at it when Nestor came up to him.

Nestor looked drawn and grey-tinged. He glanced up at the flies without apparent surprise.

'You knew about this little exploit?' Patroclus asked curtly.

'I did. Not uplifting. But necessary.'

'Necessary?'

'Yes, necessary. If we are to have any chance of victory today. Have you eaten this morning?'

Patroclus shook his head.

'Come and eat with me.' Nestor set off towards the Pylian section as he spoke, without waiting for a reply.

There was something soft about Nestor's hut. It was heavily furnished, and finely, with little inlaid tables and enamelled boxes scattered around as if it were a queen's withdrawing room. Nestor's favourite girl, Hecamede, was short and curvy, with liquid eyes and hair that was braided in a complicated mass of intertwining tiny plaits. Nestor settled down among a pile of cushions and watched her as she fussed around mixing up a potion with wine, and cheese, and barley meal, and onion in it. She brought his first, in a big fancy golden cup, and he patted her bottom as she turned to fetch Patroclus' cup.

'You fight today.' Nestor's voice barely lifted at the end of the sentence.

'You know I cannot.'

'I thought that was Achilles. You made no rash vows.'

'I made my vow twenty years ago: of loyalty to Achilles.'

'I thought your role was to give Achilles wise counsel and keep him from making a fool of himself.'

'Like Ulysses and Diomedes.'

Nestor smiled faintly. 'This morning, my dear boy, they are our heroes. It is Achilles who is reckoned dishonourable.'

'Not by the Myrmidons.'

'You think he would be right to load his ships in mid-battle?'

Patroclus scowled. 'I think that is for me to discuss with Achilles. Not with you, Nestor.'

Nestor lifted up the big golden cup and sipped. He put it down carefully. He rubbed with his finger at the tabletop, as if he saw a mark on the inlay that should not be there. 'And have you discussed it?'

He waited patiently for Patroclus' reply. At last Patroclus said, 'I am doing what I think is honourable.'

'Ah, honour again. So much honour and loyalty.'

'I was not aware you considered them optional.'

Nestor settled back still further among his pile of cushions. 'The Trojans have broken two negotiated truces this summer. They had their own spies out last night. They anticipated the attack. Therefore, they have spies in our camp who warned them of it. All in all' – he glanced across at Patroclus – 'they are playing the game very dirtily indeed.'

'So they are no better than us. What a surprise. I cannot say that knowledge inspires me to fight. Or to persuade Achilles to.'

'Not even for the girl?'

There was a long silence. Patroclus looked hard at Nestor. Nestor's hand was playing with the double stem of the beautiful cup. A heavy cup, intricately moulded and carved, with four golden handles and a pair of golden doves perched on the rim. It was an old hand, wrinkled and corded.

The deep-cut lines of Nestor's face looked suddenly like a mask. In the middle of it, the eyes twinkled. There was nothing obviously malevolent in the twinkle, but Patroclus suddenly realized that he hated Nestor. Hated him powerfully, as he had rarely felt about anyone before.

'What girl?' He rose as he spoke, making for the door where he almost collided with Hecamede as she came back in with bread and honey cakes.

Nestor had a moment to frame his reply as Hecamede neatly recovered and sidestepped to let Patroclus past her. He said it in the same level voice, with the hint of an old man's amusement deep below its surface. 'The Myrmidons are loyal to you, too. I wonder what would happen if you told them to defy Achilles and fight under you?'

Patroclus turned back, his anger open in his face. 'Neither you nor I, Nestor, shall ever know that. Because I shall never do it.' He slammed the door behind him as he left.

He had not yet given Achilles' men their orders. He did it now. They did not argue with him. They set to work on the ships, with the noise of the battle loud in their ears.

Achilles did not help. He had emerged from his hut and he now stood on the prow of his flagship. The ships stood high on the beach and from the prow he could see across the stockade to the plain. It seemed Achilles was watching the battle, though his face was expressionless and his eyes gave no indication that they saw what was in front of them.

The Myrmidons were sullen and worked in silence. They stowed rations and booty, cleared the tents and huts. They stacked their weapons on the decks last of all. They did not stow away their armour. Every man who had any was wearing it.

By midday the Thessalian section of the camp lay stripped bare below the ships. Achilles' hut alone was untouched. Only then did Patroclus board the flagship and walk up to the foredeck where Achilles stood.

Achilles did not turn to look at him. He said in a steady voice, 'Nestor just drove his chariot past with a wounded man. I think it may have been Machaon, the surgeon. Go to find out for me.'

Patroclus went to the Pylian section. Nestor's chariot was propped outside his hut. The wheels were still on, but the team had been unharnessed and led away. He walked past the chariot and through the half-open door.

In the hut, Nestor and Machaon sat. Machaon's shoulder was

bloody. There were dark stains on the pile of cushions. The two men were drinking mulled wine: mulled wine elaborately prepared, with honey and onions and herbs in it. Hecamede was heating water over the fire.

'Ah, Patroclus. Come and sit with us.'

Patroclus shook his head. 'Achilles sent me to find out who was wounded. I'll go straight back to tell him.'

'Just a moment,' said Nestor. 'Now you are here, let me tell you about the rest. Diomedes has been hit in the foot. Ulysses was speared in the stomach. Agamemnon has withdrawn with an arm wound. He fought well today. Eurypylus was pulling back with an arrow in his thigh as we were turning for the camp.'

'I shall tell Achilles all of this.'

'When I have finished. Do sit down.'

'Are there that many injured?'

'There are. And there are one or two other things I want to say as well.'

The old eyes were not twinkling any more. Machaon was watching him. Patroclus sat on the hardest chair he could see. Nestor began to talk.

Most of it was what he would have said the night before if it had been he who had gone to plead with Achilles. He said it at length. He talked of when he was young: of what he had once done, and now could do no more. Of the men who were young now, the great heroes of the Achaean army. Achilles. And Patroclus. Patroclus, whom he and Ulysses had brought to Troy nine years before. Patroclus, whose father waited, back in Thessaly, to hear tales of his son's honour and glory.

There was no mention, this time, of the girl.

Patroclus listened in silence. The old voice quavered and stilled. Hecamede stood motionless by the cauldron of boiling water.

Nestor pressed his hands to his head and then looked up slowly at the younger man. 'We are losing the battle. You know that, surely. Every sign tells the same tale. We need you. We need the Myrmidons. There is no hope otherwise.'

'I will do,' Patroclus said slowly, 'what I think it is honourable to do.'

.

'Well, let us pray to the gods that your damn honour does not kill us all.'

'Do that.' Patroclus did not say it angrily. He moved slowly as he rose to leave the hut.

On the way through the deserted camp Patroclus ran into Eurypylus. He had been hit in the leg, as Nestor had said, and was limping back to his quarters alone.

'Patroclus,' he panted. 'You're still not fighting.'

'How is it going?'

'Worse. They've undermined the stockade. It cannot hold for long. The line is broken. There will soon be nothing between them and the ships.'

'I'll take you to the hospital tent.'

'There's not a man there who can do anything. You must bind it up for me. I'll be all right then.'

'You had better come to our hut.'

Patroclus put his arm round Eurypylus, who sagged. He half dragged, half carried the man back to the Thessalian section. The Myrmidons gathered around once he reached it. He sent men for hides to lay Eurypylus on; women to heat water, and others to find yarrow powder. He helped Eurypylus to lie on the floor of Achilles' hut and began to work on his leg.

The arrow was triple-barbed, and deep in the leg. Eurypylus was still conscious. Patroclus made himself keep talking as he probed with the knife.

When the point was free he bent to suck the dirt and venom out of the wound. He sprinkled on the yarrow to clot the blood and began to bind the leg. He could hear the noise of the battle growing louder. There seemed to be a new note in it. The screams now were from men struck, not by spears or arrows, but by terror.

The doorway darkened. Patroclus looked up. Automedon stood there, silhouetted against the sky. He was fully armed and carried his helmet in his hand.

Patroclus said, 'They're through the stockade.'

'Yes, and up to the furthest ships. You'll have to try again.'

Patroclus stood up. 'Stay with Eurypylus. Or if you cannot, find someone else to.' He left the courtyard slowly, then broke into a run as he was swept into the crowd of men hurtling away from the battle and towards the black ships.

Achilles still stood on the prow of his flagship. It appeared as if he had not moved at all. It seemed nobody had dared to say a word to him.

He turned as Patroclus approached. The face was still set hard. The eyes were wide and stormy. Mad. No, not mad. The iron will was still there, the will that had made him stand and watch it all.

Patroclus began to speak even before he could draw breath freely. 'It was Machaon. And Ulysses is wounded. Diomedes. Agamemnon himself. There are dozens more.'

Achilles said nothing.

'Do we sail?'

Slowly Achilles said, 'Would you give the order if I told you to?'

'Yes. I would hate you for it.'

The cries and clashes were loud in their ears. Ajax and his men were making a stand by the furthest ships, and Idomeneus was trying to rally some of the men who had fled. Patroclus found himself shouting. 'Your damn pride. It's not honour now. Nobody, nobody honours you for what you are doing now. It's your bloody pride that has lost you her, and is losing you me, and will lose you everything that matters to you.'

Achilles' voice was low and flat. 'I am not going to fight.'

'Let me fight for you, then. The Myrmidons will follow me.'

A light flickered in the grey eyes. Behind them the Trojans were pouring with torches over the wreckage of the stockade, towards the black ships. 'Fight for me?'

'For you, for me, for Agamemnon. Who cares?'

'I care. You may fight for me. Not for Agamemnon. For me, and Briseis, and the Myrmidons. Take my armour.'

Patroclus did not move. He felt as if a cold weight had settled, leaden, in his stomach. As if, in a moment, he had wrecked something that had taken years to build. Something that could never be mended.

There was a great shout, somewhere close to them, and he saw Achilles' eyes leave his face. There was no need for him to turn. The flames were there in front of him, reflected in the stormy eyes.

'Do it now.' Achilles strode down the deck, leaped off the ship and made for his hut, where his armour and weapons had lain untouched for fourteen long days. Patroclus stood, a moment, alone on the prow. Then he followed.

Achilles helped him arm. Eurypylus had gone and they were alone in the hut. Achilles' armour was much finer than Patroclus' own. He knew each piece. The bronze greaves. The cuirass, blazoned with stars, that every man on the plain would recognize. The shield, the silver-studded sword, the helmet with its nodding yellow plume. Outside they could hear the Myrmidons forming up.

'My spear?'

'Too heavy. I'll take my own.'

'And the team?'

'I saw Automedon go to harness them.'

Achilles nodded. He hesitated for a moment, then said, 'You know what you have to do. You get the Trojans out from the ships, and past the stockade. No further. Do not try to push them back to Ilios. That is Agamemnon's war. This is ours.'

Patroclus could not hold back a last flare of anger. 'I'm fighting now. I do it my way.'

'Then you must come back to me.' Achilles turned from him to the sea-chest that stood by the wall. He rummaged in it to find his cup and went to wash it before dipping it in the winebowl. He stepped out into the courtyard, with Patroclus a pace behind him. The prayer he raised up was to Zeus. He poured the wine in a long shining stream onto the packed earth.

Patroclus made his own libation. To Apollo.

The Myrmidons had formed up in the little clearing at the heart of the Thessalian section. They did not cheer as the two men approached. They braced and tightened their ranks until a solid wall of shields stood hard and menacing before them. Achilles looked them over. He had always given the orders. He shouted above the noise of the battle, 'Myrmidons. You fight for Patroclus as you would for me.'

The cheer came sudden, deafening. Patroclus waved in response and vaulted into the chariot. Automedon swung his whip and the three horses lurched forward.

With Chryses gone to Thebe, the sanctuary was unnervingly quiet. There seemed to be no other human being alive. For the first few days Chryseis lay late in bed, the dog stretched out on the floor beside her, listening to the chatter of the cicadas and the song of the birds. Then she got up, breakfasted quickly and moved out into the courtyard. After the first day she did not touch the house, but she cleaned the cages daily and fed the mice. She settled down, then, to doze in the shade.

Until one morning she went to make her breakfast and found the grain basket empty. She went to fill it from the store and found the great pithos empty too. A spider had made its web across the top and waited motionless in a corner, as if she were a fly about to be trapped in the sticky strands.

No, she would not be trapped. In a sudden panic she worked her way through the storeroom, checking all the jars one by one. There was wine. There was a full jar of oil, hidden right at the back; she found a few dried peas and black beans; a small jar of honey, half-empty. No barley at all, no wheat, no dried fish. There had been no meat since the sacrifices when she returned.

It was late summer. There should have been harvesting in the fields, threshing in the village. The village women should have been gathering and drying figs and plums, crushing olives, salting fish and meat for the winter. But there were no village women any more, no village men. There were no village cows or goats, sheep or pigs. The Achaeans had taken them all.

There was just her, Chryseis. If no one was there to do it for her she would have to do it for herself. She made her way back to the house, found a cloth to tie round her hair, and set to work clearing out the storeroom. She threw the pieces of the broken jars on the midden, washed round the empty ones, swept the floor with Rhene's old birch broom. It was midday before she had finished. Her dress was grey from the dust, her throat parched. There would be no lunch until she found her own. She went out through the courtyard to the back of the house, where there was a plum tree. There had been nobody to pick the plums and the branches hung almost to the ground.

She thought at first that all the fruit was overripe and maggoty. Then she found a dozen good plums, which she took to the courtyard. She poured some wine, ate her plums and sat in the sun. A moment later she remembered that she had not made any libation. She poured a little more wine, raised her cup high and spilled drops of it on the packed earth. The beads of wine sat for a moment on the ground, sparkling in the sun, before the earth took them in.

She could not eat plums for supper too. She needed grain and fish. The dog needed food too. Maybe the bones from the sacrifices would last it a few days longer. Then there were the mice to think of. However she looked at it, there was a lot of work to do. She had better get back to it, or there would be no supper.

She stood up awkwardly. The baby was kicking hard, but she did not think of it. The baby was not real to her yet. It was not the baby's future she had to work for, it was her own. She went back into the house and found some thicker sandals and a tight-woven reed basket. Then she called the dog and set off on the long walk to the lower fields.

The fields dismayed her. She had never joined in the harvesting and threshing, though she knew more or less how it was done. She could see at a glance that it would be a desperate task to sort out the wheat from the tangle of tares; and then to thresh it with no help, no men and no oxen. Perhaps the threshing could wait if she gathered in the crops herself. Not today. She would need to come back with a long knife, and to find some way of carrying the grain up to the house, or perhaps to the threshing floor just outside the village. She went on, towards the harbour.

There had been no planting that year, and no harvesting the year before, but the crops had ripened untouched and spilled their seeds. The earth of the plain was rich and red. She found beans, the pods blackened but some of the beans still green inside, and some small pumpkins, eaten away by mice and insects.

Off the path there were figs to be found, and plums, and on the vines growing against the cottage walls a few small hard grapes. She filled her basket steadily with these. There were olives, but they could wait for some time. She came at last to the village and looked along the street. It was mid-afternoon and very hot. She needed shade and rest. She made for the nearest cottage.

Inside, a rat scampered into a corner as she pushed the door open. The dog forced itself past her, yelping with excitement. Chryseis backed out and tried the next cottage.

She had known the family who lived here: they had had little children with whom she had played, and boys her own age who had fished from the harbour. The room was neat, as she remembered it, but for the dust and the spiderwebs. There were the bed pallets rolled in the corner, the jars stacked along the wall, and the wood pile next to the stone hearth. The wood was still there, but there was no cauldron to put on the fire; there had been no fire to put it on. On the shelf stood a loaf of bread, half-eaten before the soldiers came, and what was left turned hard as stone. Next to it, a solid mess in a pot that might once have been stew. It had long been abandoned even by the maggots; it did not smell any more. She crossed to the pallets and touched one gingerly. It spilled open, exposing a family of mice that had burrowed into the straw. The mother squeaked and set to work burying her babies from view. No need; Chryseis turned away silently.

The spears had stood by the door in a long row. She knew they would not still be there: the soldiers would have made sure of that. But soldiers had no use for fishing nets or tridents, and there they were, stacked in the corner behind the door.

It was the tridents she wanted, they were best for shallow fishing from the shore. There were no boats to take her further out. Two of them stood there: not the bronze-tipped ones, the rough wooden ones the poorest peasants used. She took one out into the courtyard and lifted it, experimentally. The wood was smooth to the touch. It was heavy, but not too heavy.

Everyone in Chryse knew how to fish. The soldiers could not have taken the fish away.

They had not. She walked over to the shore and peered down into the cool greenish water. There were fish even there, right by the water's edge. Later. She went back to the house, found a wooden stool and settled down on it in the shade by the wall to wait till the sun went down. After a while the dog came across to join her, its mouth bloody from the rat. She reached over to pat it and it flopped in the shade beside her.

They must both have slept and when Chryseis woke the sun was low in the sky and the dog still by her side. No need to wake it. She stood up and went into the house to find a cup. A small stream fed into the harbour and she leaned over to wash the cup in the running water and fill it. The water was cool and fresh and she drank cup after cup of it, letting it spill past her mouth and down to cool her body and dampen her dress.

Back at the harbour Chryseis settled down on the shingle, slid off her sandals and then stood up to fasten her dress high round her thighs. She waded knee-deep into the sea and stood, the trident poised high in her hands, waiting for the fish to come to her.

As the days went by, Chryseis fell into a steady routine. In the mornings she would rise early and go up to the shrine to make a little offering to Apollo: some of the fruit she had picked the day before, or a few drops of wine. Then she would come down to work in the house, cleaning the pots, sweeping, seeing to the mice. After her meal she would go down through the fields to the village. She always took the dog with her. It had a name now: she called it Menon.

She searched the houses by the harbour methodically and found enough grain to last through the autumn. The soldiers had taken the main stores, but not the small jars that each housewife had kept by her fire. She found fishing nets, a couple small enough to manage; three knives, fallen where the soldiers had missed them; in one cupboard, a length of woollen cloth. The knives and the cloth she took home with her. She cleaned the house where the fisher boys had lived and used it as her base. She would sleep there in the heat of the afternoon and then at sunset she would go down to fish in the harbour before making her way home with her prizes. She supped on fish, on bread when she had energy left to make it; on thick plain stews of pumpkin and beans.

She was standing in the shallows one evening, perhaps ten or twelve days after her father had left, and whacking an octopus against the stones of the jetty to make it tender, when Menon began to bark. She did not let the sound interrupt her rhythm. Probably a rat, she thought to herself. It might even be a rabbit or a hare, on the slope behind the cottages. The dog caught something most days. Rabbit was good; she had always hated fish, peasant food, and a grown rabbit was enough meat for her and Menon to share. He was a good dog, almost as good as the old one, and he would save her her portion. Once he had taken a snake, but that was best not thought of. Nobody killed snakes on purpose, but it was not a poisonous one and she had made her supper on it. Its flesh had been firm and tasty, surprisingly good.

She felt the octopus, squeezing the tentacles. It would do. She waded slowly close to the water's edge and added it to her small pile. Mullet, most of it: one biggish red fish, and half a dozen very small ones. Just a couple more, to make up a batch for salting. She picked up the trident. The fishing was her favourite part of the day's work. There were so many fish now that there was only her to catch them.

Then Menon was right down at the shore, barking still. She looked up and saw two men standing at the foot of the path that led inland to the sanctuary and beyond.

Her blood ran suddenly as cold as the water about her ankles. Of course they had seen her. She waded slowly and carefully out of the water and went to sit on a rock close to the pile of fish. She watched, her eyes narrowed, her hand holding the dog still by her side and her mind sending up a silent prayer to Apollo as the men came past the cottages and right up to her.

They were soldiers, Ilians, and as they came closer she made out the dragons on their tunics. Priam's guards. They did not shout to her; they walked on until they were maybe four or five paces away, then stopped and looked her over. Menon growled softly and she leant to whisper reassurance to him before bringing her face up to meet the men's eyes.

'Good evening, gentlemen.' Her voice sounded strange to her: it was the first time she had spoken for days.

The soldier on her left bowed slightly. He was a sturdy man with a thatch of brown hair, thinning on top. Not young, and not an officer: an envoy, maybe, sent to the sanctuary by Priam or another Trojan leader. The other soldier was much younger, no more than a boy, with perhaps thirteen or fourteen summers behind him.

'Evening, ma'am. We thought the village was deserted.'

'Nobody lives here any more. I live up at the sanctuary, but I come here to fish.' She looked down, remembering for the first time the skirt tied high around her thighs. Her legs below it were smooth and brown. 'As you see.'

'Yes, ma'am. We came from the sanctuary, but there was nobody there.'

'That is because I am here.'

'And the priest and his daughter?'

'The priest is in Thebe. I am his daughter.'

The soldiers exchanged a glance. Chryseis watched their expressions, amused. She had caught them off balance, this pregnant fisher girl with the bare legs and grubby tunic.

She stood up and unfastened her dress calmly, smoothing it down over her knees. 'Come, gentlemen. It is almost suppertime. Would you please pick up my fish for me?'

The soldier boy gave her a sudden grin and bent to retrieve the fish. 'There is a basket for them by the rock over there. You see? And I keep the trident in the house opposite.' She stood watching, suddenly a king's mistress once more, as both men scrambled to do as she suggested. Then she led them slowly back through the village and along the path towards the house.

The soldiers cooked the supper for her, building a fire and grilling the fish. The boy made to light a lamp, but Chryseis reached out from the bench to stop him. 'There is only a little oil left. Wait until it is quite dark.' He turned to look at her and put out the taper, grinding it on the floor under his foot.

She brought out the strongest wine from the storehouse and filled the men's cups repeatedly. When both their faces were flushed in the firelight she rose to light the lamp herself and then sat down again on the bench. She spoke quietly and firmly. 'What can I do for you, gentlemen?'

The older man replied. 'Prince Hector sent us, ma'am. He heard that the Achaeans sent you back to Chryse. He wanted to know if you were well, and to hear what you could tell us. And the priest, of course.'

Chryseis considered his face in the dim light. He seemed a kindly man. Tough, experienced, but not inclined to cruelty. Neat with his hands, as she had seen when he was gutting the fish, but not sharp-witted, not a natural spy or interrogator. That was just as well. She did not trust her ability to handle really fierce interrogation. 'I am well, as you see. And Prince Hector? The High King?'

'They were both well when we left.' The man paused.

'But?'

'I was to make sure the priest knew that Prince Troilus is dead.'

She could not look at the men. She stood up, slowly, and walked over to the far end of the room. In the shadows they could not have made out her expression, but she turned her back to them anyway. All three were quiet for a long moment. The dog let out a little whine, but he did not move from his place by the fire. At length she said in a low voice, 'When did he die?'

'Last winter. In a skirmish on the plain. They say Achilles killed him.' The soldier paused and added, 'I thought maybe you'd have known, ma'am, being in the camp.'

'No.' She took a deep breath. 'He died well.'

'Yes, ma'am. He was a good fighter. Prince Aeneas was with him, maybe he could tell you more some day if you wanted to know.'

'I am not sure that I do.' She walked back into the warmth, but instead of sitting on the bench she drew a small stool away from the trestle, so the lamp would not light her face.

'We were to ask you, ma'am, if you wished to come back to Ilios. Prince Hector would be glad to see you. Lady Andromache has a son, born this spring, and there would be company for you.'

'And for my baby.' She said it in a firm, low voice. 'But I am in no condition to travel now, as you see. And I have no wish to go back to Ilios.'

'Yes, ma'am.'

Chryseis was silent. She had an urge to leave the soldiers, go to her room and cry herself to sleep in the dark. Not that she had expected to go back to Troilus. But that he had died, and so many moons before – she felt it should have changed things, more than it had. It would be stupid to leave the men, though. She knew she should make them ask their questions that night, while they were fuddled and off balance. Her voice, when it came, was loud and abrupt in the still room. 'What did you want to ask me?'

The soldier started. 'Nothing particular, ma'am. Just to find out if there was anything you could tell us. You know, being in the camp, you might have seen or heard something that would help. Something the army could use.'

Chryseis did not help him as he floundered on. She felt a sudden hard contempt take shape inside her. They had her at such a disadvantage. What they had told her had shaken her to the core, made her intensely vulnerable. Knowing that Troilus was dead she might have been persuaded, she thought to herself, to tell them everything she knew. Not because she felt any particular loyalty to Priam or Hector, more as a memorial to Troilus: to the pair of them, and their love, which had been real to her once. But she had no intention of betraying the Achaeans to a drunken fool who would not even frame the questions for her. If Hector really wanted her information, she thought, he could pay a proper price for it, send someone she could respect to get it from her. 'No, I cannot help you. There is nothing I can tell you.'

The soldier seemed almost relieved. 'I thought maybe there wouldn't be, ma'am. Being a prisoner, like, you'd not have heard anything you weren't meant to hear, would you?'

'No. Nothing I was not meant to hear.'

'I'll tell that to Prince Hector.'

Chryseis gave a thin smile. 'Yes, do. Now I think I should go to bed, gentlemen. You will sleep in here. Do you want blankets?

Then in the morning perhaps I can persuade you to chop some wood for me before you go.'

There was no telling when her father would return. Many more days passed, the moons grew and faded in the sky and the summer heat began to die down. She welcomed that. The baby gave her little trouble. She did not let herself notice the breathlessness when she worked hard. She was not worried. Father would be back, she thought, with a woman, in time for the birth. Until he came she was content to be by herself in the place of the God.

Chryses returned on a clear day at the end of the summer. He brought with him a cow, and a woman: a peasant woman, short and plump, her face worn into lines that spelled out a life of hard work and ill temper. The priest looked exhausted from the journey and its company. He stayed a few moments in the house, then retreated to his hut. The woman bustled into the house as if she owned it. She did not mention its neatness. She grumbled about the inconvenience of the cooking arrangements, the lack of herbs, the tiny quantity of wheat. Chryseis watched her, silent. This woman seemed to have taken her own energy away from her. She answered the woman's questions, but volunteered nothing.

'You're too thin, dear. When did you say the baby was due?'

'Maybe at the next full moon. I'm not sure.'

'No more of this fishing. You'll stay in the house and get everything ready. Do you have the baby's clothes made?'

Since sending her father to Thebe Chryseis had done nothing to prepare for the baby. She had reconciled herself to the rest, more easily than she had expected, but the thought of the baby still came hard to her. She said slowly, 'There is some cloth in the cupboard. I found it in the village. I'll see what I can do.'

'Less than a moon to go and nothing done! What have you been thinking of?'

What had she been thinking of? Nothing that she could tell this woman with her loud voice and roughened hands. 'I have been busy. With the house.'

'Well, you leave the house to me now and worry about the child. Now get yourself to bed and rest. I'll see about the supper.'

Chryseis felt she should have made some attempt to take back control. This woman, grumpy and forceful, seemed to be defeating her as even Agamemnon had not done. She seemed to have lost the will to fight. Maybe it would come back later. She went to bed and tried to sleep. Her body felt heavy and awkward and she tossed among the blankets, hot and uncomfortable.

She told herself, the next day and the days after, that the baby would come quickly. The clothes did not matter so much. She could soon put together a few and any child could survive a grubby dress. She did not think she could endure much more of this waiting, this discomfort, this nuisance of moving a heavy weight around with her. Not much more of the woman's badly cooked meals, of her father avoiding the house. Perhaps they could send the woman packing after she was over the birth. The days went by, though. The full moon came and waned, and still it did not come. The brown faded on her legs and arms, her face seemed puffed as large as her stomach.

The pains began one night, late. She woke and recognized them. I suppose, she thought to herself, I should call the woman. She did not do it. She lay there in the dark, letting the pains wash over her. They were pleasing at first. Sharp, just a little cruel. Then they came faster and faster, and with them came a nausea, something that was not clean at all, but vicious and messy. Something that pulled her down into the private place of darkness and anguish. I must call the woman now, she thought. I must make it stop. But it knew no limits, this pain. There was nothing she could do to stop it.

There was no thinking after that. Her hands were white on the bedpost and everything centred on the agony in her womb.

In the morning the woman came and found her soaked in sweat and beyond talking. She brought water and chatter and hard, capable hands that felt and mopped and kneaded. It went on all day, and into the night. Perhaps her father came briefly: Chryseis imagined that she heard the woman talking to him at the door of the room, but he did not enter.

When it grew dark the woman lit lamps. Chryseis was exhausted. She lay limp on the bed in the half-darkness, consumed by the tearing pain that gripped and pulled at her insides.

Finally in the still time before dawn, it came: an empty silence. And then a loud, piercing wail.

'It's a boy. A good strong one, considering.' The woman picked him up. He was streaked with bloody slime and yelled at the touch. 'And heavy. He'll do all right. I'll just wash him, then you can put him to your breast. It'll bring the afterbirth faster.'

Chryseis hardly heard her. It was over, and she wanted to sleep. She lay still on the bed as the woman bustled around her. Her body seemed to have shrivelled to nothing, though her stomach was puffed out in front of her, as if its occupant had not yet gone. A boy. The words did not seem to mean anything. And yet the tiny body that snuggled against her and the hand that gripped fiercely onto her finger were more real to her than anything she could remember.

Andromache sat up all night when the Trojans camped on the plain. She had the fire lit in the hearth in the megaron. The room echoed forlornly with women's voices. No able-bodied man was left in Ilios. The servants clustered round the fire, sleepless, waiting their turn to go and act as watchwomen.

It was what Hector had ordered, so Andromache drew up the schedule for them. She took a turn of duty herself, with one of the maids, a good-natured but empty-headed girl called Nisa, at the main watch tower by the Scaean Gate.

A canopy of stars hung over the town as they walked to the tower. It seemed dark in the streets; but it was light compared to the blackness of the tower staircase, where the torch scarcely seemed to light the step at their feet. The second storey contained the living quarters of the guards, but the old soldier who was in charge of the tower that night had settled down to sleep on the first floor, next to the great cistern. His head poked out, tortoise-like, from his roll of bedding as the two women stepped into the big room and their torch lit up its shadows. In the cistern, the water looked dark and dull, like a spillage of oil on a cloudy day.

'Go right up to the roof,' said the soldier. 'You'll not see a thing from the windows. Don't expect you'll see much from the roof either. You probably wouldn't notice a man out there if he came right up to the gate. Listen instead.'

With that, his head disappeared under the blankets. Andromache spoke sharply. She felt incompetent, and it embarrassed her. 'Listen for what?'

The man's head slid out again, only just far enough for his mouth to be seen. 'You'll know if you hear it.' He lifted the blanket back up and then pulled it down for the last time and added, with a cackle, 'And don't wake me if a rabbit hops around.'

The tower was tall and the staircase grew narrower as they went upwards. The stone walls were cold to the touch. They gave way, higher up, to brick.

On the roof the wind was high, and the air clear. The parapet barely came to chest height on the women. Andromache shivered. It had been so warm in the house, she had brought her thin cloak without thinking. It was too late to go back for a thicker one.

The two of them settled down with their backs to the rough brick of the little tower which housed the door to the stairwell. They did not dare to talk. They stood, gazing out at the black landscape and listening for strange noises in the night. All the night noises were strange to them. The wind whistling around the rooftops, the owls hooting to each other, a low splash from some nocturnal creature by the river, the high giggles of children who were too tired to sleep. Andromache separated them out automatically, her senses heightened, her mind alive with an anticipation that was not yet terror.

The soldier was right, there was little to be seen in the starlight. A distant glow from the watchfires of the army. They seemed a long way off. Dimly beyond, the black outline of the Achaean camp, a muddle of low shapes behind the purposeful stockade. And beyond even that, the emptiness of the sea. There was a lot of sea. It would not be so difficult for the sea to close over the Achaeans, wipe out their black ships as if they had never been. She could imagine it in the dark. The Achaeans tumbling, one by one, into the blue-black waters. A storm, Poseidon-sent, which would drive the waves onwards and upwards till they licked across the logs of the stockade and washed bare and clean the bloody plain. With the help of the gods something like it might happen the next day. The Achaeans could be squashed to a pulp between the wave of Trojan soldiers and the waves of the Aegean shore.

Their watch ended while it was still dark, but Andromache returned to the tower in the morning. She wanted to fit the reality to the picture in her mind. In daylight the army stood out clearly, the bronze shields and helmets flashing in the sun. She watched the mass of men, chariots and horses mill around until they resolved themselves into what was surely the shape of an attack: the front line straight and clear, the rear straggling back across the empty plain behind them, the archers strategically positioned on the flanks. Just out of bowshot the gates in the wooden stockade were thrown open, and a second army tumbled out of them. From the tower the men of the two sides were indistinguishable, black insects against the greeny yellow of the plain.

It was a bright sunny morning, but even in sunlight the sight was chilling. No birds sang on the plain; no laughter rose from the houses in the city. Andromache did not wait to see the fighting begin.

She went back to the house on Palace Square, to feed the baby and set up her loom. It would be best to keep busy and she had the plan for an elaborate cloth, a deep purple with a rose-coloured thread to pattern it. It should cheer her to start the work, she thought to herself. She ought to be in good spirits. If this day of fighting was different from so many before it was for the best of reasons.

All the same, she needed someone to talk to. She sent a servant to the palace to see if Cassandra would come. Then she set to work, fixing the warp threads and hanging the weights.

She finished the setting up and started to weave. At last the servant came. Polyxena was with her.

'You're starting a new piece?' Polyxena asked.

'I finished the white yesterday. This one will be the pattern

Hecuba gave me. She showed you too? With the rose thread.'

'You have enough purple? They were short of murex in the dyeing shop.'

'I had this batch in the storeroom waiting.'

'That's lucky. May I take just a length to mend my cloak?'

'I'll cut it off for you.'

They worked and gossiped until midday. They drank a lot of mint tea. At midday the nursemaid brought Astyanax in. The two of them played with him for a long time, tickling his toes and singing him songs. Hector had sung him a song before he set off. Astyanax had been so frightened to see his daddy in the big helmet with the plume nodding. But Hector had laughed and let him try it on himself and whistled into it so that the echo boomed. Andromache thought all this, but she mentioned none of it to Polyxena.

Polyxena said, 'I had better go back now.'

'I'll walk over with you to see if they can tell us anything. And I should see how Cassandra is.'

Polyxena frowned. 'Come if you want to. Hecuba probably will not let you see Cassandra.'

She should have guessed. Cassandra had been working up to it for days. It was almost always the same pattern: not the pattern of that day at the shrine back in early summer, but of the times when the God really did seem to talk to her. She grew restless, talked feverishly, found it hard to sleep. Then would come the explosion, the incoherent visions, the screams, and afterwards the long exhausted sleep.

'She'll not upset me.'

Polyxena made a little, impatient sound. 'You might upset her.'

Andromache looked strained today, Polyxena thought to herself. Perhaps it was just the unbecoming green of her dress that made her skin sallow and accentuated the dark shadows under her eyes. Of course she was worried about Hector. But still, she should have been livelier, with the news from the army so good.

The news at the palace was even better. The army was attacking the stockade round the Achaean camp. Hector had sent for torches, so they could fire the ships if they broke through to them. The palace women were making for the walls. There was sure to be something to see.

'I'll go for the baby and join you there.' Andromache said it on impulse, Cassandra's madness forgotten. She almost ran back to the house, her servant trailing behind her, and burst into the nursery, shaking the nursemaid and the dozing child in her arms. 'Let's all go up to the walls. We can watch the fighting from there. They say the army may manage to fire the ships.'

The nursemaid followed, protesting weakly. Andromache's sudden burst of energy had drowned her opposition. The other servants left their work and came too, through the deserted streets and up to the steep steps to the walkway. It was crowded already on the ramparts.

Even from Ilios they could see the breach in the stockade, the soldiers swarming like ants over and around the uprooted logs. The Trojans appeared to be building a causeway over the ditch between the plain and the stockade. The passage grew wider as the women watched, until charioteers as well as foot soldiers were pouring across and into the camp. In the open space beyond the stockade there was a jagged line of Achaean defence; beyond that were the irregular shapes of the huts and tents, and down towards the sea, the towering masses of the ships.

Andromache watched with the rest as the Trojans pushed forward and the line of defenders wavered and broke in front of them. The fiercest fighting now was around the nearest ships. A flame rose up, clear even in the bright afternoon light, and a ship began to burn. The fire began at its prow and spread quickly. As the flames licked around the mast, a cry rose up from the crowd on the ramparts. Andromache turned to grab her son . . . and with a swift kiss, lifted him high. 'Look, Astyanax! Look, we're burning the ships! Soon we will send all the nasty Achaeans away, and Daddy will be back home.'

The baby looked down at her, his eyes unfocussed, and began to cry, a loud, practised wail that cut through the cheers.

'He's upset by the noise,' the nursemaid said tartly. 'I'll take him back to the house.'

'No, stay here for a while. He'll calm down.' Andromache thrust him into the nurse's arms, the howls redoubled, and turned back to watch the fire rage and the mast, insubstantial as a splinter from where she stood, keel over onto the deck.

The women were shouting encouragement out across the plain. Another one, they yelled. Fire another one! But no second ship caught fire, and shortly afterwards it it seemed that a new force, tightly packed, its lines hard and regular, had entered the battle to defend the ships. The shouts died down. As the women watched, the wedge of new soldiers cut forward and began to push back the attackers.

Some of the women disappeared to their homes but Andromache stayed watching, silent. At her back the nursemaid melted away. The child, exhausted, had gone to sleep.

As the afternoon wore on the fighting worked steadily closer to the city. The Trojans moved back, regrouped, attacked, withdrew again. The noises of the battle drifted up to the city walls on gusts of wind. Andromache could now make out the shapes of the nearest fighters. The plain was littered with fallen bodies. Clouds of dust hung in the air as the chariots charged and wheeled back. The city gates opened and wounded and exhausted men poured back inside.

And, bandaged and watered, they poured back out to make a stand at the foot of the walls. The women returned to the ramparts. This time they left the children below. They were not cheering now; their voices were low and unsteady.

Andromache heard a familiar voice at her elbow. It was Polyxena.

'Have you seen Hector?' Polyxena asked.

'Over there. You can see the gilt on his chariot, look.' Andromache had not taken her eyes from him since she had first made him out.

'They have Achilles fighting. Did you see him?'

'I'd not looked. Where?'

'Down over that way. See, the stars on his shield and breastplate? It was the Myrmidons who joined the battle after the ship was fired. Now Achilles has turned the battle their way. He must have taken a dozen men or more.'

Andromache watched him for a moment. The tall man did fight like a champion. His burnished chariot was covering his rear. She said, 'I thought Achilles had three horses.'

'They've killed the trace horse. You can see where the driver has cut him free and patched up the reins.'

'It's dangerous for him to be so far from the camp, with the team shaken. Hector will attack him now.' Andromache was not afraid any more. It had calmed her, watching Hector. He was fighting powerfully too. She did not think he had been hurt at all.

'I cannot see Hector now,' Polyxena said.

Nor could Andromache. She searched the confused mass of men until Hector's tall figure stood out once more. He was bringing his chariot round, close to the Scaean Gate where the Myrmidons were pressing their attack. She pointed him out to Polyxena.

Polyxena's eyes were bright. 'This should be worth watching.'

Half the Trojan army seemed to be surging towards the Scaean Gate. The Myrmidons moved sideways to counter the defenders and beyond them Hector vaulted from his chariot, his spear poised. The Myrmidon leader jumped down too and in the same movement threw a sharp stone, hard, past Hector to where his charioteer Cebriones was reining in the horses. He caught Cebriones clean on the forehead and the man fell in a high plunging dive across the side of the chariot. Whooping, the Myrmidon ran forward, and the two leaders clashed, spears ringing on their shields, over the body of the charioteer.

Other Trojans pressed forward to try to recover the body; other Myrmidons, to defend their leader. The promised single combat faded into a general scrummage. The Myrmidons gave ground; then as the Trojans were pulling Cebriones' corpse back, they launched an attack, and another, and another. The body was safe; but each time another heap of corpses marked the spot where the first kill had been made.

The third time they pushed too far. A second force of Trojans was sweeping around their rear, and a stone, thrown in a long loop, caught the Myrmidon leader's helmet and knocked it into the dust. The man paused, stunned by the passing blow; and the Trojans attacked in a rush, taking him in the back.

'Somebody's got him.' Andromache whispered it. The man was still standing, but he staggered, his spear drooping from his hand. In a rush Hector was at him, his spear taking the

Myrmidon hard in the thigh. The man tumbled to the dust. Hector fell on his body, his eyes gazing down at his adversary. Time stood still on the battlements. Then Hector pulled his spear free, his foot on the man's sheathed thigh, and kicking the body over in the dust, thrust the spear again and again into his back.

Andromache turned away. There was a sour taste in her mouth. She felt the sickness rise up and then fall, heavy in her belly. So this was a glorious death, this the honour that men strove for. The right to kick an opponent in the dust, laugh in a man's face as his life ebbed away. Polyxena stood watching for several moments more, then turned to her. 'Are you all right?'

She made herself stand up straight. 'Yes. A bit shaken.'

'Hector's men are pushing forward. He has the body, but not the charioteer; he pulled back too fast. Hector will be safe, though. He has not gone wild.'

'No.'

'It was not Achilles.'

Andromache stared at the other woman, uncomprehending. Polyxena, calm now, repeated it. 'It was not Achilles he killed. You didn't see? When they knocked his helmet off, that man had fair hair. Achilles' is red.'

'He fought like Achilles.'

'He fought hard. I think it must have been Patroclus, Achilles' lieutenant.' Polyxena frowned. 'Still, it was Achilles' armour. Hector has it. I think he was turning to send it back to the town. He was going to cut the head off, but they drove him back before he could do it. He has his trophy, at any rate. Shall we go down to the gate?'

The sickness had subsided. It was a wife's duty to be proud of her man when he made such a kill. Even if it was not Achilles. 'Yes,' Andromache replied in a firm voice, 'we'll go there now.'

They pushed their way down the steps and walked through the town to the Scaean Gate. It stood open, a mass of wounded men just inside and guards at the ready to close it quickly if the Achaeans pressed too close. The soldiers surrounded the two women and their attendants. 'You saw, Andromache? You saw? Hector has Achilles' armour.'

'I saw. Is he bringing it back here?'

'No.' One of the guards spoke, a youngish, confident man. 'He was sending his men back with it, but now he has decided to wear it for the rest of the battle. Wait anyway. He'll send his own armour back.'

Andromache felt a quiver begin in her stomach, and radiate outwards till she was shaking from head to toe. To wear that breastplate, that shield, that he had just ripped from a dead man's body. That every man knew.

'I'll not wait. One of the women can collect it.'

She turned away and Polyxena turned with her. 'Don't go indoors yet. Come back to watch. You can tell, even from what we could see through the gate. We are pushing them back again now. Watch the victory come.'

Andromache shook her head. 'You can tell me later.'

Polyxena did not come to the house again that day. Some of the servants had stayed to watch and they brought Andromache the news. The fighting had raged around the spot where Patroclus had fallen, until at last the Achaeans had succeeded in taking his body and sending it back to their camp. There would be no fair head decorating the battlements. Then the troops had fallen back across the plain and fought once more over the bloody, dusty ground the armies had contested in the early afternoon. By sunset the Trojans were back on the territory they had possessed the previous night.

Andromache had the women place the great copper cauldron on its tripod over the fire.

'Do we need to do that, ma'am?'

She stared at Helike. 'Of course we do. We need the water to bath him when he comes in.'

'He'll not be back tonight. They'll camp on the plain again.'

'They cannot. Not after two days of fighting.' And such fighting, such losses. Dozens of the Trojan officers were dead. They had lost Sarpedon, the best of the Lycians, and several of Priam's bastard sons. She was sick of it, she could not take any more. 'They must agree a truce tomorrow. They have to rest. And the corpses.' Oh, the corpses.

'I'll send a girl up to the palace. They will know at the palace.'

'Do that. Meanwhile, we heat the water.'

■

There had been a battle. Briseis had been able to tell that from the clamour of the preparations in the camp, from Agamemnon's failure to call her after dark, and from the silence when the men had gone off to fight. It had been followed by a day of truce. She had recognized that. The sentries outside her tent had been even more silent than usual and there had been the unmistakable smell of the pyres, the burning flesh and the incense.

Then there had been two further days of fighting. Two, with no truce intervening. The bodies must have lain unburied on the plain. On the second day the sounds of battle had seemed to come much nearer, as if they were fighting within the camp itself.

She had tried to talk to Helen that morning, grabbed her arm as she turned to go. She was kept to the tent all the time, except when she went to Agamemnon's hut, and Helen was the only person she had seen. But Helen, wide-eyed, had hissed that she was not allowed to talk to her and had wrenched herself free, leaving the dish of porridge on the floor. Briseis was left to sit, and listen. And to think. Her thoughts were not comforting to her.

At perhaps midday on that second day she had heard someone arguing with her guard outside. Another soldier, unfamiliar, with a strong Southern accent and a voice that sounded raw and uneven.

'Come and fight, damn you. We need every man.'

'I'm not to leave her. Agamemnon is back at the hut. He's not so badly hurt. I dare not go.'

'A wounded man could guard her. You must come. Come now.'

'I'll come as soon as you find someone.'

'Come now, now. Zeus, they are at the ships!'

'I'm coming. Hold on.'

Then silence. Perhaps the guard had gone to fight. She had not dared to look outside the tent. If the Trojans did come, she had tried to tell herself, she was safest there. They would see that she had been kept prisoner. It was stupid to be afraid of the Trojans. They would free the captives, not butcher them. Except that freedom was not what she wanted any more; and what she did want it seemed she was never to have again.

She had heard the noise of the fighting grow louder, and then change. It had sounded more muffled, the screams had been less shrill. She had decided that the Trojans could not have broken through after all. Maybe they were being pushed back. Then the shouts and crashes had died away, and later there had come the sounds of men talking, cooking pots clanging, ordinary camp activity. It was nightfall, the fighting over for another day.

Helen had come again with her supper. Behind her the flap of the tent had stayed open as she set it down. Briseis had seen a guard, silhouetted against the stars. A new one.

That night, silence.

She was woken at dawn by voices. There were noises outside the tent, murmurs, thumps and shuffles that she could make no sense of. The sentry burst in. 'Are you awake? Quickly. You must come now.'

'Come where?'

'Don't ask questions. Ulysses is waiting.'

Ulysses? A new wash of fear swept over her. She scrambled to her feet and smoothed down the dirty and crumpled cream dress. She tied the belt with fingers that shook, fumbled with her sandals and walked unsteadily across to the tent flap.

It was the first time Briseis had been outside in full daylight for nineteen, perhaps twenty days. The sun blinded her. She closed her eyes against it. When the light through her lids no longer hurt her she reopened them slowly.

Ulysses stood in front of her, his face composed and patient as if he had been waiting for her to recover. Behind him there were the guards from her tent and a group of soldiers, all in the sheepskin jackets of the Ithacans and heavily armed. Ulysses' eyes moved behind her and she spun round, expecting to find Agamemnon there. Instead there was a group of women: Helen, and half a dozen others she did not know. Helen met her eyes momentarily. The woman looked terrified. Her naked fear quenched Briseis' own. She turned back to Ulysses. 'What is this? Where are you taking us?'

'To Achilles? There is nothing to fear. Come now.'

The soldiers moved around the women at Ulysses' signal and herded them after him. Briseis dared not think what was happening. Ulysses led the group along the short stretch of track that led to Agamemnon's hut, and to the assembly ground.

He stopped them as they reached the edge of the open space. The entire army was there — more men, it seemed to Briseis, than there had ever been before. Her eyes moved over the crowded ranks until she made out the black tunics of the Myrmidons. She could recognize Automedon, Eudorus and some of the other captains at their head. She knew immediately that neither Achilles nor Patroclus was there.

It was more of an effort to look towards the altar, for she was sure that Agamemnon would be standing in front of it with the High Priest Calchas. He was there, his arm in a thick bandage, his hands outstretched in a theatrical gesture, his eyes on the troops. At his side was Achilles.

The breath silently left Briseis. Achilles' face was grey and blank. It was streaked red and smeared with dirt, and his hair was matted with earth. Every line of his body was raw with despair.

As she looked he turned slowly towards where she stood beside Ulysses. His eyes seemed to see, and yet not see her. The look on his face did not seem to be for her at all. She stood there, cold in the long morning shadow cast by Agamemnon's hut, transfixed by the blindness of his look.

Ulysses took her arm and pulled her forward. He came to a halt barely two paces from Achilles and Agamemnon. The High King was talking, in a loud voice, to the troops,' . . . and I swear I never laid my hands on her in all the time she has been kept in my quarters.' Briseis did not take in the words. Her eyes were still on Achilles.

Agamemnon's voice died and there was a heavy silence. The High King came forward, reached out and took her arm with his uninjured hand. She flinched in his grasp, but it was firm, and he did not seem to notice. He backed a pace, drawing her towards Achilles. He took Achilles' arm too and slid his hands down their two arms until he could lock their hands together. The three of them stood like that for a moment, their hands clasped; and then Agamemnon withdrew his hands and stepped back to the altar.

Briseis gripped Achilles hard, digging into him with her finger-nails. For a moment the stormy eyes cleared and she knew that he knew her. But in his face was a wildness, a despair that told her that whatever price he had paid for this moment, it was too heavy for him. She could not share his pain. She feared and distrusted it. Her grip loosened and she looked down. She hardly noticed when Ulysses came and led her to stand back with the other women. There were horses, too, and a great pile of goods: cauldrons, tripods, bars of gold. They meant nothing to her.

Achilles turned his back to her, to watch the High King at the altar. Calchas was beginning the invocations. Ulysses tugged Briseis to her knees, and all over the parade ground the soldiers knelt with them.

A young boar had been laid across the altar, its legs and snout trussed with yellow-dyed rope. The High King took a bronze crescent-shaped knife from Calchas and cut a bunch of its bristles, holding them high in ritual offering to Zeus. He repeated the words he had said earlier – that he had never touched Briseis – with a great oath to Zeus and the other gods. Briseis understood them this time; but she could not make herself say anything, or move at all.

Calchas moved forward, bearing the double-headed axe. Aga-memnon fell to his knees as the High Priest brought it down on the animal's throat. Hot blood gushed at his feet, overflowing the golden cup. Calchas raised it high in blessing; then poured its contents on the earth. As the High King rose, and the assembled troops after him, the criers came to take the carcase of the boar. It was not for feasting on. It would be thrown to the fishes.

Then Achilles spoke to the troops. They would fight after their breakfast, it seemed. Briseis gathered that Achilles himself would fight, and his men. He was not armed yet. It seemed he must have called the assembly himself, for it was he who dismissed the men.

As the assembly broke up a small troop of Myrmidons came to take charge of her and the other women, the horses and the gifts. Automedon took her arm; again she looked about for Patroclus, but he was not to be seen.

They were taken to Achilles' hut. Automedon said nothing on the way and Briseis asked him nothing. Achilles did not come with them; Briseis did not see which way he took. Automedon paused by the gate to the courtyard.

The Thessalian women were all standing there, in the path and around the gate: Diomede, Iphis, Doris and the rest. Their faces were grimy, swollen and streaked with tears.

Iphis rushed forward. 'Oh, Briseis!' Briseis stood in the centre of the track as Iphis hugged her, tears streaming down her face. She could not speak. After a moment she pushed the other girl away and made herself walk to the gate and across the courtyard to the hut. She knew by the silence that nobody was following her.

His bed was covered in white linen. She walked up to it and pulled the linen back. He lay there, his eyes as blue as she remembered them, open, gazing blankly up at the roof. They had washed him, but she could see the raw gape of a deep spear wound that had cut open his thigh. That would not have killed him; there must have been some other wound too that she could not see. She thought all this, mechanically, as she stood and looked down on him.

So this was the price. Patroclus had fought, where Achilles had not. And the gods had taken his life. They had taken him from them, their captain and their love.

A voice came from by her side: Iphis was there. Briseis had not realized, till she turned to the other girl, that she was crying herself. The tears were filming her eyes. They dropped onto the cold body as she fell, in a single movement, onto the bed to hold him for the last time.

Achilles came back later, his face hard-set and grim. He looked around at the room full of wailing women.

'Leave us.' He spoke quietly, but they rushed to obey him. Briseis thought for a wild moment that he meant her to go too; but he crossed to the door behind the others and shut it.

She did not touch him. Nothing about him seemed to be asking for comfort. She was not ready to be comforted herself. He said, in a harsh voice, 'I would have told you, but Agamemnon held me back.'

'It was better this way.'

'The troops are forming up. I'll see you later.'

'You mean to fight today, with him not yet buried?'

'I am fighting for him. I avenge him first, then I bury him.'

'You did not fight with him?'

'How could I?' Achilles turned from her and walked to the corner of the hut, where a pile of armour lay. He began to fasten on the greaves, the breastplate. Briseis made herself cross to help him with the leather straps. The breastplate was battered, familiar, but there were no stars emblazoned on it.

'But this is not your armour.' There was too much she did not understand; too much, she was beginning to think, that she never would understand.

'Hector has mine. I think Patroclus would let me borrow his until I can claim it back from him.'

She watched in silence as he slung his sword across his shoulder and put on the helmet with its tall crest. His face beneath it was still streaked with the mourning lines.

He turned to look at her when he was at the door of the hut. 'Grieve for him. Do not fear for me. I shall not die until I have avenged him.'

She nodded, unthinking, and watched him go out of the hut and join the Myrmidons who waited for him to lead them into battle.

■

Though some of the Trojans had argued against it, Hector was determined to press on without a day of truce. Before the stockade was mended. Before the men behind it got their spirit back.

Aeneas opposed his decision. So did a dozen others. Hector

did not listen. So what, if – as the spies all said – Achilles was likely to enter the fight? His Myrmidons were as exhausted as the rest now. One man alone could not turn a battle.

To Aeneas and the rest Hector hoped he appeared hard and forceful. Privately, he was angry. The anger had taken him over when the lust of the battle died. He fed it with his thoughts, knowing somewhere underneath that he could not afford to let its fire die down and face the ashes of bitter disappointment.

To do it all, and then to have it all to do again. To fuel the fury of the men, when they had discovered what had been done to Rhesus' Thracians, then watch it flare and die. To fire a ship, just one, then to end up where they had started at daybreak. To kill Achilles; and then find out that it was not Achilles. That Achilles was still there, behind the broken stockade, working up an anger of his own.

Anger against anger, then. He would fight the real Achilles the next day. He would taunt him by wearing his armour, show him for a fool in front of his troops. And if he killed this one, then surely that would be the end. There would be no more lines of ant soldiers rising up out of the ground as the ones in front were cut down. There would just be mortal men, defeated, pushed back to the ships. The ships he would burn.

He watched the men when he gave out the orders in the loud voice that he meant to hide his anger. They were glad. They wanted to keep on killing. They knew it could be done now. Champions died like the rest, in the dust, with a groan and a bubble of blood and the sudden stench as their bowels opened. Ships burned. How brightly they burned.

Andromache was angry too when Helike came back and told her of Hector's decision. She did not want to sleep alone and come face to face in her dreams with the Hector she had seen that afternoon, the Hector who had bent to taunt the dying man and laughed as he thrust the spearhead into living flesh. If Hector had returned, surely he would have turned back into her gentle husband, the man who made Astyanax laugh with joy, the man who had watched her cry, and cried with her. That was the Hector she needed, the Hector who loved and protected them.

The anger kept her going. The water was left in the cauldron. The next night it would surely be needed. She drove the servants through a night of watches as if it were an old routine. This time they all slept when it was not their turn to watch, just like the old man by the cistern. Next morning, heavy eyed, she did not go to the walls. She stayed in the megaron and watched the purple and rose cloth grow under her hands.

In the morning the town was quiet. No sounds came through the thick walls of the tall black and white house. A low shaft of sunlight shone through the open door of the megaron on the roses as they built up, row upon row, and on the rings on Andromache's deft and steady fingers.

In the afternoon there were noises. A dull rumble. She knew what it meant now. The battle was coming closer. She bent to knot a broken thread.

'You'll not go to the walls?' Helike's voice was harsh and disapproving.

'No. I'll go to look from the window.'

She went upstairs, to her room, and crossed to the tall window, pushing the chair aside and leaning out. She could not see the fighting. It sounded much closer. It must be right up against the walls, she thought, hidden by them from her view.

Shouts came through the window, screams, and clankings. There was a burst of sound, building to a crescendo. To her left, somewhere. She went out of the room and down the corridor. There was a small window at the end. It looked away from the plain, onto the lower town, the East Gate, and the Square of the Smiths, where she had used to sit beneath the wild pear. The square was filling with men, panting. Some of them were bleeding, but not all. These were not wounded seeking shelter. It was a retreat. The army had been defeated and was falling back within the walls.

She heard a thud and saw, beyond the men, the shadow of the East Gate move slowly across the archway. Hector must be back, with the rest. It was sooner than she had expected. She hurried downstairs to order the fire lit and the water heated once more.

Then, above the murmur from the men, came new screams. A commotion on the walls; from the direction of the tower, a wailing and moaning. Mourning noises. This was not the general agony of the battle. It told of some very particular disaster.

Andromache rushed out of the megaron, lifting her skirts, and ran down the hill towards the Scaean Gate and the watch tower. The soldiers in the streets fell back to make a way for her. She hardly noticed them, or the maids who came dashing after her. She took the stone steps two at a time and stopped at their head, where the wall adjoined the tower and she could look over it.

The fighting had almost stopped. She knew that. The Trojans were almost all within the walls. Outside there were Achaean troops, standing about in disarray. A horse reared high and whinnied. Two more horses – horses she knew from the day before – pulled away at a gallop. In the chariot behind them she saw a tall man lean forward to whip the horses faster, while his charioteer by his side held high in trophy a shield and breastplate, blazoned with stars.

Behind the chariot, furrowing the plain, a body was pulled along by its heels, its head wrapped in a cloud of dust. It bore no armour, and in the place of the missing cuirass the man's chest was a morass of blood.

Andromache's eyes blurred and the world went dark. She fell back, headlong towards the steep steps, as Polyxena and the servants ran to catch her.

'I think he has gone mad.'

Diomede said it, quietly, thoughtfully, as if she were thinking out loud. She and the other women were huddled in one of the inner tents, leaving the outer tent to the women who had once belonged to Agamemnon.

'Everybody seems to think it now,' Doris agreed. 'Even Ulysses was saying it.'

'I could understand the madness of the battle. His God gave him that. It was what he needed to kill Hector and the other

Trojans and thoroughly to avenge Patroclus. But it should have vanished by now; and it has not.'

Iphis shook her head and said, 'The God still has him.'

'It was real madness, what he did at the funeral,' one of the other women said.

'And the business with Hector's body. He should have taken a ransom for it long before now.'

'He should be recovering from his grief. You have to live with deaths, everybody does. But he does not seem to want to recover.'

'Nor does Briseis.'

'She is not mad,' Diomede said. 'She just does not know how to cope with being married to him.'

There was no viciousness in Diomede's tone. Even she was not jealous of Briseis now. To Briseis' numbness the other women lent the sympathy that they were unable any more to find for Achilles.

A moon had waned and grown full again since the battle. Patroclus' bones lay beneath the great mound that Achilles intended, he said, to hold his own as well. He had a terrible certainty that he would never leave Troy alive. With them were the bones of four fine horses, two hunting dogs, and twelve Trojan captives. Achilles had slaughtered them all himself. It was an act of barely conceivable barbarity and it had not been done in the red-hot passion of the battlefield, but in icy cold blood, and with obsessive care. Achilles had consulted the oracles to determine the right number of victims. He had arranged the corpses neatly and fired the pyre efficiently, in spite of the thick thunderous air that dampened the flames. The act carried an echo of an age of heroes, an age when men had fought as Patroclus had done, not enmeshed in the sticky spiderweb of politics, but out of simple bravery, and loyalty to their families and comrades.

Hector's bones had not been buried. Achilles had refused to return his body and the Trojan envoys who had negotiated the truce had gone away pale and shaken from their brief interview with him. Every morning Achilles rose at dawn, and driving his chariot alone, dragged the mouldering corpse three times around Patroclus' tomb. Returning, he abandoned the body to the dust without a backward glance. He kept it well away from the dogs and the kites. There would have been no satisfaction in desecrating a skeleton.

There was nothing honourable in that. It was an act of shame and even those who had joined in the funeral procession without a murmur were vociferous in condemning it.

Achilles seemed oblivious to the condemnation. For him it was a private grief, a private vengeance upon them all. It was as if he had chosen his path, and meant to follow it to its very end. It was not clear if he had found the end, or if he was wandering trackless in a desert. His path had led him, it seemed, to a place where he could nurse a rage that was both more and less than honourable, a towering fury, a descent into murderous excess.

It was a place that set him beyond normal human contact. Briseis had silently returned to live in the women's tents. Achilles had not spoken to her since he went out to kill Hector. He had not slept with her, or with any of the other women. He barely slept at all: he would rise in the night and stalk alone along the shore, his eyes fixed on the white surf that hissed and bubbled in a fury of its own where the black sea broke into fragments. He talked only to his officers, and then only of the business of war. The Myrmidons he kept razor-sharp, even with the autumn drawing in.

'What can we do?' Doris asked.

There was a silence. Diomede broke it by saying, 'Briseis must do it. She has to go and talk to him.'

'She must get him to send the corpse back at least.'

'She is in no state to do that,' Iphis protested.

Diomede frowned. 'I know. But she must.'

Another silence. Doris spoke. 'If only she would tell us what happened while Agamemnon had her.'

'That has nothing to do with it,' Diomede said.

'I think it has. Whatever it was that happened, she hates him for it. Hates Achilles for standing by and letting it happen to her.'

They all considered that. At last Iphis said, 'I doubt if she hates him. I think it is he who hates her. Because she is still alive, and Patroclus is dead.'

'Because it all happened while he was trying to win her back?'

'But you forget,' Diomede said in a low, unsteady voice, 'that he never did try to win her back.'

Briseis did hate Achilles. The hatred grew as her numbness began to wear off. It tingled all over her. It was not because of the barbarity of the human sacrifices: she could understand that, in a way. It was not because of his refusal to fight for her: she had accepted that long before. It was not even because he had let Patroclus die doing what he would not have done himself. She believed she could have accepted his sacrifice of them both if it had been the right thing to do. The unforgivable thing was that he had done it and then been proved wrong. He had squandered their sacrifice, in the creation of this being who no longer seemed to be a man.

She could not say this to the other women. Certainly not to Iphis or Diomede. Not even to Doris, though she found it easiest to talk to Doris. It was Doris who took on the task of persuading her that Achilles must be approached.

Doris argued that it must be done for the sake of the women, for the sake of Hector's shade and his family, for the sake of the army. None of Doris' arguments struck home to Briseis. She found an argument of her own that did, however. She felt that the sacrifices might somehow be redeemed if Achilles were to regain his humanity.

Doris planned out with her how it might best be done. There had to be an excuse for talking to him, for they never spoke casually. Agamemnon's women would provide it. It was driving them all to distraction, the overcrowding coupled with the listless despair of the newcomers. There had even been a fight in the women's tents: no more than a petty squabble, but it could be built up into something more. It would make an opening: Briseis would have to work round from there to the subject of the corpse. Doris had no suggestions as to how she might achieve that.

Only when she had agreed to try did Briseis think to ask herself if Achilles did hate her. It had surprised her, when Doris had suggested that he might.

On reflection, she thought not. She reasoned so: there was

nothing to be deduced from Achilles' behaviour towards her. She believed there was no reason for him to blame her for what had happened: the price he had paid had not been for her at all, in his mind. It had been the price of his honour. His fateful, god-given sense of honour.

There seemed to be no point in waiting for a right time: no times were right. Diomede decided when it was to be done. She picked a cool afternoon, when there was no fighting and Achilles had returned alone to his hut.

The women dressed Briseis as carefully as if she were going to his bed. She refused to wear the cream dress, so she borrowed one of Diomede's, a long shift of fine grey wool, bordered in blue. They prayed with her before sending her out across the track to Achilles' hut. Their prayers were to the women's gods, Artemis and Athena, for it seemed to them that this was a matter for women.

The dogs barked as she pushed open the courtyard gate. They were always edgy those days, apprehensive when strangers approached. Briseis paused to see if the noise would bring Achilles to the door. It did not. She walked slowly across the yard and knocked twice before lifting the latch.

Achilles was sitting on his bed, polishing his breastplate. He had been working obsessively on it for days, knocking out the dents that it had received during the battles, persuading the smiths to re-cut the design where it had worn away, renewing the leather straps, polishing it until it shone. He waited a moment before looking up. There was no surprise on his face at seeing Briseis. After a little while he rose, setting the armour carefully on the floor, and went to shut the door behind her.

The room was dusty. There was mud on the floor and there were crumbs on the trestle. A litter of bones, discarded by the dogs, lay around the hearth. A shiver of distaste ran through Briseis.

'The hut needs cleaning,' she said tautly. 'I'll send Helen across to sweep it.'

Achilles did not reply. She forced herself to look at him. He did not seem like her husband: this was the commander of the Myrmidons. His face was set into the cold, decisive expression he assumed when dealing with his officers. His eyes did not avoid hers, but there was no light in them when she met them.

Briseis waited a moment, then went to sit on the bench by the trestle. If she was to do this at all, she was beginning to think, it would have to be as Achilles' chief slavewoman. It was a relationship she had observed between other couples. The woman asserted her little rights. She dared to sit in her husband's presence, she gave orders on his behalf. She never, ever looked for affection from him.

Achilles came to sit next to her, out of touching distance. 'There's something you want?'

She did not look at him as she worked through her tale of feminine intrigue. He replied rationally, the commander giving orders to his inferior officer, with plans for rearranging the tents.

'Thank you.' She did not stand up.

'There is something else?'

Briseis took a deep breath. 'May I send word to the Trojans that you will negotiate now? For the return of the body?'

'Do you have a way of sending word to them?'

'No.' She looked across at him surreptitiously. 'But if you tell me how, I will see to it.'

His face was still cold and calm. 'The priests can arrange it. At Apollo's shrine, neutral territory. It is too dangerous for you to go there. It will need to be a soldier. Not one of my men.'

Briseis was tempted to disobey him and ask one of the Myrmidons she had nursed the year before, but he was too proud to tolerate that and would not forgive her if he discovered it. Who else was there to be trusted? She supposed men turned to Ulysses in such situations. Achilles, she realized, would prefer not to know. She said carefully, 'I will talk to someone.'

'Yes.' He was not going to thank her. He stood up, still without touching her. He said, 'Come to me tonight,' went to the door, opened it and walked out of the hut.

Maybe he was right, she thought wearily. It would be easier for them both in the dark. She got up herself and went to find a messenger she could send to Ulysses.

The Trojan emissaries arrived the following evening. The first the women knew of it was when Automedon came across to their tents. They were, he said, to wash and prepare Hector's body, ready for its return. He and Alcimus fetched the corpse.

They did it outside the tent, by lamplight. The corpse stank. They could not close the eyes in the mouldering face and they seemed to stare at Briseis as she worked, helping the other women to wash away the grime and blood as well as they could and anoint what was left of the skin with oil. She had known those eyes alive. Hector had come to her wedding, at Mynes' house outside Lyrnessus. He and his own new bride had laughed and joked with them, shared their happiness. The thoughts would not go away and in the end she had to leave the others and go around the side of the tents to be violently sick in the long grass.

Automedon appeared not to notice and the others made no comment. By the stockade to Achilles' hut there was a mule cart full of ransom goods that the Trojans had brought with them, and Automedon rummaged through it to find a tunic for the body and a couple of cloaks that could act as a shroud. He discarded the purple cloak he came across first and selected two plain red ones, the kind that merchants wear.

Achilles appeared as they were finishing the work. Cold-faced, he helped to unload the ransom and lift the corpse into the empty cart.

He drew Briseis aside when it was done. 'We shall have to feast them. I shall have a lamb slaughtered. Give us time to eat. Then come yourself and bring Iphis, to make up beds. They cannot take the body back tonight; I'll give them an escort in the morning.'

'I'll bring bread,' Briseis said. She was conscious that Automedon did not know how to arrange it all, as Patroclus had. There had been no feasts since he had been acting as lieutenant to Achilles.

'And keep it quiet. Watch Agamemnon's women, let none of them leave the tents.'

He still thought of them as Agamemnon's women, Helen and the rest. He treated them like enemies. He never spoke to any of them, even to give them orders. Briseis could not see the danger: Helen and her comrades were far too cowed to try to escape from the Thessalian section, and she knew that they would never willingly return to Agamemnon. All the same, she obeyed him.

She understood why Achilles had spoken as he had, when she and Iphis came into the hut with the newly baked bread. There were two Trojan emissaries: one sitting in the low chair that was Achilles' own, and the other hovering, servant-like, in a corner of the hut. Her eyes were drawn instantly to the man in the chair. He was dressed in a plain supplicant's tunic of heavy oiled linen, and the cloak that was thrown over the back of the chair was of wolfskin. But the eyes in his hawkish face were dark and glittering, demanding attention, and the claw-like hands that rested on his knees were weighted down with heavy rings. He was old; but it was not because of his age, she realized, that he did not stand as she entered. He was no man to stand for others, even when forced to make a token show of humility.

Achilles crossed to Briseis, holding out his hand. He took hers and led her across to the chair. 'My wife, sir.'

She knew him now, in the firelight, though she had seen him only once before. At Lyrnessus. He had made a state visit to the town when she was a child. With her parents she had waited in the palace megaron for his formal entrance; and after the ritual prostrations she had been briefly presented to him. She still recalled the deep echoing voice that had repeated her name and asked her father if she was yet promised in marriage.

The High King. He had come himself, in disguise, to beg for the return of Hector's body. It was the greatest honour he could pay to his dead son. It was an honour to Achilles. And it was a major insult to Agamemnon that he should not have been told of this.

King Priam nodded imperceptibly and his eyes narrowed. He did not speak, but he recognized her, Briseis thought. Briefly she assumed that he remembered her from Lyrnessus, recalled her as Prince Mynes' wife. No, she realized a moment afterwards. He did not know her for a Trojan. She was a woman his spies had told him of: a Thessalian woman, whose cause had almost lost the Achaeans the war, and won it for him. She started to make the reverence – he had, after all, been her High King – then checked and did a little curtsy, as Achilles' wife would do.

After that she sat in the corner with Iphis and waited while the men feasted. Myrmidons served them, so there was nothing for her to do but watch.

King Priam was an old man, older than she had expected him to be. She could see that his face was drawn and his body bent with pain. His face was composed into a formal mask of grief. Surely it was genuine, his pain, and yet behind the mask she had the impression that he was not remotely unbalanced by the agony of his loss. Instead there was a mind razor-sharp, continually watching, calculating, measuring Achilles and planning his revenge.

Achilles, wiser in the ways of pain but not in those of intrigue, saw none of it. Briseis knew he would treat this dangerous enemy with honour, and not see the knife until it was hilt-deep in his back.

She had her honour to uphold too. She sat proud and silent, as Achilles' wife would sit before his visitors. When Achilles signalled to her she set to work with Iphis to make up beds for the two Trojans, outside the hut under the deep colonnade. It was the best place. If anyone came to the hut, another commander or a messenger from Agamemnon, they would see nothing. The torches flickered in the night air as she and Iphis piled up the purple blankets and the fleecy coverlets that were fitting for a king.

Iphis returned to the women's tents and Briseis went back into the hut alone. Automedon was there, but the other officers had been dismissed. The Trojan servant still hovered in a corner. Achilles sat at the trestle with King Priam. They were bargaining seriously now, negotiating a truce for Hector's funeral. Eleven days the Trojans would have. Achilles gave Priam his word, with nothing in his voice or bearing to suggest that this was not one supreme commander addressing another.

Still she said nothing. Not then, and not later, when Priam had been ushered to his makeshift bed and she and Achilles lay together in the shadows of the hut. The embers of the fire that Automedon had built up to roast the sheep still glowed brightly. In their light Achilles' face was warm, its hard lines softening a little as he looked at her.

He had not changed. He had come back to her, the master she had hated and learned to love. Whom she must learn to love once more; to submit to, unquestioningly, as women always do. Around them in the hut the dancing shadows brought closer the ghosts of the men, living and dead, who had come between them. Patroclus, his smile wiped away, whose loves had forged for him the brittle, golden death mask of a hero. Agamemnon, smiling still, but thinly and cruelly, his eyes cold, as he watched their every move. Diomedes and the rest, the ones who had reminded her of what she had briefly forgotten: that underneath the glitter all the Achaeans were pirates who looked on what other men had made, and stole it for their own. And the men who had made her, Briseus and Mynes, servants of the malevolent man who lay curled, perhaps asleep, on the other side of the wooden wall.

Yes, it was better in the dark. The fire did not die so easily, though. She reached to draw Achilles to her and he made love to her with a passion that was as mad, and as controlled, as his grief had been.

The night wore on, and under cover of its darkness Priam — more fearful than malevolent, naked without his kingly power on this enemy territory, and dreading the knife in his own back — rose, and without turning towards the door of the hut, helped his crier to harness the mules to the cart and set off under the stars for the only home he had ever known.

They would have a lifetime. But some lives are short, and Briseis was as sure as was Achilles that his would be one of them. There would be the days of the truce, while wails of grief rose from the towers of Ilios and the Trojan woodcutters marched off with their mules to Mount Ida to bring wood, and more wood, for Hector's pyre. There would, Briseis hoped, be the winter. It was coming already. The sun went down early, the nights were long and cool.

They had the truce. It was not enough. Neither of them could bring themselves to speak, to clean out the festering wounds. It needed more time, Briseis told herself. She expected to get that time, when the fighting died down and Achilles stayed in the camp and kept the fire burning in his hut.

But after the truce the battles began again. Achilles continued to act as if he were supreme commander, and Agamemnon appeared to do nothing to stop him. The High King had lost his own spirit after Chryseis' departure. He no longer seemed to have the will to fight his rival.

It was Achilles who forced the pace of the war, sending the army out day after day across the sodden plain. It was to Achilles' hut that the Achaean leaders made their way at nightfall. Even Agamemnon came sometimes and took his place around the trestle, leaving Achilles at the head of the table. When she could, Briseis kept to the women's tent then. Achilles did not ask why. She did not try to tell him.

When the commanders had gone he would send for her and make love to her, again and again, with a fierce lust that somehow left them both detached and alone. She rarely saw him in daylight. They barely talked, never laughed together. The harp lay untouched in the corner of the hut, dust and tarnish dimming its silver trimmings.

Briseis felt she understood him; but he seemed to have no time to understand her. Slowly it came to her that she had failed. Her own love was gone, and she did not believe any more that it would ever return. There was no trace of his either. He was alive again, but that was due to Agamemnon's other, more unexpected gift: to the thrill of power, that channelled all his anger and gave him a means of getting yet more revenge.

It was frightening to watch Achilles in command. He drilled the men to the point of exhaustion. It was gone now, the caring, the fairness that had made the Myrmidons love him. When the weather permitted it he attacked, pushing the army relentlessly forward. When it did not, he schemed and plotted. Briseis knew he had begun to treat with the spies.

The war was going well, considering how weakened the army was by the plague and the battles; but Ilios did not surrender. Even before the spring, Priam managed to buy new allies. Strange allies, from tribes who lived in the desolate lands to the far east. There were black men, their skins shining, their hair curled tight, who fought stripped to the waist even in winter. There were warrior women, the Amazons who trained their girls like men. The men who came back to the hospital tent told her of their light bows, their battle axes, which inflicted unfamiliar blows. It took a long time to learn how to counter them.

Briseis feared the plotting more than she feared the Ethiops and the Amazons. Achilles had set himself adrift in a seascape as alien to him as it was to her. She believed Priam and his sons would outmanoeuvre him as smoothly and viciously as Agamemnon had once done. The trap would come, she felt sure, in this way. Not from men who fought openly and honestly; not from pygmies and women who attacked with strange weapons; but from those who plotted in dark cellars, with snakes, vials of poison and the tricks of the underworld.

She did not think he would recognize it. He needed friends. He needed lovers, people he could trust totally, to whom he could open himself. But Patroclus was not there to make him see sense, and she no longer expected him to share anything with her. Losing Patroclus, they had lost some essence that had bound all three of them tight. Achilles ate, drank and talked with Automedon and the rest, but she did not think he spoke to them of the spies and plots. He did not share his secrets with Agamemnon or Ulysses, Nestor or Diomedes. They too felt out in the cold. From their men rumours came back even to her that Achilles was planning some treachery.

As spring approached Achilles went out on long forays with Ulysses, with Nestor's son Antilochus, with Ajax. They returned bloody, with more captured spears than jars of wheat and barley. On other journeys he went alone. The rumours of treachery intensified. Briseis still did not believe them: he had nothing to gain from treachery, not when he had sacrificed so much on the altar of honour and loyalty.

The women had a different theory. They had watched and recognized Briseis' failure with Achilles. He still did not call any of the others to him. It must, they whispered, be some other woman who drew him from the camp. A Trojan, not a captive. Some said it was King Priam's daughter, Princess Polyxena; a few believed it was Helen herself. Briseis listened to these whispers too: the sympathy was waning now, and they meant her to hear them. She believed them even less. Achilles was not looking for new passions to spur him, he had had his fill of the old ones. He was not looking for warmth, for sympathy, for love. He seemed to be beyond reach of any of it.

She ought to try again, she supposed: find some way of

breaking down the barriers he had set up. But how? When she did see him he was preoccupied with the problems of the war and barely listened to what she said. And looking at his hard-set face, the cold grey eyes sunk into hollows of sleeplessness, she could not feel any spark of warmth. There had to be a grief there, somewhere deep inside her, but she could not reach it. She had no urge to cry, no urge to touch him gently. He would not have responded, anyway: there was no gentleness left in him.

They had something. A husk, a shell. Once, Briseis reminded herself, it had been the form that bound together a captor and his prisoner, a master and his slave. Now, it was – not the outline of a marriage, but the harder, more brittle shell that wrapped around two lovers who no longer ached to stay together, but who could no longer part. Perhaps they had put too much into their love. Or perhaps, she added to herself, remembering Patroclus, remembering Achilles' face as he had watched Agamemnon's envoys lead her away, they had not given it enough. Perhaps it was not their fault at all, but that of the jealous gods, who do not like to see men and women happy for too long.

There was no happiness any more. There was just a slow slide towards the ultimate destruction.

It would come, soon. Daily, as he left, she found herself expecting that he would never come back to her again.

Part Four

HONOURABLE MEN

AENEAS BROUGHT A FAIRLY LARGE company back with him to Ilios. It had surprised him that so many men were willing to fight, when he was reluctant himself. Some of them had been ready to leave nearly a moon before, but he had delayed till spring was well underway.

He stopped them in the foothills of Mount Ida, in a small copse close to a stream. They were just out of sight of the citadel.

'We camp here tonight,' he said firmly to Gyrtius.

Gyrtius scowled. 'If we march on, we could be at the camp before nightfall.'

Aeneas shook his head. 'Tomorrow.'

It was not just fear of the encroaching dark and the Achaeans it might hide that prompted his decision. He felt he needed a day to assimilate the nearness of Ilios, and to come to terms with what he must do in the next phase of the war.

He lowered his pack from his shoulders and dropped down onto the rough ground. The movement jarred his side slightly and he felt the dull ache where he had been grazed by Achilles' spear in the great battle towards the end of the previous summer. It seemed a portent to him. Whatever he found in Ilios, he did not expect the coming summer to be anything but painful.

The Dardanians arrived at Ilios before midday and made straight for the camp. Aeneas looked up as he passed through the gate in the stockade. Above his head the standards flew: the Thracian sunflowers, the Mysian poppies, the Lycian crossed swords. Two or three of them were not familiar to him. He asked Deiphobus, who greeted him just inside the camp, and Deiphobus lazily explained that the blood-red standard was that of the Ethiops, the white and gold of the Amazons, while the black cross belonged to a contingent of Carian mercenaries.

'You will have heard,' Deiphobus said, 'that Priam has enlisted many new troops.'

'I heard.'

'Your old quarters have been taken by Memnon and his men. He has been here since midwinter. Paris has found you a space to the north, near the stockade.'

Aeneas looked Deiphobus in the eye. The taller man gave a sly smile. 'Though I am sure,' he added, 'that you will be able to change it if you would prefer to be elsewhere.'

Aeneas shrugged. 'It will do for now.'

'Paris will see you tomorrow. Not too early.'

'And the High King?'

'He has no wish to see you at present.'

An Ilian welcome. Aeneas turned without another word and gestured to Deiphobus' boy to show him to the huts that had been cleared for his men.

In the morning, early, he went to see Andromache. It was a decision he had made after much thought. It seemed to him that it was necessary to mend his alliances within the citadel and he felt that to start with Andromache would entail the least risk. Andromache was never less than friendly to him, usually forthcoming. It was not in her nature to keep secrets. Though she was not an acute judge of other people's opinions and attitudes, Aeneas reckoned she would be able to advise him where his efforts would be likely to bear the most fruit.

He was in a cautiously optimistic mood by then. His new quarters were more spacious than Deiphobus' welcome had led him to expect. Clearly Paris had not intended to antagonize him unduly. And he could see advantages in being placed at the edge of the camp, where his messengers could come and go unobserved.

Aeneas barely glanced towards the palace before crossing the square and pushing the half-open courtyard gate to the house that had been Hector's. The housekeeper, as alert as ever, was at his side before he had ventured two paces into the yard. 'I'll announce you,' she declared, eyeing Aeneas' feet as if she were willing them to be still.

Andromache emerged from the megaron a moment later. 'Aeneas. How good to see you.'

Her pleasure sounded genuine to Aeneas, but he could see

the ghost of long-indulged misery lingering on her face, matching the widow-wanness of her dress.

'I came back yesterday.'

'With your men?'

'Close on five hundred of them. And I have new horses from my father to replace the pair Diomedes took last summer.'

Andromache frowned. She did not care to remember the last battle in which Aeneas had fought. She turned, more abruptly than she had intended, to send a servant to fetch wine. Aeneas followed her indoors and they sat together in high chairs, lost in the echoing spaces of the megaron.

'You will find a lot of changes in the camp,' Andromache said.

'And Ilios is changed. Perhaps I see it more clearly than you, coming back.'

'Not for the better.'

No, not for the better. In the lower town, many of the battle scars had still not been patched over. In the citadel, the stucco on the buildings was soot-blackened, the paint of the palace pillars peeling. The camp was full of foreign troops, whose languages Aeneas did not speak, and whose appearance he found disconcerting. He picked his words with care. 'It seems everyone is enthusiastic about the new troops. Penthesilea's Amazons have done wonders, even after losing her. And this Ethiopian Memnon is evidently a remarkable man.'

'Oh, Memnon. We never seem to hear about anyone else. His troops are good, but he is so self-satisfied. And have you seen his train of women?'

'My dear Andromache, Priam's family can hardly accuse anyone else of pride or self-satisfaction.' Aeneas gave a thin smile. 'I heard about the women. It seems he is adored by every female in Ilios. Except you?'

Andromache looked down. 'I have no interest in men.'

'Priam and Hecuba have not pressed you to remarry?'

'Not pressed it, no. They are too concerned with Cassandra. You knew? Eurypylus brought his troops from Teuthrania on condition that Priam would give her to him, and now she is refusing to go.'

'You sound as if you sympathize.'

Andromache gave him a sharp look. 'Of course she should

not cross the High King. She is not strong, though, and . . .'

'And she dislikes men,' Aeneas finished for her.

'That one, at least. I think she might have taken you.'

That surprised him. He had half-expected Andromache herself to look to him. Evidently not. 'You flatter me, Andromache. I am afraid I cannot rescue Cassandra now, though. I married, myself, this last winter.'

'Oh. To a Dardanian girl?'

'Yes. She will stay in Dardania until the war is over.'

Andromache regarded him coolly. He had been expecting the usual questions: her name, her character, the colour of her hair. None of them came. Finally Andromache said, 'So you do not plan to challenge for the generalship.'

'Why, do you think marriage to Cassandra would have given it to me?'

Andromache's silence implied that she did think it, or something like it.

'I doubt if Priam would have contemplated it.'

'He will not consider it now.'

'Paris is not such a bad choice.' Andromache started in annoyance and Aeneas went on quickly, to cut her off. 'I know he's no Hector on the battlefield, but he is a good schemer. The war will be won with spying and trickery now, not through battles.'

Andromache rose abruptly and crossed the room. In the corner her women servants were busy spinning and kneading dough. A couple of them looked up, but she did not seem to notice them. She spun round to face Aeneas. 'The war will not be won now. That is what you mean, isn't it, Aeneas?'

Aeneas felt his temper begin to fray. He had expected a gentle, comforting meeting; but this Andromache, straight and cold-faced, was very different from the plump chatterer he had known. His voice had an abrasive note as he replied. 'If I thought that, I would not be here. True, I would much prefer to try to negotiate an honourable peace, and there is no hope of that while Paris heads the army. But I think there is a chance of winning outright. We pushed as far as the ships last summer, don't forget. Memnon has almost done as much already this year. If Paris could eliminate Achilles I think the Achaeans would be badly shaken, and then we could press home. From what the spies tell us, Agamemnon is a spent force. With Achilles gone the other leaders would split into factions, and they would be in no state to counter-attack effectively.'

Andromache walked back towards him. She did not sit, but stood, looking down on Aeneas, with a frown on her face. 'Paris is planning something, then. Against Achilles.'

The strength of her reaction told Aeneas that the vague rumours he had heard in the camp had a real foundation. He played for time, hoping that Andromache would give him a clue as to where he might learn more. 'We are always fighting against Achilles. That is nothing new. You want to avenge Hector, surely?'

Andromache's lip curled. 'Is that vengeance, to "eliminate" his killer?'

Aeneas' annoyance was open now. He turned his head up past her to the gilded rosettes of the ceiling. With Hector in this room, he had never noticed such details. With Andromache, he did. 'Do not delude yourself that the war was clean when Hector was fighting it, Andromache. Hector was not above a bit of dirty work when it was needed. Though Paris will do it rather better.'

'He will have to, to get Achilles, won't he?' She wheeled away, then turned to add icily, 'Don't let me keep you from the palace, Aeneas.'

'I won't.' He slammed the door behind him.

Andromache watched him leave in silence. It struck her afterwards that she had not offered to bring down the child. Oh well, she thought to herself, Aeneas never had liked children.

The sun was well above the rooftops by the time Aeneas strode up the steps to the palace and into the men's megaron, his sword clanking at his side. He had made the decision on the journey from Dardania never again to go unarmed in the citadel.

It was galling, though not unduly surprising, to hear from the guards that Paris and Priam were still closeted in a private meeting. Helenus greeted him instead. 'I had not expected to see you so anxious to get back to our little quarrels.'

'I am escaping from one. With Andromache.'

'That explains everything. I cannot offer you wine. Andromache might have plenty, but the palace is almost dry and there is no hope of getting more till the autumn, if then. There's cistern water.' Helenus' smile was neat, even diplomatic. 'It has an interesting tang. Clears the head very effectively.'

'Why don't you requisition Hector's cellar?'

'What an uncivilized suggestion.' Helenus propped himself sideways against a pillar, with an air that was remarkably civilized, in spite of the confusion of his clothing. His left hand, shattered by a spearthrust in the great battle, hung useless by his side. 'If you want Andromache's wine you will have to marry her.'

'Is that what Priam is hoping?'

'Yes and no. He intended her to take Deiphobus, but she declined. I gather she offered to settle for me, but on the whole I prefer to stick to the water.'

'She would suit you. Bring you down to earth. And in spite of the nose, she is pleasant to look at, when you get to know her.'

'Maybe. I would not suit her, though. She would find me damnably unreliable on better acquaintance.'

'You don't think the same of me?'

'Oh, she would never notice your treacheries, any more than Hector would have done.'

Helenus' voice was light and easy. Aeneas was not sure whether he meant it to be taken seriously. In fact, it ran close to home, for Aeneas, rigidly correct in the earlier phases of the war, had recently begun to dabble in the underhand. He had set up a network of spies of his own over the winter and had been negotiating privately with Achilles from Dardania.

He held Helenus' eye a moment and then replied, 'Perhaps she sees as much as you do. It's no good, though. I married this last winter, in Dardania.'

'Really? Passion, or convenience?'

'I think I would describe it as love.'

Helenus smiled again. 'How touching. Perhaps I should track down some wine after all, to drink to the occasion with you.'

Aeneas swallowed his retort. 'I shall need it, before I face Priam.'

To his slight surprise, Helenus repeated Deiphobus' earlier verdict. 'You will not face Priam. He has not appeared in public since Hector was killed. He tolerates Paris in private, but not the rest of us. Hecuba handles the marital entanglements, and Paris does the rest.'

'And Memnon? Eurypylus?'

'Sensibly stick to the camp, and keep clear of the citadel.'

'I think I shall follow suit.'

Helenus put on an exaggerated expression of disappointment. 'But Aeneas, you enjoy the intrigue. Stay and play spies with us. No, don't spit at me. I'll go to find the wine.'

Aeneas was in no cooler a temper when he went back to the camp. Paris had played him like a fish, throwing out hints, but not any details of his plans. Helenus did not stay for their meeting and was not to be found in the palace when it ended. Aeneas did not like to be ignorant. He went over to the Mysian section to find Ennomus and perhaps discover what was really going on.

Ennomus greeted him calmly and replied thoughtfully. 'Helenus was asking me, the other day. I doubt if he would know either. There's some messy scheme that Paris is keeping to himself. I hear Deiphobus is involved, but that's all that has spread as far as us. I doubt if anyone in the camp could tell you more.'

'You don't think Helenus is playing a double-blind on you? That he too is involved in the plan?'

Ennomus considered. 'No. Helenus may be choosy about giving out his information, but I have never caught him lying. He serves Apollo, remember? Knowledge and truth.'

'Snakes and mice,' retorted Aeneas. 'The God of dirty tricks. Don't tell me that is why Paris is keeping him out of it.'

'Why are any of us out of it? Faction-mongering, that has always been Paris' game, and Priam's. Why do you need to know, anyway? Do you plan to sweep in and rescue Achilles, or do you just want to be in at the kill?'

Aeneas did not reply and Ennomus added, 'You know the rumour in the Achaean camp is that Achilles himself is a traitor.'

'There are rumours like that about everyone now, on both sides.'

'True. Helenus spread it about that you were suspect yourself. Not that anyone believed him, of course.'

'Perhaps we should start believing it of Helenus.'

'He makes sure some people do. It suits Helenus to know everything, and do nothing. He has no wish to be drawn into plots, just to hear about them. Forget him. Come and drink with Memnon.'

Memnon. The new dominating force in the Trojan camp, together with his two thousand pitch-black troops. Memnon, who had so deliberately placed himself where he could see and be seen by everyone. Memnon, who was perhaps intriguing himself for the generalship that Paris held so precariously. Memnon, who might yet become the focus of the opposition to Priam's policies within Troy. Memnon whom, it seemed, he could avoid no longer.

Aeneas stalked with Ennomus across to the centre of the camp. He had expected the Ethiopian leader to have taken over his own hut, but Ennomus told him Memnon had found it too stifling and used it only for stores. He used a tent instead, which he had pitched in front of the hut, at the very head of the parade ground. Ennomus lifted the flap and gestured to Aeneas to follow him.

Inside, the tent was resplendent with woven hangings and reeked of incense. There were no chairs, no trestles, not even any weapons in evidence. The Ethiopian king reclined on a low bed. About him, a dozen slave girls giggled and cooed. He gave a regal wave at his visitors. He did not stand. 'Ah, the augur himself. And this must be the famous Aeneas. Come and make merry, for tomorrow we fight. The girls will bring wine.'

Ennomus dropped onto a pile of cushions, seemingly perfectly at home. Aeneas stood, regarding his host. Memnon had the polished perfection of an ebony statue of a god. He wore only a short kilt. As he stirred, jewels flashed at his ears, his neck, his wrists. He wore a queen's ransom in gold and rubies and he smiled up at Aeneas with the charm of a high-class hetaira. And yet the effect was not womanish, but powerfully male. Satisfied, Aeneas sat. 'We fight tomorrow? I did not hear that from Paris.'

'Paris fight? That would be a sight worth seeing.' The girls tittered around them. 'I have not the slightest idea what Paris intends. Should I care?' Memnon said it to the nearest girl, who gave a tinkly laugh. 'I fight. I have plans for a little encounter.' He reached a hand over to the girl and drew a neat circle with his finger on her bare tummy. Then jabbed, hard, in the centre of it. 'With Achilles.'

Aeneas said steadily, 'You have hopes of killing Achilles?'

Memnon grinned lazily, as if the sudden jab had been an illusion, and slid his hand down the girl's leg in a liquid movement. 'I think it would be a kinder fate than the one Paris plans for him.'

Did Memnon know more about Paris' plans? Aeneas knew, as soon as he thought it, that the Ethiopian was the last man in whom Paris would confide. The very threat to pre-empt Paris' plot was proof that Memnon too felt alienated from the citadel and from Priam's interminable family. 'A more honourable one, I imagine. I shall look forward to fighting with you.'

'You would not prefer the Amazon ladies?' The girls tittered again, but Memnon's face was still. 'They had the better of the Myrmidons when they arrived.'

'And need a new leader? I do not think so. If my Dardanians do not join up with your contingent I think we would be more at home with Eurypylus' Teuthranians.'

'They are good men too,' Ennomus said. 'Paris did a first-rate job this winter, hunting out new allies.'

'So I see. And there are no fresh troops to boost the Achaeans.'

'None at all. We are holding them back. But we should be winning.'

'Tomorrow, Ennomus.' Memnon did not disagree with the Mysian, Aeneas noticed, but the diagnosis did not seem to upset him. 'Tomorrow, we go for Achilles.'

The following evening, Memnon was dead.

■

Cassandra left the palace for Ennomus' funeral. It was the first time that Aeneas had seen her since he had returned to Ilios.

He had expected her to come. Like Helenus, she had cared deeply for the little Mysian who had had such skill in reading signs in the flight of birds. While she had accepted her exclusion from the other funerals – and there had been many, that summer, since Memnon's troops had carried his bones back to Ethiopia – she would not have endured being kept away from this one.

Aeneas mourned Ennomus too. He would not have disturbed the rites for the sake of talking to Cassandra. He had spoken many times with the Mysian, though, of the possibility of inducing Cassandra to provide the information that they had been able to obtain nowhere else. He did not think Ennomus would take it ill if he used this opportunity to approach her.

It became clearer and clearer to him, as he edged his way through the mass of Mysian troops and towards the palace contingent, that Cassandra was at the funeral under guard. She was surrounded by Hecuba's women, priestesses and wives of palace officials. Only by making a conspicuous effort could he have had any chance of speaking privately with her.

Had Paris deliberately wanted to keep her away from him? Aeneas wondered. The idea seemed to him ridiculous. Paris and Deiphobus both appeared confident and assured, in spite of the continuing disasters of the war. Neither man had given Aeneas any reason to think that they considered him a serious threat to their plans.

He settled for taking up an inconspicuous position perhaps a spear's throw from Cassandra. As the crowd broke up, and the flames of the pyre began to burn lower, he watched while a succession of other people crossed to make their assault on her guard.

She was being kept from Andromache, he realized to his amazement, and from Polyxena. Helenus did not even attempt to talk to her. Chromis was politely diverted by one of the priestesses. Deiphobus was allowed through, and so was Helen – though Helen herself was also guarded, rather less obviously.

Aeneas moved a little closer. He could see Cassandra's face clearly now. Her hair was as short as she had cut it in mourning for Hector, her face marred by the grief stripes. But the changes that alarmed him were in her expression and her bearing. She no longer stood tall and confidently, she no longer moved with the absent-minded assurance that had been so uniquely hers. Her chin drooped and there was something slack about her mouth. He decided even before he met her eyes that she had been drugged. She was barely awake, moving trance-like through the rites of the funeral.

There was no sign of Eurypylus, Aeneas noticed belatedly. Was the Teuthranian too forbidden to speak to her? He asked, when he was back at the camp, and was told that Eurypylus had decided some time earlier to withdraw his offer for her hand.

Aeneas did not suspect Cassandra of being directly involved in Paris' plot. He was certain that she was not. But the very pattern of her guarding convinced him that Paris and Hecuba were not afraid only of her general indiscretion, of her wilder prophecies; they believed that she might reveal something specific: something that would, directly or indirectly, affect what they were planning.

He was still deeply concerned to know what they were planning. The unknown plot had become a focus for all his unease about Ilios. It was not that he disagreed with its objective. Achilles had been even less forthcoming than he had expected in their private negotiations, and after seeing Memnon and Ennomus fall at his hands, Aeneas would have been perfectly happy to see the Achaean champion killed. But there was something about the way the matter was being planned that made him convinced that while the fact of Achilles' death could hardly fail to be a triumph for Troy, the manner of his killing might prove to be their undoing.

He knew by now exactly who was part of the plot. He no longer suspected Helenus of any involvement. Paris and Deiphobus were the ringleaders. Their men he had been able to guess at, and little indications, marks of favour from Paris, knots of men who broke up when he approached, had made him certain. It was a group large enough for an ambush, large enough to lead a well-planned attack. But there was something central, he suspected, that he did not know. It was not going to be just another attack on Achilles. It was a plot. And he did not like it.

It was Deiphobus who brought the news to the camp of Achilles' death; Paris had gone straight to Priam. He made for Aeneas, but before he reached the Dardanian's quarters half the camp was at his feet, drawn by his air of excitement and his bloody sword. They held an impromptu assembly and Deiphobus made his announcement with an uncharacteristic rush of enthusiasm.

And, Aeneas noted, very little detail. Deiphobus seemed happy to let the sword tell its own tale, and the common soldiers were too delighted to ask questions. This was the news they had all been waiting for. Uproar broke out and Deiphobus stood watching, his smile less catlike than usual, as the troops shouted and cheered in front of him.

Aeneas stepped in to order an extra wine ration in celebration, and to dismiss the army. They went more than willingly: few of them seemed to be interested to hear more. Aeneas himself was very interested. If he had not been able to uncover the plot beforehand, at least he could discover now what it had all been about. It was easy for him, looking for the signs, to be convinced that there was something worth uncovering. The hint of guilty delight in Deiphobus' look told him that; and as far as he knew, there had not been any fighting on the plain that day.

'Come to my tent,' he said curtly to Deiphobus.

Deiphobus' eyes narrowed as he took in Aeneas' expression. The smile faded, slowly, though a lingering smirk stayed behind on his face. 'Not now, Aeneas. I have to get back to Paris at the palace. If there is more you want to know there will be a council meeting tomorrow, I expect.'

'I don't want to report to the council. I want to know what really happened.'

'Achilles is dead. That is what happened.' Deiphobus turned on his heels.

'And there were no other casualties? You do not have his body, or any trophies?'

'We lost half a dozen men. The Achaeans had a few injuries. They got his body back.' Deiphobus smiled, the panther once more, and waved his sword so that the blood glistened in the sunlight. 'You do believe me, Aeneas?'

Aeneas ignored the question. 'It was a big skirmish, then? Why was the army not called out?'

In the bright light, Deiphobus' eyes had turned to slits. 'You ask too many questions, Aeneas. It almost makes me think you did not want Achilles killed.'

'What exactly are you trying to accuse me of?'

'Curiosity, cousin. Or jealousy, because it was not you who took him.'

The smirk hinted at a different answer. Aeneas found his arm lifting. Deiphobus parried it, deftly, with the bloody sword. Aeneas turned sharply and went back alone to his hut.

He did not drink the wine ration. None of the commanders did, once he had called them to his hut. Instead they argued, heatedly. They saw too many possibilities, had too little information. After the altercation with Deiphobus, Aeneas himself could hardly go up to the palace and demand to know more. Ten days before he would have sent Ennomus. The Mysian's death had left him even more isolated.

Finally Chromis offered to talk to Helenus. There were no other suggestions; it would have to do.

It was a long afternoon. Towards dusk they made up a wine-bowl from the rations. At dusk Chromis returned, with no information: except that Helenus had gone to Apollo's shrine to make enquiries.

Acamas groaned. 'Zeus. We might as well have asked Cassandra.'

Aeneas swallowed his retort. 'It makes some sense. Perhaps he reckons the priests will get the truth out of the Achaeans. Did he say that, Chromis?'

Chromis shook his head. 'He didn't tell me why. He was very evasive. Maybe he guessed something, or has some source he didn't want me to know about.'

'Maybe.' Aeneas dipped a cup in the winebowl and handed it to Chromis. His hut was still crowded. Outside they could hear the troops celebrating drunkenly. Their commanders, apprehensive, had not bothered to restrain them.

Helenus came himself when it was already dark. He doused his torch outside the hut. Inside, he looked around at the assembled men, then threw himself carelessly onto the ground. 'You have some wine after all.'

'A little. I brought it back from Dardania.'

'Thanks.' He drank it down, slowly and steadily. As he lowered the cup, Aeneas said, 'I trust you are going to earn it.'

'With information? Yes.' Helenus set the cup beside him on the beaten earth and squatted on his haunches. 'First, it is true. Achilles is dead. And Paris and Deiphobus did it. They took a troop of men, mainly soldiers from Priam's guard, and I think Polyxena too.'

'Polyxena? On a raid?'

'It was not exactly a raid. I would call it an ambush. They got Achilles alone and tried to cut him down. Made a fair muck of it, he must have killed half a dozen men. There is no scratch on Paris, or Deiphobus. I suppose they closed in just in time to give the final blows. Then some more Achaeans surprised them and they made a run for it, leaving the bodies. They have not been back yet for their own casualties. The Achaeans left them, so the priests are cleaning them up.'

'I don't understand,' Antiphus' deep voice broke in. 'Where did all this happen?'

Helenus looked round at the circle of waiting men. He spoke in a low, level voice. 'In the shrine. They killed Achilles in the shrine of Apollo's sanctuary. Lured him there on the pretext of a negotiation and hid the men till he had come into the grove alone.'

The laughs and shouts from outside the hut wrapped round the sudden silence within, holding it still and perfect. Finally Aeneas broke it. 'You had no idea how it was going to happen?'

Helenus' face in the lamplight looked old, every line cut deep with shadows. 'No idea, no. I knew it would be . . .' – he groped for a word – '. . . terrible. But not this. I did not know it. Nor, I am sure, did any of Apollo's servants. You know they would not have permitted it.'

Chromis said quietly, 'The army will not stand for it.'

'They will,' Aeneas corrected him. 'After Troilus, and Hector, and Memnon, and Ennomus, and all the other men Achilles killed. If they see that we accept it. If they were to see that we do not . . . I think they would still go along with Paris, if he did enough to appease the God. They don't give a fig for honourable methods, they want to get a sniff of victory. They will believe that this could turn the tide and give it to us.'

'It will not.' Antiphus spoke. 'It will unite the Achaeans. It gives them the justification they need to plot an underhand victory over us.'

'So you will stand up to Paris over this?'

'Do not oppose him openly, not now.' Helenus' voice had a note of command in it. 'Aeneas is right, we cannot bring Paris down in the wake of this. There is no need, the Achaeans will take their revenge on him. Then we shall have the opportunity to influence Priam's next choice of general.'

Silence. Then Chromis said slowly, 'Can we take it that you would support Aeneas' claim? To the generalship?'

Helenus considered for a long time before answering. 'If Priam will consider him. If Priam will not, Aeneas and the rest of you must undertake to back my claim against Deiphobus.'

The silence this time hid a stunned surprise. Nobody had expected Helenus to covet the command for himself. It seemed to Aeneas that they could not afford to question him at this stage. Aeneas said rapidly, 'Done, Helenus,' and reached to draw the other man to his feet. Before Helenus relit his torch and set off back to the citadel they had all laid their hands upon the bargain.

Aeneas had never seriously anticipated winning the generalship. He had never schemed or bribed with that aim in view: he had known too well that it was unlikely ever to pass out of Priam's immediate family. It would have been pointless to set up a serious challenge to Hector; and for different reasons, nobody before that time had challenged Paris. He had not let himself dwell on the situation that might arise after Paris' death or downfall, since both of those had seemed unlikely contingencies.

Now, with the unlikely becoming a probability, the question

had to be taken seriously. It surprised Aeneas slightly to realize how clear the issues were in his mind: as if unconsciously, his ambition had been far more powerful than he had ever permitted it to appear on the surface. He was forced to confront the fact that he did covet the command for himself. Even with Ilios veering daily closer to defeat, he would have taken it without hesitation.

It had always been apparent that Deiphobus would be too poor a candidate to step into his brother's shoes unopposed. If Paris lost the command it had long been certain that there would be two candidates: Deiphobus as Priam's obvious nomination, and a rival candidate, supported by the allies. Aeneas, not given to false modesty, was not surprised to find himself the automatic choice as the allied challenger.

But a challenge from Helenus! Nobody, surely, had anticipated that. If Aeneas had never pretended to himself that he understood Helenus completely, he had at least thought that he understood him better than that.

He had no doubt that Helenus intended it as a serious challenge. He would not have offered such a bargain otherwise. And wanting it, and being in the citadel, and having Priam's ear when Aeneas did not, and support from the allies when Deiphobus did not, he would be in a strong position to get it. He might not even be such a bad choice; he was popular with the commanders, and a good tactician.

But surely Helenus had never coveted the command before. There had been no hint from anyone that he was canvassing support in anticipation of a bid. He had never shown any inclination to be seen as a leader, any more than he had been interested in fighting. What had made him suddenly change his mind?

Aeneas ran wearily over the list of people who might be able to give him an answer. Hector: dead. Troilus: dead. Ennomus: dead. Chromis: he doubted it. Cassandra? He knew she was in no state to discuss such an issue rationally, even if he could now have gained access to her. No other names came to him. It was done now, anyway. He had no option but to support Helenus' bid as he had promised.

Paris was still general, though: there was nothing to be done yet. Aeneas watched and waited. He updated the instructions to his private network of spies and messengers. They began to sound out Ulysses and Diomedes — who seemed to have the upper hand among the Achaeans — and to circle warily around Agamemnon.

In the camp the euphoria at Achilles' death faded like a rainbow. In its place came the rumours.

Of course, Aeneas listened to them. There was not, as far as he could tell, any serious reason to doubt Helenus' version of the killing. Paris was busily spreading his own version, however. His was certainly audacious: it had the Achaean champion falling at the Scaean Gate. Anybody who stopped to think about it knew it could not possibly be true. Still, the tale gained currency.

Until Paris' death. That happened barely a full moon after the truce negotiated for Achilles' funeral came to an end. Paris, whose unpopularity had plumbed new depths, led the troops in the battle that followed. An Achaean archer took him full in the chest. One or two of the men who had seen it suggested that his guard had deliberately drawn back, exposing him. A sacrifice, men whispered, to appease Apollo.

Inevitably, there was talk of returning Helen. Priam would not tolerate it, it seemed. Nor, to Aeneas' greater surprise, would Helenus advocate it; and nor would Deiphobus. Before the talk in the camp had either built up or died down, events in the citadel had overtaken it.

Helen tried to escape. She gave her maidservants the slip and tied a rope to the battlements, on the sheer north side of the citadel. Perhaps it was more a token than a serious attempt because the sentries caught her before she had even reached the top of the wall. They led her before Priam; and the High King, to enforce her loyalty, made her marry another of his sons.

Helenus, so Aeneas' informants told him, pressed his own case. Priam did not listen. He gave Helen's hand to Deiphobus, and with it the generalship of Troy.

There had been no council meeting, no consultation of the allies and their leaders. A single night had thrown away all of the plans made in the camp. If it had been Deiphobus whom

Priam had intended to impose on the army all along he could not have planned it better. It was even rumoured that Priam had staged the entire incident, for just that purpose.

Aeneas would have liked to hear Helenus' side of the story. Helenus was not to be found, though. A few days later the rumour was circulating that he had left Ilios. It was not clear if he ever intended to return.

Some of the allies were willing to give Deiphobus his chance. Others were not. The Amazons evaporated like dew on a hot morning. Chromis, muttering, made an excuse to take his troops back to Mysia. The Lydians and Lycians were restive. And Aeneas, who had been back in Ilios for less than three moons, was seriously considering leaving it again.

What Priam's reaction to the defections was he did not know. The High King had emerged from his bedchamber to deal with Helen, but had retreated straight back to it. Aeneas' request for an audience with him was brusquely refused by Deiphobus, with Hecuba at his side. Deiphobus did not look like a man hard pressed, though by all the gods he should have done. Perhaps, Aeneas thought sourly, it was the sweetness of the nights with Helen that unclouded his brow.

The nights with Helen. He saw it suddenly with cold clarity. It had been inevitable that the next general would receive Helen's hand with his command. Helenus had never wanted the command for its own sake. He had merely been willing to shoulder it, knowing it would bring him Helen.

It was the deceptive simplicity of his motive that had blinded Aeneas to it earlier. Helenus and he were, it seemed, even less alike than he had thought. The thought came to his mind that if he had indeed married Cassandra, as Andromache had suggested, he would have won the command after all. He dismissed it with barely suppressed fury.

Deiphobus treated the defections calmly, as if he had positively planned them. He described it as a reassessment of the defence requirements. There was no railing at the defectors, no mention of treachery or even disloyalty. Aeneas asked his spies what the new general was up to, but little information came back to him. He could hardly be negotiating a surrender. His marriage to Helen had made it quite impossible.

Aeneas waited seven days, then another seven. A messenger from Ulysses came to tell him that the Achaeans had promised Helenus safe conduct to any country he chose, in return for certain information which they did not specify. Aeneas was offered safe conduct too. The information Ulysses asked from him was trivial, barely enough to ensure his commitment. He gave it to the messenger with hardly a qualm; then went to visit Andromache.

Andromache was more than surprised when he was announced by the servant. She remembered every detail of their quarrel. Had Aeneas come belatedly to admit that she had been right? There was enough chance of it to cause her to greet him with reasonable warmth.

Aeneas, stalking into the megaron, had the look she recognized. A new look that united almost everybody in the citadel. A dull complicity, the face of men and women who have forgotten what honour ever meant, who have realized that they can do the unthinkable, and survive to do it again. The wary eyes that people have when they know that whatever course they take, it will mean betrayal for someone who once trusted them. Andromache had expected his face and words to be guarded; who was not, these days? The surprise was to find them rather less blank than she had expected.

'I need to talk with you in private. Will you take me up to your room?'

'It is quite private here. The servants will not listen.' There were three or four women in the megaron, but none were within easy earshot.

'You are too trusting. There are spies all over the citadel.'

'Aeneas, you can hardly accuse my own servants of spying against me.'

He gave her a shrewd look. 'You can hardly be on the same side as all of them.'

'I am on the Trojan side. I have done nothing to be ashamed of. And I will say nothing, to you or to anyone, that needs to be hidden.'

'Then you are more fortunate than most of us.' He looked around for a chair and Andromache motioned to one of the women to bring him one. A second one was brought for her and they sat, awkwardly.

'You did not see Astyanax last time you came. Let me send for him now.'

'Later.' He waited while another servant brought them mulled wine, thick with honey and barley meal, and smelling sweetly of thyme. When she had retreated he said, 'The child is not safe in Ilios. Have you not thought of taking him back to Thebe?'

Andromache looked disconcerted. She examined his face for a moment before replying. 'No. He belongs in Ilios. He is Priam's heir, and it is right for him to stay here.'

'There is too much danger. You should both think of leaving for a while. Then when this phase of the war is over, you would be able to come back in safety.'

The euphemism did not fool her. Obviously he expected the Achaeans to break into the citadel very soon. 'There is nowhere safe, Aeneas. It is not safe in Mysia, is it? Or in Dardania?'

'Safer than it is here. You know Helenus has gone to Mysia? To Chryse.'

Andromache spoke slowly and carefully. 'I had the impression that Helenus was regarded as a traitor.'

'I think his opinion about what happened in the shrine of Apollo is pretty much the same as yours.' Aeneas thought of mentioning his conjecture about Helenus' other, more private motive for leaving Ilios, and decided against it.

Andromache looked into her wine, reached out a finger to stir the barley into it, and with an action that was childlike and yet consciously adult, licked the finger afterwards. 'Helenus does not know what happened, Aeneas.'

'And you do?' He had not expected her to. It would have been a real surprise if Paris had ever confided in her, or Deiphobus.

'No.' Her head was bent over the cup, but she lifted her eyes and looked at him through her lashes. 'You are wrong if you think nobody told me. Deiphobus told me some of it. Helenus told me the version he heard. Polyxena told me too. What they told me was what they believed, what they saw. At least Deiphobus and Polyxena saw it, they were there after all. And yet they did not know what had happened. Nobody knows, nobody ever will know. They saw what they wanted to see, fragments of what they had and had not expected to see. But they did not see everything, did not understand half of what was in front of them anyway.

'Polyxena went there, you know, because Paris tried to persuade her that Achilles was interested in marrying her. And yet she did not know if Paris was telling the truth, if he believed it. Even if Paris had believed it, she did not know if Achilles really intended it, if he planned to betray the Achaeans, or if he expected her and Paris to betray us and save their own skins, or if he had meant it as a trap that went wrong. I do not know, I doubt if she knew herself, which side she was supposed to end up on.'

'You don't think she was planning to turn traitor?'

'Maybe some people will think it. They thought it of Achilles, and yet it was Trojans who killed him, when if he were a traitor they had everything to gain from keeping him alive. They have said it of Helenus. Of course, they are saying it now of you.'

'I have caused you embarrassment by coming here.'

'No, not really.' She paused. 'You remember the time we talked before, when you told me that Hector too had fought dirty?'

'You said then that you thought assassinating Achilles in cold blood would be unforgivable.'

'It was. It is. If that is what happened. And yet we have to forgive it.'

'So you are still on the side of the men who did it.'

'What is the alternative, Aeneas? To be on nobody's side? To decide that it was all in vain, everything Hector did, and all the others who have died? It is not that I support Deiphobus. I dislike him. I did not support Paris in that sense. It is just that I belong to Troy, and so does Astyanax. It will all be his one day, if anything is left at all. That is worth holding onto, whatever Deiphobus does in Troy's name now.'

'There are many people who would disagree with you.'

'There are some who agree. Ilios has not fallen yet.'

'Not yet, no.'

'You are so sure that it will. Well, if it does, I will fall with it.'

'A hero's end.'

Andromache turned to look full at Aeneas. 'I make a strange hero, don't I?'

She made a better one than she realized, he thought. Even impending heroism could not make her beautiful, but there was a luminosity about her, as if she walked in a clearer air than that of the citadel. She had the confidence of someone who does not bother to watch her back, the ease of someone who knows she is doing nothing to be ashamed of. It was enviable. He looked down as he answered, 'I make no kind of hero at all.'

He half expected her to press him, worm a confession on his treachery out of him. Andromache recognized it and thought briefly of doing just that. For what, though? To tell Deiphobus, whom she despised? Instead she said gently, 'It was kind of you to try to save me.'

'Will you at least let me save the child? Take him with me to Dardania?'

Andromache did not answer straight away. She finished her drink, stood and crossed to the fire; then, too warm, she moved back to sit down again. 'I don't think I could bear to lose him. I would not have the strength to go on, staying here without him.'

'If the Achaeans do come they will kill him, Andromache. They will not kill you. You will be a prisoner, a concubine. Ulysses' slave, perhaps, or Agamemnon's. Will you forgive yourself then?'

'Will you forgive yourself? Will any of us who survive it and have to live on afterwards?' Aeneas did not answer her. 'Let me call for Astyanax now. Then perhaps you will understand.'

It was the last thing Aeneas wanted, but he waited while the servant girl hurried off and returned with the child and his nurse. Astyanax was just learning to walk. Aeneas watched Andromache's face as she encouraged him to stagger a few steps on his own for them. The child, happy and trusting, fell laughing into her arms. Andromache laughed back, bent to kiss him, then looked up, over his head, to where Aeneas sat.

It was not reason that drove her. He saw that clearly now. It was love. Love for the child, love for the future that she longed to give it. She wanted that future so badly that she would not let anything break her vision of it. Astyanax would stay here, in Ilios, with his mother at his side, until the Achaeans came and shattered Andromache's determination.

Aeneas envied that more than anything. It was not love that was sending him back to Dardania, in spite of the new wife waiting there. He was leaving in a thick cloud of suspicion, hatred and depression. He sat there, enveloped already in it too thickly to think of escape, and watched Andromache until she rose to send the child away. Then he stood too and politely, formally, said goodbye. He knew as he did so that he would never see her or Ilios again.

Helenus came to the shrine bearing roses. It was a glorious day in early summer and the bushes had been in flower, pink and white along the track that led from Thebe to Chryse. He had left his servant waiting with the mule while he gathered an armful of them, abstractedly. He was not thinking particularly of Chryseis as he did it; but she came into sharper focus in his mind as he neared the sanctuary.

He had been there once, many summers before; and he recognized the low house with its courtyard, walled with stone and brush, and the hill rising gently beyond. There had been a housekeeper, an elderly woman who had made a fuss of him as a young boy. But no housekeeper came to greet them as the two men and their mule circled around the fence looking for the gate. The bees buzzed, the cicadas clicked; and somewhere inside the house, a baby cried.

Helenus found the gate and went in himself, leaving the servant to wait once more. The courtyard was neatly swept, and shady even in the midday sun. Along the wall to his right he saw the sacred mice in their cages. Opposite them, the main door to the house was open. He went through it without bothering to call out. The room was plainly furnished, bare even, but there was a smell of new-baked bread, and there were more roses in a chipped bowl with a design of fishes, on the trestle.

Chryseis appeared a moment later, from a door at the side. There was a black dog with her. She carried the baby on her hip; she did not seem surprised to see him. 'Helenus. I didn't hear you come.'

'You say it as if you were expecting me.'

'Should I have been?'

'No.' Though she had recognized him so readily, he did not think he would have known her had he not been expecting to see her. There was a stillness about her that had not been there two summers before. She moved less lightly, but with more grace, and there was a softness in her face and hair that he did not remember. There was none of the vividness that had been his clearest impression of her in Ilios.

'You came alone?' She sat as she spoke, on a low wooden bench.

'There is a servant outside. I will call him in a moment.'

'My father is working. I will call him too, once I have seen to you both.'

'You have no servants?'

'A housekeeper. She is down at the fields. We dislike each other, so she does not stay in the house when I am here.' Chryseis smiled lightly, as if it had been easy to deal with the unpleasantness. 'And there is a boy Father brought from Thebe two moons ago to serve at the shrine. You came here before, didn't you, when I was a baby, and there were lots of servants at the shrine? But of course things are different now in Mysia.'

'So I have seen.'

'Did you stop at Thebe, or have you come straight here from Ilios?'

'From Ilios. I left eight days ago.'

It was a long time, eight days to get from Ilios to Chryse. Sailing, in peacetime, he could have done it in a day. With a chariot, two days. He must have been walking, and hiding too perhaps. Chryseis took a second look. There were fresh scratches on Helenus' legs, half-hidden by the dust, and arcs of fatigue beneath his eyes. Underneath the easy boyishness was a hint of hardness that she had never noticed in Ilios. Not that she had taken much notice of Helenus once she had seen that he did not look out for her as Troilus did. It seemed she would have to take more notice of him now, at least for a while. 'I'm talking too much, I'm sorry. It's a long time since we have had a visitor. Go and fetch your servant and I'll heat water to bathe you both.'

When Helenus returned with his boy the flowers were set in water; the baby crawled around on a rush mat on the floor, a wooden rattle in its mouth; and the cauldron was simmering over the fire. Chryseis offered them fruit and wine, and set them to mind the baby while she went to clean out two of the rooms in the other wing of the house, kept for visitors to the shrine.

'I am not used to babies,' Helenus protested.

'Just stop him from crawling in the fire. I'll hear if he cries, and be straight back.' She was in command; he recognized it, and sat down to do as she said. The baby crawled over to make friends. He was a plain, sturdy child, with a fair freckled face and a hint of red in his hair. He bore no resemblance to the cool Chryseis. Helenus had not known there was a child. It was Agamemnon's, presumably.

He did not ask. Chryseis had set the tone of his reception, charmingly rustic, friendly and yet reserved. She had not asked why he was in Chryse, or what he wanted from herself and her father. When she returned she washed him, in a tub on the floor in front of the fire. Her fingers traced the lines of his body thoughtfully as she rubbed in the warm oil. He was suddenly and acutely conscious of the sexual presence that had turned so many men's eyes to her. The boy watched them, a hint of laughter about his mouth, and Helenus sent him out until it was his turn to be bathed. He did not think she lingered about the boy's body in quite the same way.

The housekeeper, when she came back, turned out to be a grim-faced woman, not the cheery one he remembered. Her gaze sent streaks of hostility cutting through the warm atmosphere of the house. She went immediately to fetch the priest, who was not hostile, but more openly surprised than Chryseis had been. He held back his questions too, but was careful to let Helenus see that he had difficulty in doing so.

Of course, they had to be answered. After supper – a bean stew, for Helenus had brought no animal to sacrifice, and there were no sheep or goats to spare in Chryse – Helenus related to them both the events in Ilios. He told the tale plainly, with no mention of his own part. His listeners were silent and attentive.

Chryses was the first to respond. 'The priests did not condone all this, you say?'

'They knew nothing about Paris' plans. Nothing at all. Afterwards Paris and Deiphobus went through the proper rites and the priests absolved them.'

'And Cassandra?'

It was not a question he had expected. 'She sees disaster coming. Priam had her shut up in the palace many moons ago and nobody listens to her.'

'Do they listen to you?'

'I do not say anything.'

Chryses frowned and looked down. Did he think, Helenus wondered, that the priests would have followed his lead if he had protested? Helenus had not intended to try to justify himself to a priest and a woman, but something about the silence made him say more. 'In the town they think that Apollo supported the plotters. Without the God's help, people argue, Achilles would not have been killed.'

'The priests should have told them better. And you among them.'

'The priests support Priam. And Priam supported Paris, and Deiphobus after Paris was killed. I did challenge for the generalship when Paris died, but Priam was determined to give it to Deiphobus.'

'So you do not support Priam any more.' Chryseis spoke in a quiet, firm voice.

Helenus hesitated, then answered. 'No. I follow what I believe the God tells me. The gods have deserted Troy. So have half the allies. The thing now is to end it quickly.'

'And make sure you are one of the survivors.'

There was an edge to her voice that Helenus did not like. 'Do you think the world would be better if I were not?'

Chryseis regarded him in the dim light without replying. He had given no proper indication what he intended to do next. She was in no doubt, he felt, that he intended to turn traitor. There was condemnation in her look. In her father's there was only the familiar tired tolerance. It was Chryses who finally spoke. 'Do you intend to stay here, as a priest of Apollo?'

Helenus had not realized that Chryses would even hope for it, let alone expect it. It was suddenly clear that he did. He wanted a successor: not one of the local lads, but someone to whom Apollo really was believed to speak. This was a marvellous opportunity for him. He was not a man who would plot to force events, but he would be deeply disappointed if he were denied. Helenus could not afford to deny him yet. He answered simply, 'Perhaps.'

'But that is not why you came here,' Chryseis challenged him in a sharper voice.

'No. I came to find a safe place from which I could negotiate with Ulysses.'

Her face barely changed. The faint surprise that she did show was due not so much to his plan, Helenus suspected, as to his failure to mention Agamemnon. Watching her, he was taken aback by Chryses' quiet voice. 'Every visitor is given shelter here. So long as they serve the God faithfully, and do as his priests demand.'

What would his priest demand? Helenus did not ask. 'I am glad to know it,' he said, and rose to bid them both goodnight.

The pallet was not uncomfortable, but he found it hard to sleep. He was forced to admit to himself that he was disappointed that Chryseis did not come to him. Not that he had expected it, after the evening; but her touch in the afternoon had made him think of it, and the thought refused to go away. She was, he reckoned, a woman who found it hard to do without a man. It must have been early in the previous summer when she had last slept with Agamemnon, and there could not have been anyone since. She would not have settled for any altar boy in Chryse, or field hand in Thebe. She would have settled for him, for that night at least, if he had not spoken as he had after supper. He did not know her well enough to judge how readily she would forget it and let herself be seduced by him.

He could, he supposed, afford to offer to marry her. She was beautiful and kept house well. He would enjoy her sharp wit. It was no good thinking of Helen any more. Strangely he had not thought of Helen at all since he left Ilios, though he could have persuaded himself just before leaving that it was because of his failure to win her that he had decided to go. It was not a motive that he wished to mention to Chryseis or her father, and he doubted if they would hear of it from anyone in Ilios. In time, it was perhaps not a motive that would be real to him either.

Helenus had sent word to Ulysses before he left Ilios, but it was some time before the Ithacan arrived at Chryse. He had, he explained, travelled to Scyros after Achilles' death, to bring back to Troy Achilles' son Neoptolemus. It was only the lad's twelfth summer, so nobody could expect much of him as a fighter; but the oracles demanded it, just as they had demanded that Philoctetes be retrieved from his exile on Lemnos. That had already paid off: it had been Philoctetes' arrow that had killed Paris.

There were other things the gods demanded, if Ilios were to be taken. Helenus divulged them, expressionless. He already had Ulysses' promise of a safe conduct out of Troy when Ilios fell. Ulysses – who did not pretend to like him, any more than he liked Ulysses – added to this an offer to take Helenus to Ithaca. Ithaca seemed to have little to recommend it, even as its king described it. It was just a collection of little rocky islands and a stretch of barren shore. Another offer was conveyed, from young Neoptolemus. Phthia was horse country, and might perhaps be similar to Troy. There was a certain appropriateness to his going there, when it was outrage at Achilles' murder that had nominally driven Helenus from Ilios. He accepted the offer. Neoptolemus would send a ship for him after Ilios fell.

He did not say so to either Chryseis or her father. The priest had treated him kindly. They had seen to the business of the shrine together, just as if Helenus had agreed to become the next priest. They worked together, most days, on the documents from Babylon in Chryses' hut. The eclipse Chryses had awaited for so long had come earlier that spring. It had perhaps been on the day of Achilles' death; they had not managed to agree the day for certain. Amid the chaos in Ilios, nobody had noticed the small bite from the sun. The priest did not seem disappointed: he believed another eclipse would follow and was bent on predicting the exact time and form of it. He did not pretend that his knowledge would make any difference to the rest of the world; it was, thought Helenus, his way of escaping. By concentrating on this work he had succeeded in ignoring Ulysses' visit completely.

Chryseis did not come to the hut, though Helenus knew she had been used to doing so: he recognized her bold hand on some of the leaves of calculation. She was avoiding him, he knew. He in turn was watching, waiting, trying to arouse her in ways that she might think were accidental. He had never seduced a woman before, being used to the Ilios whores, and he would have found it an enjoyable game had he wanted her a little less, or been more certain that he would eventually get her.

He lost patience with the game a few days after Ulysses had left. He caught her alone in the courtyard at dusk. The servants had gone to bed, the dog and the baby slept too, and Chryses was back in his hut, burning a single lamp as he bent over his cluttered table. Chryseis came out to see to the mice. One of them had just had a litter, and they needed to be separated. Helenus came up behind her and waited until she had finished rearranging the mice. She fastened the first two cages, then slowly and deliberately took her hand from the front of the third cage and left it hanging open as she turned to him.

The look told him that she knew why he was there. There was no sign of surprise when he caught her about the waist and pulled her into his embrace.

He expected her to fight a little, for the sake of her dignity; he was betting that, for the same reason, she would not scream. In fact she did neither. She kissed him back, warm and yielding, and arched her body up against his. There was not even a whisper of protest when he drew her towards his room. She untied her own belt, helped him to pull off her shift and made love to him with blatant abandon.

She was gone when he woke in the morning and when he found her in the house she treated him with the same coolness she had shown ever since the first evening. A nod to show she had noticed him coming in, and she turned to her father. 'I am afraid I had an accident last night, Father. My hand slipped as I was fastening the cages, and some of the mice escaped.'

'That is unfortunate, my dear.'

'Yes. Of course there are still plenty of mice, with the new babies coming along. I'll come up to the shrine later this morning with an offering, to make amends to Apollo.'

'I will give the prayers,' Helenus found himself saying.

'Oh, there is no need for that. Father will do it very well.' She met his eye, but he could not read the message in her look. Maybe there was none.

He had no idea if she planned to share his bed that night. He walked through the day in a haze of desire, hardly able to wait for the dark.

If Chryseis felt the same impatience she did not show it. She spent the evening talking with her father in the house. Finally Helenus came up to her, drew her a little apart and whispered, 'Come to my room.'

She smiled, as if she were taunting him with his lust. 'My bed is more comfortable.' He was still taking in the words when she turned to her father and said in a louder voice, 'I think I will go to bed now, Father. Goodnight.' She kissed her father gently and left without a word to Helenus. Defeated, he went to his own room. She was already there, naked, waiting for him.

They continued in this way until the ship came. She was not quite like the whores he was used to in bed, and not only because she was more skilful and had tricks none of them had known. Unlike them, she demanded her own pleasure in return for giving him his. She did take pleasure in him, Helenus had no doubt of that. He believed it was just as intense as his pleasure in her.

She did not want words of love. When he offered them she turned on him abruptly. This was not love, she said brutally, and it was not necessary to pretend that it was. Once or twice he tried to discuss the future with her, but she refused to talk to him on that subject too and would seduce him back into silence.

Helenus told her father that he wished to marry her. Chryses showed no surprise. He did not agree either. It was, he said, for Chryseis to choose. And if Chryseis had chosen she was not yet ready to discuss her choice with anyone.

Chryses' boy was down at the harbour fishing when the ship

came. He came scrambling back to the sanctuary to tell them of it. Just one, coming steadily down the estuary towards the harbour: a black ship with a Myrmidon standard.

'Ilios has fallen, then.' Chryses' voice was quite calm. It was what they had all been expecting: that Ilios would fall. The ship had not been expected by the priest and his daughter, as far as Helenus knew, but they showed no surprise, either of them, at the boy's news.

Chryseis turned to him, impassive. 'Did you choose Thessaly, or is that what Ulysses offered?'

'He gave me a choice. I opted for Thessaly.'

'You go as a prisoner?' They were standing in the courtyard and Chryses' voice crackled in the midday heat.

'No, it is what I have chosen.' He could not think of words that would soften the blow. 'May I talk to Chryseis alone?'

'There is no need for that. I am not coming with you.'

'My safe conduct will cover you too if I take you as my wife.'

'Can you not marry her and stay here? We shall be quite safe in the sanctuary.'

Chryseis and Helenus both turned to look at Chryses. Helenus saw the confusion on the priest's face; then, turning to his daughter, a mixture of anger and compassion on hers. She did not like to see her father begging, especially when he did it misguidedly.

'There is no need to suggest that, Father. I would not take him if he offered it.' She turned to look full at Helenus and he saw that she was not speaking out of pride. She meant every word. On her face was a casual contempt for him. It roused his anger.

'Do you expect a Mycenaean ship to follow this one up the river?'

'Not a Mycenaean one, no.' She smiled cruelly. 'I think perhaps a ship will come. But if it does it will go away again without me.'

'There is nothing for you here.'

'That is where you are wrong, Helenus. The Mouse God is here. I shall be his priestess.'

'That is not what your father wants.'

'I imagine he would prefer to have you.' She turned to smile at her father, without troubling to wipe the cruelty from her face. 'It is the God who chooses, though; not his priest. And I believe Apollo has chosen me.'

Helenus, who had believed all his life that Apollo spoke directly to him, could think of no reply. His silence did not appear to bother Chryseis. She went on calmly, 'You should get your things together; the ship will be at the harbour in a few minutes. I hope you will leave us the mule. It will be useful here. Your servant, too, if he prefers to stay.'

'Of course.' He turned to go to his room and gather his belongings together.

Chryseis came after him a moment later and stood in the doorway watching him. There was no sign of Chryses or the servants. He had the chance to speak with her alone now, but there seemed to be nothing left to say. He did not expect her to speak either and her voice when it came was a surprise to him. 'How much of this did you foresee? Of what happened here?'

He thought it a strangely naïve question from so knowing a woman. 'Very little. You know the God does not work like that.'

'But you saw a future in Thessaly. Without me.'

'Yes.' He had seen much of that, but he did not think she deserved the details. She did not ask for them.

'So we are both being true to Apollo.' She said it thoughtfully, with no trace of irony.

Helenus finished tying his bundle, stood and turned to her. 'Was that why you slept with me, to gain some of my power with the God?'

She laughed out loud. 'What a child you can be, Helenus. Was it not enough to take pleasure from it? Why pretend to love, or give other reasons for doing it?'

Because, he wanted to say, the clear light of Apollo's knowledge is too bright for us to live under all the time. We have to make shadows of our own if we are to survive. Instead he replied, 'I think it is you who are being naïve. You cannot forgive me, can you, because you think I have been treacherous? And yet I have been true to what I thought was most important all along.'

Chryseis moved back a pace to lean against the door jamb. It looked as if she were escaping from him, and perhaps she knew it; she did not seem to care. She took her time about answering.

'You think I do not understand betrayal? You think I do not know the murkiness of it, the excuses we make to pretend that what we betrayed was not worth our loyalty? You think I have not done that myself? If I had not, maybe I would believe you.'

'Have you forgiven yourself?'

She seemed to look through him. 'I see a future too. In fact, I see two futures. I see you and me, Helenus, together. Two survivors, who have paid too high a price. Who have forgotten what honour is, who despise themselves too much to love each other. I see us growing old hating each other. I do not know if Apollo put the vision in my mind, but it is there. And I see myself here, in Chryse. Tending the child, whom I have never pretended to love, and worshipping the God, whom I do not need to love. Because he is there, and will be there whatever I do, however I do it. Since I have never betrayed either, they can be cruel to me and I can afford to be hurt by it. In time, who knows, I may even remember what it is to love.'

'Did you ever know it?'

'I thought so, once or twice.'

'And Chryses?'

'He loves me. In time, he will forgive me.'

It was something, Helenus supposed, that she knew she needed his forgiveness. 'Help him to forgive me too, if you can.'

'Ah, but if the God truly calls you to somewhere else there is nothing to forgive.'

She deserved the last word. It was the last victory she was likely to have for a long time. Helenus picked up the bundle and crossed to the door. Chryseis did not move; he made himself bend to kiss her. She deserves to be loved, he thought, but she is right, I do not love her. She did not follow him as he made his way down to the harbour.

The Myrmidons brought their spears to the assembly that Ulysses called after Achilles' funeral. They watched in silence as he held up Achilles' armour, which he, Ajax and Diomedes had brought back with the body to the camp. Why the three of them had been following Achilles, and whether he had known they were there, was not clear. At the assembly nobody asked. Ulysses and Ajax both made their claim to the armour; after much discussion Agamemnon awarded it to Ulysses. There was a rumble from the Myrmidons. It was better than Agamemnon himself wearing the starry breastplate, but not much better.

It had been rumoured that Agamemnon would go on to distribute Achilles' prizes of war among the living commanders. It was the usual thing for the officers to get a dead man's goods, and for his women to be handed over for common use. At the sight of the Myrmidon spears Agamemnon evidently thought better of it. That was not the way to block up the anthill. Instead he called on Calchas, the High Priest, to pronounce on the indications for the war.

Calchas rose hastily, as if to get his announcements over quickly. The gods had decreed, he said, that the war could be won only if Achilles' son Neoptolemus were brought to Troy. A voice or two protested that he could be barely more than a child. They were drowned in a chorus of approval. It would solve so many problems. Nobody asked what auguries had driven Calchas to such a conclusion; the spears had been a sign clear enough for the least-gifted augur to interpret. Maybe this was not what the Myrmidons had had in mind, but the boy would be a commander – albeit a token one – under whom they could not refuse to fight.

Calchas stopped to enjoy the reception and before he could continue Ulysses reached for the speaker's staff, to announce that he would go in person to fetch Neoptolemus. He offered to take Phoenix along, to appease the Myrmidons, and added that the boy should have the disputed armour. On the surface, it was profoundly generous. Perhaps Calchas thought so too. When he got the staff back he calmly added to Ulysses' burden a second task: to fetch Philoctetes from Lemnos, where he had been abandoned with a festering snake bite years before. Ulysses, outmanoeuvred for once, was forced to agree.

As soon as Ulysses dismissed the troops the Myrmidons retreated to hold their own council of war. They were not deceived. It did not please them, the prospect of a commander with barely twelve summers behind him and Ulysses hovering at his side, demanding gratitude and insisting that his tactical advice be taken. They decided to distribute Achilles' trophies among themselves. If Neoptolemus proved to deserve them they could be rediscovered and properly presented to him. Whatever happened, they were damned if Ulysses would have the ugliest slave girl or the smallest bronze cup.

Neoptolemus was too young, anyway, to have any use for the women. The men drew lots for them.

That left the problem of Briseis. Not a Myrmidon was going to treat her as part of the booty. It was essential to every man's honour that Agamemnon, Ulysses and the rest see that she had been dealt with as befitted Achilles' widow. She would have to remarry, and quickly, before Ulysses or Diomedes got round to making any other suggestions. The officers undertook to arrange it.

Briseis was duly summoned to the hut. She asked Diomede to come with her for support. The two of them found all the Myrmidon officers waiting. Phoenix was delegated to convey the decisions: he was the oldest and the least likely, the others reckoned, to be chosen by Briseis. Flustered, the old man could not recall to whom Diomede had been allotted. No matter. The point he had to get across was that she had no choice; and that Briseis did.

Briseis took in that much. She looked past Phoenix at the rest of the officers. They were still dressed for the assembly, in their black tunics with swords slung across them, though they had left the spears by the door. Their faces still bore the sullen, combative expressions they had assumed for Agamemnon and Ulysses. Apparently they intended to act as her protectors, but they looked to her more like her enemies.

'I am not sure I understand. I must marry a Myrmidon?'

Phoenix did not reply and Automedon, taking pity on his confusion, took over from him. 'You are to marry whoever you choose. Not that we would like it much if you did not choose a Myrmidon.'

'I see. May I take some time to decide?'

'Don't take too long. Agamemnon may award you to some other commander.'

'I would not want that.' Briseis did not want to marry again at all. But if any prospect was more awful to her than that of choosing one of these hard-faced men it was that of being given to one of the men who had used her in Agamemnon's hut. She had an urge to pick a common man, one of the lads she had nursed and who had laughed and joked with her. If she had been given her choice in front of them all it might have been allowed her. However, that was not how the officers had planned it. Perhaps they were right. This was not being done for her pleasure, but for the sake of Achilles' honour.

It would have to be a man Achilles had cared for, then. Automedon had been closest to him. No matter that she did not much like him; at that moment she did not like any of them. It would be best if she did not appear to consider it too long. She said carefully, 'I will take you then, Automedon. You were Achilles' friend.'

'I will be yours too, I promise you that.'

Briseis did not look at him. It had struck her, after she had said it, that she might have chosen Phoenix, who was old and would not have troubled her much in bed. She would have had a respite, too, while he was away with Ulysses. It was too late to change her mind. Automedon moved forward and took her hand. She remembered now the time he had touched her before, in her father's house, when he had struck her to bring her to her senses. His touch now, firm and confident, had much the same effect. He would behave decently, and make sure she did the same. He was not a green boy who would expect her to love him.

There had been no rites with Achilles, but the men were adamant that there must be this time. None of them had the authority in the camp to make the marriage stand up without. Phoenix went in search of Calchas and returned with him after a long interval. It was hardly surprising that the priest was reluctant: it would not make him popular with the rest of the men if he had anything to do with the Myrmidons' insubordination. On their own territory, though, these men were not to be opposed. They stood guard around the room as Automedon and Briseis spoke the words that bound them together.

When it was done the priest hurried off and Automedon dismissed the other officers with an air of authority. Evidently they would treat him as acting commander now that he had married her. At least her choice had been accepted by everyone. If any of the others had particularly coveted her they must have appreciated that she would bring more than enough problems as her dowry.

Briseis made herself meet her new husband's gaze. There was a hint of sympathy in Automedon's look, and more than a hint of lust. Automedon smiled at her. He was apparently not dissatisfied with his new position.

After a moment's hesitation, she smiled back. He was not handsome: his square peasant's face had none of the distinction of Achilles' or of Patroclus'. But he was an honest man, and a sensible one. So Achilles had always reckoned. Whatever she suffered from him, he would protect her from worse threats from outside.

He intended, it seemed, to make it as easy for her as possible. He led her to the bed that had belonged to Patroclus, not to Achilles'. Perhaps he took her shiver as a suggestion of desire. He took her quickly, straightforwardly, without disguising his pleasure, or pretending that it was anything more than it was. She did not pretend to enjoy him, but she knew it could have been far worse. He slept afterwards, heavily; and after a while so did she. When he woke he made love to her again, more slowly, with the same uncomplicated directness. He waited for her to get aroused, and to her surprise the tremors came, long and sweet, before his own.

'You enjoyed it that time.'

'Yes, I did.' There was no ecstasy in his touch, but it had soaked the tension out of her body, and she was grateful.

'We'll get by together.' He did not wait for her to reply, but heaved himself out of the bed and began to dress. 'I shall be seeing to the horses, and then there are a few things to sort out with the men. I'll be back by sunset.'

'I will have supper ready.'

'Arrange it for the other officers too. No point my getting too far above them, the lad will knock me back to my proper place when he arrives.'

'I'll do that. Have you met him, then?'

'Neoptolemus? Nobody has. I'm not expecting a second Achilles, if that's what you mean. But then I'm no Achilles myself, am I?'

Maybe, Briseis thought, that was no bad thing. She did not say so, though, and it did not seem as if he expected her to.

Not long after the marriage to Automedon she found that she was pregnant. She reckoned the child was Achilles', not Automedon's. Automedon, when she told him, took the news easily. He had another girl in the camp, so it would not cause him undue inconvenience. Briseis moved back to the women's tent without regrets. She did not like the prospect of bearing a child in the camp, though there were plenty of others there, but there was nothing to be done about it unless Ulysses forced a sudden breakthrough.

Neoptolemus turned out to be a sulky boy, with Achilles' red hair, but with no sign of his will or temper. He was already a couple of fingers taller than Ulysses and perhaps that was why he gave the impression that he looked down on the Ithacan. Ulysses, unruffled, continued to give his advice and handed over Achilles' armour as soon as the boy was installed in the camp.

The Myrmidons took him out with them to the battlefield a couple of times. He fought passably, Automedon told Briseis. His guard were careful to throw their spears when he did and Neoptolemus accepted the kills that were credited to him without any fuss. Automedon had the impression that he enjoyed the blood and gore, but after those first sorties he showed no further interest in fighting and spent much of his time with Ulysses, who was evidently engaged in some complicated intrigue.

Many of the Achaeans believed that it was Ulysses' fostering of Trojan traitors that would bring about Ilios' downfall. The Myrmidons, who had always preferred a straight fight, ignored this thesis and with Automedon in the vanguard they continued to attack head on, as if the walls of the citadel would crumble under their charge. The Trojan allied forces had visibly crumbled, but there was no sign of the walls following suit and, it seemed to Briseis, no immediate prosepct of the war ending.

As it happened, Ulysses' negotiations had little to do with the breakthrough — as far as Briseis could tell. It was not a Myrmidon victory either. The gods brought Ilios down in their own fashion.

Briseis woke in the middle of the night, into an unearthly stillness. No noise at all cut through the darkness. She was rising to her feet, suddenly frightened, when the ground shifted beneath her. It jolted and then rolled in great waves, smoothly, as if the earth had turned to sea.

The timbers of the makeshift tent creaked and gave way. A mass of hide and canvas enveloped her. She struggled with its folds until she was free of them. There were shouts and cries from all directions now, from men and women escaping from the debris, from the trapped and from the injured.

The women were unharmed, but for bruises and scratches. The tents had not been sturdy enough to injure them. They huddled together among the wreckage, whispering consolation to each other in the dark, until Automedon and the rest came with torches, and orders to move onto higher ground. They moved slowly, feeling out each step and stumbling occasionally over fallen logs and piles of debris.

The light came slowly; they were wide awake and waiting for it. They made out the destruction of the camp first. Poseidon had let the Achaeans off lightly. Only the low ground by the harbour was flooded and most of the black ships looked to be untouched. The tents were in ruins and a few fires still smouldered among the wreckage near the cooking areas.

'Achilles' hut has not been damaged,' Diomede said. She pointed to where it loomed above the wreckage, like a wooden ship that had sailed the storm that pulsed through the soft earth.

'Nor Agamemnon's quarters.'

'I don't think many men are injured at all.'

'It will be worse,' Briseis said slowly, 'in Ilios.'

The others turned to look at her, and consider this.

'It is still too dark to see. We are too far away.'

'It is true, though. The ground is harder, it will have cracked, and tall stone buildings take earthquakes badly.'

'They must have done something to anger Poseidon.'

'Or Apollo has kept his word and given us our victory.'

Briseis said, 'Not today. The men cannot fight today, surely.'

'Of course they will,' Diomede said brusquely.

They would. The troops were already forming up at the edge of the camp. They set off across the plain in the hazy red light of the morning after the earthquake. News came back swiftly to the casualties at the camp. They had found great chasms in the walls, and devastation within them. The tall houses and high towers had tumbled to the ground. By sunset Ilios had fallen.

The sack of the city was bloody, Agamemnon made sure of that. Priam and his sons were butchered. Of the other defenders, only those Ulysses named were spared. There would be new women prisoners to set alongside the old ones. Agamemnon took Cassandra for his own. He must have reckoned Hecuba too old, and Andromache too plain; he gave Hecuba to Ulysses, who was not grateful, and Andromache to Neoptolemus, who accepted the honour gravely. Andromache's child was a nuisance. As Hector's son, he might have grown up to become more than a nuisance. Some men said it was Neoptolemus who had calmly tossed the boy from the battlements, at a point where they still stood high. Others reckoned Ulysses had done it for him, in a fit of fury. None of the Achaeans cared much. The gods had given them Ilios; they reckoned the gods must be to blame for the carnage that the victory brought in its wake.

Polyxena killed herself. That caused considerable anger, for there were fewer women in Ilios than the Achaeans had hoped, and it was a waste of a young and pretty one. To make the best of it they tossed the body on Achilles' tomb, as his share of the spoils.

If Automedon had been in the camp he might have kept the worst of these details from Briseis. Other men came back first, though. They were still high on the wildness of the bloody orgy; they told the women everything and laughed at their tears. Briseis cried with the rest. She was not sure if she was crying for the Ilians, for their victors, or for herself. It did not seem to matter which it was; they had all lost more than anyone can bear and still stay sane afterwards.

Automedon, when he got back, was more sane than most. He was not even drunk: they had found no wine in the city. Neoptolemus was nowhere to be found, so he arranged the feasting himself. They would begin to load the ships the next day; and fire the remains of the citadel before they left, the day after.

It was the second day before Briseis could manage to talk with him. He had enough on his hands, keeping the troops in order and the prisoners guarded. He turned her away at first, and only when she caught at him and pleaded did he take her back to the hut. 'Well? What is it, woman?'

'I wanted to say . . . must we go back to Thessaly?'

'Go back? Of course. There's nothing here for me.'

'Yes, there is. There is my house, in Mysia. It is good farmland, and far enough from Ilios. We could settle there.'

'You must be joking. I've had enough of Troy. I want to be home. You are not far gone with the child, you can stand the journey. This is all nonsense, you will be treated well enough in Phthia.'

'Think about it, Automedon, please.'

'What, become a farmer in Mysia? I'm a fighter, and I'll stay one. Enough of this, I'm getting back to see to the ships.'

The door slammed, and she was left alone, with only a couple of dogs sniffing around the desolation of the hut. They had stripped it already, leaving only the beds till the morning. Briseis sat down, heavily, on the bed that had once held Achilles.

She knew what it would be like, back in Thessaly with Automedon. He was a fighter, as he had said. He was not a grower, a man who made things for himself. He was a pirate who took other men's things by force. She would sit at home, waiting, as he ravaged the world with his men and brought its booty back home again. The child would grow up perhaps, and in time he too would become a bloody pirate. Never forget it, her father had said. She had forgotten, for a while, but she remembered again now.

A woman could not live without a man, she knew that. But how was any woman to live with men like these? Perhaps she too should go and stab herself on Achilles' tomb. He could have the baby as well. It should be sacrifice enough for any man.

The door opened and a soldier burst in. A young Myrmidon, a man she barely recognized. 'Oh, sorry, ma'am. Didn't know you were here. I just came to fetch the captain's spear, he reckoned he left it here.'

Briseis looked at him blankly. The man went on cheerfully, 'Can't see it. Maybe he made a mistake.'

Maybe he had. She stood up slowly. 'He keeps it here, behind the door.' She went to fetch the spear and turned to hand it over to the man. He looked at her, the cheery grin wiped out. 'You're crying, ma'am. There's nothing to cry about. We're going home.'

She managed to say, 'You are. I'll never get home,' before the flood of sobs overwhelmed her. The man took the spear awkwardly and set it by the wall. Then he put his arms around her and held her gently while she wept.

How they agreed it she did not know. But it came out, somehow, how little he had to go back to. How sick he was of war, how he had always longed for a patch of land and a few cows of his own. There were no grand prizes of war for common soldiers like him: no women slaves, no oxen, no cauldrons or golden cups. Mysia was enough to offer him. He took it.

The sentries were all guarding prisoners and there were none around the stockade. They did not dare to take a horse or a mule, but he had a dagger and kept the spear, and she took the food that was in the hut, enough to last for a day or perhaps two. By nightfall they were nearly at Mount Ida and the camp was more distant than the glow of Ilios burning. They made a fire to keep off the wolves and slept under the stars. In the morning, she remembered that she had not even asked him his name.

Adamas, it was. He wondered out loud if he should change it, but there seemed no point, no one was likely to come after them.

It took them ten days to get to Lyrnessus. They saw other fugitives sometimes, but kept their distance. Nobody would welcome the sight of his black tunic, so she went alone to beg for food from the farms they passed. Most of the wives gave her a little, and Adamas caught a couple of rabbits as well. On the sixth day they poached a donkey from a farmer who had turned her away, and after that they travelled faster.

She knew Lyrnessus when they got there. So did he, but she did not ask him about that, and he did not say anything. It was deserted. The walls were crumbling low and the grass grew up high over the debris of the houses. They did not stop there.

The house that had been Mynes', when they came to it, was changed less. Some of the servants had returned there after the town fell. They had patched the roof the Myrmidons had fired, and rounded up the animals that were left. There were a pair of goats, a dozen sheep. In the orchard the apples were ripening. One of the fields had been replanted, with beans, onion and celery growing in neat rows.

It came as no great surprise to the servants to see Briseis. They had not exactly been waiting for her, but they cleared their belongings out of the room that had been hers and killed one of the sheep to feast her return. She was thin after the journey.

She did not remember the treasure in the orchard until several moons later. Adamas took one of the field hands out with him and they set to work with picks on the dry earth. The man had known just where it was, but had seen no point in digging it up. He had no idea where to sell bronze now that Lyrnessus was a ruin. Nor did Briseis, but it pleased her to see the things she remembered about the house. Later, when Adamas had learned to speak better Trojan, he took a couple of the dishes up the mountains to Scepsis and bartered them for a cow.

The baby was a boy. It was born in midwinter, a skinny child. When his hair came it was brown; but his eyes were a dark and stormy grey. He called Adamas father, and they never told him any different. It was not a good thing for any man, Briseis believed, to know that he was the son of Achilles.

Author's Note

This is a work of fiction, and I do not pretend to be a classical scholar or archaeologist. It should be read as such. However, the background to my story and many of the descriptions and events in it are taken from archaeological and classical literary sources. The notes here are intended to explain broadly what in the book is derived from outside sources, and what invented.

Though the Trojan war has been a source of historical legend for three thousand years, there is still no absolute proof of its existence. There are ruins of a town that may have been called Troy or Ilios, however, close to the modern village of Hissarlik in Turkey, near the mouth of the Dardanelles. It has been extensively excavated, originally by Heinrich Schliemann, and most recently by an American team led by Carl Blegen, and there are a variety of detailed and general accounts of the excavations. My prime source for the details used here has been Blegen's *Troy and the Trojans*.

Of the many settlements on that site, I have taken Troy VIa to be the inspiration for the Ilios of this story. Troy VIa, like my Ilios, was probably destroyed by an earthquake in the late twelfth century BC. Many archaeologists subscribe to this theory, though some – including Blegen – prefer to think of the later Troy VIIa as Homer's Troy, and others doubt that either is an entirely suitable candidate.

Though some of the foundations of Troy VIa remain, no trace has survived of the centre of the citadel, and the details of the palace and of Hector and Andromache's house are invented, or adapted from the information available about contemporary sites in Greece. Archaeologists have uncovered no written records, and only limited indications about the society of the people who lived there. I assume in this book that the society was similar, but not identical, to the contemporary society of Mycenaean Greece, about which a little more is known. Of course, life in the Achaean camp outside Ilios would itself have been very different from life in the major cities of that period. Inevitably, life in the historical Troy, if it ever existed, will have borne only a very general resemblance at best to my fictional Troy.

The prime literary and historical source for anyone interested in the Trojan war is, of course, Homer. All of my major characters are mentioned in the Iliad, and so are many of the minor ones. The outline of the central part of the story is also taken directly from the Iliad, and some of the scenes in this book — including, for instance, the assembly at which Agamemnon and Achilles quarrel, and Ulysses' and Diomedes' night raid — are deliberate echoes of the Iliad. I have, however, changed some details of the story, and particularly where Homer introduces the gods directly into the action I have deviated from his version.

It would be impossible to improve on Homer, and at a few points in the book I have consciously echoed his words rather than attempt to do so.

Troilus gets only a brief mention in the Iliad, though Chryseis plays a vital part in its plot. The love story of Troilus and Cressida is probably not classical in its derivation: it was popularized and elaborated in the Middle Ages. Shakespeare's *Troilus and Cressida* was the original inspiration of this book, and Shakespeare's shadow hangs almost as heavily over it as the equally monumental shadow of Homer. I have tried to echo some of the themes that Shakespeare explored, though my Troilus and Chryseis differ in many ways from Shakespeare's characters. In Shakespeare, Chryseis is ransomed by the Greeks from the Trojans; I have followed Homer in ransoming her the other way around.

The Iliad ends with the death of Hector, and I have used other classical sources for the later stages of my story. Many of the legends are mutually incompatible, and it is virtually impossible to tell which version, if any, reflects historical truth. I have not attempted to judge which tales are true; I have simply used a set which I find reasonably consistent and convincing. There is no classical indication of Briseis' eventual fate, which is invented. That Chryseis stayed in Chryse with her son is also not certain.

As far as possible, I have used Homer's names for the characters derived from the Iliad. There has been no attempt to set up a consistent system of given names and patronymics. Most characters Homer refers to by their given names, but for some minor characters – including Chryseis and Briseis – he provides only patronymics, and I have adopted these as if they too were given names. I appreciate that can lead to confusion where several characters and places have very similar names, for example Chryse, Chryses and Chryseis, Briseus and Briseis. I hope that this does not make the story too difficult to follow. The Greek names can of course be rendered in English in a variety of ways, and I have tried to use the most familiar versions throughout.

I have made no attempt to judge which of Homer's human characters are historical, and which mythological.

I am also broadly following Homer when I call the Trojan capital Ilios, and the territory which it controls Troy, rather than using the same name for both. 'Achaeans' is Homer's word for the people of present-day Greece in this period.

Commentators on Homer have been arguing since classical times about the sites of Thebe, Lyrnessus and Chryse, and about the names and territories of the peoples whom Homer describes as fighting with the Trojans. Here I have taken the name 'Mysia' to apply very generally to the territory to the south of Mount Ida, which I assume here to be under Priam's overlordship. My Thebe, Lyrnessus and Chryse are all located in this territory, around the modern-day gulf of Edremit. I have not identified any of them precisely with the very scant ruins that are to be seen in this region. These placements are derived primarily from the classical geographer Strabo. Strabo is not an entirely reliable guide to the geography of Asia Minor – he slightly misplaces Troy itself, for example – but on these points I find him convincing. The locations he subscribes to also fit in reasonably well with Homer's account of events. I know of no classical indication that Chryseis and Andromache were related, but it seems to be a reasonable assumption that they might have been if their homes were so close together.

Andromache is described in the Iliad as a Cilician. The land later known as Cilicia is well to the south of my Mysia, but some Homeric commentators have argued that Homer's Cilicians and similar peoples may have occupied different territory in the Late Bronze Age, or that there may have been Cilician colonists closer to Troy.

One of the most attractive features of the Mycenaean type of society, as we understand it to have been from Homer, is the freedom allowed to women, and the vital role they played in national and international affairs. This is, of course, in strong contrast to the comparative seclusion of women in classical times. I assume in this book that the women were only a little restrained by primitive taboos, and that they mixed quite freely with men in society, though I do not subscribe to the theory that promiscuity before marraige was the norm. With women so freely available, I see no reason to assume that love was equated with homosexual relationships, as it was, by and large, in classical Greece.

That Achilles married Briseis after a fashion seems to me to be clearly stated in the Iliad. Many commentators argue that this is a misinterpretation, or even that his proposal was intended as a joke. I find it difficult to accept this reading, and I believe I am following Homer in taking the marriage seriously, though the details in my version are different from those Homer gives. Homer also hints at a close relationship between Briseis and Patroclus, and gives Briseis a moving speech on Patroclus' death. However, the nature of that relationship, as set down here, is entirely my own fiction.

Finally, worship of Apollo as the Mouse God has historical justification. There were a number of shrines in the Aegean, in classical and pre-classical times, to Sminthian Apollo – 'sminthos' being the Greek word for mouse. Extensive remains of one classical temple can still be seen to the south-west of Hissarlik, near the modern-day Turkish village of Gulpinar. (This is close to the site of Hamaxitos, where the mice are said to have eaten the armour of Teucrian invaders – a story mentioned in classical texts.) Strabo and others say that the village around this shrine was also called Chryse. It is not my Chryse, and the ruins that remain are more recent than the imaginary shrine in this book, but the temple and its surroundings have undeniably influenced my descriptions of Chryse.

Strabo says that in this temple stood a statue of Apollo with a mouse under his foot. I do not know of any further details of how or why the mice were involved in ritual. The connection between mice and plagues has frequently been mentioned elsewhere; the suggested link with eclipses of the sun is my own invention.

Details of religion in this period are in general very hard to come by, and it is by no means certain that the Mycenaeans and Trojans did worship all the classical Greek gods. For the purpose of this book, I assume that they did.

Susan Curran
Norfolk, 1985/6

Fontana Paperbacks
Fiction

Fontana is a leading paperback publisher of both non-fiction, popular and academic, and fiction. Below are some recent fiction titles.

- ☐ FIRST LADY Erin Pizzey £3.95
- ☐ A WOMAN INVOLVED John Gordon Davis £3.95
- ☐ COLD NEW DAWN Ian St James £3.95
- ☐ A CLASS APART Susan Lewis £3.95
- ☐ WEEP NO MORE, MY LADY Mary Higgins Clark £2.95
- ☐ COP OUT R.W. Jones £2.95
- ☐ WOLF'S HEAD J.K. Mayo £2.95
- ☐ GARDEN OF SHADOWS Virginia Andrews £3.50
- ☐ WINGS OF THE WIND Ronald Hardy £3.50
- ☐ SWEET SONGBIRD Teresa Crane £3.95
- ☐ EMMERDALE FARM BOOK 23 James Ferguson £2.95
- ☐ ARMADA Charles Gidley £3.95

You can buy Fontana paperbacks at your local bookshop or newsagent. Or you can order them from Fontana Paperbacks, Cash Sales Department, Box 29, Douglas, Isle of Man. Please send a cheque, postal or money order (not currency) worth the purchase price plus 22p per book for postage (maximum postage required is £3.00 for orders within the UK).

NAME (Block letters) _____

ADDRESS _____

_____

_____

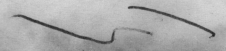